W9-BYG-575

ALSO BY SUZANNE ENOCH

Something
in the
Heir

SUZANNE ENOCH

St. Martin's Paperbacks

This is a work of fiction. All of the characters, organizations, and events portrayed in this novel are either products of the author's imagination or are used fictitiously.

Published in the United States by St. Martin's Paperbacks, an imprint of St. Martin's Publishing Group.

SOMETHING IN THE HEIR

Copyright © 2022 by Suzanne Enoch.
Excerpt from *Every Duke Has His Day* copyright © 2023 by Suzanne Enoch.

For information, address St. Martin's Publishing Group, 120 Broadway, New York, NY 10271.

www.stmartins.com

Library of Congress Catalog Card Number: 2022019285

ISBN: 978-1-250-88996-6

Our books may be purchased in bulk for promotional, educational, or business use. Please contact your local bookseller or the Macmillan Corporate and Premium Sales Department at 1-800-221-7945, ext. 5442, or by email at MacmillanSpecialMarkets@macmillan.com.

Printed in the United States of America

St. Martin's Griffin edition published 2022
St. Martin's Paperbacks edition / June 2023

10 9 8 7 6 5 4 3 2 1

For my sister Nancy—
thank you for helping me find the time to
write this, and for watching all those old
Cary Grant movies with me (even though that
part was pretty fun).

And thank you to Monique and all the wonderful
people at St. Martin's who figured out how
to navigate the craziness, keep me on schedule,
and still let me have the most fun ever
writing this thing. This book took a village,
and that's you guys.

PROLOGUE

Emmeline Hervey caught her mother by the elbow. "Did I just hear you tell Cousin Penelope that we're vacating Winnover Hall?"

Lady Anne Hervey nodded. "We have that lovely cottage in Bath now. There's no reason to keep it a secret."

"There's *every* reason to keep it a secret, Mother, for heaven's sake," Emmie whispered, pulling the duke's daughter further away from the dance floor of the ballroom. "Especially from Penelope. I've only been out for three weeks, and you've just announced that Winnover Hall is up for grabs."

"Precisely. I've already given you three weeks to plan, without anyone else knowing."

"Yes, but—"

"They were bound to find out soon enough. I wrote the duke at the beginning of the Season, and you know *he* can't keep a secret."

"Couldn't he make an exception for me? Winnover is my home. I don't want to live in Bath."

"You know he won't. That's the way it is with Winnover Hall. It has been, since the third Duke of Welshire acquired it in 1635. Do I need to recite the rules to you?"

"I know them. I've lived them. 'The first Ramsey

descendant to wed after Winnover is vacated wins the use of it for five years. If said descendant produces a child within those five years, they may keep Winnover for their lifetime.'"

"Or until they decide to live elsewhere." Lady Anne peeled Emmie's hand off her arm. "Consider that if your father and I had kept it until I died, you would be already married and not eligible to live there. We've done you a favor, waiting until you turned eighteen and began your Season. You have marriage proposals already."

"Yes, but I haven't decided on any of them yet."

"Well, since your cousin became engaged a week ago, I suggest you do so quickly. Otherwise, Winnover will land in Penelope Ramsey's hands."

Penelope. "She would have all the walls smothered in pink wallpaper and use the library to display her bonnets." Just saying the words left a bad taste in her mouth.

"Then I suggest you seriously consider the three proposals you've received, and settle on one of them. Posthaste." With a swift almost-kiss to her daughter's cheek, Lady Anne glided away to converse with their hostess.

Emmie stayed where she was, her gaze on the filling dance floor. Despite her protests, she knew it would do no good to appeal to her grandfather, the current Duke of Welshire, to give her Winnover Hall, even though she'd lived there her entire life. Not only was he famously intractable, but he detested most of his own family—which was odd considering his demand that they all procreate in order to receive any kind of boon from him. He wanted his bloodline to continue, he said, in the hope that at least one of his descendants would be worth a damn.

But for heaven's sake, this was Winnover Hall. Those halls and pastures were the center of her life. Her parents might have given her a few more weeks, at least. By tomorrow every unmarried member of her large, competitive family would know that Winnover was available for the first time in twenty years.

Penelope had a year's head start on her, and while their age difference hadn't mattered much previously, it did now. Or rather, it mattered that Penelope had had a year to fish, and that she'd landed Howard Chase, the puffy-faced second son of a viscount. Stupid Howard Chase.

As she digested all of that, a hand slid around her arm. "My condolences," Penelope Ramsey said, giving her arm a squeeze. "I imagine you'll find residing in Bath much to your taste, though."

Taking a breath, Emmie smiled and gave her cousin a kiss on the cheek. She would *not* be residing in Bath with the wig-wearing set of gray-hairs. Neither was she about to let Penelope know that, though. "I have to say," she said aloud, "I'm glad we've found a situation that agrees with Father's health. That helps set my mind at ease."

Penelope narrowed her eyes just a touch. "I expected to see you on the floor and flailing your arms about over vacating Winnover. You can't be this content about losing it."

Oh, Penelope. "I'll miss it horribly, of course. But I can't ignore the very obvious situation before me. I've only been out for three weeks. You are already betrothed. While I wish my mother might have kept our circumstance hidden a while longer, we all know that that was never going to happen." She sighed. "I intend to be horribly jealous of you, and I hope you will invite me to come visit Winnover—and you, of course—from time to time."

Giving her arm a last squeeze, her cousin straightened. "Of course, you must come to visit Howard and me at Winnover. But not right away; I already have so many ideas for improvements, and I want you to see it at its finest."

Emmie allowed her smile to slip. "I don't know that it needs much improvement, but it will be yours. I wish . . ." She brushed at one eye. "Well, I wish you all the best, Pen."

That made her cousin happy. Emmie could see the unabashed avarice in her toothy smile. "Aren't you a dear," Penelope cooed. "Oh, and there's Howard!" She sent him a wave. "I must go tell him the good news."

With that she twirled away, resplendent in pink silk and taffeta. Emmie watched after her cousin for a moment, then blew out her breath. "Silly thing," she muttered. And now Penelope and Howard could return to taking their time to plan their glorious wedding and their even more glorious future at Winnover Hall.

Except that Winnover Hall belonged to *her*. Emmie knew that, felt it, with every bit of blood and bone she possessed. She breathed it and dreamed it and loved it. Penelope couldn't have it. And that meant she had one course of action. Marriage. And quickly.

She did have three proposals already, and she'd put them all off; that was what a young lady did when she still had most of the Season before her. Now, though, thanks to her chatty mother, she had a deadline.

Squaring her shoulders, she toured the ballroom and neighboring salons. She hadn't attended two finishing schools and learned three languages to be drummed out of her own home by bad timing—or her very gaudy cousin.

Ten minutes later, though, she had to concede that she wouldn't be accepting any of her gentlemen tonight, because none of them were in attendance. She could arrange a coincidental meeting with one of them tomorrow, but at any moment Penelope might realize that Emmie would never give up Winnover without a fight. And with a special license she could be Penelope Ramsey Chase three days from that moment.

The trill of a waltz began, and she didn't even have a partner. And there was Penelope, all smiles and excitement as she dragged Howard onto the floor. *Dash it all.*

"If someone had wagered me that Emmeline Hervey would be standing at the edge of the dance floor while a waltz played, I would have lost a great deal of money."

Emmie turned around, smiling despite the distraction. "You don't wager, Will Pershing."

William Pershing inclined his head, his mop of dark brown hair falling across one eye and the rest of him looking nearly as disheveled, as if the cravat had been an afterthought and his coat the one that happened to be nearest the door. He even had ink stains on his fingers. "True enough," he said. "I do dance, however, if you're willing to risk your toes."

That was Will, absentminded, but always good-hearted. And tonight, saving her from looking like a social pariah. "You are a godsend, my friend," she said, grinning as she took his outstretched hand.

"You are the only one to think so," he commented, his smile almost making her forget that they were practically siblings. "My mother took one look at me earlier and just shook her head."

Emmie laughed. "That's only because you are so very close to being dashing. A haircut, a bit of tidying up, and that eyes-half-closed brooding look, and you'd be irresistible."

Will lifted an eyebrow as he put a hand on her waist. "If that's the only difference between me being swarmed by females or not, I'm rather happy to remain myself."

"Well, I've always adored you, so I have no complaints about that."

He gazed at her for a heartbeat before he twirled her onto the floor. "You do have a way with words, Em."

She bit back her smile a little as they swung past Penelope. She was supposed to be gloomy and distraught and not looking for a husband, after all. "I saw your mother earlier," she said once her cousin had passed by. "She's still trying to convince my mother to join her at a coffeehouse for breakfast."

"Yes, I'm afraid drinking coffee makes her feel daring, and she's determined to drag all her friends into the habit with her."

As they turned and the other dancers flowed past, she returned to her quest. Another half dozen gentlemen came to mind, but not a one infatuated enough with her that he could be induced to propose tonight. "You haven't been about much, Will. I've had to find new riding companions."

Will shrugged. "Oxford, and an apprenticeship with Lord Howverton. I could manage a ride or two, though, if you've a mind. We are neighbors."

Only half listening, Emmie nodded. "Of course. Does Lord Howverton ever smile? I must know."

"Not in my presence," he said, grinning. "He's been lobbying to widen every canal between London and Wales. It'll improve shipping speed and lower costs of both coal and iron. He's up against every Tory in Parliament, but the longer we put off this sort of progress, the further behind we'll fall."

Will Pershing was only two years her senior but serious as the grave when it came to politics and the state of the kingdom. If only he paid as much attention to his dress. "An apprenticeship? Surely you're worth more than that, Will."

"I'm a nobody, I'm afraid. And, I quote, 'far too young to have a grasp of the difference between necessity and fashionable folly.'"

"Nonsense. All you need is someone to remind you to take a moment to charm a fellow before you try to convince him to open his purse, and perhaps a young lady acquainted with a great many wives of departmental secretaries and parliamentarians."

"Ah. You and I should become partners, then, Emmie. You could charm Midas himself into donating gold for a good cause."

She smiled again. "I have missed you and your compliments."

When he smiled back, amusement touching his light green eyes, her attention snagged. Will Pershing *was* a handsome young man beneath his disheveled surface, tall and well-built if still a bit gangly. All her friends thought him serious and shy, not adept with flirtations or conversations about the weather, while she reckoned he just couldn't be bothered. Everyone knew his future lay in the government, either in Parliament or on some Department Secretary's staff. She wouldn't have been surprised to hear one day that he'd been elected prime minister. They'd been neighbors and friends since childhood; he'd even proposed to her in Seasons gone by, though she hadn't paid him any mind.

Oh. *Oh.*

William Pershing.

Why not her and Will Pershing? She wanted to keep her home, and obviously he needed a wife who could encourage him to dress more carefully and make the effort to be charming, to help him open whichever doors he might find closed because of his age or his lack of deep familial pockets or pedigree.

She shoved down the responding electric flutter of her nerves. Rationally, she was more than adequately prepared for married life; aside from her formal education, she knew how to make herself—and her spouse—popular among the *haut ton*. She knew how to speak to her social betters and lessers, she'd discovered precisely how much ratafia and Madeira she could imbibe and still keep all of her wits about her, and she could hostess a dinner party for two or for two hundred with equal aplomb. Really, she was a veritable artist, and a social calendar her medium.

Other ladies her age might pine for true love, but by becoming Mrs. Pershing she would get the one thing her heart truly desired—Winnover Hall.

"Penny for your thoughts," Will muttered, tilting his head a little as he gazed down at her.

Oh yes, Will. She did need him for all of this. Closing her eyes for just a moment, Emmie took a deep breath. This was only the rest of her life. "I've told you about Winnover Hall."

"Yes. I've always wanted to see it. You describe it quite vividly."

"I'm about to lose it. Forever."

His brow furrowed. "What's happened? Are your parents well?"

"They're moving to Bath, for my father's health. And Winnover is actually owned by my grandfather."

"The Duke of Welshire."

"Precisely. And he has . . . rules about who may live there. It's to be the next member of the family who marries."

As he took that information in, she watched his face.

He'd always been quick-witted, and she hoped he didn't fail her now. If there was one thing she didn't want, it was to look foolish.

"Your cousin, Penelope Ramsey, just accepted Howard Chase's offer, did she not?"

Emmie nodded, surprised he knew even that much Society news. "She did."

"So Winnover is hers now?"

"Not yet. She's betrothed, but she isn't yet married."

"Ah."

He turned her about the dance floor in silence. Was he looking for a way to turn her down without hurting her feelings? Or had he not yet caught on? She took another breath. Subtlety was for people with time. "We should get married, Will. You and I. Winnover Hall would be ours. It's only a day from London, much more practical than your Arriss House in Yorkshire for a man who means to work for the government."

His face paled, and she felt his shoulder stiffen beneath her hand. "I—"

"And I would be the perfect partner for you," she pressed. "Just think of it. I know everyone, I have a duke for a grandfather, and we'd have Winnover's substantial income. Our political dinners would become the hit of London. We'd have the prime minister himself dining with us every Wednesday."

"So y—"

"I will devote every waking hour to your success," she continued, before he could free himself and run away. Yes, she'd ambushed him, and yes, she was being horribly selfish *and* foolish, but she meant it. In exchange for keeping Winnover Hall, she would do everything in her power to help him to political success. "You wouldn't regret it, Will."

"Th—"

"Please consi—"

"Shut it, will you?" he protested, pulling her off the dance floor and barely avoiding a collision.

"I know it sounds mad, but—"

"Emmie. Allow me a moment to think, will you?"

"Oh. Yes. Of course."

"Thank you." He drew a breath. "Now. You want to marry me in order to keep Winnover Hall as your home, yes?"

The time for romance in her life had passed before it had begun, but for Winnover she would take friendship and a business partnership. "Yes."

"And our marriage would accomplish that?"

"If we marry before Penelope does. And we'd have to produce an heir within five years in order to keep it."

"Your grandfather is mad, Em."

"I agree, though Winnover's been passed down this way for ages."

"Why me?"

He wouldn't believe her if she flung something about long-simmering romantic feelings at him. While she'd been rather smitten by him as a child, that had been ages ago. They'd barely spoken in two years. "Because you're my friend, and because you'll put my talents to good use," she said. "We don't need to do any courting, we can wed quickly, and we understand each other's motives. Political success for you, and Winnover for me."

"You have other suitors." He glanced about the room again. "Ah. None of them are here, are they?"

So much for not sounding desperate. "William Pershing, I will help make you a valued member of our government. I swear it. In addition, you will reside at the loveliest home in the world, and you will not regret a moment of your decision. But I do *need* your decision. Tonight."

Returning his green-eyed gaze to her, he grimaced. "This is not . . ." He shut his mouth again, and she could almost see him thinking, no doubt debating the logic and consequences of any decision. Then, straightening, he held one hand out to her. "Do I need to ask your father's permission, or do we just tell them we'll be marrying as soon as I procure a special license from Canterbury?"

Emmie took his fingers, just barely refraining from planting a kiss on his cheek. "Oh, thank you, Will. You have no idea . . . Thank you." She could keep Winnover. Even more, she would be mistress of Winnover. It would be hers—and Will's—for the rest of her life. Smiling, she met his gaze, but for once she couldn't quite define what she saw looking back at her. He was doing her a very great and unexpected favor, though.

"We will have a good . . . partnership, I think," he said. "You won't have cause to regret this, either."

"Of course I won't." She'd done it. And now all they needed was a license, a parson, and a church before Penelope could realize she'd been outmaneuvered. And if she could manage to find a husband in one evening, which she had, the rest would be easy.

CHAPTER ONE

Eight years, four months, and thirteen days later

Emmeline Pershing sipped her tea, then set it down with a smile. "Your success with the miners' charity is remarkable, Barbara. I have no idea where you find the patience to deal with all the bureaucracy."

Barbara, Lady Graham, smiled back at her. "It's mostly a matter of nodding at the right moment, my dear. Allow the men to argue until they're exhausted, and then nod at the one whose idea makes the most sense. A following smile nearly always secures support and agreement."

With a chuckle, Emmie waved away their waiter. They were nearly done here. The Blue Rose Inn kept its tables far enough apart that even on the busiest of afternoons, one could have a reasonable conversation without being either drowned out or overheard. That made it perfect for luncheons such as this one. "Oh, the degree of patience that must take. Does it work with Lord Graham, too?"

"On all but the rarest of occasions." Barbara took a sip of her own tea. "Don't tell me you can't also bend Mr. Pershing with a smile, Emmie. I'll never believe it."

"My chance to do so depends on whether Mr. Pershing ever looks up from the papers he's always obsessing over. I daresay if I could assure him that he's not the only one who understands that a single silly road in Africa could improve not just Britain's spice trade but our relations with half of Europe, he would be much more amenable to holding a soiree for our friends and neighbors, for example."

"I do love your soirees, Emmie." The baroness leaned forward. "I'll have a word with Edmund about that road. He's stubborn as a mule, but he does love Britain making money. And me, of course."

Oh yes, Lord Graham doted on his wife. Which was why Emmie lunched with Barbara, despite Lord Graham's very conservative politics. She put a hand to her chest. "If Lord Graham were to support Mr. Pershing's road, Barbara, I daresay the resulting Winnover Hall soiree would be talked about for a Season or more."

They stood, and Barbara took her hand. "If you promise to have Mrs. Brubbins bake her delightful blackberry pie, you may consider it done, my dear."

Emmie inclined her head. "Perhaps I'll have my cook send you a pie tomorrow, and you needn't wait."

"And that is why I adore you, Emmie."

As she left the Blue Rose Inn, in the heart of the village of Birdlip, in the heart of Gloucestershire, Emmie was joined by her maid, Hannah. "It went well, I presume?" the maid whispered.

They climbed into the waiting coach. "It did. And after dinner with the Hendersens this evening, I think Mr. Pershing may have the support he requires for his road."

"That's splendid news, Mrs. Pershing."

It was what she'd promised Mr. Pershing: to aid his efforts in the government and see him succeed. Thus far, if she said so herself, it had all gone quite swimmingly. She sat back to look out the window as the coach wound along the road and up the long, sloping hill to Winnover

Hall. The method she and Mr. Pershing had developed over the past eight years worked well. With a mere note or two, they flawlessly coordinated their separate calendars, his causes, and the points where the three merged for such things as this dinner. Here in the countryside those joint ventures were of course less common, but she did enjoy the time off from the busy London social and political Season.

As they stopped at the head of the drive, the butler pulled open the carriage door and handed her down. "I hope you had a pleasant luncheon, Mrs. Pershing," Powell said, following her into the house and taking her shawl. "I've seen the painting replaced in the dining room as you requested, and I reminded Mr. Pershing that the Hendersens will arrive at six o'clock tonight for dinner. He does tend to misplace time when he's out hunting."

"Yes, he does. I daresay he would sleep out beneath some shrubbery or other if he could, just to gain an earlier start to his morning."

Emmie didn't hunt, but she did enjoy the woods and meadows surrounding Winnover Hall. After all, she'd grown up walking the trails and picking apples from the orchard and, until her mother had deemed it unladylike, climbing trees and fishing in the large pond beyond the garden. No other place in England could match the view, with the soft, rolling hills, the green pastures set amid copses of oak and elm trees, the wildflowers growing along the lanes . . . Nowhere and nothing in the world made her heart as happy as this thousand acres in Gloucestershire.

Earlier she'd put a bouquet of fresh autumn roses in the morning room, and the warm, spiced scent of them filled the entire front of the house. Yes, this—Winnover Hall, with its wooden beams and brick fireplaces and yellow Cotswold stone—was the very best place in the world. And she was its mistress.

"Please remind Mrs. Brubbins that the Hendersens are teetotalers; no wine in the broth. Or on the table. Have her start brewing some of that Moroccan coffee at half five; the scent will be delightful for our guests. Then we'll set it out after dinner. Oh, and I've promised Lady Graham one of her blackberry pies for tomorrow."

The coffee would provide an opening for Mr. Pershing's over-dinner discussion regarding North African trade routes and treaties. He'd left her a list of things he wished to discuss with Mr. Hendersen, a rather influential member of the House of Commons, and Africa had again been right at the top.

While she wasn't well-versed in any African dishes, there were other ways to turn a conversation to a particular topic. That was why she'd asked Powell to remove the Thomas Lawrence painting hung in the dining room, the pastoral landscape of Gloucestershire she and Mr. Pershing had received as a wedding gift from her parents, and replace it with the painting of wild elephants her great-uncle Harry Ramsey had left behind in the attic. That would suit the evening's theme much better.

The butler nodded, the ring of hair that began at his temples and circled round to the back of his head nearly a solid gray now. "I'll see to it. And the mail just arrived; you have a letter from His Grace." He retrieved the silver salver from the side table, the letter resting atop it.

Her heart stuttered. She and her grandfather did correspond, but she couldn't say it was anything she looked forward to. Still, duty was duty. Taking the missive from the tray, she turned it over. The Duke of Welshire's seal, imprinted in red wax, held the letter closed. It always looked very impressive, even if the contents were more often than not of the "I don't approve of Lord So-and-So's politics, pray do not socialize with him more than is strictly necessary" variety.

She broke the wax seal. "Oh, thank goodness," she murmured, skimming through the first paragraph. "I'd nearly forgotten His Grace's birthday next month. Luckily, the Duke of Welshire has never been one to pass by the opportunity to be fawned over."

"It's his seventieth, is it not?" Hannah asked.

"It is." As she read on, though, her relief twisted into a deep, hard knot. *Oh dear. Oh dear, oh dear, oh dear.*

"Mrs. Pershing, are you well?" the maid asked, fanning at Emmie's face with her hands. "Should I fetch you something? Do you need to sit down?"

Emmie grabbed on to the wall for balance. "I—The— No, thank you, Hannah." She forced a smile. "Nothing worrisome. Just something I need to see to. I'll be in the morning room. Please do not disturb me except to notify me the moment Mr. Pershing returns."

"Of course, ma'am. Are you certain you're well?"

"Yes, yes. I'm perfectly fine."

With a swift curtsy, her expression a mix of worry and badly disguised curiosity, the maid retreated, and Emmie walked through the morning room door and shut it behind her.

The moment she found herself alone, Emmeline strode over to the window to read through the letter a second time. The last thing she wanted was to misinterpret an innocent turn of phrase and see ruination where none existed. In her grandfather's spare handwriting, though, the words remained—the damning, damnable sentence right in the middle of the page, where she couldn't excise it without its absence being noticed, where she couldn't pretend that she'd missed seeing it and still respond to the rest of the missive's contents.

Oh, this was very bad. For eight years she'd made her union with Mr. Pershing a successful one, and indeed they were universally praised and admired. She had her charities and her friends, most of them carefully chosen depending on the political leanings of husbands, fathers, or brothers; he had his clubs and his work with the government; and they both comported themselves like the proper, correct-living people they were.

Now it was gone. Not yet, because at this moment she was the only one who knew of the destruction. This was one thing, however, that she couldn't see to without informing her marriage partner. And then . . . Oh, God, it would all be over. She would be ridiculed, ruined, gossiped about, and, finally, ignored and forgotten. Reliable, gentlemanly Mr. Pershing, who hadn't done anything to deserve such censure, would face the same consequences.

Emmeline stood up, the letter clenched in one hand, and paced until she ended up at the liquor tantalus against one wall. As a rule, she didn't drink anything stronger than ratafia, but pouring herself a brimming glass of whiskey, she decided that her private comportment didn't signify. Far more public and less excusable flaws were about to emerge.

That wasn't even the worst of it, though. This letter meant her—their—days at Winnover Hall had ended. Her house. Her home. The large library with its half dozen windows overlooking the garden and the pond beyond. The scent of orchard apples that came with the autumn's afternoon breeze. This lovely morning room with its warm yellow wallpaper and cozy green-and-yellow-striped chairs. All gone now to the devil—or to her cousin Penelope, which was nearly the same thing.

She jumped when someone rapped at the morning room door. How long had she been in there? Emmeline finished off her second—or was it the third?—glass of the horrible-tasting liquor before she answered. "Yes?"

Hannah leaned into the room. "Mr. Pershing is at the stable," she said, her eyes widening at the sight of the half-empty bottle. "Would you like some tea, ma'am? Or Mrs. Brubbins is brewing that coffee you mentioned, if you'd like something stronger."

Emmeline waved her hand. "No, no. We're saving the Moroccan coffee for our guests. That's why I purchased it. Just tell Mr. Pershing that I wish to speak with him. I shall remain here." She felt steadier now; perhaps the whiskey wasn't so bad, after all.

Once the door shut again, she walked to the window, leaning against the sill, then repositioned herself by the fireplace with one elbow on the mantel. No, perhaps sitting at the pianoforte would be more strategic. She smoothed out the letter she'd managed to crumple, pressing it against her thigh. *There*. Now she looked composed.

The door opened. "You wanted to see me?"

William Pershing, she thought unhelpfully, was a fellow whose face would have been supremely handsome if it wasn't always so serious. His dark hair was windblown, and he still wore his hunting jacket. His very well-fitting hunting jacket. The faint odor of gunpowder mixed with the heavier scent of her autumn roses, the combination a bit unsettling.

"What is it, Mrs. Pershing?" her husband prompted, one hand still on the door, as if to make it clear that he was on his way elsewhere. "I'd like to clean up before dinner with the Hendersens," he added unnecessarily.

Emmie opened her mouth, then shut it again. How did

one go about destroying one's life, after all? Begin with a success, of course. "Lady Graham is confident stuffy old Lord Graham will support your road."

He tilted his head, his mouth briefly quirking. "Are you drunk?"

"What? Of course not." She smoothed the duke's letter again. "I—we—have a partnership that works well for both of us. Wouldn't you agree?"

"Yes. You have been an invaluable asset, just as you promised. Why?" Mr. Pershing took a full step into the room and quietly shut the door behind himself.

Yes, he was as mindful of gossip as she was, yet another reason their partnership worked so splendidly. "I keep an impeccable household, don't you think?"

A frown creased his forehead. "Yes. You manage the household perfectly. The servants, our meals, parties, and our joint social schedule. Why are you asking?"

Emmie cleared her throat. "One of the conditions for the Duke of Welshire giving us this home was that we continue the family bloodline. You know he's obsessed with that."

His jaw jumped. "We did make an attempt," he reminded her. "For seven months after our wedding."

Oh, she remembered that. She'd promised him a friendship and a partnership, but then three days later they'd been married. And good heavens, partners didn't . . . do those things. Not her disheveled, earnest friend who'd stripped off his clothes and had that . . . thing jutting out at her and then put his mouth all over her. And then it had . . . erupted before . . . And his nakedness, the bare all of him . . . Her cheeks burned at the recollection. They'd later managed to complete the deed on several occasions in the hope of producing offspring, but only with the candles out and her eyes shut. Every time he stepped into the bedchamber, she couldn't help recalling their wedding night, the way he'd unbalanced their agreement and made their partnership about an intimacy she certainly hadn't been ready for. "Yes."

"And you informed him that we did so. He accepted that."

For a moment she contemplated holding her breath until she fainted, just to avoid saying the words. This was it—the moment of her destruction. "I have made an error." *Doomed. Doomed.* "I told him we were successful," she blurted.

The seconds seemed to stretch for hours, the silence so profound she imagined she would have been able to hear the church bells all the way in Gloucester.

Mr. Pershing sank into a neighboring chair. "I'm sorry," he said faintly, "I didn't quite catch that."

"My grandfather would never change his mind about the agreement, and I much prefer living here to some tiny cottage in the middle of Yorkshire," she stated, folding her arms.

"Arriss House is *my* inheritance."

"Yes, I know. And Winnover Hall is, or was, mine, ridiculous conditions attached or not. But you've said yourself that Yorkshire is too far from London for it to suffice."

"So you—you told him we had *a child*?"

"He's a recluse living all the way up in Cumberland," she shot back. "For heaven's sake, we've barely seen him twice in eight years. What's the harm? This is a splendid arrangement. We've achieved everything else we attempted, just as I promised. Why should we have to leave Winnover Hall simply because of an accident of nature? So I fixed it."

For heaven's sake, she had done everything possible

to fulfill the second part of the Winnover agreement. She'd gone to the doctor her mother had recommended. She'd listened as he'd told her that if she hadn't conceived in seven months, she likely never would, and that some women weren't meant to be mothers—a sentiment her mother had shared, and claimed to envy. And if her mother regretted being a mother, Emmie wasn't about to regret *not* being one. This way was much simpler, kept her attention from being divided, and made her a much more efficient mistress of the household and partner to her husband.

"You fixed it," he repeated.

"Yes."

Abruptly he stood again, striding over to the whiskey bottle and pouring himself a drink. "So, Mrs. Pershing, you've delivered us a child," he said, downing the contents of the glass. "Given your current . . . agitation, I'm assuming our status quo has altered?"

"It's the Duke of Welshire's seventieth birthday," she stated, waving the letter at him. "In forty-three days. He wants all of his offspring and their offspring and *their* offspring gathered at his side so he can"—she lifted the paper to read the line—"'be assured of the immortality of my bloodline as I look toward the grave.'" The enormity of the disaster she'd caused hit her once again, and she flung her hands over her face. "I've ruined everything!"

He made a sound from across the room, but didn't say anything more. No doubt he was busily wondering whether a marriage of eight years could still be annulled.

Emmie lifted her head. "I'm so sorry," she wailed. "I shall make it clear to His Grace that you had nothing to do with the deception, or the lack of children. There's no reason you should be blamed. I will go to my parents' house in Bath, so you may enjoy Pershing House in London in peace when we are cast out of Winnover."

Silence. "What did we have?" he asked abruptly.

Blinking, she tried to catch her thoughts up to his dialogue. "What?"

"Our imaginary child. It had a name and an age and a sex, did it not? Though I presume it would have been a boy."

"Yes. A boy. He would be seven now. Named Malcolm, after His Grace."

Her husband gave a brief nod. "That was a nice touch."

"Well, once I began, I had to make it all as useful as possible. But it doesn't signify now." She lowered her head into her hands, disliking the way the room had begun spinning. "And we have a daughter, too, you might as well know. Cousin Penelope bragged that she had another little one on the way—she has three now, you know—so I decided that we needed another one. She's . . . five, and is named Flora after His Grace's dear mother, my great-grandmother."

Silence. "Are there any more little blessings I should know about?"

"Two is enough to damn us, Mr. Pershing."

He blew out his breath. "So it would seem." She heard him set down the glass and risked a peek up at him to find his gaze on her. "I would have named the girl Louisa, after my grandmother, but as I wasn't consulted . . ." Mr. Pershing visibly shook himself. "Well, it doesn't signify, does it?"

"I should have asked you, of course."

"I don't think that would have helped." He fell silent again, his mind clearly miles away. Finally, he stirred. "Well. As we have roughly six weeks until we're to be evicted, I suggest you have a lie-down before the Hendersens arrive for dinner. I will compose a letter to my solicitor to see if there's anything to be done about keeping Winnover Hall."

There wasn't anything that could be done. Emmie was certain of that. Everything had been put into writing and signed by her and Mr. Pershing, after all. The Duke of Welshire, and all the previous Dukes of Welshire, had been very specific about this gift—or loan, rather. She and her husband were expected to produce a child within five years of their marriage, or they couldn't stay.

The letter pulled from her fingers, and she looked up again to see Mr. Pershing perusing it, his brow furrowed. "Winnover Hall has been a splendid home," he said quietly. "I've certainly never found finer fishing anywhere in England. And I know how much you adore it."

Another tear joined the hundred others running down her face. "At least our children gave us eight years here, I suppose."

"Eight very pleasant years. Ages seven and five, you said?"

"Yes."

"Ah, here it is. 'I expect you and William to attend the festivities, along with young Malcolm and Flora. I would have all my relations gathered around me so that I may be assured of the immortality of my bloodline as I look toward the grave.'" He glanced up at her. "He actually did write that. It's quite morbid, isn't it?"

"It makes sense when you consider that he's been looking toward his grave and demanding descendants for at least the last forty years."

"I suppose so."

She watched as Mr. Pershing finished reading the letter

and set it atop the pianoforte. For eight years he'd been a calm, solid presence in the house, amiable but not intrusive, and—after she informed him of her infertility and the lack of need for them to continue attempting to procreate—visiting her private rooms only rarely and only after giving her advance warning. She'd seen to it that every action she took was done with the betterment of his career in mind—while she had the status of marriage, his impeccable reputation, and, of course, Winnover Hall. The arrangement had been perfect. "I am sorry, Mr. Pershing," she said, another tear running down her cheek.

"As am I. Damnation."

He walked to the window and stood looking out over the front drive, hands at his sides. She couldn't begin to decipher his thoughts, but if they were anything like her own, Mr. Pershing was in deep despair. She wanted to tell him she'd spent hours this afternoon trying to think of a way around the consequences of her lies, but nothing at all had come to mind.

Finally, he turned to face her, his green eyes meeting her gaze. She nearly told him that he had pretty eyes, but that stank of pandering, and she'd only had the thought because of the discussion of their . . . physical union. "All of this aside," he said, "Mr. and Mrs. Hendersen will be here within the hour, and as you know, I could use his support. We must focus on that."

Emmeline wiped her eyes. "Yes, of course."

As he left the room, she sank her head onto the cool top of the pianoforte. Yes, her duty as hostess remained, whether they were about to be drummed out of their lovely, lovely home or not.

At least for the moment she had her duties. Once he'd heard from his solicitor that there was no possible way to retain use of Winnover Hall, he might well decide that her role in his household was no longer sufficient to recompense him for the loss.

Oh, the last thing she wanted to do this evening was entertain stuffy Mr. and Mrs. Hendersen. The only bright spot was that their insufferably proper children wouldn't be attending to remind her of her own failure—her twice-over failure.

Mousy little Maxwell was what, six years old now? Nearly the same age as her own Malcolm would be. And . . .

Oh. *Oh.* What if—Oh. She straightened again, then stood to pace to the door and back. *No.* She couldn't. But what if . . . Her grandfather was a known recluse. His house party was to last a week, according to the letter, but she wouldn't be surprised to see him send all his relations away after a single day. It had happened before. He didn't like them nearly as much as he liked the idea of them. Which meant that he would be seeing his hundred or so children, grandchildren, great-grandchildren and grandnieces and grandnephews and God knew who else for a matter of hours. Minutes for each one, really.

Surely it would be possible to borrow a pair of well-bred neighbor children for a few days. One tiny, additional falsehood in exchange for the rest of her life at her childhood home and for the salvation of Mr. Pershing's career. Who could object to that? *Good heavens.* Yes, it was rather brilliant, if she did say so herself.

"Hannah!" she called, and rushed over to the writing table to extend an invitation to the Hendersens to bring their two darling children along to dinner this evening.

"Mrs. Pershing?" the maid asked, hurrying into the room.

"Have this delivered to Black Oak Manor at once, if

you please. And inform Mrs. Brubbins that we will be six for dinner. I shall have her make her famous lemon biscuits. Children like biscuits. Yes, they do."

"I believe that to be true, ma'am," Hannah said, taking the missive. With a bewildered look at her employer, she left the room again.

There. She hadn't figured it all out, of course, but why wouldn't it serve? Two borrowed, perfectly polite children for a fortnight or so, with the prize being a lifetime at Winnover Hall. *Well done, Emmie.*

Then she grabbed for the vase of autumn roses, flung the flowers away, and cast up the contents of her stomach into the pretty etched-glass container.

CHAPTER TWO

Gregory Hendersen gestured with his fork. "That's all very well, Will, but spending blunt on African roads and African bridges when the London mail coach throws a wheel every two miles? It's frivolous."

He was a round and serious man, matched well by his wife's rail-thin presence and tendency toward overextravagant praise of her own offspring. Will Pershing didn't like to use the word "insufferable," but the adjective fit the Hendersens. He glanced down the table. Why Emmeline had invited the children to join them, he had no clue. With her ability to set the perfect scene for whichever project he'd laid before her, he had to trust her decision. Children and transportation routes through northern Africa, though, didn't make for any kind of puzzle he'd ever pieced together.

"I had a thought, Mr. Pershing," Emmeline said, as soon as he finished his statement about roads and bridges not being as important in themselves as they were to trade and building alliances.

He glanced at his wife, hiding his surprise behind a practiced smile. She left the business negotiations to him and utilized her considerable talents to ease his pathway.

This felt a bit direct for her. "What thought was that, Mrs. Pershing?"

"Well, it's just marvelous." She leaned forward, taking Mary Hendersen's hand across the table. That in itself was a faux pas of the sort she simply didn't make. "Mr. Pershing and I will be holidaying in Cumberland next month," she said to the Hendersen matriarch. "Wouldn't it be delightful if young Maxwell and Prudence were to join us?"

What? Will frowned, glancing from her to the children and back again. Abruptly it dawned on him—they needed two offspring in order to keep Winnover Hall. And there they were, a boy and a girl sitting politely, using all the correct utensils in the proper order, just like miniature adults. *Good God.* He lifted an eyebrow. "You think Maxwell and Prudence should accompany us. To Cumberland." It seemed obvious that was her plan, but it never hurt to be certain.

"Why, yes! Don't you agree?"

Gregory Hendersen sent Will a quizzical look. "Why in heaven's name do you wish to take our children on holiday with you?"

With a shrill laugh, Emmeline squeezed Mary Hendersen's hand, thereby breaking several more rules of etiquette. "We haven't been to the Lake District in ages, and as both Mr. Pershing and I are fond of the youngsters, I thought, well, why not ask the Hendersens if their young ones might wish to see it with us?"

"I . . . don't know what to say." Mrs. Hendersen sent her husband a look that suggested they'd agreed to dinner with Bedlamites as she retrieved her hand from Emmeline's grip. "Prudence and Maxwell off on holiday without us? That's very irregular."

"Nonsense," Will countered, trying to keep up. Emmeline might have mentioned her intentions beforehand, at which time he would have pointed out several things she seemed to have overlooked. Still, in for a penny, as the saying went. "I was but eight when my uncle took me to stay with him in Scotland all summer."

"What does that have to do with anything?" Mrs. Hendersen commented.

Emmeline had come up with a rather clever idea, dash it all. Will wished he'd thought of it. "Maxwell, you must be what, seven?" he asked, refocusing his attention. It was damned audacious, and that appealed to him. Audacity could well be the only chance they had to keep hold of Winnover Hall. The blow to his reputation and his career—he'd only just begun to realize how significant the damage from her lie could be, but if they could manage this one problem at the heart of the spider's web, it would solve all of the others.

"I am six years and three months old," the black-haired youth said, setting aside his fork and sitting up straighter. "Nearly seven."

Hmm. Seven was the exact age of the son Emmeline had created from the ether. "Nearly seven," he echoed. "What a delightful age."

"Yes, it's perfect, isn't it?" his wife seconded.

"'Perfect'?" Mr. Hendersen repeated, scowling.

"I'm nine," Prudence, black-haired like her brother, piped in.

"Prudence, mind your manners. She's such a chatterbox."

The girl ducked her head. "I apologize, Mama."

Yes, Prudence was definitely a problem. She was older by four years than the fictional Flora, and better than a foot taller than her brother. Perhaps they could convince the duke that it was Flora who was the seven-year-old, and Malcolm the five-year-old. Pigtails might make her look younger.

It all depended on how detailed Emmeline's description of their fictional offspring had been. The Hendersen children were well-mannered, and while their coloring wasn't ideal, with Will having dark brown hair and Emmeline being an attractive fire-touched blonde, there were certain to be some black-haired relations in their ancestry. Enough to explain these faux offspring, anyway. No doubt that had been his wife's thinking—though he had the suspicion that her thought process was still suffering from that bottle of whiskey.

Emmeline smiled broadly at the girl seated beside her father on the far side of the table, then smacked her hand loudly against the mahogany surface and turned to the butler. "Powell, I think the children would enjoy some of Mrs. Brubbins's biscuits." She looked back at the children's mother. "Our cook makes splendid lemon biscuits."

The butler nodded. "Of course, Mrs. Pershing." He gestured at one of the footmen, who darted out of the dining room.

Biscuits in the middle of dinner seemed like another one of those rules Emmeline Pershing would rather fall on a sword than break, but she'd clearly put all of her eggs into the Hendersen basket. Her gentle, elegant, guiding hand, her masterful reading of every room she entered and every occupant therein, had vanished in favor of a wildly swinging cricket bat of half-finished ideas. *Fascinating.*

"I thought you were spending hunting season here, Will," Mr. Hendersen put in.

"I was," he took up, "but Mrs. Pershing's grandfather

has an estate in Cumberland, and there's rumored to be splendid pheasant and grouse hunting there." He *did* like to hunt, and that made for a solid reason to go on holiday. The Hendersens couldn't be allowed to know that their children were needed for the purpose of lying to a duke.

Mrs. Hendersen sat up straighter, which in itself was a feat considering how ramrod-like her spine was on the most casual of occasions. "The Duke of Welshire? That grandfather?"

"Well, yes," Emmeline conceded. "He's invited us—"

"Oh, I say, I wouldn't mind joining you for a fortnight at Welshire Park," Gregory Hendersen broke in. "I've heard tales of the fine pheasant hunting to be found at Welshire. Famous, it is. What say you, Mary?"

"No," Emmeline blurted, before Will could come up with a logical excuse that would prevent the parents from joining them.

"I beg your pardon?" Now Mary and Gregory Hendersen were both frowning at her.

Will cleared his throat. "I believe what Mrs. Pershing meant to say was that we—"

"What, that you only wanted *our children* to accompany you?" Gregory broke in. "I think not, Pershing."

"It would only be for a fortnight," Emmeline pressed, facing the youngsters. "If that. Don't you wish to see the Lake District with your aunt and uncle Pershing, darlings?"

"You're not our aunt and uncle," Prudence said, scowling.

"Prudence! Please. The adults will handle this."

The girl subsided again. "Yes, Mama."

"You are not their aunt and uncle," Mary Hendersen stated. "In fact, Emmie, I can't recall a single instance where you've taken any previous interest in our children."

"How could I not? They're all you ever talk about."

Will snorted before he could stop himself.

"Well! I never. Gregory?"

"The answer is no. We must decline your . . . invitation." Gregory stood just as the footman reentered the dining room, a platter of biscuits in his hand. The two men collided, the lemon-scented confections flipping into the air before they thudded like buttery raindrops onto the blue and gray Persian throw rug.

"That's disappointing," Prudence observed.

"I don't know what's afoot here," Mrs. Hendersen stated, standing to grab her son by the arm and drag him out of his chair, "but this is very peculiar."

"I assure you, Mrs. Hendersen, Gregory, that we have nothing but the purest of motives for making our offer," Will protested, rising from his own chair. It was far too late for negotiating, but perhaps he could still salvage their reputations—and the African trade routes. "What child wouldn't wish to be able to brag that they've met a duke?"

"I don't want to go with them, Papa," young Maxwell whined, stepping over cookies with a mournful look on his round face.

"And so you shan't, my boy. Will, I trust you do have some sort of method behind all this madness. Perhaps offer it to me in writing, so we may be friends again. If you wish my name to be joined with your northern Africa roads cause, especially."

"I give you the same suggestion, Emmie," Mrs. Hendersen stated stiffly. "Good evening."

Powell hurried after the Hendersens to assist them out the front door. The two footmen lowered themselves to their hands and knees and began searching for bits of lemon cookies beneath the table.

"Leave it," Will said. "Out. Everyone."

Emmeline set her napkin aside and stood, turning for the door. God, what a mess she'd made. It was remarkable. But another dinner or two like that, and they would both be ridiculed as societal outcasts even without her lie becoming public knowledge.

"Not you, Mrs. Pershing. You shall remain."

"I don't blame you for being angry," she stated as the staff vacated. "After all, I've been lying to the Duke of Welshire for seven years. On the other hand, you viewed the agreement for Winnover Hall at the same time as I, and you don't seem to be cursed with a failing memory. You had to know that without children to appease him, eventually the duke would demand Winnover's return."

"Sit," he said, noting the more logical tone of her argument. This evening's catastrophe seemed to have somewhat sobered her up.

"I may be the one to blame for lack of offspring," she said, seating herself primly, hands folded in her lap, "but at least I am attempting to aid our situation."

Will shut the dining room doors one by one. "We're at the moment where we fault me for not also deciding to conjure imaginary children, then?" he asked mildly, facing her again.

"I—No, of course not. I only mean that at least my fiction gave us three years in residence past the original five."

"I did see and agree to the contract. Since we continued to live here, I thought your grandfather had decided not to abide by the terms of our residency, especially after you informed him of our unsuccessful efforts. I had no idea, of course, that we were raising two children."

Emmeline shrugged. "Not those two children. Selfish Hendersens."

"You were acting like a madwoman, Mrs. Pershing. I can't blame them for fleeing."

"I am not a madwoman." She folded her arms over her chest.

"No, I have always found you to be sensible, even-tempered, and highly intelligent," he agreed, meaning every word. He could add a few more: beautiful, for one, and as of this afternoon, surprising. "In the future, however, when you decide to abduct children, I would appreciate a bit of advance notice."

"We are in desperate circumstances."

"And if you had troubled yourself to recall that in addition to being rather charming I negotiate with obstinate, unyielding people on a regular basis, our odds of success might have improved."

Emmeline lowered her arms again, her mouth opening and closing. "You . . . don't disagree with my plan? It wasn't at all logical, I'm afraid, and you—well, if they built a statue to logic, it would look like you."

He sighed, not the least bit flattered. "How much did you have to drink, anyway?"

"I . . . I may have had a glass or two of whiskey, but it was only to settle my nerves, because I dreaded telling you that we are about to be removed from our home."

He lifted an eyebrow. "Two entire glasses of whiskey?"

She grimaced. "Perhaps it was three."

Or four. "Ah. Plainly I should have inquired about that beforehand. We might have begged off tonight and made a better attempt tomorrow."

Emmeline stared at him as if he'd sprouted a third eye. "You're not opposed to borrowing someone else's children?"

"In truth, Mrs. Pershing, I thought it was quite brilliant."

Her cheeks blushed a pretty rose. "Oh."

"I am fond of Winnover Hall, and I know quite well how much it means to you. I don't wish to lose it over a failure to meet an absurd requirement any more than you do." Not only was Winnover her beloved childhood home and a lovely place, it was close enough to London that he could still be available to the trade ministry, and far enough away that he could set work aside once he arrived in Gloucestershire.

With its multiple sitting rooms and movable ballroom walls, it was perfect for large or small gatherings. Aside from all of its various physical attributes, residing at Winnover Hall felt . . . peaceful, and he was loath to give it up because nature had decided to spite the Pershing household.

She continued to eye him. In all honesty, he did understand her surprise. While he didn't agree that he and logic were interchangeable and statue-like, he did have a good head for facts and figures. Flights of imagination weren't something in which either of them was accustomed to indulging. Not for the past eight years, anyway. And yet there they both were, flapping their wings.

"As I consider it, those Hendersens were the wrong ages," she stated, waving a hand in dismissal. "Well-behaved, yes, but the girl could never pass for a five-year-old."

"I had that same thought, after I caught on. The boy would have done, but without a daughter we're no better off than if we had no children at all to present."

"We *have* no children to present."

He grimaced. "Yes. I find, however, now that you've hatched this scheme, I rather approve. And the Hendersen children are not the only young ones in this corner of Gloucestershire."

"I . . . You want to continue with this . . . stratagem?

After the mess I made of things? With your African trade routes?"

"I do, by God." He wanted to be able to remain here, and not only because the Arriss House property was up in Yorkshire. She wanted to remain, with him, and once upon a time he'd been desperately in love with her. So long ago he'd nearly forgotten it, but then at odd moments, like the present one, he remembered. "But do *you* wish to continue? Because as you just so cleverly demonstrated, this task will take both of us."

Her pause made him wonder if she'd sobered up enough to reconsider her mad plan. "Who would we ask?" she queried after a moment. "Lady Graham's daughter Elizabeth is some fourteen years too old, and Lord and Lady Baskin have a babe of but one."

"There are other children about, Mrs. Pershing. Farmer Dawkins has seven or eight, at the least." It was more than that, but he'd stopped counting after eleven.

"Dawkins?" she repeated, her curved eyebrows lifting. "There are at least twelve children now. But our son and daughter are meant to be the great-grandchildren of a duke."

"Our son and daughter do not, at present, exist. And no one else would believe anything to be odd about their parentage, because *we* would be the parents."

Emmeline gazed at him, her features, he noticed, more elegant and slender now than they had been when she was eighteen, and she'd been stunning then. Her pretty brown eyes mirrored her surprise and, unless he was greatly mistaken, approval. "You know, Mr. Pershing, I think this conversation may be the longest we've shared in better than a year."

"Yes, I believe it is. It is definitely the most . . . unexpected." *And rather delightful, actually.* He couldn't remember the last time he'd attempted more than a compliment on a fine soiree. Shabby of a husband, but she'd declared this to be a partnership, and nothing more.

"Well. It's pleasant to have an ally. And as we've already demonstrated, together we have a much greater chance of success. You are, I have found, brilliant at times."

"Well, if I'm to be a logic statue, I suppose I'd prefer to be a brilliant one."

Squaring her shoulders, she stood. "Very well. I shall go have a word with Mrs. Dawkins. Perhaps I'll bring her the remainder of Mrs. Brubbins's biscuits."

"You will remain here," he cut in, "because it is well after dark. Go to bed, Mrs. Pershing."

Her cheeks reddened. "I am not some recalcitrant child."

"No, you aren't. But this has been a day full of surprises, already. I rather expected that it wouldn't take me seven years to realize I had a child, for instance. Children, rather."

She made a face, her pert nose scrunching up. "I did not mean to cause you trouble, you know. I only did what I thought was best for the both of us."

He paused. "I do not like the lie," he said, even though the idea that she'd done something so out of character captivated him, "but I do understand the reason for it. And given that the lie has happened, the direction of most benefit to us would seem to be to make it appear to be the truth. Therefore, first thing in the morning we will make a plan, and we will call on the Dawkinses. Together." If this was to be the last act of their partnership, at least it would be a memorable one.

Whatever the devil his wife had gotten them into, this

looked to be an autumn utterly different from every previous one spent in her company. In fact, he hadn't been so surprised since the evening she'd proposed to him. Evidently, he still liked a good surprise every now and then.

CHAPTER THREE

They took the coach to the Dawkins farm; if they convinced the farmer and his wife to lend two of their children, Emmie and Mr. Pershing would require them at once. Forty-two days, which included the three or four days they would take to reach Welshire Park, was not much time to teach children who weren't of the aristocracy the art of polite and proper behavior.

"We're in agreement about our offer, then?" Mr. Pershing said, flipping his dark green beaver hat between his knees and catching it again. "This will be an opportunity for two of the children to better their positions in life."

"Absolutely," Emmie agreed, wishing she'd kept a list of names and ages of all the Dawkins children. One never knew when a bit of information might prove useful.

"I don't see how they can refuse," her husband went on. "If nothing else, it will be two fewer mouths for them to feed for better than a month."

"I daresay they'll all be eager to go, and we'll have a bounty of youngsters from which to choose." Another flutter of nerves greeted that thought; simply acquiring faux offspring would be only the beginning. There would be lessons and clothes, and of course the meeting with His Grace to get past. Thank goodness the duke's birthday wasn't during the Season, or her calendar would be in shambles as she tried to balance lessons and her social maneuverings on Mr. Pershing's behalf.

"Do you suppose either of them will be literate?" he asked. "I would hate for your grandfather to think us behindhand in educating our own children."

That had occurred to her, as well. As far as she knew, neither of the Dawkins parents knew their letters. "I believe several of the older ones attend the local school, but their actual meeting with the duke will be extremely brief, regardless. We only need to be certain they can write their names, on the chance there will be a birthday card to sign or a game they will be expected to play."

Mr. Pershing nodded. "Well considered as usual, Mrs. Pershing."

Her cheeks warmed at the compliment. The Will Pershing she'd known as a youth would have been flustered and appalled by this mess, and the one since then should at least have been angry. But there were moments last evening when he'd seemed almost . . . amused. It made no sense. Her task, her job, was to see that every event, every dinner, every conversation, was perfect. This marked a colossal failure.

Also baffling was the way she kept catching herself looking at him this morning. Perhaps it was the shock of all this, or the realization that they would have to figure out this large problem together, but with his black, well-fitting coat, green waistcoat, and buckskin trousers, he did look quite attractive. Once she'd found him a good valet she'd been able to stop worrying about his disheveled hair and how well his clothes fit, but at some point she'd just stopped . . . noticing him. But for goodness' sake, she was noticing him now. It was very distracting. And rather annoying. "I appreciate that you've agreed to help," she said, "even if you only see Winnover Hall as the most strategic place to reside."

"We began as partners," he said. "Partners we remain."

"I'm glad to hear that."

"I hope none of the Dawkins youngsters are gingers," he offered after a moment. "There are no gingers in my family as far back as we have portraits to recall them." He tilted his head as he glanced at her. "Your hair has a touch of fire to it, though, so perhaps that would do, after all."

She touched her hair. It wasn't a compliment, though. Only an observation. "Anything between dark brown and blond would be acceptable—and believable. I wrote that both Malcolm and Flora have brownish hair with a hint of gold, though I believe children's hair may change as they grow older."

His hat stopped flipping. "You invented hair colors for them?"

"Well, yes. In Penelope's letters, she's forever talking about how lovely and curly young Lucy's hair is, and how her oldest boy, Frederick, is towheaded. In retrospect I should have left their appearance a blank canvas, but I never thought about actually having to produce them."

"What about eye color?"

She met his gaze. "As you have green eyes, and mine are brown, I said they had hazel eyes. I suppose we may choose children that have any of those three colors and it would still be believable."

Her husband glanced out the coach window. "That is fortuitous," he said, his lips twitching. "Well done once again."

"Does this amuse you?" she demanded, telling herself to stop looking at his blasted mouth. "Have I been a silly, dim-witted female? Because I am very worried about losing Winnover."

He looked back at her. "Mrs. Pershing, yesterday we were but a twosome. Now I find that I have two children of brownish hair and greenish eyes, and that they have names and genders. It also strikes me that I am about to be a father, temporarily or not. That appeals to me. You enjoy a challenge. Doesn't that aspect, at least, appeal to *you*?"

Some women simply aren't meant to be mothers, Lady Anne Hervey had said to her, seven years ago. *I wasn't. Messy, inconvenient thing, you were. You did allow us to keep Winnover, though, so thank you for that, I suppose.*

She shook herself. Considering that she'd mastered the intricacies of both Society and politics, temporary motherhood would be just another task. "A challenge needs a plan."

His responding grin warmed his face and lit his eyes. "A plan of attack. Yes. And considering I once saw you charm Lord Avington into contributing his own money toward constructing the Paddington canal branch, I don't think either of us has a thing to worry about."

That was nice to hear. She shrugged. "You needed it to succeed."

"And it did, thanks in great part to you. In fact, I owe most of my success to you."

"That was our agreement." He'd given up every possibility for a marriage with a wife who could bear him children, whom he might love, in order to help her keep her home. Aiding his way into his chosen career had been the best and only way she could repay him.

The coach bumped as it left the well-traveled road. When it rocked to a halt, Mr. Pershing stood, pushing open the door and setting his hat back on his head as he stepped to the ground. "Mrs. Pershing, I believe we are only moments away from our latest success."

Mr. Pershing had never been one to exaggerate, and Emmie smiled as she took his outstretched hand and descended to the small front yard of the Dawkins cottage. A rooster herded a dozen or so chickens away from the coach and toward their coop, while a trio of geese hissed at the pair of blacks harnessed to its front. As a lone pig trotted past them, she had the oddest feeling that they'd landed in the middle of some artist's pastoral painting of simple life in the country.

She started when the cottage door flew open. "Oh, oh!" Mrs. Dawkins, her blond hair in a haphazard bun and an infant on her hip, ran outside to greet them. "Mrs. Pershing! Mr. Pershing! Good morning to you!"

"Good morning, Jenny," Emmeline said, mentally squaring her shoulders as she put on her best smile and reached out to brush the baby's grubby cheek with one finger. This would be a performance, just like every occasion she'd ever hosted. "Who is this little one?" She held out her hands.

With a brief, quizzical look, more than likely prompted by the fact that Winnover Hall's mistress had never asked to hold one of the Dawkins children before, Jenny Dawkins handed the baby into Emmie's arms. "This is Joe. My youngest."

Then, children began appearing. Some came from the barn, others from the house, and still more from the direction of the field where Harry Dawkins's head popped up above a flowing crop of wheat. Good heavens, they were everywhere.

While she bounced the baby on her hip and cooed at it, Mr. Pershing waved at Dawkins, motioning him to join them. She doubted the farmer needed the encouragement, though; while her husband visited their tenants on a regular basis, and she attended church social gatherings and village charity functions, the two of them there together—and in the middle of the week—would make for something unusual.

"Aren't you a dear, Joe?" she murmured, and the infant gave her a damp smile. *Well, this wasn't so difficult.* And the imaginary Malcolm and Flora weren't infants, relying on her to feed and bathe and dress them. "Are all of these yours?" she went on, turning to Jenny Dawkins again.

Two of the younger girls had attached themselves to the woman's skirts, while one of the boys dragged the pig about the yard by its back feet. As the pig didn't protest, Emmie assumed this to be a regular occurrence.

"Yes. All of 'em. Oh, wait. Sally and Walter, there, belong to the Youngs. The rest, though, is all mine and Harry's. All fourteen of 'em."

"Fourteen?" Emmeline repeated, disregarding the unexpected jealousy that tightened her chest. Being fertile certainly wasn't Jenny's fault. Aside from that, for all her pretty blond hair and slender figure, Jenny Dawkins looked . . . tired. Old, despite her being only one-and-thirty. Good heavens, the woman had given birth once a year since her seventeenth birthday.

"Good morning, Mr. Pershing!" Harry Dawkins boomed, emerging from the field and sticking out his big hand. "And you, as well, ma'am. What brings you here?"

Mr. Pershing shook the farmer's hand. "We—Mrs. Pershing and I—have a proposal for you."

"You've been a good landlord. I'm more than happy to listen."

While she made an effective hostess, Mr. Pershing

had become at least as gifted a negotiator. Content to leave this bit to him, Emmie looked around again. The Dawkins brood were all similar-looking, with ears that stuck out from their heads, a pronounced widow's peak, and a larger front left front tooth that pushed the right one crooked.

In the little ones it was darling, though not so much so for the older ones. None of them looked anything like her or Mr. Pershing, or anyone in their families, but at least the hair was a brownish blond, and the eyes somewhere in the spectrum she'd written to her family about in her letters.

"Say that again?" Dawkins frowned, his hands on his hips.

"It's quite simple, really," Mr. Pershing said, donning his best smile. "Mrs. Pershing and I are beginning a new project. We would like to take two of your children for a month or so, teach them some skills such as dancing and conversation and comportment. Our hope is that this will lead them to have greater employment possibilities when they come of age."

"You want two of my little ones."

"For a month, yes. If our mission is successful, we will of course look to do it again, with additional children."

"Harry, what do you think?" Jenny Dawkins asked, her eyes widening. "Two of our babes learning to be fancy? They could grow up to be ladies' maids or footmen. Or even a butler like that grand Mr. Powell up at the manor house!"

Young Joe began sneezing goop from his nose, and keeping her smile firmly on her face despite the abrupt urge to vomit, Emmie handed the baby back to his mother. Good heavens, the quantity of mucus really was astonishing. Jenny seemed to think it was normal as she absently wiped her son's nose with her apron, all of her attention still on the conversation between the two men.

"What we'll have, then," the farmer was saying, "are two young ones too high up for us, and all their brothers and sisters jealous. There will be no peace in the house if you make two of the children fancy."

"It's not making them fancy," Emmie countered. "It's only teaching them a few skills. And bringing them with us on our holiday to Cumberland."

"Oh, so now they'll be high-and-mighty about traveling to faraway lands, too." Mr. Dawkins scowled. "I'll not have my own children thinking they're better than me."

"That's not it at all, Dawkins," Mr. Pershing said. "It's only an opportunity for—"

"Harry, it'll be two less mouths to feed," his wife pointed out helpfully.

The children began a game of tag around them, churning up the yard and frightening the chickens all over again. The volume of screeching and yelling and laughing was incredible. True, Emmie had been an only child, as had Mr. Pershing, but this seemed far beyond anything she and her nonexistent siblings would have dared in the presence of their parents or guests.

The farmer blew out his breath, lowering his hands from his hips. "Well, if they'll be back in time for harvest, I reckon I can let you have Kitty and Daisy. Kitty! Daisy! Stop chasing the chickens and get over here to meet your betters."

Two girls, one perhaps thirteen and the other eleven, broke off from the game and ran up to join them. *Oh dear.* They would never do. Emmie sent Mr. Pershing a glance, to find him looking about the yard, his attention going from one child to the next. No doubt he was attempting to figure out which boy looked like he could pass for a seven-year-old, and which girl could be five.

"We had in mind a boy and a girl," he said aloud, and pointed at the young man going after the pig again. "That one, perhaps? And the girl with the brown chicken."

"Samuel and Betty? Why them?"

"They're a good age for learning new things," Mr. Pershing answered smoothly.

"But whatever they learn from you, they won't be able to use for a good five or six years, at best. I reckon they'll forget it all. Plus, Samuel's a bit simple."

"Harry Dawkins, don't you say such a thing," Jenny Dawkins chastised him. "He takes his time, is all."

Baby Joe began to wail, and the woman handed him off to the older girl, Kitty. Just from watching, Emmie could tell this was something that had happened so many times before that no one even noticed it any longer. The chaos, the crying, the older children stepping in to look after the younger ones—everyone had a role, and she abruptly wondered what would happen if she and Mr. Pershing removed, even temporarily, two of the players.

"No," Dawkins stated. "I can't let you have two, to lord it over their brothers and sisters. Especially two of the younger ones. If you're taking one, you'll have to take them all."

Emmeline blinked. *All of them?* The brief image of children hanging off the railings and climbing the curtains of Winnover Hall crossed her mind, making her shiver. Even if they could somehow pretend that two of the Dawkins children were Malcolm and Flora, by the end there would be no Winnover Hall left to save. *She* would certainly be dead of an apoplexy. "We—"

"We couldn't possibly deprive you of all your assistance," Mr. Pershing cut in. "Two seems a much more reasonable number for you to do without. We could compensate you for their absence, if that eases your mind."

Oh, well said, she wanted to tell him. She'd been on the verge of running away before any of the sticky children could attach themselves to her.

Dawkins cocked his head. "You'd pay *us* to take two of our wee ones and teach them manners?"

"Of course. I know how useful all of them are to your farm."

"And you've no idea how loud all of them are. No, Mr. Pershing. It's to be all or none. That's my final offer."

A muscle in Mr. Pershing's jaw tightened. "Give me a moment to confer with my wife, Dawkins." He angled his head toward the coach, and with a murmured apology to Jenny that the woman would never hear over the noise, Emmie followed him over to the vehicle. "I don't suppose we could bring them all, and claim two as our children and the rest as their friends," he said in a low voice.

"We might manage that with a half dozen or fewer," she returned, "but I doubt any reasonable seven-year-old boy would claim either a fourteen-year-old girl or a six-month-old babe as fast friends. Aside from that, we would need to hire six additional carriages for children and luggage."

His mouth quirked. "We would make an impression, but not the one we require, I fear."

"How can you continue to be amused by this?" Frowning, Emmeline looked past him at the child-filled yard. "I've already considered the remainder of our neighbors. There are children, but either they're the wrong age, or I don't know the parents well enough to attempt to borrow them."

Nodding, her husband followed her gaze. "I've likewise considered my friends at the trade ministry. I can't think of any who have children of the necessary age." He swore under his breath. "Taking better than a baker's dozen worth of children with us won't suffice. And if I were Dawkins and considering a holiday from the horde, I don't think any amount of money would persuade me to change my mind."

"That's that, then. We're finished." They'd made an attempt, just as they had to produce children in the first place. They'd failed twice now. Three times, she supposed, since she still owed Mrs. Hendersen a letter of apology.

"I'll make our excuses. Wait here."

She could tell the moment he gave the news to Mr. and Mrs. Dawkins. Jenny's shoulders sagged, and Harry's arms crossed back over his chest again, his lips thinning. She could sympathize with them wanting a holiday from their offspring, but for heaven's sake, they were the ones who'd produced so many of them in the first place.

When her husband returned to the coach, he handed her in, had a word with Roger the coachman, and joined her inside. "Back home, then. It seems God gives some a bounty beyond their ability to appreciate, while others he passes by for reasons beyond their ability to comprehend."

Emmie looked at his profile, leaner and more angled now, as if chiseled by some master sculptor. Yes, they'd tried to have children. But it had all been so confusing and he'd seen her in a way she . . . hadn't been ready to be seen, and she'd been relieved to tell him they were wasting their time, as she was barren. The idea that he'd *wanted* children had never occurred to her. He'd certainly never even intimated such a thing before now.

"I'm sorry," she said aloud.

He whipped his head around to look at her. "I was not complaining," he stated.

The sharp tone startled her. "Very well, then." Emmie looked down at her hands, considering whether this was a conversation she truly wished to have. "I never asked, I suppose, but am I to infer that you did wish for children?"

"I won't say the thought of young ones never crossed my mind," he said slowly, no doubt measuring his words. He always measured his words. Mr. Pershing tilted his head. "Did you wish for children? Other than to satisfy your grandfather's agreement, that is?"

"It may have crossed my mind," she admitted, deliberately echoing his words. She *had* thought about it. Mostly how it would have changed things. Made her less effective with her duties. Made her responsible not for a perfect party, but for an entire human or two. She stifled a shudder.

He nodded, but didn't ask her to elaborate. "Well, at the moment, we *need* a couple of them. The Dawkinses aside, none of our neighbors or friends have been obliging enough to produce offspring of the proper age. Any other ideas?"

Emmie shook her head, sighing. "I've spent the last two days trying to conjure one. There are shops for everything. Couldn't we find one for children?" She pointed, waving her finger. "I'll have that boy. Yes, the towheaded one. And I do like the look of the girl in the green dress. Wrap them up, if you please."

He snorted. "Do you have any that play the pianoforte?"

Even as she chuckled, it struck her again that she'd lost her home. For seven years she'd knitted a tale that had kept them under Winnover Hall's roof, but a tale wouldn't keep them in Gloucestershire any longer. She lowered her head to her lap. "I don't want to leave."

"Neither do I. Damnation. A shop for children might be highly improper, but it would also be exceedingly useful. We could just rent a pair for a month or two, and be done with it. The . . ." Mr. Pershing trailed off, then thudded his fist against one knee. "There is such a shop, you know."

Emmie straightened. "What are you talking about? A shop that sells children?"

Mr. Pershing shook his head, leaning forward. "An orphanage," he announced.

"An . . ." Emmeline gasped. "We couldn't."

"Why the devil not? Borrow two for the next few weeks, teach them some manners and polish. They would certainly be better off for it."

She stared at him, a hundred thoughts bashing about against each other in her mind. "For someone who didn't approve of me lying about offspring, you've adapted rather quickly."

"Necessity," he replied crisply. "Are we of the same mind, here? This is a project where both of us will be necessary for success."

She'd been to orphanages during the Season in London. Bringing old clothes or treats for the children was part of her charitable duties. Her father was even on the board of one of them.

Perhaps Mr. Pershing had the right of it. They would make it known that this was a short-term adventure. What child wouldn't want a holiday at a grand house, lovely clothes, and a visit to the Lake District? As he'd said, once they were returned, their chances of being permanently placed would be much improved.

"My father is on the board at St. Stephen's Home for

Unfortunate Children in Charing Cross," she said aloud. "We could offer a donation to the orphanage, and explain that we're attempting a new sort of . . . charitable venture."

"'Charitable venture,'" he repeated. "I like that. The more concisely we can word something, the more practical and logical it sounds. We're bound for Charing Cross, then. It's a day to London, and the same back again. Pack for two days, and we'll leave within the hour. It'll give me a chance to inform Lord Stafford that I'm taking an extended leave of absence. You'll need some help with the lessons."

She ran through it in her mind. If they had to visit several orphanages, it could take an additional day. There would be paperwork to complete, and other things neither of them could anticipate. Aside from that, this was the first time in years Mr. Pershing had asked her to accompany him on one of his frequent off-Season trips into London.

"Doing this in London could actually save us time," she said. "We'll need to find someone out-of-the-way to make them some clothes. Out-of-the-way is much more easily accomplished in London than in our little village. The less gossip that gets out about what we're doing, the better."

That made him frown. "Hold a moment. What about your other relations? Your parents? They'll be at the party. Do they not know we are without children? Our ship will be sunk before we leave the harbor."

Emmie grimaced. "They don't know any such thing."

Lifting an eyebrow, he sat back. "How have you managed that? We've gone to visit both sets of our parents."

Oh dear. "As far as the rest of the family is aware, we *do* have children, but they are sickly, and it is a tender subject you don't wish to discuss." And yes, she'd felt more than a little satisfaction when she'd written to inform her mother that she had managed to have a child, even if it had been an imaginary—and sickly—infant. At the same time, she'd proven to be an exceptional and much-admired hostess. *So there*. Except that everyone was about to discover that she'd been lying all along.

He stared at her. "*I* don't wish to discuss it. You did mean to keep our offspring from me, then. And you've made me the villain of the piece."

"No, I didn't, and no, I haven't. I simply didn't wish you to be surprised by someone mentioning our children, and I needed a long-term excuse to keep them out of sight." She shrugged. "It hardly seemed necessary to pull you into this mess, or to possibly compromise your work."

"If you'd asked my opinion, I might have disagreed about that." The coach stopped, and they stepped down onto Winnover Hall's white crushed-oyster-shell drive. "As I know now, you should enlighten me about any other particulars you've told people."

Nodding, Emmeline joined him to head into the house. "I've made a journal."

This time both eyebrows went up. "A journal. About our nonexistent offspring."

"Well, yes. One for each of them, actually. I correspond with myriad family members and friends, and I didn't want to contradict myself. People do talk, you know."

For a moment he stood regarding her. "I should like to read these journals. So that I don't contradict the tale, either."

Now she hoped they wouldn't seem too fanciful. Everyone thought their own offspring perfect, but she worried that she had made hers too much so. "I'll lend them to you." She nodded to the butler as he opened the front door. "Powell, please have Hannah join me in my bedchamber. And I will need one of the medium-sized trunks brought down from the attic."

"Very good, ma'am."

Mr. Pershing delivered his own request, then faced her again. "I'm glad we are allies," he said. "All this has made me realize you would make for a rather formidable foe."

"Thank you," she said, smiling. "And likewise." That was quite possibly the most complimentary thing anyone had ever said to her. "Being feared would be very nearly as useful as being admired. But we still need to find some offspring, or our formidable partnership will serve only to make us the laughingstock of London."

"And homeless, unemployed ones, at that," he added, his half smile diving into something grimmer.

Yes, that would be even worse.

CHAPTER FOUR

"I beg your pardon?" The nun—Sister Mary Stephen, according to the others of the flock who'd guided Emmeline and Mr. Pershing to her tiny office—lifted her eyes from whatever it was she'd been pretending to read. "Could you repeat that? I don't think I heard you correctly."

Mr. Pershing nodded. "A brother and sister. Ages seven and five."

"With brown or blond hair," Emmie added.

"Yes," he affirmed. "Do you have a pair of children here matching that description?"

"I heard that part," the nun returned. She looked very much like a nun, if that was possible. Black, protruding eyes in a severe face with prominent cheekbones and a straight, thin mouth. Terrifying, in a way nuns were supposed to be. At least their visit hadn't merited the attention of the Mother Superior. That woman, Emmie recalled from her occasional visits, was the stuff of nightmares. "I meant the part about you and your missus wanting to *borrow* two youngsters."

"In exchange for a substantial gift to your facility." Mr. Pershing sent a pointed glance at the paint beginning to peel from the drab corners.

The nun's eyes narrowed. "While we have received requests for children of a particular age, we as a rule make the arrangement permanent, ensuring that the child or children in question will be fed and clothed and raised in a proper Christian home until adulthood. And while we are happy to accept a donation from the adopting family, we do not *sell* children—or the use of them—here."

Permanent. The idea of suddenly, in a literal blink of an eye, becoming an actual, forever parent, a mother, of all things, and one responsible for the care of two young people, made Emmie sit up straight, her heart hammering. "We—that is to say, I—we aren't—I mean, we cannot—"

"This is to be a temporary arrangement," Mr. Pershing persisted with a slight frown that she still somehow found attractive. She definitely couldn't blame it on the whiskey, then. "We have not made any secret of that fact. This is a charitable project for the benefit of the youngsters. It will be for a period of eight weeks, during which time the children will be clothed and fed, and instructed in the ways of proper Society. I daresay that will improve their prospects of finding a permanent residence in the future."

Once again, Mr. Pershing managed to make the whole enterprise sound reasonable—which, of course, it was. "They will be well cared for," she put in, trying to catch her breath up. "And it is in the children's best interest. Here they might find themselves fit to be bricklayers or washing women. With our guidance, they might become shop clerks, or companions, or household servants. A vast increase in employment opportunities to hand."

Sister Mary Stephen tapped the end of her pencil against the desktop. "I should consult the Mother Superior about this, but she, unfortunately, is in Canterbury for the next week. Perhaps you could call again on Tuesday?"

"My schedule is such that we cannot remain in London for that long," Mr. Pershing countered. "Time is money, as they say."

"What was the figure you had in mind for your donation?" the nun asked, clearly understanding what was happening. "You never said."

"I think two hundred fifty pounds wou—"

The nun cleared her throat.

"As I said," Mr. Pershing resumed smoothly, "five hundred pounds would see every child here with improved meals, clothing, shoes, and beds, as well as affording new paint, roof repairs, and a donation in St. Stephen's name to the Church, if you should so choose. All of that, not in exchange for, but rather in addition to, two of the youngsters receiving lessons in comportment and propriety."

"It does make a certain amount of sense, when you put it that way," the nun said. "*If* we have two young ones who meet your requirements."

The woman in novice's robes by the door made a waving motion. "I had a thought that Peter and Lotty Wevins might serve," she said in a whispery voice. "They're both sweet children, and—"

"Nonsense," Sister Mary Stephen interrupted. "They are both too young, and that pleasant carpenter and his wife from Kent have expressed interest in Peter."

"What about—"

"I have it," the black-eyed nun cut in again. "The Fletcher children."

The novice drew in a breath. "The Fletcher children?" she repeated.

"I think they will suit your requirements," Sister Mary Stephen said with a smile that stretched her mouth.

"George is eight and small for his age, and Rose just turned five. They are darlings. Little angels. And both would benefit from a lesson or two—for the sake of their future adoption by some appropriate family, of course." She steepled her fingers on the desk in front of her. "If your donation is as generous as you say, that is."

"I have a bank note to hand," Mr. Pershing answered.

"I shall fill out the papers, then," Sister Mary Stephen said, pulling a pair of sheets out of her desk. "Sister Mary Christopher, please fetch the Fletchers."

The younger nun bobbed a curtsy and scurried out of the room. A new worry tightened the muscles across Emmie's shoulders. If these two children wouldn't suit—if they were curly-haired or clubfooted or, worse, French— they would have to begin all over again, elsewhere.

There were a frightful number of orphanages across London, of course, but only three where her connections and her charitable work would warrant them an immediate audience. As she looked around at the gray walls and small, infrequent windows and listened to the stern nuns walking about in loud shoes and the subdued children's voices, she made a mental note to donate more of her time and efforts here in the future. No child should grow up surrounded by gray walls.

"We do not sell our children here," Sister Mary Stephen repeated, as she wrote out the children's names and the address of both Pershing House in London and Winnover Hall in Gloucestershire. "I am pleased, though, that you are so insistent on offering a gift to St. Stephen's."

"Mrs. Pershing and I are pleased to be able to support our less fortunate fellows," her husband said smoothly.

Finally, the nun turned the sheets to face him. "If you'll sign here, then, Mr. Pershing, the children will become your responsibility."

"For the next eight weeks," Mr. Pershing corrected, not moving. "And we would like to meet them before we accept responsibility."

"Ah. Yes. My mistake." The nun turned the paper back and crossed out a line, replacing it with another. "For the next eight weeks." The door to her left opened. "Here are the little darlings now. George, Rose, say hello to Mr. and Mrs. Pershing. You're to live with them for the next few weeks."

The smaller mop of brown hair pulled her simple gray skirts out to either side of her knees and gave a clumsy, two-footed curtsy. The taller one, his hedgehog hair a lighter brown and sticking up crazily from his head except where it looked like someone had wetted the mess and attempted to pat it down, just looked at them. The novice sister flicked him in the ear. "Good afternoon, Mr. and Mrs. Pershing," he said, taking a half step sideways.

Good heavens, they were small. Things too tiny and delicate to be left alone in the world, certainly. The girl's face was more oval than her brother's, her dark eyes enormous as they peered from between strands of her unkempt hair. Little Rose barely would come to Emmeline's waist, and Emmie was petite herself.

George looked a bit . . . sturdier than his sister, though also too thin. He was a head taller than Rose, and his eyes were lighter—a green very close to Mr. Pershing's. As they continued to stare between her and her husband, they narrowed. Assessing? Frightened? Angry? It could have been any one, or even all three.

"Hello," she said, staying seated so she wouldn't tower over them. "As Sister Mary Stephen said, we would like to bring you home with us for a time. I'm sure we'll all be fast friends, and we'll have a grand time together. Would you like that?"

Both sent glances at the imposing-looking sister. "Yes, ma'am," they recited.

Poor, frightened babies. These children weren't simply props for the play she'd written about the nonexistent Pershing family. They were actual . . . children. Youngsters without parents, who'd clearly been browbeaten enough that they were afraid to set a foot wrong.

"Mr. Pershing, I am satisfied," she said, keeping her hands clenched in her lap against the temptation to flick both nuns on *their* ears.

"As am I," he said crisply, an undercurrent of something hard in his voice that made her give him a look. Had he seen the same thing she had? Had he come to the same conclusion? Had he abruptly become as determined as she was to give these young ones eight weeks' worth of hot meals and soft beds and a splendid holiday in the Lake District before they returned to London?

Sister Mary Stephen slid the amended sheet of paper back around and handed Mr. Pershing the pen. "Sign here to indicate that you are taking responsibility for the children, and we'll call this finished."

He signed, and at the nun's nod the novice set a small sack down beside each child—presumably their belongings—before she stepped back. "We'll see you in eight weeks, dears," the nun stated, that stretched smile of hers reappearing. "Learn all you can, and mind your manners. When you return, we'll see about getting you put somewhere permanently."

For some reason that sounded ominous, but the entire orphanage unsettled Emmie. Before she knew it, she and Mr. Pershing, along with young George and Rose Fletcher, had been ushered down the hallway, down the stairs, and out the front door. It shut behind them with a heavy, reverberating thud. Back in the depths of the orphanage, she swore that for just a moment she could hear the sound of female laughter.

"Are you going to sell us to gypsies?" the little girl, Rose, asked from her seat in the coach.

"Rosie, shut it," George cut in. He held his sack of belongings on his lap, his body perched forward as if he meant to leap out of the coach the moment the vehicle stopped.

"No, we're not selling you to gypsies," Emmeline answered with a smile. "Or to anyone else."

"Deirdre said her cousin got sold to gypsies," Rose went on, craning her neck to look out the nearest window.

"You got to stop believing everything people tell you," her brother stated, offering Mr. Pershing beside him a sideways glance.

"Deirdre knows things."

Emmie cleared her throat at that pronouncement. With the frightening Sister Mary Stephen well behind them, the children had visibly relaxed, thank goodness. "Would you like to kneel on the seat so you can see outside?"

"Sister Mary Francis says sitting is for arses, and praying is for knees."

"Well, this is a new adventure, so we can make an exception," Emmie replied.

Without waiting to be asked a second time, Rose bounced up onto her knees to rest her forehead against the window glass. "I was just a baby the last time we was this far away from the stone jug."

"I'm sorry, the what?"

"St. Stephen's," George clarified.

Across from Emmie, Mr. Pershing shifted. "I believe

'stone jug' is a colloquialism for Newgate Prison," he supplied.

"That's horrible. Did you hate it at St. Stephen's?"

"Mrs. Pershing," her husband said, before either child
could answer, "I believe we should be discussing new
clothes and shaved ices."

The look he sent her said more than that, though. She
frowned. *Of course.* They would be returning to that stone
jug in a few short weeks. No encouraging them to detest
it any more than they probably already did. "Shaved ices,
indeed," she said, putting a smile back on her face.

"I don't want new clothes," George stated. "These is
fine."

"These *are* fine," Mr. Pershing corrected. "And they
are not fine. The grand adventure we have in mind for you
will require a more extensive wardrobe."

"You can't turn George into a dandy," Rose observed.
"I would be happy to be a princess, though." She turned
around and sat down again, her feet dangling well short
of the floor of the coach. "I have a very important question."

Emmie sent Mr. Pershing an amused glance. *Little
darlings.* "We're listening."

"I need a pink gown. With yellow stripes. And a bonnet that matches."

While not a question, it was certainly adorable. "I believe we can manage that," Emmie answered. "And some
pretty shoes, as well."

"Oh yes. Shoes. Shoes are very important."

"So they are. What about you, George? Do you have
a request?"

The eight-year-old shook his head. "Do you live in
London?" he asked.

"During the Season, we do. Our main residence, though, is Winnover Hall, in Gloucestershire. That's where we'll be heading in the morning."

"How far away is that?"

"It'll take us most of a day to get there," Mr. Pershing continued. "We'll stay overnight at our house here."

"They don't have orphanages in Gloucestershire?"

Her husband's brow furrowed. "I imagine they do. Mrs. Pershing's father is on the board of St. Stephen's, though, so we thought to travel here to find you."

The boy's head swiveled to examine Emmie again. "I thought I seen you before. You bring sweets, sometimes."

She nodded. "I do." And in the future, she would also be bringing a selection of clothes, blankets, and books.

"You never borrowed no one before, though."

"No. This is our first time."

"But you'll borrow more after this?"

Well, that wasn't very likely. "I suppose we'll see how this turns out. How do you think it will turn out?"

George shrugged. "That ain't for me to say, Mrs. Pershing."

Oh, that wouldn't do. She sat forward a little. "For the purposes of our adventure, what say you and Rose call us Mama and Papa? Is that acceptable?"

"But you said we had to go back," Rose protested.

"Yes, but not for eight weeks. And in the meantime, I hardly want to spend all of my time explaining to everyone we meet that no, these aren't my children, and yes, they are supposed to be accompanying me. It's so much easier to just call us Mama and Papa, don't you think?"

"I don't—"

"We can do that," George interrupted his sister. "So we're supposed to be George and Rose Pershing?"

Not exactly. "Well, it's quite silly, but—"

"Yes, that'll do for now," Mr. Pershing cut her off.

She opened her mouth to argue, because names would be the one thing they couldn't afford to stumble over. But giving them a few moments to accept one oddity before she sprang another on them made sense. Especially since that oddity included changing their names from George and Rose to Malcolm and Flora.

The trouble was, she'd never spent much time conversing with children. She would figure it out; she'd once successfully orchestrated a dinner with both the Prince Regent and the Duke of Wellington while convincing each that he was the guest of honor, after all.

"We've arrived, Mrs. Pershing," Roger's voice came from above them in the driver's seat. "The dressmaker's. And the tailor is just down the street."

Emmie leaned over and unlatched the door. "Very well. The coach will circle back around for us, yes?"

Her husband nodded. "George and I will manage a hack."

"Rose and I will meet you at Pershing House at two o'clock, then, shall we?"

"Wait," George said, sliding forward on the seat. "We ain't going together?"

"I'll be taking you to a tailor, my boy," Mr. Pershing said. "Trousers, breeches, waistcoats, shirts, and coats. Not very exciting, and nothing in pink or yellow, but we'll make do. And then shaved ices."

"I'm supposed to look after Rosie," the boy countered, scowling. "She's just a baby."

"I'm not a baby, Georgie. I'm five years old. And I want a pink gown."

Reaching out, Emmie touched the back of George's clenched fist. "I give you my word that I will look after your sister. And that you will be returned to her company by two o'clock this afternoon."

He gazed at her, green eyes serious and unblinking, before he spit on his palm and held it out for her to shake. *Oh.* Generally, she would have refused to touch anyone who spit on his hand, but this was, she sensed, an important moment. Emmie pulled off her glove, dry-spit into her own hand, and shook the little boy's.

Before she could decide what to do with her unsavory damp palm, Mr. Pershing pushed open the coach door and stepped down, holding out his own hand to help her to the street. "Well done," he whispered, and slipped her his handkerchief.

Emmie nodded as Mr. Pershing rejoined George in the carriage. He'd complimented her before, of course, but this felt more . . . personal. That made the boy's spit she surreptitiously wiped from her hand more tolerable, though she had no idea why children seemed determined to drool on her.

As the coach continued down the street to its next destination, she pulled open the door of Mrs. Palorum's Gowns for Ladies. She'd never visited the Knightsbridge shop before, as it was firmly in the center of a community of bankers and merchants and solicitors—a clientele who simply didn't move within her social circle. And that was precisely the point. There would be no one to gossip about running across Emmeline Pershing with a young girl dressed in rags.

"Oh, welcome, welcome!" a plump, impossibly red-haired woman said, swishing out from behind the counter of the shop and wearing what, if she'd been feeling uncharitable, Emmie would have described as a harlequin's tent. "I am Mrs. Palorum."

"Hello," Emmie returned, while Rose scooted behind her skirts, her small hands grabbing into the light blue material. How odd, to have gone from being a complete stranger to a trusted protector in twenty minutes' time. "We have need of several gowns for my daughter here. Demure, tasteful, and at least one of them must be pink with yellow stripes." She twisted around to view the girl behind her. "That's correct, isn't it?"

Rose, her face still buried in skirts, nodded. "Yes," she said, her voice muffled. "And a matching bonnet."

"Ah. I understand perfectly. Do you have specific occasions in mind? That does help with the decisions on style and material."

Hmm. "At least one gown fit for al fresco dining, two for formal dinners, three—no, four walking gowns, and four for mornings at home. And nightwear, of course."

The hands detached from her derriere. "That's so many gowns!" the little voice said. "How many is it?"

"Eleven, plus a night rail." Emmie recalled the spit she'd just acquired from Rose's brother. "Two night rails."

"That's diamond! I'll be all the crack!" Rose exclaimed, jumping up and down on her toes. "Can they all be pink?"

"No, they cannot," Emmeline returned, smiling and deciding to ignore the street-sounding slang. Thus far being a parent wasn't so difficult. Clearly, she'd spent too much time worrying about her ability to manage young ones, and for no good reason.

"I may close the shop early today," Mrs. Palorum chortled, swirling back behind the counter for paper and a measuring string. "There are biscuits on the table there, dears. Do help yourselves."

"Oh, biscuits." Rose lifted one off the tray and had it

halfway to her mouth before she froze, casting a glance up at Emmeline. "I want a biscuit, but I want a shaved ice, too. I never had one of those."

"Then you may have one biscuit."

The five-year-old favored her with a broad smile. "Thank you, Mama."

Oh, goodness. That alone made Emmie want to give her an entire bakery of biscuits. Still smiling, she turned to see Mrs. Palorum looking from her to Rose, a quizzical look on her face. Rose was dressed in rags, after all, and she . . . well, she was dressed like the mistress of one of the finer homes in Mayfair.

"I should explain," she said aloud. "I am Mary Jones. My husband and I just adopted Rose, here."

"How wonderful," the seamstress exclaimed, clapping her hands together.

Rose, though, tilted her head up to look at Emmeline. "I'm Rose Jones now?"

Emmie chuckled. "Yes, dear. Rose Jones." *For the next hour or two, anyway.*

"This is very complicated," the little girl observed, and wandered off in the direction of a selection of bonnets and hair ribbons, still muttering "Jones" to herself.

That might have gone more smoothly, but, Emmie reminded herself, this was new to both of them. The strategy she and Mr. Pershing had concocted on the way to London had been about gaining the children. What to do with them afterward had been a much smaller portion of the discussion.

As Mrs. Palorum measured the waif and jotted down her dimensions, Emmeline divided her attention between the little girl and the collection of small-sized hats and bonnets the shop boasted. To think, she'd never really spent time noticing such things before, though until now she hadn't had any reason to do so.

The already-made muslin dress that fit Rose was a pale green rather than pink, but at least the girl wouldn't have to go about London wearing the shapeless, worn gray smock given her by St. Stephen's. The way the little one twirled about in front of the dressing mirror pinched her heart a little, and she turned around to find the dressmaker watching her.

"We'll need a few things sent to us early tomorrow morning," she said, as Mrs. Palorum abruptly began digging through bolts of fabric. "The rest can be sent on to Winnover Hall in Gloucestershire."

"I'll send for two of my girls," the dressmaker said, nodding and turning again to make further notations. Despite her girth, the woman was a whirligig. "We'll have a day dress or two and something for a nice evening all ready for you first thing. I have a night rail that will fit, I think, and I'll order another. Where should I send the items in the morning?"

"We're staying at Pershing House on Leicester Street just now," Emmie answered. "With some dear friends."

"How nice that they're here to welcome you, even with the Season well over," the large woman commented.

"Yes, it is. Especially with young Rose joining the family."

The price quoted, eleven pounds fifty, was exorbitant. It seemed Mrs. Palorum suspected their tale to be not entirely true. As it wasn't, Emmeline gritted her teeth in a smile, and handed over the money. "And an extra pound," she said quietly, handing over a coin, "if you see to it that the pink and yellow dress is the first one finished."

"It will be indeed, Mrs. Jones."

That was that, then. One task, finished. "Come along, Rose," Emmie said, offering a hand to the little girl and accepting the bundle of night rail, hair ribbons, old shoes, and gray smock in the other. "We're off to Pershing House."

As she passed the counter, she noted that the plate of cookies sat empty. No wonder Mrs. Palorum had such a round figure; the dressmaker must have eaten twenty of the treats, since young Rose had only taken one of them.

CHAPTER FIVE

Will sat in the small Pershing House foyer, young George Fletcher on the bench beside him with as much space between them as the lad could manage without tipping onto the floor. "Are you certain you don't wish to see where you'll be sleeping tonight?" he suggested for the second time.

"I'm waiting for Rose," the boy returned again, shifting a little and flexing his fingers around the mouth of the cloth sack holding his possessions, held on his lap. "I look after her. Why is that fart-catcher staring at me?"

Landon, standing stiffly at his post by the front door, stirred, cheek twitching and jaw clenched. "I am not . . . one of those," the servant said crisply. "I am the butler. And while the master remains in the foyer, so do I. As for the staring, I was not informed the house would be entertaining . . . guests."

That pause had a great many questions attached to it, but the house was Emmeline's realm, and he would leave her to decide what the servants needed to know, and what they should say if questioned by the neighbors—or more likely, given the time of year, the neighbors' reduced, off-Season staff. "It's only one more night, Landon. We don't expect perfection."

"Mrs. Pershing does. And I do. We have only opened the two main bedchambers. Will more be required?" The butler sent another pointed look at George.

"Yes. Please air out the two southerly rooms," Will decided.

"Of course, sir." With a nod the butler stirred again, glancing at the front door as if he expected it to fall off its hinges if he stepped away.

"I'll remain here until Mrs. Pershing's arrival," Will said. "She will not have to open the door herself."

"Very well, then." With an audible sigh Landon vanished in the direction of the kitchen and the servants' quarters.

Will cleared his throat. "Are you hungry? I could send to the kitchen for a bite."

"Rosie and I eat together. Is it two o'clock?"

Will pulled out his pocket watch. "Four minutes till."

"If that frigate sold my sister to gypsies, I'll go find J—"

"No one is selling anyone, George. I promise you that."

The boy narrowed one eye. "Liars make promises, too."

Evidently George Fletcher was a wizened old grandfather trapped in an eight-year-old's body. "They aren't even late yet," Will observed, sending up a quick prayer that Emmeline wouldn't turn them both into promise-making liars.

"Yet."

Before he could conjure a distraction, wheels rattled to a stop outside, and a moment later the narrow window to the left of the door darkened. Will stood, crossing the foyer in one long step, and pulled open the door. "Mrs. Pershing," he said, bowing.

"Oh! Mr. Pershing." Her quick, excited smile made him

grin in return. She'd been successful, then. And timely, though he hadn't doubted for more than a moment that she would be. Since their marriage, perfection had become her byword.

"Look at me, Georgie!" Rose exclaimed, spinning in a pale green circle, arms out and a new pink bonnet held in one hand. "I'm a lady!"

"It's pretty," her brother said, tugging at the sleeves of his new dark blue coat. "But you ain't a lady."

She stomped her foot. "I am! Look at me. Lucifer's balls."

"Rose!" Emmeline chastised, covering her mouth with a hand that didn't quite hide her grin. "A lady does not use such language."

"I told you that you wasn't a lady." George folded his arms over his chest.

"Well, you look like the man who drives the hearse," his sister retorted.

"That's it." George stood up and began shedding his coat. "I ain't a carrion hunter!"

"I think you look very handsome, George," Emmeline countered. "We will be the envy of everyone who sees us when we go get our ices."

Will nodded. "Now, perhaps you two would like to see where you'll be sleeping tonight before we head out?" he suggested. "George insisted on remaining in the foyer until his sister appeared."

"Ah. I made you a promise, George," Emmeline said, gently tugging the boy's coat back up over his slender shoulders. "As you can see, I kept it."

"As I said you would," Will seconded. "I had Landon open two more rooms for tonight, by the way."

"Two rooms?" Rose whispered, moving closer to her brother.

Her tone, equal parts awestruck and worried, hit Will in the gut. No doubt they were accustomed to a dozen or more children sharing sleeping quarters. "Yes," he said aloud, while Emmeline handed over her shopping acquisitions to Hannah as that young lady arrived downstairs. The maid sent only one quick glance at the children, so she'd been told something. He wondered what it might have been. His wife had stories ready for every occasion and contingency, it seemed. "One for each of you," he said. "They have a connecting door, which you may of course leave open if you wish."

The siblings exchanged a look, and George nodded. "As long as the door stays open."

"We'll make certain your bedchambers at Winnover Hall also adjoin," Will went on, now that he understood the sticking point. George and Rose each needed to know where the other one was. He had the feeling they'd had only each other to rely on for some time. "Shall we go see them?" He motioned them toward the stairs, taking Emmeline's hand and wrapping it around his forearm.

"This is going well, I think," she murmured, as they led the way upstairs.

He leaned his head down by hers, the delicate lavender scent of her hair intimate and arousing. It was almost as if being forced to admit a lie, an imperfection, had brought her back to life. Whatever it was, she had him wishing all over again that she saw him as other than a project and a partner. And it had him wondering how long it had been since they'd shared a bed. "I have a suspicion they're worried we mean to change our minds. George made a point of asking me more than once how far away Winnover is, and when we would be leaving London."

"That makes sense. Sister Mary Stephen is the stuff of nightmares." She gave an exaggerated shudder.

"She did seem rather . . . stern," he said with a half grin. "We need to tell Landon something, as well. I presume you spoke to Hannah?"

"I did. I'm still figuring the tale out, but I'll take him aside. They are sweet little things, aren't they? It's almost a shame we have to return them." She sighed. "But Lady Graham and Lord and Lady Baskin and the Hendersens and all our neighbors in Gloucestershire know quite well that we've never been seen with or mentioned children. They're expected not to be seen in London, but back at Winnover suddenly appearing *with* them could ruin everything just as much as appearing *without* them at Welshire Park."

The logic was faultless, if a bit cold. "You're correct, of course."

"So many windows," Rose marveled as they topped the stairs. "And I ain't never seen so many doors!"

"The open doors on either side of the suit of armor there are yours," Emmeline said, pointing. "Choose whichever you like."

Holding hands, the children ran into the first room, Rose making happy squealing sounds. "Look at the bed! It's grand! And so many pillows!"

Evidently Rose hadn't seen "so many" of a great deal of things. The fact that pillows could so easily delight her was both charming and sad. If Emmeline didn't instruct the staff to give the girl piles of pillows, he would do so himself. A pair of maids took the last of the coverings off the dressing table and the yellow-and-red-striped chair set before the fireplace, and Rose twirled about the room, green skirts akimbo, while George gazed out one of the windows.

"I'm assuming you've chosen this room, Rose," Emmeline said. "Come see yours, George." Gesturing, she headed for the adjoining door and opened it.

The boy turned away from the view to join her. Both children needed a good scrubbing, and George a haircut. Luckily Will's valet was a proficient barber, and Davis had made the trip to London along with Hannah.

"Do you like it?" his wife asked, allowing the boy to precede her into the second bedchamber, Will trailing behind them. The walls were a pale blue broken by wide strips of brown and yellow wallpaper, the curtains a darker blue, and the bed, currently being uncovered and the pillows fluffed, matched the blue of the walls.

"It's grand," he said, reaching out a forefinger to touch the dressing table. "Rose and I could share a room, though."

"Mr. Pershing and I wish to spoil you."

He looked over his shoulder at the two of them. "You're married, ain't you?"

"Yes, of course. Why do you ask?"

"The mumbler said you had two rooms opened last night. For the two of you. My mama and papa shared a bed. And they called each other Martin and Mary. Or lambkin and darling." He made a face. "It was silly, but they wasn't Mr. Fletcher and Mrs. Fletcher. Not to each other. Are you new married?"

Emmeline's cheeks turned pink, but Will only shrugged when she sent him a pleading look. He had no idea how to explain their arrangement to an eight-year-old boy and his five-year-old sister. Sleeping separately had been her idea, after all. Not his.

"Mr. Pershing and I have been married for eight years," she finally said.

"Don't you know his Christian name, then?" The boy faced Will. "What's your Christian name?"

"William," he answered promptly. "Or Will, preferably. Mrs. Pershing is Emmeline, though her friends call her Emmie. It's a pretty name, is it not?"

Her blush deepened. "Mr. Pershing—Will—and I have a partnership."

"Like a business? You get money to be his wife?"

"I don't want to be a wife," Rose said, joining them. "I'm going to be a duchess."

"To be a duchess you have to marry a duke, Rosie."

"Oh. Then I'll marry a duke, if he pays me to."

"Good heavens," Emmeline muttered, and lifted one hand. "That is not—"

"We have a partnership in that I see to some tasks, and Mrs. . . . Emmeline sees to others, to make certain the household, my work, and our friendships and social engagements all entwine harmoniously with each other," Will interrupted, the taste of his wife's name exotic on his tongue. The formalities had begun drifting into place at the same time she'd announced that she couldn't have children. Her obsession over seeing him succeed in the government had begun by the time of their wedding, but after they'd shifted to separate bedchambers she'd become relentless.

Odd, the difference between thinking a name and saying it aloud. He hadn't called her Emmeline or Emmie in years, but that was going to change. As far as explaining the exchange of money, he'd leave that to her, if she cared to delve into it. They had each received something—status, security, Winnover Hall and its property income—from the marriage, after all.

"Harmoniously. Yes, precisely," Emmeline said, the

hint of a smile touching her mouth. "And Rose, while a lady may marry for money, we would never admit to such a thing."

"So he can pay me as long as we don't talk about it."

For a five-year-old, that seemed a fairly reasonable summary, but Will wasn't about to say that aloud. Instead, he caught most of his grin as his wife sighed. "Yes, my dear," she said. "Men may also wed for money. We don't discuss that, either."

George rose on his toes to look through the window and down to the small garden below. "I'm going to marry someone rich. Then we can have beef stew every night."

"And fresh apples," Rose contributed. "And fruit pies."

"It so happens that our cook at Winnover, Mrs. Brubbins, makes an excellent blackberry pie." Emmeline gestured toward the hallway. "Shall we go get some shaved ices now, or would you prefer to keep exploring here?"

"Ices!" Rose yelled. "I want a lemon one."

"Strawberry for me," George said. "Deirdre says they make strawberry ices."

Evidently Deirdre at St. Stephen's did know things, as Rose had declared. Things about shaved ices, anyway. "They do," Will confirmed. "Let's leave the staff to put your things away, and we'll be back here in time for dinner. We want to make an early start in the morning." Their deadline had already shrunk by three days.

George clutched his old sack hard against his skinny chest. "I don't want no one's grubby hands nicking my things."

"George, I assure you that Betsy and May will not make off with anything that belongs to you," Emmeline said, gesturing at the upstairs maids. In response his fingers dug so hard into the sack that his knuckles turned white, and she gave a sympathetic cluck. "However, if you place your personal items in that trunk there," and she pointed to the mahogany box they used for spare blankets at the foot of the bed, "no one will touch it. I promise."

The boy ran his fingers across the heavy mahogany lid. "I can put all my things in here? And no one will touch them?"

"Yes."

"Can it come with us to Winnover Hall?"

It was a rather large trunk to be carrying an eight-year-old's small sack of property, but if it gave him some comfort to have a safe place to put his things, Will certainly had no objection. At Emmeline's sideways glance, he nodded. "It can and will."

"Do I get a trunk for *my* things? I think I need one." Rose turned around and vanished back into her room. "Oh, there is one! Can it come with us?"

"Yes," Emmeline said, raising her voice to be heard in the other room. "They now belong to you."

Rose leaned back into the doorway. "For ever and ever? Or just for eight weeks? This is very important."

"For ever and ever," Will stated, his jaw clenching in abrupt anger at the unmet Fletcher parents who'd had the temerity to either die or abandon their young ones. If St. Stephen's or Sister Mary Stephen didn't like it, well, another small donation should see that the children had a spot to put their trunks. They would need a place for their new clothes, anyway. A cloth sack would certainly never do.

"Oh, thank you!"

"You're quite welcome. Now, put your things away, and Mr. Pershing—Will—and I will meet you downstairs in the foyer in five minutes."

With Betsy and May still pulling sheets off of the furniture, the children wouldn't be left completely to their own devices, but they could likely use a moment or two to acclimate themselves.

"I wonder what George has in that sack," his wife whispered as she led the way downstairs. "He's very attached to whatever it is."

"He barely set it aside to be fitted for clothes," he returned. "It had to be in his sight at all times." Will sighed at the weight the boy seemed to be carrying on his slender shoulders. "I suppose it could be something of sentimental value from his parents. Rose doesn't seem nearly as attached to her belongings."

"No," Emmeline agreed. "They are darlings, aren't they? With a bit of polish no one will ever know they aren't ours."

"They do seem to have been cowed by the nuns. I'm pleased they're well behaved, and Rose seems sprightly enough, but I don't want them to be frightened of us."

"At the moment I think they're more suspicious than frightened, but I hope by the time we reach Winnover they'll realize we can be trusted."

He nodded. "And we need to tell them everything, even if we leave the more detailed explanations for later. I don't want them thinking we're abusing this trust of theirs that we're after."

"Absolutely. The ices should help with that."

Will stopped beside her in the foyer. "Agreed. And I asked Mrs. Hobbs to make beef stew for dinner. George has mentioned it at least thrice now. I hope that wasn't overstepping."

Generally, he had no doubt that she would have been offended that he'd barged into her household duties, but she knew that the success of this project—this lie she'd begun—would benefit both of them. "No," she said unsurprisingly. "It was a good idea. Another good idea."

He sketched a shallow bow. "We are in this together, Mrs. Pershing. Emmeline. Partners."

They had indeed been in a partnership for the past eight years, but this task would clearly have them working more closely than they generally did. Given the madness with which it had begun, he looked forward to it. The Emmie of his youth had been a fun, adventurous companion, and he missed her. For the first time in a while, he missed being in love with her.

Finding shaved ices turned out to be more of a task than he'd anticipated. During the Season, vendors stood in at least two different locations in Hyde Park. Now, though, they had to take the coach from Leicester Street to the park and back east to Covent Garden before they found someone selling a selection.

"What color is my tongue?" Rose asked, sticking it out at her brother.

"Yellow," he answered, sticking out his own. "What color is mine?"

"Very red," she said, wrinkling her nose. "If you eat it fast, your brain will freeze. That's what Deirdre says."

"Deirdre doesn't know anything." With a smug look, George scraped off a large spoonful of shaved ice and plopped it all into his mouth. A moment later he squeezed his eyes closed and dropped the spoon to press the heel of his hand against his forehead. "It's frozen! Oh! I'm dying!"

Stifling a grin, Will patted the boy's knee. "Steady there. It'll pass in a moment. Evidently Deirdre does know some things."

Thus far this parenting thing wasn't all that difficult. The Fletcher children seemed clever and eager to learn. Teaching them the bits that would be necessary to pass them off as Pershing offspring would be the matter of a few days. In six weeks' time when they were to be presented to the duke, they would be perfect.

And once they had been seen by all her relations, the children's absence could be explained away forever after—or at least until her grandfather passed away. By then, no doubt his enterprising wife could invent a tale of how the youngsters had left for America, or one or the other had perished, or married poorly, or any of a hundred things.

At worst, they could certainly put off another in-person meeting between either of their families and their children for two or three years, or until they could find older youngsters to portray Malcolm and Flora. Children's appearances did alter greatly from year to year.

"Better, George?" he asked.

The boy tentatively lifted his face from his hands. "That was horrible. I'm never listening to you again, Rosie."

"I said you *shouldn't* do it, gundiguts."

"Goodness. Rose, ladies do not say that word." At George's responding snort, Emmeline faced him. "And neither do gentlemen."

"I ain't a gentleman."

"Ah, but you will be one," Will took up. "Best begin practicing now."

George frowned again. "You know I can't really be a duke, because my papa wasn't a duke. He was a sailor."

"In His Majesty's navy?" Emmeline asked.

"No. On a whaling ship. He was a harpooner."

"Georgie said that Mama said a whale split his boat in two with its tail, and dragged Papa down to Davy Jones' locket," Rose added.

"Locker, Rosie. You're such a baby."

"I am not a baby. You heard Mrs. Pershing—I mean, Mama. I'm a lady."

"Our *real* mama was a washerwoman. That means you ain't a lady."

George knew some of the rules of heredity, evidently. What they hadn't been told yet, and needed to be informed of soon, Will reflected, was that they were about to stand in for the great-grandchildren of the Duke of Welshire. If this *had* been an adoption, it would all but guarantee George's future membership in the best gentlemen's clubs in London, and invitations to all the best parties. And while Rose wouldn't be a duchess, she would certainly be a lady. All that, though, was a handful of very high-flying fantasies.

"When a woman behaves correctly and politely," Emmeline said on the tail of his thought, "she is a lady, no matter her social status."

"See?" Rose stuck her lemon-yellow tongue out at her brother again.

And for a few weeks, at least, she *would* be a young lady.

CHAPTER SIX

"George?"

The flaming sword George Fletcher had been wielding to stave off the horde of giant rats chasing him and Rose down a dark alley vanished from his hands. In the same breath the tall, hooded rat king gestured, and one of the unusually large rodents lunged at his face. "Rats!" he shrieked, flailing.

"No rats, Georgie!" Rose yelled from a long distance away.

His eyes flew open. Rose, safe and seated across from him. In a coach. Late-afternoon sunlight in the windows. The frigate looking at him with a concerned expression on her face while the swell checked his pocket watch. The Pershings. The nuns weren't turning out the beds looking for hidden food or baubles, and the rat king was at least as far away as London. "I'm awake," he grumbled.

"He's afraid of rats," his sister said in a matter-of-fact voice.

He sat up, wiping drool from one corner of his mouth. "No, I'm not, you pudding-head."

"We thought you two would like to look out the window," the lady said with a too-big smile. "Being that we're on Winnover property now, and the house is at the top of the hill."

George shifted to the window, pushing open the glass to lean outside while Rosie did the same on the coach's other side. "This is Gloucestershire," his sister reminded him. "We've never been so far away."

"I know. A whole day away from London. I can't even smell it, anymore." Or hear it, which could be nearly as overpowering. He liked being this far away, even if it would only last for eight weeks.

"I still smell horse shite," his sister answered.

"Rose!" Mrs. Pershing said, as sharply as Sister Mary Stephen. "Ladies do not say 'shite.'"

"You just did," Rose pointed out.

"As a matter of instruction. We say 'horse manure,' if we must mention it at all."

"Can I say 'horse shite'?" George asked, turning his head to look at Mr. Pershing.

"Yes, but not in female company," he returned promptly, his expression much less ruffled.

"Oh, is that it?" Rose yelled, leaning far enough out the window that the missus grabbed on to the hem of her pink-and-yellow-striped dress. "It's sterling! Georgie! Look at all the windows!"

George leaned out the opposite window again, letting the breeze blow away the rest of his nightmare—afternoonmare—and tangle into his hair. "The whole orphanage could fit in there. Even Fatty Crunkle!"

"Who, pray tell, is Fatty Crunkle?" Mr. Pershing asked.

"He's one of the long-haul boys," George said, counting windows at the front of the giant house. They had to pay taxes on every one of those windows. The Pershings must be rich as Croesus. "And he's enormously fat."

"What's a long-haul boy?" the missus queried.

"One that's never going to be adopted. He's already twelve. Fat as he is, nobody wants him even to clean shi— manure—out of their stables. He eats more than he's worth, I reckon. He'll go to the workhouse next year." He didn't like thinking about long-haul boys, so he reached out with one hand to point. "Look, Rosie! A pond! Are there fish?"

"There are," Mr. Pershing answered. "Do you like to fish?"

Oh, he would probably be a magnificent fisherman. "I think so."

Rose ducked her head back into the coach for a moment. "We never been fishing," she explained, and returned to her view.

Mr. Pershing cleared his throat. "Well. We shall have to remedy that at the earliest opportunity."

Fish. Fishing. No London stink, no snoring Fatty Crunkle and the other badgering long-haul boys, no being scratched at by the big people who thought he and his sister could help them nick a quid or two, and no damned nuns trying to get Rosie adopted while he got left behind. George whooped into the wind. "No more London!"

"No more London!" Rose echoed, hopping up and down.

He waited for one of the grown-ups to remind them that they would be back in London in eight weeks when they were finished playing mama and papa, but neither of them said anything. It didn't matter to him, anyway, because he'd already decided they weren't going back. No, they were making other plans, he and Rosie were.

The coach rolled up to the front of the house. Even before it could stop, a tall, stout cove in green and black livery emerged from the house, two more fart-catchers at his back. "Welcome home, Mr. and Mrs. Pershing," the fancy one said, pulling open the coach door.

"You don't have much hair," Rose observed. "Are you the butler?"

The big man stared right back at Rosie.

"Powell," Mrs. Pershing said in a too-loud voice, "these are our children, George and Rose. Children, this is Powell. Yes, he is Winnover Hall's butler, and a very fine one at that."

"Your . . . children, ma'am?" the butler said faintly.

"Yes, our children. Please have Edward show them to the gold and green rooms."

"They adjoin, like you said?" George jumped down to the crushed-oyster-shell drive.

"They do."

"And our trunks?"

"They will go up with you. No one will open them."

The second coach turned onto the drive, its roof stacked high with blanket boxes and clothes and other things from London. The maid and the valet, Hannah and Davis, emerged, and all the other servants mobbed them. George wished them luck figuring out what was going on, because he didn't have a clue.

He kept an eye on his trunk all the way inside the house, up the wide staircase, and down two lamplit hall-ways to a gold-colored room where maids were already lighting more lamps, even with the edge of the sun still above the horizon. It was bigger than the shack all the Fletchers had shared when he'd been little. It was bigger than the dormitory room where he and fifteen other boys slept and kept all of their earthly belongings—at least the ones the nuns didn't take—in a wooden box beneath each bed. The windows weren't so high up the wall that you couldn't see—or get out of them—without turning a bed on its head and climbing it like a ladder.

"Have you chosen a room yet?" the lady asked, walking into the gold room.

"I like the green one," Rose answered, plunking herself down on each chair by the fire and then jumping up again to race through the connecting door to do the same in the other bedchamber. "It has roses on the walls! That's my name!"

"Is this one acceptable to you, George?" Mr. Pershing asked.

George took another look out the window. Still visible in the fading light, trees, pastures, some fields down in the valley, and maybe a river beyond them. Acres and acres without anyone hawking their wares or trying to lure rich shallow pates into some dark alleyway or other. No alleyways at all. "Is that all yours?" he asked, gesturing.

Joining him, the husband nodded. "Those are our pastures that way, and beyond that the wheat fields and cattle pastures used by the farmers who rent the land from us. Over that hill there is the village of Birdlip, which marks the border of Winnover land on the west."

"'Birdlip'?" George repeated. "That's a stupid name. Birds don't have lips."

"It's called after Birdlip Manor on the far side of the valley," Mr. Pershing explained. "Where Lord Birdlip got his name, I have no idea." He leaned back against the window casement. "Perhaps one of his ancestors had a mouth like a bird's beak."

George stuck out his lips, pursing them together. "I reckon that could be it," he said. "I wager he was one ugly bustard."

"What are you doing?" Rose asked, bounding back

into the bedchamber and immediately scrunching up her face in an imitation of George's bird beak.

"Making bird lips," he explained. When he turned around, the footman was pushing the new blanket box, *his* blanket box, into the dressing room. Out of sight. "I want it here," George said, pointing at the foot of his bed.

"You might trip over it out here," the fart-catcher said. With a quick glance at Mrs. Pershing and an even quicker grimace, though, the servant pulled the box back into the room and over to the foot of the bed. "There you go, sir," he said, inclining his head. "All nice and tidy."

Freezing in place, George stared at the tall, thin servant as he left the room. Then he spun to face Mr. Pershing. "That cuffin called me 'sir,'" he whispered.

"You're our son for the next few weeks," he explained. "That makes you a 'sir,' or 'Master George.'"

"What am I?" Rose demanded, lighting on the edge of the bed like a cricket, pausing for a moment but not finished yet with hopping about.

"You are 'miss' or 'Miss Rose.'"

"Ooh, I'm a prime article!" she exclaimed. "Deirdre won't ever believe it!"

Mrs. Pershing made a sound. "George, Edward will help you put your clothes away in the wardrobe there, and you may arrange the room however you please. Rose, I'll have Sally assist you, and you may do the same. When you're ready, come back downstairs and Powell will show you to the dining room where we'll have dinner and begin making our plans."

So they were Master George and Miss Rose now, and the fart-catchers and mop squeezers and even the pantler, Powell, had to do what they said. They'd never had it so soft and splendid, but George could see that it wouldn't take more than a few days to get them as spoiled as chickens in a pile of corn. When the chicken was happiest, that was when the butcher lopped off its head.

While the children hurried about opening drawers and wardrobes and exclaiming at all the space they had, Emmeline slipped up the hallway to her own room, the second-largest bedchamber in the house. Good heavens, they were loud. She doubted Winnover Hall had experienced such a ruckus since her mother and her aunts and uncles had been small, if then.

"I have your gowns back in the wardrobe," Hannah said, emerging from the dressing room. "But I can't find your abalone hairbrush. I don't recall leaving it behind, but I was helping Miss Rose, too."

Emmie sank into one of the chairs by the crackling fireplace. "Don't fret. When I have a moment, I'll send a note back to Landon. I believe Mr. Pershing left at least one shoe behind, and his hat."

The maid set the emptied portmanteau by the door so it could go back into the attic until they required it again—which would be in just under six weeks when they began the trip up to Cumberland. "I've told everyone who's asked just what you said—that the young ones are a charitable project and we're all to address them as your children."

"Thank you."

"But . . . Well, I've been in your household since you were sixteen, ma'am. I mean to say, it's none of my affair, but if I had some idea—"

Ah, that. Of course, all of the servants would have questions, and not a one of them had reason to believe the tale they'd been handed. Of everyone employed there, Hannah and Powell had been at Winnover the longest. The butler had kept her secrets as a young girl, and she had no doubt he and Hannah would do so now. "Would you ask Powell to join us?" she said aloud, folding her hands onto her lap.

"Yes, ma'am."

Once the maid and the butler had joined her in her bedchamber, she blew out her breath. "Have a seat, why don't you?" she said, gesturing at the pair of chairs opposite her.

Hannah, looking as if she would rather chew nails, perched herself on the edge of an overstuffed chair. Powell, though, remained stiff-shouldered and on his feet. "I have never sat in the presence of my employers, Mrs. Pershing," he stated. "If you deem it necessary I shall do so now, but I—"

"No, no," she interrupted. "Stand if you wish. I—"

Hannah popped to her feet again. "I wish to stand, as well."

"Fine." Emmie sat there for a moment, looking for a way to explain this so she and Mr. Pershing didn't look like the scheming bamboozlers they clearly were. "I don't know if you two are aware," she ventured slowly, "but there were conditions attached to Mr. Pershing and me remaining at Winnover Hall. Our marriage earned us five years of residency. By the end of that time, we were to . . . procreate. Produce a child. A descendant of the Duke of Welshire. As you know, we have not done so."

"Madam, this is none of my concern," the butler said, jaw clenched and his cheeks turning red.

"But it is, Powell. My grandfather's seventieth birthday approaches, and he wants to meet his great-grandchildren." She looked down for a moment, feeling like a schoolgirl caught in a lie. "You see, I may have informed him—I *did* inform him—in order to keep Winnover Hall—that

Mr. Pershing and I had a child. Children. A boy and a girl."

Now even the butler looked shocked, and given the usual granite of his expression, that was quite the feat. Hannah glanced over her shoulder in the direction of the children, her eyes widening. "That's why you—"

"Yes. That is why we've borrowed two children from St. Stephen's orphanage," Emmie finished. "For the moment you may address them as Master George and Miss Rose. Sometime before the party, they will become Malcolm and Flora Pershing. I will inform you when this occurs, so that you may inform the rest of the staff. We will all require some practice."

"Oh my," Hannah breathed.

"I know this is highly unusual. And it is imperative that the true story not spread to the rest of Society. If word should get back to His Grace of the actual circumstances, we will be removed posthaste from Winnover Hall. The estate will, I assume, go to Cousin Penelope and her husband and their brood."

"This is *your* childhood home, ma'am," Powell said stoutly. "We will do whatever is necessary to see that it remains in your possession."

"Thank you, Powell," she said feelingly, though she had a good idea that part of his loyalty owed to the fact that he didn't want to be at the beck and call of the high-handed Penelope Ramsey Chase and her overbearing husband and their three hellions—if they even kept the butler on.

"Mr. Pershing knows you invented children?" Hannah asked, then put her hands over her mouth. "That is none of our business either, of course."

"Mr. Pershing didn't know until three days ago," Emmie said, deciding that if all of this did gallop off the road and into the hedgerow, her husband should not have to bear the weight of any blame. It was her love of Winnover that had led to this mess in the first place. "We have agreed that this is the least disruptive solution."

Both servants nodded. "They are both darling children," she went on, "and while they seem a bit subdued after their time in the orphanage, I'm certain they will be happy to be in such a lovely home and to learn about being a gentleman and a lady."

"I would hope they would be exceptionally grateful for the opportunity to mingle with their betters," Powell stated.

"None of that, now, Powell. For the next few weeks, they are Pershings. The rest of the household will follow your example."

The butler sketched a stiff bow. "Of course, Mrs. Pershing. We shall not fail you."

"No, we shan't," Hannah seconded.

"Thank you." She smiled, flexing the fingers she'd been gripping far too tightly together. That had gone better than she'd expected. "That's all, then. We'll be having dinner within the hour. Powell, please let Mrs. Brubbins know that I will sit with her tomorrow to go over a revised menu for the house."

"Ma'am."

Once the servants had gone, Emmie sank back in the chair and closed her eyes. Every time she looked too closely at this little gambit her head threatened to explode, so she forced her mind to the two points of all this—keeping Winnover Hall, and not damaging Mr. Pershing's position. They'd taken the first step, she and her husband, and now they had a pair of sweet, unfortunate children. Everything after that would be much, much simpler.

Knuckles rapped at her door. Emmeline opened her

eyes and sat up straight. It wouldn't do to be caught napping before the children had even settled in. "Come in."

Her husband pushed open the door and strolled into the room. His presence filled her private retreat, unsettling and reminding her of those rare nights he'd used to come visiting. Indeed, he hadn't called on her in her bedchamber in months, and never this early in the evening. "I didn't mean to intrude," he said, his gaze on her. "I thought we should have a discussion about strategy before dinner."

"You're not intruding. And yes, I was thinking the same thing. All of my attention has been on obtaining children. Now we have under six weeks until they're presented to the Duke of Welshire and all my relations as our offspring." She frowned, rubbing her palms over her thighs. "And it just now occurs to me that the Fletcher children will have a lifetime to hate us for showing them opulence and luxuries they will never experience again."

Mr. Pershing sank into the chair opposite hers. "We're not doing them harm," he said. "We're expanding their potential futures."

"Yes," she said briskly, "and that didn't sound rehearsed, at all."

He tilted his head, narrowing his eyes. "You're not the only one to have second and third thoughts, Emmeline. This will be good for them, though."

It was reassuring that he felt guilty, too, and even more surprising that he'd tolerated this madness. No, not tolerated. Embraced. Had he done so to save his own career, or to help her keep Winnover? Perhaps it didn't matter, but for heaven's sake he'd married her so she could keep her home. Will Pershing, a brilliant man with a formidable future, had said yes when she'd been goose-headed enough to propose to him.

And now she'd learned that he'd wanted a family.

With her. Certainly, he didn't view her as a mere business partner, then. And she hadn't seen him as the fine-looking gentleman he'd become until he'd surprised her into looking at him by agreeing to this scheme. Oh, she'd gotten so many things wrong. Abruptly she wondered— had he been one of them?

She shook herself. "Will learning manners and which fork to use keep them out of the workhouse?"

"I hope so. At the least, they will have some fond memories of their time here."

"Fond memories are good," she agreed. "And we haven't lied to them about any of the circumstances." They had neglected to mention one or two of them as yet, but this was only their second day of acquaintance, and they would be told the rest without delay. "I am glad they're so enthusiastic about it."

"As am I. And they *should* be happy. We're giving them the run of the most beautiful house in England."

Indeed, they were. Winnover Hall was a part of her. She wouldn't have proposed to Will Pershing otherwise. She wouldn't have conjured a pair of youngsters otherwise. Having the children here, though, forcefully reminded her of one important fact. This wasn't just about her and Mr. Pershing and Winnover Hall any longer. "As vital as it is they learn propriety," she said, "we do need to see to it that they have some fun, then."

Nodding, he stood again. "I agree. And I'm beginning to think we were lucky Farmer Dawkins didn't take us up on our offer."

"Or the Hendersens, for heaven's sake. We could never pass that Prudence off as a five-year-old."

That earned her a chuckle. "We do still need to make amends with the Hendersens," he reminded her.

"Keeping things frosty for the next few weeks might

be to our advantage," she countered. "The Hendersens have a large social circle."

He shrugged. "If we cross paths with them, we'll simply tell them that they're a cousin's children, here for a visit before we take them with us to Cumberland. Oh, didn't we mention that they would be joining us on our holiday?"

She snorted, belatedly putting a hand over her mouth. "William Pershing! I'd quite forgotten you were so wicked."

Mr. Pershing looked over at her. "I know. I am a bit, though. Wicked."

What did that mean? His green-eyed gaze remained on her as he offered her a hand, and a small shiver of . . . something warm trailed down her spine. Oh. *Oh.* "We have a strategy, then," she said, taking his fingers and rising, then swiftly releasing him again as she turned for the door. *Goodness.* Or not goodness, rather. "Useful lessons, and as much fun for the darlings as we can reasonably manage."

"Agreed again."

Afterward, their well-orchestrated, parallel dance could resume. Would resume. Everything would return to calm, order, and perfection, and not one thought about how long it had been since he'd last kissed her. Since she'd kissed him.

CHAPTER SEVEN

Clearing her throat, Emmeline set her palms over the pair of journals she'd brought downstairs. "Now that you've eaten, I have a story to tell you before bedtime."

"Are you certain you wish to do this now?" Will asked. He understood that she wanted to explain her—their—motives. But these weren't imaginary children, and they were tired after a long day. At the same time, *she* was the one who'd begun laying the plans to save Winnover seven years ago. Perhaps a bit of faith was called for.

"I love stories," Rose said, yawning. "Does it have ducks in it?"

"No." Emmeline opened the first journal. "A few years ago, we—"

"Is there a giant? Or a beanstalk?"

"It's not that kind of story, Rose."

The girl slumped. "Oh."

Emmeline looked over at the little one, then took a deep breath as she shut the journal again. "It does have a prince and a princess."

Will lifted his eyebrows. "It does?"

"Yes. You see, a prince and a princess married, and the old king, the princess's grandfather, gave them a wedding gift. Th—"

"Oh, a magic one?" Rose straightened. "Was it a chicken who grants wishes?"

"Chickens aren't magic," her brother stated. "Nothing is magic."

Damn, but the boy was cynical. "That's a rather broad sta—"

"Mornings are magic, I've always thought," Emmeline countered, before Will could conjure his own argument.

"See?" His sister stuck out her tongue. "So was it a magic chicken?"

"No. The gift was a beautiful, perfect home. A home with a garden, and big windows, and a large pond filled to the brim with fish."

"Oh, like this house," Rose breathed.

"Very like," Emmeline agreed. "In exchange for this perfect house, though, the king had one demand to which the prince and princess had to agree. And—"

"Oh, I know this one," Rose interrupted again. "Never go into the woods at night." Her eyes widened. "Did they? Was there wolves?"

The matchup between Emmeline's rarely ruffled sense of order and Rose's very loose hold on her imagination was rather hilarious. And would quite possibly end in fist-icuffs. "Were there?" Will asked.

His wife shot him an annoyed look. "No wolves. The demand was that the prince and princess have children. And they tried, but they couldn't."

"Oh dear. It must have been a witch's curse. Deirdre said her uncle was cursed by a witch, and it made his boy thing fall off. Witches are nasty creatures."

"Good heavens! No, it wasn't a witch's curse. It was just . . . bad luck. But anyway, the king never came to visit, and the prince and princess never told him they had no children. In fact, after a time the princess pretended they *did* have children, and she made up stories about how wonderful they were and sent letters about the pretend children to her family, and everyone was perfectly happy that way. It went this way for years, until one day, the king sent word that he was holding a grand birthday party for himself, and that he wanted to meet his great-grandchildren."

Rose gasped. "Oh no! Did the king cut off the prince and princess's heads?"

"Now it's getting interesting," George commented, putting his elbows on the table and his chin in his hands.

Will agreed. With a grimace, Emmeline curled her fingers around the edge of her journals. Considering that an hour ago she'd meant to give the children a summary of the actual facts, Will doubted she'd had time to construct the ending of this fairy tale. Hell, they still didn't know how it would end.

"You see," she began, "the prince and princess were clever. They were able to find some children who perfectly matched the descriptions she'd written, and they all went to the king's birthday party and were able to fool everyone. And so they were able to keep their house, with no one the wiser. The end."

"No witches at all?" Rose said, frowning. "And no magic?"

"Wait a minute." George straightened. "You're the princess and the prince, ain't you? We're the children."

"What do you mean, Georgie?"

Clever boy. "Yes, you are," Will said aloud. "Emmeline's grandfather is the Duke of Welshire. He is going to be celebrating his seventieth birthday in just under six weeks. He lives in Cumberland, and wants all of his family to join him there for a grand party."

"And you was supposed to have children, and you

never did. So you borrowed us from the stone jug so you can keep this house."

"Yes," Emmeline said crisply, smiling her charming smile. "All of the duke's children and grandchildren and great-grandchildren, cousins, nephews, nieces—everyone will be there."

George dug the tip of one forefinger into the tabletop. "You lied. To a duke."

Rose continued to look dissatisfied. "I still think this could be a witch's curse. Are you certain there's no evil witch?"

"No witch, I'm sorry to say." Will picked up his glass of port and took a swallow, mostly to cover his grin. The little one was relentless. "As Emmeline explained, the problem is that without children, the duke *will* take the house from us. She grew up here, and we both adore it."

"I'm confused," Rose said. "Are we your children now?"

"No, Rosie. They only need us for the party."

That sounded . . . horrible. And yet there the children were, all set to be returned to St. Stephen's in eight weeks. "Perhaps you could think of it as a holiday from London," Will said aloud. "Fishing, fine clothes, fine food, and then for a few days at the end George will be Malcolm, our imaginary seven-year-old son, and Rose will be Flora, our five-year-old daughter."

Rose put her hands on her hips. "Wait a moment. If I'm choosing a name, I wish to be Lydia."

"Don't be a goose, Rosie. The point is, this is why they only need us for a few weeks." He glanced at Emmeline. "At least you told us that."

"Oh, George." She put a hand on his shoulder. "You will have fun here. And we will teach you *so* many things that will help you find a family, and work."

He shrugged out of her grip without bothering to be politic about it. A boy unaccustomed to having comforting arms wrapped around him. "Things like what?"

"Riding a horse," Will stated, aiming for winning them over. "Shooting and fencing. Fishing."

"Oh, I want to learn to fence," Rose said, shifting to put her folded legs under her bottom. "That's swords, ain't it?"

"Rapiers." Will narrowed one eye. "Yes, swords."

"Rose, you're to learn embroidery, dance, and the pianoforte." Emmeline sent him another look, as if Rose's wishes were his fault. That said, he could practically read her thoughts—they didn't have time to allow Rose to muck about with swordplay, or either of them with horses. In Emmeline's mind, fun would be arranging flowers, no doubt.

"Someone brought a pianoforte to the stone jug and played it for us once," George said. "I liked it. I'll learn that."

Emmeline blinked. "I hadn't planned on instructing both of you."

"I don't want that. I want to sword." Rose picked up her fork and stabbed it into the air.

"That sounds grand, of course, but we only have a few weeks until we leave for the Lake District. Fishing for George because boys enjoy that sort of thing, and dance for Rose because you're already very good at twirling. You'll have fun with those."

"What about horses, though?" Rose insisted, pressing her palms together. "Mr. P—Papa said horses. Please?"

"We didn't have a riding habit made for you."

"But if I'm to be a lady, I need to ride a horse," Rose pressed. "All the other ladies ride horses, I wager."

"Ladies don't wager."

"What about horses, though?"

"I—"

"Rosie, don't be a baby. We'll do what they say. It's for our own good."

Will took another swallow of port, his glance at Emmeline's exasperated expression nearly making him choke. Never one for flights of fancy, she'd become a book of orderliness and purpose over the past eight years, and he would have been willing to wager that she hadn't put "arguing with children" on her well-organized list of tasks for the day.

"I suggest we all consider our choices tonight, and we can begin tomorrow," he said.

"I'll consider about sword fighting," Rose said. "And riding."

Emmeline sent them off upstairs, then finished her glass of ratafia and stood. "Good evening, Mr. Pershing," she said, inclining her head.

"You're annoyed I didn't take your side regarding Rose and fencing. And riding." Will swirled the glass in his hand and sat back.

Her shoulders rising and falling with her deep breath, she sat again. "Yes. You might have said something. I know we want them to have some fun, but we also have a finite amount of time. If we take on those extra recreations, when will we have time for geography for George and embroidery for Rose, and manners and conversation and dancing lessons for both of them, and—"

"They don't need to be perfect," he interrupted. "Only passable. And if we don't give Rose her fencing lessons and teach George a song or two on the pianoforte, they will never have a chance to learn them. What did you mean to add to the mix to give them those fond memories? One day of fishing or a single afternoon playing tea party?"

"So as usual, you set an impossible task and expect me to see to it."

Will blinked. "You've managed every one of them thus far," he said. "And done so with elegance, efficiency, and, if I may say so, brilliance. If I've come to rely too much on your expertise, I apologize for not realizing how difficult I've made it for you. In my defense, you unfailingly make it all look effortless."

She opened her mouth and snapped it shut again. "I forget sometimes how effective you are at wielding words and soothing ruffled feathers."

"I'm not trying to manipulate you, Mrs. Per— Emmeline," he countered, for the moment ignoring the fact that she'd suggested at least half of the events they'd hosted. "For God's sake, I would never place you in the category of a simple vote or a banknote." She was far too complicated, and too important to him, whether she would ever feel the same way about him, or not. "I am very aware that I would not have the position I currently enjoy without your tireless efforts. That was therefore an apology."

The silence stretched for a good number of seconds. "We have a partnership," she said finally. "You allowed me to have Winnover Hall, and I've hopefully aided your career. This muddle . . . I'll see to it, and things will return to normal. So I also apologize."

That was it, then. The tit for tat. Eight years, and it hadn't changed a whit. "I have Winnover as well, you know."

"Yes, of course." Emmeline sighed. "Generally, we work in parallel, the two sides of a coin. This will be . . . different."

"Yes, it will. And I'm certainly willing to enter the fray at your side."

"You still have your work, Mr. P—Will. That must come first."

"I am on leave, with Lord Stafford's permission. I am free to wade into the muck with you."

"But—"

"As I said, Emmie, we are in this together."

A soft blush spread across her cheeks. "Well, I suppose it's beneficial every few years to turn everything on its head."

"We're overdue, I think. Eight years into a marriage is not when a husband is supposed to discover that his wife is a fine storyteller, or that she's been single-handedly keeping a roof over our heads by inventing offspring." He tilted his head, gazing at her pretty brown eyes. "For God's sake, Emmeline, we've known each other for most of our lives. I had no idea you possessed such an imagination."

"That's a nice way of saying that I'm a complete, useless fraud."

"You are no such thing. We are both proficient at playing our parts. And I will do my part with the children." He put his hand over hers.

Her fingers were warm and soft, and the caress made him want to kiss her, made him wish all over again that before he'd signed the wedding register, he'd told her that he adored her. But he hadn't. She'd said friend and partner, and now he was stuck. And still wishing and dreaming.

A slow smile touched her mouth. "I'd stopped imagining children in this house, but if they continue to be as eager for new experiences as they have been, we should be able to manage it. Together."

"Yes. Together." Briefly squeezing her fingers, he climbed to his feet again. God's sake, perhaps she'd begun to catch his interest all over again. But he wasn't that young idiot any longer. If he'd learned one damned thing, it was the necessity of being patient where Emmeline was concerned. "By the way, as the children seem to find the way we address each other odd, do you have any objection to me continuing to refer to you as Emmeline?"

Another soft, attractive blush touched her cheeks, and his fingers twitched in response. "I do not object. I can't quite remember when we stopped using our Christian names."

He could; it had been when she'd returned from the physician in London. "Neither can I," he said anyway.

"Then do you still prefer Will, or is it to be William now?"

"Will." He smiled. "Perhaps we might find some benefits to this that we'd never have expected, after all. Good night, Emmeline."

"Good night, Will."

"Rose. Rosie. Wake up."

Rose opened her eyes. "What are you doing?" she asked her brother. His face looked big and ghost-white, looming over hers in the dark. "I was dreaming about horses. I was riding a white one with a horn on its head."

"That's a unicorn," he said, standing upright and then yanking the warm blankets off her.

"Hey!"

"Shh. We're leaving."

She sat up, but gave up trying to get her sheets back. "We can't leave. You promised Sister Mary Stephen we wouldn't run."

"This ain't the stone jug." He picked up her dress for tomorrow from where it rested over the back of a chair, and tossed it at her head. "But in eight weeks it will be again."

Making a face, she straightened out the dress over her lap. It was the pink and yellow one, and that was good, but it was dark outside, and that was bad. "It's nighttime. And I want to learn to sword."

He came back to stand beside the bed. And he had his sack of treasures with him. "Didn't you hear the missus?" he asked. "They want you to learn to curtsy and say 'yes, please' and 'no, thank you' and be able to embroider a flower. That's it. Only what you need to know to pretend to be fancy for an hour."

"But swords. And horses." They hadn't promised, but she'd asked in a very nice way. People gave her pennies sometimes when she asked for them in that same nice way.

George sighed. "Even if they did teach you riding, we'd still end up back at the stone jug. They ain't got horses there. Or swords. All they have is folk who want to adopt you and leave me behind to be a long-haul boy. And we're well rid of London." He moved closer to whisper. "And you know who. We got to stay together, Rosie. You know that."

She did know that, and she knew it was good to be far away from some of the everyones in London. Especially the ones they couldn't trust. "Where are we going, then?" Sliding down from the soft bed, she pulled off her night rail and wiggled into her dress. Nighttime or not, she was going to wear her bonnet, too. And her new shoes.

"We'll go to Birdlip," he said. "There should be wagons and such there. We can get a ride to Gloucester, or Birmingham. Those are big enough we could find a place to stay. When we get enough money, we can rent a room."

"Are you certain we don't need to learn to sword fight before we go?"

Instead of answering, he opened her blanket box and pulled out her treasure sack. It was heavier than before, she knew, because now it had a new brush, a pair of pretty earbobs, and a dozen biscuits from the fat lady at the dress shop. She'd meant to eat some more of them tonight, but the lemon biscuits Mrs. Brubbins had made them for after dinner had been very good. And now she could save the dress-shop cookies for breakfast. She was very practical.

"Ready?"

"Just a minute." Taking her sack, she added the pretty silver candle holder from beside her bed, and the fluffiest of the pillows.

"Can you even carry that?"

"I can carry it. And I still think the Pershings are nice."

"Of course they're nice," her brother returned. "They need us so they can keep their fancy house, and then they'll send us back to St. Stephen's. They'll be riding horses and dancing, and we'll be fighting Fatty Crunkle for stew rations and wondering if *he's* ever going to reappear."

What he said made sense, and Georgie always made sense, anyway. And he always made sure she had food and a blanket. Sister Mary Stephen had probably given away their beds the minute they left, and if they went back, they'd have to sleep on the floor until enough children who'd been there longer were adopted and a bed opened up again. She hated sleeping on the floor.

"Let me make the bed, and then I'll be ready."

"Rosie . . ."

"It's a nice bed. And ladies don't leave messes."

While he kept listening at the door like he expected hounds to burst in, she pulled the blankets back where they belonged and set all the pillows in place. Then she picked up her sack and followed her brother into the hallway and down the stairs.

The front door was latched, but George went up on his tiptoes and reached the lock. Once he had the bolt slid, he pulled open the door and they went out into the night. Georgie would make sure everything was all right, but she did wish she'd been able to bring more than two of her new gowns with her. She'd been well on her way to being a lady, and she didn't want to give that up. Not even to avoid going back to the stone jug and London.

"Good morning, Mrs. Pershing." Hannah pushed open the pretty green curtains of the window that overlooked the front of the house, and sunlight flooded into the room.

Emmeline sat up, shaking off an odd dream in which her husband kept asking her to dance and it was always a waltz, and they kept spinning and spinning until she was so dizzy she couldn't see straight. She still felt unbalanced. "Good morning. How are the children?"

"They haven't risen yet," the maid answered. "You didn't say if one of the staff should wake them, so I thought perhaps you would want to."

"Yes. That would be lovely. Thank you."

Bobbing her head, Hannah fetched the kimono-style dressing robe Emmie favored and held it open for her. "I asked Mrs. Brubbins to be certain she had fresh rolls and fruit on the sideboard for the little ones this morning. I hope that's acceptable."

"Hannah, I had no idea you were so knowledgeable about children."

The maid blushed. "I'm no expert, to be sure. I did have two younger sisters, and I recall them both liking butter and marmalade and apples in the morning."

"I appreciate your thoughtfulness. No doubt George and Rose will, as well."

She tied the dressing gown around her waist. However short their stay would be, she did want the children to be happy and comfortable while they were in Gloucestershire. It was simple guest etiquette, and it felt more comfortable to hold on to that idea rather than the one where she was now responsible for two children.

Even that thought, though, didn't seem as fraught with horrors as it had been yesterday. Mrs. Hendersen, for example, always went on and on about how her every waking moment was devoted to her two young ones. For heaven's sake, either Mary must have been exaggerating, or the woman was horribly ineffective.

If Emmie could manage a solid partnership with Mr. Pershing—Will—for eight years, she could, she reasoned, do the same with two youngsters for a handful of weeks. Beginning this morning. For goodness' sake, she'd married Will on a whim and still held up her end of the bargain. And when she looked at him over the last few days, that gangly, distracted boy he'd been seemed very far away. The man who'd taken his place—the mature, thoughtful, handsome, witty one—she didn't know quite what to make of him yet. But she was definitely curious.

With the scent of bacon and fresh-baked bread in the air, she walked down the hallway and knocked on Rose's door. The girl didn't answer. Not wanting to startle her, Emmie began speaking softly as she pushed down on the handle and opened the door. "Good morning, my dear. I hope you slept well and had sweet, sweet dr—"

The bed was empty. It had also been made, albeit rather sloppily, as if by someone who didn't quite know what to do with the dozen pillows and the quilted coverlet. Her heart hammered for a bare moment, until she spied the open door connecting Rose's bedchamber with George's. *How sweet.*

Walking on tiptoe, she reached the connecting door and leaned in, a smile on her face as she imagined how darling they must look snuggled up together. But George's bed was empty, as well.

It hadn't been made, pillows and blankets scattered across the bed and the floor. A cold, biting alarm pinched deep in her gut, a sensation she'd never felt before. "George?" she called. "Rose?" Only the subdued clatter of servants readying the house for the day answered her. "George! Rose!"

Whirling around, she nearly stumbled into Hannah. "I'll go see if they've gone down for breakfast," the maid stammered, and ran toward the stairs.

"Yes. They're downstairs," Emmeline breathed, a hand over her chest as she tried to slow the frantic beat of her heart. It made sense that they would have smelled breakfast and gone to eat.

Her mind thought that perfectly logical, but her heart refused to slow its hard pounding. Sinking onto her knees, she peered beneath the bed. The only resident down there was another stray pillow. Standing again, she strode back to Rose's room and did the same thing. Nothing.

The panic shooting down her muscles was paralyzing. She'd been through crises before and had never felt the like. It made her want to scream and run and cover her eyes and hide all at the same time. "Hannah!" she yelled, hurrying to Rose's doorway again. "Have you found them?"

"No, Mrs. Pershing!" came the answer. "Powell hasn't seen them. Nor has Mrs. Brubbins!"

"Keep looking! Everyone, search!"

"Yes, ma'am!" Powell's yell answered her.

She needed to wake Mr. Pershing. As she hurried up the hallway, it belatedly occurred to her that he might have taken the children down to the pond to go fishing, or something. *Oh yes*. That must be it. Steeling herself, one hand still over her chest to keep her heart from leaping onto the floor, she knocked at the door to his private rooms.

"Come in," his low voice answered.

"Oh no, you're here," she rasped, shoving the door open.

Will, his waistcoat still unbuttoned and his coat across Davis's arm, lifted an eyebrow. "Beg pardon?"

Capable. That was the immediate thought that struck her. He looked very capable. And not at all like a disheveled, gangly boy. "I'd hoped—that is, I thought you and the children might have—oh, that doesn't signify. I can't find them. George or Rose."

Before she could even finish her sentence, he'd moved past her out his door. "You checked their bedchambers?" he asked, striding down the hallway. "Of course you did. The breakfast room?"

"Hannah's just been there. No one's seen them."

He glanced into each of the children's rooms as he passed, then without pause headed for the stairs and trotted down to the ground floor. "Rose's bed is made," he muttered, "but George's isn't. She wasn't frightened into fleeing, then."

"Do you think George was? And she followed?"

He shook his head. "She wouldn't have stopped to make her bed under either scenario."

That made sense. "Yes. Logic. Logic is good. If they weren't frightened, it stands to reason that they're here somewhere. Perhaps exploring."

"Powell," Will barked, and the butler skidded into the foyer. "Divide up the staff and search every room. Begin with the attic. If I was a boy, that would most interest me."

"Or the stables." Without waiting for him to concur, Emmie pulled open the front door and strode outside. The garden had its lures, as well, and changing her mind, wanting to look everywhere at once, she hurried around the side of the house. Then she remembered the pond, and she broke into a run.

"The pond." Will's voice came from behind her. With his longer stride he passed her up, making for the small dock and the punt tied up there.

She didn't think she'd seen him run since they'd been children, but he ran to the pond, sprinting along the reed-lined shore. It was so tempting to stop, to let him do the searching while she spent her time thinking up every possible disaster that might have occurred. That was both useless and unfair, though, so she gathered up the hems of the cumbersome robe and headed back toward the stables. Five grooms and drivers there meant five more pairs of eyes to help the search.

"Billet!" she yelled, yanking open the smaller door into the building.

The head groom emerged from the tack room. "Mrs. Pershing? What's am—"

"Have you seen the children? The boy and girl who arrived with us yesterday?"

He frowned, a rag gripped in one hand. "No, ma'am. They're missing?"

"Yes. We can't—We don't know where they've gone."

"The boys and I will saddle up and take a look about the property. They might've gone into Birdlip. The bakery smells like God's own heaven in the mornings."

"Thank you. Take Topper and Willow if you need them."

As much as she wanted to supervise that, to make certain they divided up the property into searchable areas, she turned and ran back to the garden. With its central fountain and pair of follies at opposite corners, it had a great many places for small people to hide—though if this was some sort of hide-and-seek game, someone was going to get a spanking.

When she climbed up onto a bench to look over the low wall, she spied her husband in the boat, punting back and forth across the length of the pond. Nothing so far then, thank God. The gardeners joined her search, but she couldn't come up with a logical reason the children would continue to hide among the roses and shrubberies when they had to have heard everyone calling for them.

If they'd bothered to leave the house at all, it would be for some actual destination, wouldn't it? Somewhere in particular they meant to go. Birdlip? Perhaps, but Billet would be searching there. What would they want from the village that they couldn't get at Winnover, anyway? No, that didn't make sense.

The two of them had never even left London before. Could they have headed back to Town? No, that wouldn't be it. Mr. Pershing had said that George had asked her several times how far away they would be from London. And they'd sounded so excited at being away from St. Stephen's.

They certainly wouldn't be looking for an orphanage. The last place they wanted to be was back at the "stone jug," as they called it, or any place even resembling it.

Wait a moment. Emmie hopped down from the bench and sat on it instead. The children were presently as far from St. Stephen's as they'd ever been. Last night they'd been told the plan for her grandfather's birthday, what they were being asked to take on. They'd already known that at the end of this they would be returned to London and the orphanage, and then she'd piled on dancing and propriety lessons.

They'd run away. Standing again, Emmie returned to the shore of the pond. "Will?"

"I don't think they're here at all," he said, turning the boat with its single pole and heading back to the dock.

"We told them we would only keep them for eight weeks. Then we said we expected them to learn dancing and embroidery and manners that would satisfy a duke."

Her husband, still supremely capable-looking and handsome in shirtsleeves and with his waistcoat unbuttoned, stepped back onto the dock and tied off the punt. When he straightened, his worried look had shifted into something more thoughtful. "We're idiots."

She nodded. "I think we may be."

"They've run away, haven't they? Damnation."

CHAPTER EIGHT

Emmie felt useless. Running hither and thither and fainting everywhere would only make her the worst sort of heroine, though, so she stayed in the foyer to take reports from the staff of where they'd searched and sent them out again to where no one had yet been.

Even though flight made the most sense given what little she and Will knew of the children, she made certain the staff checked every room and every wardrobe and beneath every bed twice. Outside was much more problematic, and the stable boys, the gardeners, and even Mrs. Brubbins the cook were presently working their way through the garden and the surrounding fields.

Will had gone up to the widow's walk on the roof for a better view of their surroundings, while she abruptly wondered if keeping track of offspring wasn't why one of her ancestors had built the thing in the first place. "Donald, please make one more check of the wine cellar," she said, noting that instruction on the paper she'd been using to keep track of everyone's whereabouts. "And Edward, I need you to search the billiards room again. As before, lock the doors after you leave. At least we can narrow down where they're not."

"Yes, ma'am."

A loud whistle echoed into the house through the open front door. Shouts of "he's got them" and "there they are" began from outside and the upper floors.

"Oh, thank God," she muttered, running out to the front drive.

A moment later Will, a relieved look on his face, joined her there. "I caught sight of them coming up the hill from Birdlip," he panted. "Billet and Roger have them."

"Was that you whistling?" she asked, glancing up toward the widow's walk.

"It was. Haven't done that since I was a boy." He flashed her a grin.

"I thought I recognized it." And for the first time in quite a while, she also recognized that exuberant, gangly youngster in his demeanor. God, she'd followed that boy everywhere. Somewhere along the way, though, she'd lost sight of him, and he'd become a thoughtful, logical man. And now, even a bit dashing. When—and why—had she stopped appreciating all the aspects of him?

Before she could decipher any of those questions, two riders emerged from around the bend and turned up the hill. A child rode with each of the men, Rose sidesaddle in front of Roger, and George facedown like a sack of turnips over the front of Billet's saddle. Faint words reached her, growing more distinct as the riders approached.

". . . fat-faced dog booby, you let me down or I'll bloody thrash you," George growled, flinging his fists backward in the head groom's direction.

"Hush now, boy," the groom returned in a smooth tone. "Your mama and papa will hear you."

"They ain't my mama and papa, you damned scapegallows. I'll give you two quid to turn around now. Otherwise, I'll bloody your conk, you Captain Huff!"

"Good heavens," Emmie murmured. Her uncle Harry

had been fond of profanity, but he was an amateur compared to George Fletcher.

"I thought he was the quiet one," her husband noted, stepping forward to haul the eight-year-old off the front of the horse.

As soon as George's feet touched the ground he tried running, but Will grabbed him by the top of his trousers and held him in place. "Let me go!"

"No."

Billet dismounted, walking over to lift Rose down from the other horse. "Keep hold of him, Mr. Pershing," he said, gripping the little girl's hand. "I spied him in the middle of plucking the billfold right out of Lord Graham's coat pocket while the little one sat in the middle of the road and wept that she'd fallen from her papa's wagon."

"*What?*" Emmie stared at the girl's angelic face.

"It usually works," Rose said, shrugging.

"You want us to lie, too, so don't get all high-and-mighty, you bloody frigate."

"Manners," Will said, shaking the boy a little.

"He makes a point." Emmie took a breath, still trying to reconcile her image of the little darlings with the hellions standing before her. They were supposed to be her children! But *her* children were well-behaved and well-mannered; she'd written them that way. *Oh dear.* "Whyever did you run? Good food, clothes, a few lessons in how to be proper—what's so horrible about that?"

"That's what I said," Rose put in, swiping one forefinger beneath her nose. "We should have stayed until we learned something, Georgie."

"The question is, why leave at all?" Will shifted his grip to the boy's shoulder, turning him to face them as the servants pretended they weren't ogling the proceedings.

"Because we ain't going back to London. I promised Rosie we would leave damned St. Stephen's as soon as we could and now we have, and we won't go back to that devil's stewpot."

"That's an odd thing to call an orphanage overseen by nuns. But wait a moment; we can have a more honest conversation in private." Will leaned down a little, to meet George's still-angry gaze. "Agreed?"

"I don't agree about anything," the boy snapped. "We got no reason to stay here one more damned minute, and no reason to trust you."

Another fair point. Emmie and Will had both overlooked several important points in their plan, in fact, the main one being to find a reason for the children to cooperate. Not something they might find useful later, but an actual thing that would convince them to remain when a return to the orphanage loomed but a few weeks away.

"Have you eaten breakfast, at least?" she asked.

George narrowed his eyes. "No."

"A few biscuits, and we got some eggs, but George had to throw 'em at a dog that was chasing us." Rose sniffed again.

"Well, we have fresh rolls and butter, and apples and oranges. Would you care to join us?"

"I *am* a little hungry," Rose said. "Georgie?"

The boy lowered his shoulders. "Fine. We'll eat. But that don't mean we changed our minds."

Emmie inclined her head. "Of course not."

"And we want our things back."

At Will's nod, Roger unfastened the two cloth sacks from the back of his saddle and handed them over. Each child took one, though how they knew which belonged to whom, Emmie had no idea. They looked bulkier now, but both youngsters had additional clothes, and she wouldn't have been surprised to discover that Rose had taken a pillow or two with her. The girl adored the things. Pillows, though, didn't explain the metallic clanking sounds coming from the depths of the bags.

The groom handed Rose over to Emmie, and the four of them—along with most of the staff—headed back to the house. In the doorway George paused. "Hey, Billet. You'll never catch us next time," he called over his shoulder.

Billet snorted, sounding a great deal like one of his four-legged charges. "I'm on to you now, scamp. You won't get past me again."

As they dug into their breakfasts, Emmie looked from one child to the other. Yesterday she'd thought them darlings just beginning to find some spirit again after being nearly crushed by the misery of St. Stephen's. They were still those children, except that they weren't as subdued and crushed as she'd thought. But it was more than that. George had been picking the pocket of a baron, and Rose had been distracting said baron while her brother robbed him. From what Billet had said, the two would have been successful if he hadn't interrupted them. They didn't look like criminals, but she doubted this was the first time they'd attempted such a thing.

Was larceny the reason the younger nun had seemed so surprised at Sister Mary Stephen's choice of orphans to lend? And that laughter she thought she'd heard from behind the door after they'd left . . . *Well.* That opened a whole box of new questions.

"I have a question," Will said, before she could figure out how to word her own query. "Are the two of you hardened criminals who've been pretending to be children? Does Rose sleep with a loaded blunderbuss beneath her pillow? George, do you have a knife in your shoe?"

From their confused expressions, the children didn't know how to take that question. They would have been expecting yelling and accusations, threats to return them to London as soon as the coach could be readied. Humor, though, clearly baffled them. *Well done, Will.*

George stared at the mister. Rose couldn't lift a blunderbuss, much less put one beneath her pillow. And Pershing didn't seem like a half-wit, even if he and his wife were odd and thought borrowing children to lie to a duke was a good idea. Dukes could get people transported. Or hanged. Maybe the mister was trying to be funny, which was better than yelling and threatening to throw them in jail like the nuns did.

"I don't have a blunderbuss," Rose said, slathering her roll with near an inch of butter.

"Well, that's reassuring. George?"

"I have a fipenny," he stated around a mouthful of bacon. If they got mad and locked them in their rooms, he at least wanted to begin on a full stomach. "It don't fit in my shoe. But I ain't telling you where it is." They wouldn't find it by searching, either, and he'd scream bloody murder if they tried to take off his smallclothes.

"I'm sorry, but what's a fipenny?" the lady asked.

"A folding knife," her husband answered.

The mister knew some things, then. Where he'd come by that information George had no idea, because the swell didn't look like the type who frequented buttocking—or sleek and slim—shops. The nice-seeming ones, though, were sometimes the worst.

"How long were you at St. Stephen's before we came by?" the missus asked.

"About six months the last time, I reckon. That was when that Philistine nabbed us and took us straight to the stone jug. Said it was for our own good, the bastard."

The lady frowned, but didn't complain about the profanity this time. "You escaped the orphanage, then? And a Bow Street Runner arrested you?"

Rose nodded. "I thought the law would send us to Australia, but after the second time George promised the nuns we wouldn't run if they didn't give us back to Bow Street. I don't really remember before that, except for when we lived in that hole under the church."

"A hole under a church," the missus whispered, her face turning a little gray.

"It wasn't *under* the church," George countered, scowling again. "It was a hole that led to the cellar where they kept the wine and such. I liked it there. Twice a month they gave away food, and we got first pick because they kept it down where we was."

"Which church?"

"I don't know. It had a big stone cross outside, and a tall, square part in the middle."

"We used stepping-stones to get to our hole without our feet getting wet," Rose piped up. "I'm good at jumping."

"Those weren't stepping-stones, goose," he informed her. She was five now, and could stand to learn the truth.

"Well, what were they, then? You said they were stepping-stones."

"Because I didn't want you to know they were gravestones. Laid out flat in the grass, they were, all over the grounds. No standing ones at all."

"St. Quiteria's?" Mr. Pershing muttered.

"That was it, I think," George affirmed.

"I was walking on *people*?" the five-year-old screeched.

"Dead people. They didn't care."

"It sounds as if you did quite well for yourselves," Mrs. Pershing said, looking like somebody'd put a plate of bugs in front of her. "What gave Bow Street cause to pursue you?"

"Oh, some damned cully caught me in his pocket," George grumbled, leaving out the part where their supposed lookout had taken off running. "His collar was so high I didn't even think he could turn his head, but there he was, glaring at me. Grabbed me by the hair, he did. I yelled murder and Rose kicked him, but there was a Runner right around the corner and he nicked us before we could get away."

"In all fairness," the mister commented, "you were trying to steal from him."

"Just his pocket watch. We could've gotten some good rhino for it. He shouldn't have been standing there, sneering and watching Rosie dance, with her not even five years old. If I'd had a knife in my shoe then, I would've shown him, the whore's bird."

The two adults looked at each other. George didn't know what surprised them so much—Rosie was too little to be able to dig into pockets, but most grown-ups stopped to look at her when she danced or cried, calling her waif and darling and sprite. Some of them, though, didn't look at her the same way, and that was why he wouldn't let the nuns get her adopted without him.

"You said your father died at sea. May I ask what became of your mother?" The missus still looked sympathetic, which was more than he'd expected.

"They said it was the miasma," George answered, grinding a fist into his thigh. "But I saw that well was a horror. Rosie got sick, too, but I went and stole her some milk and then we left there. Better wells where the fat culls live." He grimaced. "No offense."

"None taken." Mr. Pershing stroked his chin. "You're a rather remarkable young man, George Fletcher."

It took a few seconds for George to realize he'd been complimented. His face felt warm, and he hoped he wasn't blushing like a girl. Pershing, Mr. P, seemed like a good cove, and the missus asked questions instead of yelling. That was good, but it didn't mean he trusted them. No good ever came of trusting somebody. "We done what we had to. Rose is my responsibility."

Mrs. P cleared her throat. "Well. Now we know each other a little better. Where do we go from here?"

"Not back to St. Stephen's."

"We could look for a more . . . pleasant place for you," Mr. P offered, a brief scowl making lines on his forehead.

"I don't want to go to a different orphanage." Rose dropped her spoon, bent down and made a show of looking for it, then straightened with a shrug and resumed eating with her fork. Not as good as he could do it, but she was getting better.

"Me, neither," he said.

"They make us do prayers to be forgiven for trespassing and clean the floors all the time. Me and George only trespass a little, and besides, if we didn't have to kneel, nobody would need the floor so clean."

"No orphanages." George planted his coiled fist on the table. "Rosie and me ain't going to learn to be a lady and a gentleman if you're going to send us back to an orphanage. And we're done with London, too." That was hard to say, because they knew London, knew the best alleyways for running and which farmers at the market didn't mind if they nicked an apple. But there were people in London it would probably be better if they didn't run across again. Just him and Rose. That was better.

"We could stay here," Rose suggested.

That made Mrs. P's face go white. George pushed his chair back from the table before he would have to listen to either of them making more excuses why they were only borrowing children. "I don't want to stay here," he said. "Too many people looking sideways at us." He headed toward the hallway, Rose skipping behind him. "And whatever you borrowed us for, we didn't sign nothing. And we ain't your trained monkeys."

"Whether you like it or not, we are responsible for your safety and well-being for the next eight weeks. As you are not . . . trained monkeys, in one hour we will meet in the library to negotiate the terms for your cooperation. If you attempt to flee again, you will lose the advantage you currently have." The mister sat back and picked up his teacup.

If they had an advantage, George meant to keep it. "We'll stay here to negotiate, then. You have good food."

"Thank God for Mrs. Brubbins and her excellent cooking," Emmeline whispered as the children tromped up the stairs. "Donald, please ask Billet to have one of his grooms or a gardener stationed below the children's windows, on the chance they do make another run for it."

The footman bobbed his head and hurried out the door.

"We're not attempting to use them as our trained monkeys, are we?" Will said once they were alone. "Because it does smack of that, Emmeline."

"I don't think so," she said. "In all honesty, I think they're too young to understand the value of what we've offered them."

"Then we need to offer them something they *want*," he suggested.

She scowled. "They're children. Should we trade their cooperation for a bag of sweets? *That* would be treating them like trained monkeys."

"They're children who are clearly cleverer than we were at that age."

"Will, they were robbing Lord Graham. And Rose stole that spoon from the table just now. Are we supposed to reward them for that?" She gulped down the rest of her tea. "I may not be a parent, but I do recall something about thievery being unacceptable behavior."

"They are still children whose cooperation we need, and clearly no amount of etiquette lessons will persuade them to behave. Yes, they tried to steal from the baron. The fact remains, though, that we need them. What do we offer them to gain their assistance?"

"A bribe?"

He sat back, gazing at her. "A trade. And yes, perhaps a bribe to convince them not to steal the Duke of Welshire's trousers when we arrive at Welshire Park."

"I'm delighted you still find this amusing," she retorted, "but I didn't expect we would be attempting to reform felons. This was supposed to be which fork to use, and how to curtsy and bow." Emmeline blew out her breath. "I thought you'd permanently lost your sense of humor when you left for Oxford, anyway."

That hurt a bit. "If we had bothered to speak more than two sentences at a time to each other over the past eight years, I imagine we both would have made some interesting discoveries." Will took a breath. "You began this lie, but we are attempting to find a solution to it. Together. It's merely a bit bumpier than we anticipated."

She stood. "Bah. I'm trying to find a solution to a problem, not a way for our lives to come crashing down around us."

"You expected perfect, well-behaved, spiritless children, I assume? And that the lies you told would not come back on us in any way at all, and we would slip through all obstacles like a hot knife through butter?"

"I certainly hoped for a few of those things." Emmeline strode for the door. "I am only attempting to save Winnover Hall—and your career, by the way."

"Thank you for saying so. I actually wasn't certain I figured into your calculations at all."

"For heaven's sake, how many times do you expect me to apologize for lying to my grandfather? And everything I've done since we married has been for your career. You would certainly not be more comfortable at your tiny house in York. We would have to live at Pershing House all year round, and you could wave goodbye to all your hunting and shooting and fishing excursions. And your weekend fetes where you try to charm parliamentarians into funding roads and canals."

"I'm aware of the consequences."

"Of course my actions were meant to benefit both of us. And I did apologize for entangling you without your knowledge. I saw a problem within the household, and I managed it. That's what I do. And so now you get to do your favorite thing and negotiate. I would suggest mentioning something about no more pickpocketing, but since you find them amusing and this problem originated with me, I suppose I'll be the one to correct their behavior."

"Stomp off, then, but I still want to see your journals. I believe I have a right to know our children, even if they only exist on paper."

"Fine. There they are. Have at them." Gesturing at the pair of leather-bound books on the table, she left the small dining room, and a moment later Will heard her bedchamber door close.

"Sterling, Will," he muttered.

He knew she'd become obsessed with perfection. How perfect were their lives, though, if two days of living with children, two days of spending time together, could up-end so much, and set them at each other's throats? Will finished off a last piece of bacon. Perhaps their lives hadn't been perfect, as much as they'd been . . . simple. Easy. Uncomplicated.

Well, they weren't any of those things at the moment. Nor could they return to those times until they'd managed to navigate their way through this mess of pint-sized pick-pockets and confidence men.

Taking a breath, he slid the journals closer, choosing the one with "Malcolm" written in neat letters across the front and opening it. He expected lists, paragraphs of characteristics, dates for important milestones.

This wasn't lists, though. The very first line made that clear. "We have a son," it read. "We've decided to name him Malcolm, after my grandfather. He's a sweet thing, with a mop of hair the color of Mr. Pershing's, and blue eyes that I'm certain have a bit of green in them already."

He flipped through another few pages. "Malcolm may have begun walking today, though Mr. Pershing and I are in disagreement over whether they were an actual trio of steps or merely fortuitous stumbling. As I was the witness while he had to hear about the momentous event after the fact, my opinion, I believe, weighs more heavily."

As he read on, he realized that Emmeline Pershing led two entirely different lives. The one he could see, with her efficient, deft hand serving up a perfect confection of conversation, food, and charm to influence his guests to-ward the conclusion he wished for, and the one he couldn't see, which was filled with smiles and laughter, charming incidents carefully arranged in order to evoke enjoyment in whoever read about them in her letters, and a pair of darling little angels who said clever things and whose greatest misstep was getting mud on their clothes at the most amusing moment possible.

Will sat back. They had quite the task before them, if they meant to turn George and Rose Fletcher into the precocious and flawless Malcolm and Flora Pershing. And he'd be damned if he was going to remain the distant, work-consumed, barely involved Mr. Pershing of his wife's stories. More than anything else, that man—and her view of him—annoyed him.

None of them were perfect, and she was about to discover that. And if her written version of him was rather . . . accurate, well, that stopped now. From this moment he meant to be a very different flesh-and-blood husband.

CHAPTER NINE

"You can't keep it."

Rose twirled the silver spoon in her hands. "Why not? I hid it perfect."

Her brother pulled off his shoe and removed a gold pin with a green stone on one end. "I got this off that fat baron before Billet nicked us. I can keep it because nobody seen me do it." He held it out to her. "You can have it. But you can't keep the spoon because the Pershings saw you drop it on the floor. You should've seen Mrs. P's eyes bug out like a frog's." He made his own big.

Giggling, Rose looked at the spoon. They could get a few pence for it, but if pretend Mama and Papa *had* seen her take it, it could mean the end of swording lessons, and she wanted those. "Should I put it back in the dining room?"

"No. You got to give it to one of them, and be sorry you done it. Then they can't use it against us later to make us eat tomatoes or something."

"Blech, tomatoes. I'll give the spoon to the missus. She bought me pink dresses."

She climbed out of the big chair by the fireplace in the room with roses on the walls, just like her name. Her bedchamber. The biggest place she'd ever had to herself.

She did try to listen to George, even if she wasn't a baby like he thought she was. They might have seen her get the spoon, but nobody knew about the little dog statue or the hairbrush or the three blue buttons she'd found in the dressing room she shared with George. Her favorite was the pin her brother had just given her, because the green stone was very shiny. Like a jewel. George could sell the other things if they needed to, but she was keeping the pin. It might have come from pirates.

She walked down the hallway to where the mister and missus had their two bedchambers, which still seemed odd. It was a big house, though, so maybe they had decided to take turns sleeping in every single room. That would be fun. Balling her fist, she knocked at the door on the left.

"Enter," Mrs. Pershing said.

It abruptly occurred to Rose that if they'd seen her take the spoon, they might be mad at her. *Oh dear.* She inched the door open and peeked her head into the room. "This is yours? It's very grand."

The lady of the house sat in a chair beneath one of the windows. She didn't look happy at all, but grown-ups spent a great deal of time not being happy. "It is mine," Mrs. Pershing said after a few seconds. "Yellow is my favorite color."

Rose gazed about the room, at the yellow-and-white-striped walls, the yellow bed hangings and yellow and green quilted spread, the big mahogany furniture, and the trio of windows bordered by green curtains along the back wall. "You have a lot of it. Yellow, I mean. And green."

"Yes. Did you need something, my dear? I have a bit of a megrim."

Holding her breath, Rose walked up to the chair, produced the spoon from behind her back, and set it into the lady's hands. "I took this. George says we have to look after ourselves and you only needed some children for your house, but you feed us good and gave me some pretty dresses."

"Well," Mrs. Pershing whispered, closing her fingers around the spoon. "Thank you."

No yelling yet, and that was good. "Are you still going to send us back to St. Stephen's? Because George says I'll end up being a Covent Garden nun, and he'll just be a long-haul boy and then an out-and-outer, and I don't want to be a nun. They frown *all* the time." She screwed up her face into a dour scowl. "Like this."

"I . . . don't think a Covent Garden nun is the same as a church nun," her pretend mama said, a sad look on her face. Then she smiled again. "I believe we can find better accommodations for you, Rose. I hadn't realized the orphanage was so horrible."

"Why not? You said you visited there."

"Yes, I did." Mrs. Pershing looked down at her hands for a minute. "I think I tried not to look too closely. I shall do better from now on. And I am sorry for not paying as much attention as I should have."

"That's all right. I didn't know you then. Anyway, I would still like to learn to sword. And maybe ride a pony. I told George that, but he's very stubborn." She leaned closer to whisper. "I think he's scared of horses." Straightening again, Rose smoothed her skirt. "I'm not scared."

"We'll see what we can do," the lady said. "And whatever comes of it, we will try to make sure you and George enjoy yourselves here."

The nuns would've made them stay in bed for three days, and given them nothing but water and stale bread. This was much better. "I thought you was mad at us."

"I believe, my dear, that I am angrier with myself. You and your brother are not to blame for your circumstances. Or for your ability to survive them."

"That sounds good. I have to go get ready to negotiate now." Skipping, Rose left the room again, shutting the door behind her. George had been correct again; they had seen her nick the spoon, and they wouldn't be able to get swords in the negotiation if she kept it. Next time she would be more careful and not get caught at all.

"You can't say you'd trade us food for being proper, because you have to feed us, anyway." George crossed his arms over his chest, just like Mr. P across the table from him. He could look like a negotiator, too.

"Yes," Mr. P conceded, inclining his head, "but we could make your meals nothing but bread and water."

"That's worse than St. Stephen's," Rose said, folding her arms, as well. "We at least get boiled potatoes there, unless we're being punished."

"Very well, then. Boiled potatoes." The husband unfolded his arms, made a note on the paper in front of him, and crossed them again. "In exchange for not running away, you may have bread, water, and boiled potatoes."

"Rosie, stop helping," George grumbled. He'd only negotiated once before, and that had been to not run away from St. Stephen's again in exchange for not being transported to Australia—if they would do that to two babes as young as he and Rosie had been. But as the running away hadn't been his idea the last time, he reckoned they'd done fairly well for themselves.

"I got us potatoes."

"We've been eating better than potatoes since we left the stone jug. You got us worse than what we already had."

"No, I didn't."

"Now that your staying put is settled," Mr. P went on, "our next point of negotiation is . . ." He sat forward to eye his papers. "Ah, there it is. Cursing. Profanity and slang."

"We'll say 'damn' and 'shite' for free." George grinned. "See, you ain't such a slyboots." *Ha.*

"Ah, very clever. This agreement, however, says there is to be no cursing, and that you will avoid using colloquialisms. Slang. Name your price, Mr. Fletcher."

The missus sat beside her husband, but she seemed happy to leave the parleying to him. George could see why; Mr. P was good at it. The nuns riled up much more easily than he did. But George wasn't a half-wit, either, and he and Rose needed to get as much as they could, and a way to stay out of orphanages and London.

"Well," George said slowly, stroking his chin the way Mr. P did when he was thinking about something, "we both curse a lot. Especially me. And if you mean for us to remember to say 'shoes' and not 'kicksees' or 'stampers,' I reckon that'll cost you . . ."

"Biscuits," Rose whispered. "Please say biscuits."

"Hush, Rosie. All we have now is bread and potatoes," he whispered back. "It'll cost you beef stew once a week, and a roasted chicken with gravy. And—" He leaned over for a whispered conversation with his sister. "And two times of veal cutlets and gravy."

The two adults exchanged another look, and the mister made a note on his papers. It was a lot of meat, but Rosie was little and she needed better meals than they had at the orphanage, and for as long as possible.

"Hmm," Mr. P mused, tapping his pencil against the

table. "I might possibly agree to one veal cutlets and gravy, but two? That's a bit much."

"If I may," Mrs. P said, "I think we could offer one cutlets and one venison pasties, with a dessert of raspberry ice cream."

Rose lifted up on her knees, her eyes widening. "Ice cream? I've heard of ice cream. Deirdre says it's like eating clouds."

"Rosie, stop making th—"

"I want ice cream!" The little girl bounced on the library chair. "I won't call anybody bottle-headed if I can have raspberry ice cream!"

"Stop giving in to everything, you baby!"

Rose's expression fell, her mouth turning down at the corners and a fierce furrow emerging between her brows. "I am not a baby!" she shouted, banging her small fists against the tabletop. "And if you want me to sew or embroider, you have to show me how to use a sword. And if you want me to learn the pianoforte, you have to teach me dancing."

With her face red and her jaw jutted forward, she looked ready to take on the entire British army. George kept his mouth closed—sometimes Rose had a way of getting what she wanted that not even the nuns could stand against. He hoped this was one of those times.

"That seems reasonable," Mr. P said after a moment.

George let out his breath as his sister jabbed a finger at the paper. "Write it down, then, please," she said. "Swording and dancing."

"Fencing," the missus corrected mildly.

"Fencing," Rose repeated, and plunked her bottom back onto her chair. "You negotiate your own stupid things, Georgie."

"You picked stupid things," he retorted. Dancing might

be useful, but she wouldn't be using fencing at all, unless they became highwaymen.

"I chose what I wanted. And I'm not a baby."

George scowled. He knew one thing he needed, so grown-ups would stop taking advantage. "I want to learn to read," he said aloud. "And write. The nuns are always writing things, and I want to know what it says."

Mr. P stirred in his chair. "That's a tall order for just a few weeks, I'm afraid."

"It's what I want," George insisted. "If you teach me to read and write, I'll do dancing."

"And geography." Mr. P lifted an eyebrow, the pencil poised over the paper. "And manners, for both of you."

"That's three things to one. That ain't fair."

"I already got dancing," Rose put in.

"Reading and writing," Mrs. P said, "are the most time-consuming of tasks. It makes sense to count it as three things."

"Then you have to feed us at least three times every day. Good food. And not bread and water and boiled potatoes. Plus, the meals we asked for. And that venison pasty Mrs. P said. And the ice cream." He leaned both elbows on the table. "And you have to find us a place to live, together, that ain't an orphanage."

He'd nearly forgotten that part, because as soon as this agreement was ended, he and Rosie would be going their own way. But he couldn't let the grown-ups know that, or they would be locking the doors and posting guards, and that would never do.

Mr. P inclined his head. "No orphanages. Very well. I agree. Emmeline?"

"Yes. That sounds fair."

"Good. Because I ain't letting nobody take Rosie without me, and I'm already getting too old. I'll be a long-haul boy in another year or two." George leaned over to tap his forefinger against the paper. "You write it down, then, just like we said. And read it to me."

"To us," Rose amended. "I made a good negotiation."

"You certainly did." Mrs. P sat back, making a show of fanning herself. "I need to go speak with Mrs. Brubbins. She may need to hire another cook to assist her."

Rose put her elbows on the table, her chin in her hands. "Is that because I got us ice cream?"

"The ice cream and the venison pasties, and all of the other very good meals we're going to have to provide for you two."

"Are we in agreement, then?" Mr. P finished making a note and then set his pencil down. "We don't have a great deal of time. This morning's search and our negotiation have already taken up half the day."

"I'm in agreement." Rosie steepled her fingers.

"I suppose so," George said. They had *some* good things, especially the reading and writing, but dancing still seemed like wasted time. Still, it was better than the orphanage. "But I ain't sure we won."

"Ah. In an ideal agreement, I believe," Mr. P intoned, "neither side is entirely happy. We've each had to give a bit of ground."

"Damna—I mean, oh, bother." George grimaced. "I forgot about painting. I saw a man in the middle of Hyde Park painting a man's face on a canvas. It was very good. I could paint people, and they'd pay me for it." And that would be useful. "What do you want for painting?"

"Well, that's Emmeline's area of expertise," Mr. P said, looking over at her. "If you teach George how to paint, what do you think you should ask of him in return?"

George looked at her, too, to find her already looking back at him. "Hmm," she mused. "Painting is tricky. I am willing to give you some instruction in drawing, if, in return, when we journey to the Lake District, you will both agree to be addressed by the names Malcolm and Flora. Malcolm and Flora Pershing, our son and daughter. And if as of now you will *both* start calling us Mama and Papa for practice."

"I agree," George said quickly, and jabbed a finger at Mr. P. "Write it down." He watched the pencil moving for a moment. "That was a good negotiation for me. I reckoned we'd have to be Malcolm and Flora, anyway, or your whole jig would be queered."

Mr. P tapped his pencil against the paper. "Our what would be what?" he prompted.

George sighed. "Your trick would be found out," he amended, trying not to grind his teeth. This was going to be annoying.

Emmie stifled another smile as Will stood. "I will go write this up more neatly," he said, picking papers off the table, "and then we will all sign it as best as we are able. Most important is that you both agree to what I'm about to say—that for as long as Emmeline and I keep up our end of the bargain, you do not run away again. Is that clear?"

Both children nodded, Rose more enthusiastically than her brother.

"And no stealing anything from our neighbors."

George looked at Mr. P's face and decided he shouldn't ask for something in exchange for them not dipping into some cove's pockets. There were more than enough valuables just here in the house to fund them for a year or more, anyway. He nodded. "We won't nick anything from your neighbors."

"Good."

Emmie wasn't certain she believed them; the whims

of any youngsters seemed a shaky foundation on which to build anything. Nevertheless, it did feel as if they'd accomplished something. The children knew what was expected of them, and they'd agreed to it.

Sitting back, she watched Will walk out of the library. The man could negotiate. That was why he was so valued by the trade ministry, and why the prime minister himself had become a regular dinner guest during the Season, why there'd been talk of making him a Secretary of the Department. No one who sat across the table from Will Pershing could possibly fail to come to an agreement with him. He radiated charm and good humor, and a deep empathy that, while the children might not understand or see it, they certainly responded to. Yes, she'd helped his career along, but he was precisely where he was meant to be. And that felt . . . good. With the children here now, even her largest failing as a wife would be erased.

"Well, we negotiated," Rose said, walking over to look out the window. "What do we do now?"

"We sign our names on the agreement to make sure everyone keeps their word," her brother stated.

"Are you really going to learn to read? When Sister Helen Stephen reads, her face gets very frowny."

"Yes, I'm going to learn to read. It's important, so no one can say one thing and write down another thing, and then we get stuck somewhere horrible."

That statement caught up Emmie's thoughts. Being doomed because of a skill he'd never thought to be given the opportunity to learn—granting him that chance seemed much more important than her and Will finding fun things for the children to do. "Reading makes you powerful," she said aloud. "Both because it keeps other people from taking advantage of you, and because it allows you to see other worlds and learn about things you might never have a chance to experience otherwise."

"I want to be powerful," George commented. "I'll read every book there is."

"But have you seen how many books there are?" Rose asked. "There are five million books just in here, I think." She glanced about the library, then turned around to face Emmie. "Have you read all of these books, Mama?"

Good heavens. It wasn't the first time Rose had called her "Mama," but the word slammed into her like a hammer every time. Just the ease with which the little girl called a woman—who only four days ago had been a complete stranger—"Mama" felt . . . sad. It was as if Rose had no connection either to the title or to what it represented. Either that, or she was a far more masterful actress than Emmie had imagined. She fixed a smile on her face, pretending that being called anyone's mother didn't send her into a panic. "No, I haven't read them all. They're a collection gathered together by my parents, along with assorted aunts and uncles."

"Oh." Clearly bored by the explanation, the five-year-old stepped to the next of the tall, narrow windows. "Do you have ponies, or only big horses? I know horses didn't get negotiated, but I'd rather practice riding on a pony."

The little girl flitted from topic to topic, from serious to silly, with the swiftness and ease of a dragonfly. Emmie almost needed a map to keep up. "No promises about riding, but why don't we go visit the stable while we wait for Will?"

"Oh yes. Come on, Georgie. I'll protect you."

Emmeline's chestnut mare, Willow, resided in the stable along with Will's bay gelding, Topper, two older geldings for the grooms and errands, two pair of coach horses, and a team for the phaeton. They'd never had need of ponies. They still didn't, as riding would take up a great deal of time they didn't have. But the children needed to be kept occupied right now, and she would prefer they not begin robbing the staff.

CHAPTER TEN

Emmie and the children walked out to the stable, and Billet introduced the youngsters to the horses and, at her request, gave them a quick lesson on tack. While Roger handed out apples to be given as treats, Emmie motioned at the head groom.

"They're clever babes, ain't they?" he muttered, looking on as Rose giggled and fed Will's Topper, and George winced every time Willow wiggled her ears. "They remind me of my brothers and sisters, always trotting away to have an adventure down at the mill stream."

She hadn't even realized Billet had family. She didn't even know his first name for certain, actually. Peter? Or Adam, perhaps. Hannah would know, but the maid would only blush and mumble, because no one, apparently, was supposed to notice that she had an infatuation with the sandy-haired head groom. "How many siblings do you have?" Emmie asked aloud.

"Nine. I'm the third oldest." He chuckled. "My next younger brother once tried to sell the youngest in trade for a basket of kittens. Thought no one would notice, with so many of us."

"Someone did, I assume?"

"Took an hour and one of the kittens pouncing on my ma, but yes."

"George, don't throw it," Rose instructed. "Hold it in your hand, open like this, so she won't eat your fingers."

"She can't eat my fingers when I'm back here, either," her brother grumbled.

"Thank you for finding them this morning," Emmie said, following the groom's gaze. "We have managed to come to an understanding. There's shouldn't be any more attempted escapes."

Billet doffed his cap, his light hair clean-looking but windblown. "If you say so, missus."

Well, she understood his skepticism. "I would appreciate if you would continue to keep an eye on them when they're outside the house."

He smiled. "I can do that, Mrs. Pershing."

"Thank y—"

Topper snorted, bobbing his head and stomping as Rose shrieked and jumped backward.

"Ha!" George snorted. "You got horse snot on you."

"You're gonna get horse shite on you!" The little girl stalked out of the stable.

"The little angels," Billet murmured with a grin.

Oh dear. "George, you're the older brother," Emmie said, walking over beside him as he tossed a last apple into Willow's stall. "You're to protect Rose, not tease her."

"I do protect Rose. Every dam—every day. But she said I didn't like horses, and now she's got snot all over her. It's funny."

"Not to her."

Leaving the stable, Emmie went out into the yard to find Rose standing at the water trough and running wet hands down her front. "It's ruined," she sobbed. "My pink and yellow dress."

"It's not ruined," Emmie said stoutly. "Let's get you inside and changed. All your dress needs is a good scrubbing and some time to dry."

Rose wiped her hand across her face. "Do you think so?"

"You're not the first lady to have a horse snort on her, my dear."

"Oh, thank goodness." Sniffing, Rose came at Emmie, her small arms outstretched.

Stifling a gasp, Emmeline sidestepped the slick embrace. "Let's get inside," she said quickly, and started off toward the house. No sense damaging two gowns.

"Don't leave me in there with Billet," George said, trotting up behind them. "He says he and his grooms sleep under horse sh—manure to keep warm at night."

"I'm certain he was only teasing."

"Well, I dropped his coat in a bucket of shite, so we'll see if he notices."

"George!"

"When do I get my drawing lessons?" the boy asked, clearly attempting a subject change.

"Will is making up a schedule now. Along with the agreement for all of us to sign."

"If you was bamming me about teaching me to read, then nothing else about the agreement matters. And I reckon you need us more than we need you."

That was true. And a bit unnerving to realize the children knew it, too. "We were not bamming you, George. And we will keep to the agreement, just as I know you will. But we can't do everything at once. A schedule is vital."

"You can't learn to read now, George. I need to clean my dress."

"You need to take a bath," her brother returned. "You're half dirt and half snot."

"I am not! At least I wasn't scared! He's scared of horses!"

"No, I ain't! You take that back!"

"George! Rose! That is enough!" Now Emmeline wanted to flee. But the Fletchers were the best—and only—way she had of keeping ownership of Winnover Hall. A damp hand gripped hers, and she glanced down, startled. Rose looked up at her, an expression on her oval face that even the most hardened of hearts could only describe as endearing.

"We're very sorry we yelled at each other," the girl said solemnly. "Please don't send us back to the stone jug."

That was the key. They *all* had something to gain here. They all needed each other. Emmie tightened her fingers around Rose's. "I think you and I may be glued together with horse snort now," she observed, lifting their joined hands. "Oh dear."

Rose laughed. "Oh no! We *are* stuck!"

"I got horse slobber on my hand," George announced. "From Willow. That could be sticky, too."

"Well, let's find out, shall we?" Hardly daring to breathe, Emmie held out her free hand.

George slapped his into it, gripping her fingers. "Oh no! We're stuck!"

"We'd best make for the kitchen, and hope Mrs. Brubbins can pry us apart with a spoon and some water."

"Your smile is good today," Rose observed. "I believe it."

How did one reply to that? Though since the girl was occupied with imagining all the things and people she and her brother might now become stuck to, Emmie supposed she didn't have to respond. And for heaven's sake, she smiled fake smiles all the time in London—at dinners, parties, walks and rides through the park. She was good at it. It was a mark of politeness to smile even if hearing the same tale from the same baron for the seventh time. Her smiles didn't look false. If they did, she would rightly be accused of failing in her duties.

"I wasn't pretending to smile before," she said. "This is just very funny."

"Yes. I can tell, because you ain't frowny in your forehead." The girl made an exaggerated scowl, then gestured with her free hand at the lines above her eyes.

So that was the girl's vision of her, was it? Frowny and fake. And if there was anyone who would speak the truth about something like that, it was a five-year-old. Perhaps it was time to practice her smiles in front of a mirror again. "I shall try to be less frowny from now on."

They stopped in front of the kitchen door. "How are we going to open it?" Rose exclaimed. "Georgie, you'll have to do it. Don't get your hand stuck to the door!"

"What do we have here?" Mrs. Brubbins exclaimed as the three of them edged sideways into the kitchen.

"We're stuck together!" Rose shrieked, giggling. "We need a spoon and some water!"

"Oh dear, dear, dear. How did this calamity happen?" the round cook asked, whirling around to snatch up a wooden spoon with one hand and a bowl of water with the other.

"A horse snorted on me."

"A horse drooled on me."

"And I'll need to wash this spoon after we're finished here." With a flourish, Mrs. Brubbins dipped the spoon in the water, flipped it in her hand, and then slid it between

Rose's hand and Emmie's. "Is it working?" she asked, making a show of moving it back and forth.

"No. . . . Wait! I think it's working!" Rose held on tight to Emmie's fingers, then released them to stumble backward. "You've unstuck us! Now you must free Georgie."

While the two cook's helpers giggled behind their hands, Mrs. Brubbins dipped the spoon again and pushed it in between Emmeline and George's palms. To Emmie's surprise George held on to her for a moment before he yanked his hand away.

"Oh, you've done it, Mrs. Brubbins," Emmie said, grinning and appreciative of the cook's quick wit. "Thank goodness. And now we must wash our hands or we'll be stuck again."

A bit of soap and water later she, at least, felt less . . . slimy, and both children were back in good spirits. She sent George to find Will and see if he was ready for the agreement signing, and escorted Rose upstairs to change her dress. Hopefully Hannah knew the secret of removing horse snort from a young lady's gown.

As for her, she *would* make an effort to be less frowny. And to keep in mind that, miniature criminals-in-the-making or not, George and Rose were, above all, children. And like it or not, prepared for it or not, suitable or not, over the next few weeks she and Will would be their role models.

Will emerged from his office and headed toward the foyer. "Powell, where might I find Mrs. Pershing?"

"With Mrs. Brubbins in the morning room, sir," the butler answered, jumping to straighten a vase in the foyer as the children ran past, headed for the kitchen. Changing course, Will made for the half-open door on his right. Partway through, he stopped, his attention snared.

"Strawberries will have to be ordered from a hothouse at this time of year," the cook was saying, as she jotted down notes on a piece of paper. "I could probably have them by Thursday, but you will have to pay for the accelerated delivery."

Nodding, Emmeline wrote something in her own well-organized calendar. "Then let's begin with the honey biscuits for dessert, move the strawberries and cream to Friday, and the raspberry ice cream on Saturday."

"And the beef steaks?"

"Let's move those to Saturday, as well. They'll pair well with the ice cream, I think."

"Yes, ma'am."

"And I know the additional food is exceeding your budget; I will see to it that it is increased. The first priority is feeding the children well and memorably."

The round cook bobbed her towering bun of graying black hair. "If I have my way, those two darlings will be saying 'that dish was my favorite' every evening."

"We all benefit, then." Emmeline chuckled, turning a page of her book. "Sally's birthday is next week. Wednesday. I believe she likes cherries, yes? Perhaps a cherry dessert for the staff in her honor?"

"Oh, that would be lovely, Mrs. Pershing. I have a few things in mind. Might I have you choose one tomorrow?"

"I leave it to your discretion, Mrs. Brubbins. But do be aware the children will smell your baking from miles away and expect a helping, as well."

Laughing, the cook looked up, her eyes widening as she caught sight of him standing there. "Mr. Pershing," she squawked, jumping to her feet.

"Don't mind me," he said, deciding he might enjoy observing menu preparations more often. Fascinating things, they were, rather like planning a negotiation—or a battle. Emmeline made for a splendid hostess, but it had never occurred to him how much effort went into the preparation for something as . . . banal as a meal. And likewise, how much industry had gone into what he thought of as her obsession with his work. No wonder she didn't smile as much as he remembered.

"That'll do for the rest of the week, Mrs. Brubbins," she said, closing her calendar book. "We'll strategize again on Saturday."

"Yes, Mrs. Pershing. Thank you." The cook bobbed at Emmeline, whirled around and bobbed again at Will, then slipped out of the room.

"The agreement is ready, then?" Emmeline asked.

"It is." Will shut the door behind him and strolled to the couch, where he sat beside her.

"I thought I might speak with Father John, and ask him if he knows of any local families willing to take in a brother and sister," Emmeline said, twisting the ring on her finger.

"Be certain to tell him that any candidates should have their valuables under lock and key."

"Will." She scowled at him. "While I don't approve of their past activities, if we continue to treat them like thieves, aren't we forcing them to remain precisely that?"

Stacking the papers against his thighs, he sat back to gaze at her. "We've known each other for better than two decades, and we've been married for eight years. How is it that you've suddenly gained the ability to utterly astonish me?" In a given situation, she reacted in a given manner. Even the flights of fancy from her journal were well-orchestrated moments of darling behavior.

"Perhaps neither of us is as well-acquainted with the other as we thought," she suggested.

The idea fascinated him. "Indeed. But what happened between pickpocketing and Rose stealing that spoon and now?"

"She gave it back to me. I don't know if she or George realized that we'd noticed the theft, but she apologized, and quite prettily. And then we all got stuck together when Topper snorted on Rose and Willow drooled on George."

Will looked at her, at the smile that touched her eyes, at her open, expressive hands as she demonstrated what she meant. "Attacked by horse spittle. That wasn't in your journals, Emmeline."

"No, it wasn't. Honestly, I could never have imagined such a thing."

"Surprise, the unexpected, aren't always a bad thing, are they?"

"It depends on the setting." She shifted a little. "I'll admit, though, that parenthood, even this temporary parenthood, isn't . . . I thought I would be terrified and horribly incompetent. My mother did tell me that women who can't have children weren't meant to be mothers, and that I should be glad I possess a talent for hostessing."

He took her hand. "That is a bloody horrible thing to tell someone. Writing to tell her about baby Malcolm must have been supremely satisfying."

"It was. I was very gracious about it." Emmeline shrugged. "It was all a lie, of course, but at the time I was desperate. Now hopefully she will never realize just how much of a fraud I've been."

"I knew Winnover meant a great deal to you," he said, "but I'm beginning to realize it's not just the property. You, my dear, seem to feel the need to be . . . perfect."

She took a breath. "Looking at me—and our situation—now, I don't think I could be any further from perfection. But I will, at least, see those children settled somewhere that meets with their approval. I don't know if that qualifies as perfection, but it does seem the correct thing to do."

"Yes, it does." Will glanced toward the closed door. "I intend to abide by this bit of paper, legally binding or not. Do you?"

"Yes."

"Good. Your idea of speaking to the pastor is a good one. While most of my connections are in London, there are a few letters I can send, discreetly mentioning some children who need a good home."

Emmeline nodded. "A good idea, Will. The wider we cast our net, the better."

He looked at her for a moment. "I want to say again that it's pleasant to address you by your given name again. We are married, and we've been friends for a very long time. Aside from that, I've always liked your name, Emmeline. It reminds me of springtime."

"I . . . Thank you." A soft blush touched her cheeks. "But you used to call me Emmie."

"Emmeline has more curves and shadows to it. And I'm beginning to realize you have more mystery to you than I knew. It suits you." Her renewed sense of humor pleased him. The way she'd welcomed sticky hands despite her perfectly crafted faux children pleased him. *She* pleased him, when he'd stopped . . . hoping, some time ago. "So. Shall we find the Fletchers and sign our promises?"

"Yes."

Conversation finished, but still he held on to her hand. *Stop being an idiot, Will,* he told himself. Then, before he could think better of it, he leaned sideways and kissed Emmeline on the cheek.

"Oh." She stood up a little too quickly to make it graceful, and Will stifled a grimace. Yes, he'd botched their first night together, to the point that she very nearly fainted every time he came calling. When she'd suggested separate bedchambers he'd immediately agreed, but if she still meant to jump every time he gave her a kiss on the cheek . . . "I didn't mean to upset you."

"I . . . You didn't. I was only surprised."

He smiled. "Good. That you weren't upset, I mean."

"I wasn't. I . . ." She cleared her throat. "I thought it best we begin with something the children especially requested," she went on, stepping to the door and opening it again. "Perhaps I'll do letters and drawing with George this afternoon, if you'll—"

"Ah. Fencing with Rose. Or 'swording,' as she calls it." He nodded. "Yes. That should put a bit of sweet to disguise the sour of making them learn manners." Will forced a grin, hoping he looked charming and not like an idiot. "I certainly never liked that bit, and my tutors were able to stretch it into a decade or more."

"I always looked on manners and propriety as learning how to sculpt," she said, staying by the door, but at least facing him again. "Which smile and which nod evoked the wished-for response. I doubt there has ever been a conflict in the world that couldn't have been solved by someone applying a compliment or a kind word at the precise right moment."

"Hmm." His months of work seeing one trade agreement with Egypt signed wouldn't concur with her statement, but he understood what she meant.

Her soft blush deepened to an embarrassed red. "I didn't mean to insult your work, Will, for heaven's sake.

It *is* an art, don't you think?" she retorted. "I've seen you paint a masterpiece or two, yourself."

He climbed to his feet. "Thank you for saying so. And yes, I do take your meaning."

"I . . ." Emmeline swallowed. "Why do you suddenly seem to be looking at me all the time? I worry I have pudding on my face, or something."

The one thing worse than being caught staring—gazing—at someone was having to explain it. "You're my wife, Emmeline. I believe gazing is not forbidden."

"Of course it's not. But . . . you never used to do it."

Will blew out his breath. Negotiating with hostile foreign dignitaries was simple, compared to this. "I did used to gaze at you. You just never noticed."

"I—"

"It's just . . . I thought I—that is to say . . . I thought I knew all your facets, Emmeline," he interrupted, before she forced him to confess that he'd been moonstruck over her since she'd turned sixteen and he'd realized she wasn't just . . . Emmie any longer. And that they were neighbors, not siblings. "It turns out, I do not."

She smiled again. "Thank you, I suppose," she said. "And since we're being honest, you've become so upstanding that I thought you would flee the moment you discovered I'd been lying. You're more . . . naughty than I'd realized."

"'Naughty'?" He lifted an eyebrow, stunned and supremely flattered. "How does being invested in my wife's activities make me bad? Not that I object to a bit of naughtiness."

She blinked, a grin touching her fine mouth. "I meant knotty, as in complicated. A Gordian knot, as it were."

Now his face felt hot. "Ah." Will stood and walked

to the door, making certain his hand brushed hers as he passed her. "Perhaps I'm both kinds of knotty."

Her fingers curled, prolonging the touch for just a moment. "And perhaps I'm beginning to like that about you," she whispered, just loudly enough that he could hear.

CHAPTER ELEVEN

George knew most of his letters by sight, but Emmie wrote them all out and had him copy what she'd done as they went over the sounds each one made. Meanwhile, outside the library at the top of the garden, Will and Rose faced each other, both armed with broomsticks. While George scrawled out letters, his tongue between his lips, Emmie strolled to the center window and pushed it open.

"How are you doing?" she called.

Will turned to look at her. "I'm just explaining the rules and history, how traditionally opponents would exchange verbal ripostes in an attempt to rattle each oth—"

Rose lunged forward and caught him in the ribs with her broomstick. "En garde!" she yelled.

"We're forgoing the verbal jousting, I see," he said, grunting and rubbing his chest, "and moving directly to the bloodletting."

"I won!" Rose crowed, jabbing her broomstick into the air. "This is so easy!"

"Well, of course it's easy if you don't follow the rules," Will countered.

"If we followed the rules, you couldn't hit a little girl."

He lifted both eyebrows. "We're not following the

rules, then?" Twirling the broomstick in one hand, he flicked it out and tapped Rose on one foot, then on the other.

With a delighted squeal the little girl danced backward, then swung her stick through the air, well short of Will. "Show me that!"

"No more trying to put holes in me while I'm talking to my wife, then," he returned, grinning as he made a show of sheathing his pretend weapon against his hip.

"I agree. But you have to show me how to thwack people on the feet."

From the window, Emmie watched. Not the giggling five-year-old, adorable as she was, but her grinning, out-of-breath husband. She knew he could fence but hadn't seen him do so in years. The way he moved, all grace and skill, that had been part of his world, where he went to clubs and boxing and fencing matches with friends, and she shopped or visited or embroidered with hers.

He wasn't that gawky, gangly boy with whom she'd chased frogs, nor was he the awkward, earnest one who used to propose to her every Season, or even the one whose . . . fumbling on their wedding night had made her wonder if he hadn't also been a virgin. He wasn't eight or twelve or even twenty, any longer. He was eight-and-twenty, and every inch a fit, brilliant, attractive man.

"I did all the letters," George said from the table behind her. "Why are there two different shapes for each stupid one?"

Taking a breath, Emmie returned to her seat. "There are uppercase letters, the big ones, which are for the beginnings of sentences, names, and titles. Then there are the lowercase letters, which are for everything else."

"But why?"

Why, indeed? "It makes understanding what you're

reading easier. You know when you're reading a name, or a place, just by which type of letter is used."

"Seems like shi—a waste of time to me," the boy stated, frowning.

"If you mean to learn to read and write properly, it isn't a waste of time," she countered.

"I'll learn it, but it still don't make sense."

She regarded him for a moment. Then she wrote out a short sentence. "Let me demonstrate," she said. "This says, 'A rose wilted in the garden.' This"—and she wrote out another sentence—"says, 'A Rose wilted in the garden.' Do you see the difference? One means a plant needs water, and the other means your sister fainted."

Rose ran by the open window, Will on her heels. "Varlet!" she yelled, laughing so hard she nearly choked.

George looked up. "I don't think she's learning fencing," he observed, and went back to studying the sentences. "That's Rose's name. Do mine."

He wanted to see his own name in writing. Emmie leaned in and, in her neatest printing, wrote "George Fletcher." "This is 'George,'" she said, underlining the word, "and this is 'Fletcher.'"

"With uppercase letters at the beginning of each word," he muttered, carefully copying what she'd written.

"Yes. Because they are names."

As he finished the two words, he put a clenched fist over his head. His joy at being able to write his own name felt contagious; eventually he would realize it meant he could put his name to contracts rather than signing an X as he'd done earlier, that his name on paper had weight and legal standing.

For Emmie it meant that if the children at her grandfather's party decided to make the duke birthday cards, well, he would be able to sign the wrong name. Yes, she should have been teaching him to write "Malcolm Pershing," but for heaven's sake that could wait a few days. This moment was important for him.

"You're doing very well," she said, smiling as she wrote out a few simple words with which he would be familiar. "Do you wish to take a few moments and go see how Rose is progressing?"

"I can hear her," he said. "Do you think if I can write, that one day Rosie and me might be able to open a shop, and folk will come in and buy things and give us money?"

He'd omitted several steps there, but she nodded anyway. "Of course. Though you may find yourselves with parents who own a farm, or a mill, and wish to follow in their footsteps."

George shook his head. "Rosie can't be a potato picker. Or a washerwoman like Mama. Seven different families tried to get her from the orphanage, but I told the Mother Superior that if anybody tried to separate us, I would tell everyone how the nuns lock us in cabinets and sell off our belongings to buy cigars for themselves."

"*What?*"

He went back to tracing. "Oh, they don't do any of that, except sometimes some of our things go missing, but I had to make sure that if Rosie and me go anywhere, we go together. No one else will look after her like I do. And I know we're nearly out of time. Another year or so and I'll be a long-haul boy. The nuns will give up on me ever leaving, and they'll start bartering me out to bricklayers and canal diggers in exchange for repairs to the stone jug."

Goodness gracious. Even without his letters, even being only eight years old, George Fletcher had managed to stand up against nuns and God knew who else to keep his sister with him. And he was very aware that his own adoptability faded as he grew older. When she'd been eight years old, she'd spent half a year nagging her parents for a new doll that she'd seen in a shop window—and that had been the most important thing in the world to her.

"If any nun looks like she smokes a cigar, it's Sister Mary Stephen," she said aloud.

He snorted. "She reminds me of those stone gargoyles they put on churches."

The resemblance *was* striking, when she considered it. "I'm glad you're not going back there. We will find you a good family, George. For the two of you."

"It's in the agreement." Shrugging, he went back to scrawling letters.

Considering how adamant he'd been about not returning to St. Stephen's, or even London, and how much effort he'd put into not being separated from Rose, his nonchalance now was a little surprising. Emmie hid a scowl. It was unexpected if they actually meant to abide by the agreement, she amended.

This was a clever, wily young man, and he probably had a plan at the ready for things she couldn't even imagine. If he wasn't concerned about which family might adopt them, then he'd already decided they weren't going to be adopted.

Tapping the pencil against the table, she watched him copy words. "You know, you should learn numbers, as well," she mused aloud.

George sat back. "Numbers? We didn't negotiate that. And I already gave you dancing."

"We never discussed baths," she returned.

"Baths?"

"If you're going to own a shop, you should know numbers. How much money customers will give you, and how much change they should get back. What things cost, and how to make a profit."

Glancing from her to the window, outside which Rose was finally imitating an actual fencing position with Will, George made a face. "Numbers is important."

"Yes, they are."

"How many baths?"

"However many we think you need. You and Rose."

He sighed. "Do we need to make another agreement?"

"We can just shake hands on it, I think. No spitting, though."

"We might get stuck together again." With a brief grin he held out his hand, and she shook it. "Baths for numbers."

"Baths for numbers."

Will wiped the remaining shaving cream from his chin and set the cloth back on his dressing table. His gaze remained on the mirror in front of him—or rather on the fireplace mantel in the mirror's reflection.

"Davis," he said, as the valet helped him into his jacket, "did I not have a blown-glass bird on the mantel? The one I brought back from France this spring?"

The stocky valet turned around and looked. "Yes, sir. The blue and red one. It was right there. I . . . I shall notify Powell that someone on the household staff either broke or stole an item from your private rooms."

"Let's not do that," Will countered, turning around. "I think we both know who the most likely culprit—or culprits—are."

Color touched Davis's cheeks. "I would never presume to—"

"Davis. I'm not about to sack one of the staff because Rose, most likely, took a fancy to a glass bird."

It meant the little one had snuck into his private rooms, and while he wasn't happy about that, he also knew he'd been the one to suggest borrowing children from the orphanage. Complaining about the consequences of such a rash action felt petty.

"As you say, sir." The valet looked toward the small table beside the window. "That scrimshaw box of your grandfather's, Mr. Pershing, is a delicate, lovely item if I may say so."

Will followed his gaze. The box had been sitting there for eight years, since he'd made Winnover Hall his home. The table was in the corner, and the box one of several items displayed there, but at the same time . . . "Let's put that in the wardrobe for a time, why don't we?" he suggested. "Beneath the neckcloths."

"Yes, sir."

While he had faith in this experiment, he wasn't an idiot, either. "Thank you."

He left his bedchamber and started down the hallway. Emmeline's door was already open this morning, which would have been unusual except for the fact that everything about the household was now unusual. He'd slipped out of his room twice last night himself, just to make certain the children remained where they'd been deposited at the end of the evening. She'd told him about her conversation with George, and his worry over both Rose being adopted without him and of neither of them being chosen.

George's door was open, as well, but Rose's was shut as he passed by. He hesitated, then backtracked and walked into the boy's bedchamber. "George?"

Nothing. With a quick glance over his shoulder, Will

crossed the room, squatted down, and opened the boy's blanket chest. As he'd suspected, several items from both Pershing House and Winnover Hall lay inside. Small things that weren't worth a great deal, but that all together would no doubt buy food enough to keep an eight-year-old boy and his five-year-old sister from going hungry for a time. No robin, but that would be in Rose's chest, no doubt.

What a weight the lad carried. Shaking his head, Will pulled all the coins from his pocket and slipped them into the folded handkerchief that already held what looked like three or four pounds. Whether he meant for the children to ever have to use their ill-gotten goods or not, if he could lessen George's burden a little by adding to their treasury, he would by God do so.

He was halfway down the stairs when he passed George heading back up. "Good morning," he said, smiling, then gave the boy a sharp second look. The youngster had clearly bathed, his cheeks pink and his hair slicked back against his skull.

"Good morning. Have you seen Rose?" George asked, continuing up to the second floor. "She likes to sleep in, but if I could smell the baking bread this morning, I know she did."

"I have not seen her." Little Rose didn't seem likely to flee on her own, but as the thought had occurred to him, Will turned around to follow the boy back upstairs. Just as he reached the upper landing, though, Rose's door slammed open. Shrieking, the little girl, wearing nothing but a thin shift, ran up the hallway, Emmeline and Hannah on her heels.

"I didn't agree to no damned bath!" Rose yelled, diving under a hall table.

"Oh, good God." Will didn't know whether to avert

his eyes or jump forward to assist. Clearing his throat, he pulled out his pocket watch to give himself something else to look at. "Do you need any help?" he called, half turning away.

"No, we're fine," Emmeline answered. "Merely a disagreement."

"Deirdre says baths give you the ague and then a physician puts leeches on you and they eat you!"

"Leeches don't eat you," George said. "They suck out your blood. Take your bath, Rosie. It's not so bad."

"Rose, you will not get the ague from taking a bath," Emmeline said, leaning one arm on the hall table so she could bend down to view the girl. "You will get clean, and you will smell very nice. I put lemon in the bathwater."

At the top of the landing Powell cleared his throat, making Will jump. For a large man, the butler moved more silently than a blasted cat. "Sir," he said, "there is a person in the foyer. He doesn't have a calling card, but he says he needs to speak with you." He leaned closer. "Regarding the Fletcher children, he said."

Will glanced at them, Rose still under the table and George not looking the least bit surprised at his sister's aversion to bathing. "He said 'Fletcher'?"

"Yes, sir. I did not confirm their presence, as Mrs. Pershing said they are serving as young Pershings, but he insists on speaking to you." His chin lifted. "Shall I send him away?"

"No." Will gestured for Emmeline, and she straightened to join him. "We may have a problem," he said, and told her what Powell had relayed to him.

"Perhaps he's from the orphanage," she suggested, "here to see how the little ones are being treated."

"That makes sense, I suppose." It didn't, but he had no

better explanation. Best, then, to stop speculating. "I'll go speak to him."

She put a hand on his arm. "We'll both go. Hannah, George, please see what you can do with Rose."

"Death first!" Rose yelled.

The fellow stood in the foyer, Edward unobtrusively changing out a bouquet of flowers nearby and no doubt keeping an eye on the stranger. A brown greatcoat, too large, some good-quality Hessian boots, black trousers, also too large, and a black beaver hat, too small and held in his hands, made him look well-dressed but a little . . . off plumb all at the same time.

In addition, his hair needed a stern cutting, while nothing could be done for his beak of a nose. A young man, he was, somewhere between eighteen and twenty, Will would guess, though the oversized greatcoat made him look younger. "Good morning."

The fellow twitched like a dog that thought it was about to be kicked, and spun to face the stairs as Will and Emmeline descended the last few steps. "Good morning. You would be Mr. and Mrs. Pershing, wouldn't you? Thank you for seeing me."

Thin lips, a bright smile, and a missing bottom front tooth, hazel eyes, and dirty fingers pinching the brim of his hat—Will took it all in, the same way he would evaluate anyone who sat opposite him at a negotiation. This one he would sum up under the category of "dressing above his station to impress his social superiors," but generally most guests who came to call at a grand house wore their best, be they ambassadors or farmers.

"You have our names," Will said aloud, nodding. "What do we call you?"

"Oh, a thousand apologies, Mr. Pershing. Your butler asked for a card, but I don't have one on me." The young man patted his coat pockets as he spoke. "The name is Fletcher. James Fletcher."

Emmeline made a small sound beside him and wrapped her arm around his, but Will kept his gaze on the stranger. "Is it, now?"

"Since I was born. You see, I had to let my younger brother and sister, George and Rosie, go off to St. Stephen's orphanage, on account of me being too young and not approved by the magistrate to raise two babes. But I've turned eighteen just last week, and, well, imagine my surprise when I went to the orphanage to collect the little ones, and they wasn't there any longer."

The hand around his arm dug in hard enough that she was going to leave a bruise. "Will," she murmured under her breath.

"I see," Will commented, keeping his voice cool and level. "Would you happen to have any proof that you are who you claim to be?"

The lad spread his arms. "Just myself. Ask 'em, if you don't believe me. Didn't they tell you they had a brother? I'm hurt."

"Why don't we go into my office, where we can chat?" And so he could figure out what the devil was going on without alerting the children or the rest of the household. A brother of age meant that George and Rose weren't precisely adoptable any longer, and even though he and Emmeline had only borrowed them, he imagined—even without a solicitor's understanding of the law—that they didn't have the standing to do that, either.

This was bad. Very bad.

"No offense, Mr. Pershing," the young man said with another wide smile, "but I don't intend to be bought off or threatened." He cupped a hand to his mouth. "George! Rosie! Guess who's found you, lovelies?"

"We do not shout in this house," Will stated. "My office. Now, if you please."

Footsteps pounded on the upstairs landing. As he turned to look up, George peered over the balcony railing. A moment later Rose joined him, ducking down to see through the balustrade. "It's James," she said after a moment. "What are you doing here, James?"

"Come down and see your brother, my darlings!" he said. "I told you I'd be back to collect you when I was old enough. You shouldn't have let the nuns hand you off to anyone."

"My dears, would you tell us who this is and how he relates to you?" Emmeline asked, stepping back toward the stairs.

George blew out his breath, taking Rose's hand as they started down. "He's our brother, James Fletcher. I thought you was in St. Giles Parish or somewhere, James."

That was interesting. St. Giles was overflowing with thieves and pickpockets. The location didn't make James Fletcher a lawbreaker, of course, but given the larceny being perpetrated by his siblings, it didn't speak well for him, either.

"Nonsense," James said, chuckling. "I've been on the docks, finding work, earning blunt so's we could be a family when I was old enough. And here I am. Come down and give your brother a kiss."

When the children reached the foyer, James Fletcher knelt and pulled them both into his arms. Will's attention remained with the young ones—George especially. He didn't seem frightened, but neither had he run forward or smiled. Not precisely a joyous family reunion. Then again, Will and Emmeline needed the children, so perhaps he was hoping something underhanded was in the offing.

"What is your intention then, Mr. Fletcher?" he asked. If this James did leave with the young ones, he and Emmeline would have to start from the beginning again, returning to London, finding another two children of the appropriate age, gaining their cooperation . . . and damn it all, he liked George and Rose. He didn't want to have to begin again.

"You hear that, Georgie?" their brother said, standing again. "I'm a 'Mr. Fletcher' now." He tugged on the lapels of his greatcoat. "Well, I did come here to bring the little ones back to London, as that's where we're from," he said, rocking on his heels. "But first I'd like to know what's afoot. The nuns said the babes were only borrowed."

"Yes. They're borrowing us to be their children," Rose said. "I have pretty dresses now." She looked down at her shift. "Except I'm supposed to take a bath, and I don't want the ague."

"You're pretending to be their babies?" James lifted a straight eyebrow. "Perhaps we should have that chat after all, Mr. Pershing."

Will put a hand on Emmeline's shoulder. "Of course. Would you mind seeing to George and Rose, my dear?"

The look she gave him said that she would much rather have been in the office conversing with James Fletcher, but with her charming smile she nodded. "Certainly not. Let's get you dressed, Rose. Perhaps the bath can wait until this evening."

"I'll get the ague worse, if I take a bath at night," the little girl said, but took the hand offered her and headed back upstairs, George behind them but looking over his shoulder at his brother.

Once they were safely away, Will led the way to his office, halfway down the long main corridor of the house.

He and Emmeline hadn't done anything wrong; if anything, it was the nuns who should never have allowed them to borrow two children with a family member waiting to collect them. But they were here now, and they'd made a great deal of progress already, and he couldn't think of a single positive thing about George being back in St. Giles Parish and its environs. It could be even worse for Rose.

"You've got a lovely home here, Mr. Pershing," James observed, flopping into the chair facing Will's desk. "Soon as I got to Swindon everyone knew how to find Winnover Hall just outside Birdlip."

Wonderful. Fleetingly Will wondered if James Fletcher had also asked where to find his two orphaned siblings, who were residing with the Pershings at Winnover Hall. *Damnation.* "Thank you," he said aloud. "I would first like to say that my wife and I had no idea that George and Rose had any living family to speak of. They did not mention you."

James shrugged. "George likes to pretend they're alone. Gets him more sympathy, I think. But the fact is, they ain't alone, and they do have family. Me." He sat forward, crossing his ankles. "But I have to say, this business of borrowing them don't sit right. And dressing them up fancy? You do mean to give them back, don't you?"

No, because they'd specifically asked to go somewhere that wasn't an orphanage—and somewhere that wasn't in London. *Hmm.* "It's somewhat complicated," Will ventured, "but Emmeline's grandfather dotes on children. His mind, though, is . . . dimming. He continues to believe *we* have children, which we don't. We're going to visit him in a few weeks, and we thought to bring George and Rose for what might be our last time with him."

"Ahh. I see. Because he loves children so."

"Yes. Exactly."

"Well, that's very kind of you." James sat back again, his thin lips pursed. Abruptly he slapped his knee with one hand. "I'll tell you what, Mr. Pershing. What say I stay hereabouts to make sure you're doing right by the little ones? If nothing looks . . . unseemly, maybe I'll see fit to let you take them to visit old Grandpa. I've no wish to curdle a dying man's last chance for a bit of sunlight."

Unseemly. It wasn't precisely an accusation, but the stench of it lingered. "Where, hereabouts, do you mean to stay?"

"I heard there's an inn in Birdlip. That might do, though I spent some blunt coming out here to find the babies. Eight weeks in an inn might just clean me out, and who knows where we'd end up then." He narrowed one eye. "Seems to me I'm doing you a favor here, Mr. Pershing. Perhaps you'd see fit to pay my stay at the Blue Rose Inn, is it? The little ones could come visit me there."

And that would raise more questions that he and Emmeline couldn't answer. "No, Mr. Fletcher," Will said, digging his fist into his thigh beneath the desk, "I insist that you stay here. We could do no less."

"With you? Good glory, Mr. Pershing, that's very kind of you. Especially with me hurrying out here and neglecting to bring a stitch of luggage. It does make me see you and the missus even more kindly, though. Thank you."

"Of course." Pushing away from the desk, Will rang for Powell.

The butler appeared so quickly that he must have been poised just outside the door. "Yes, Mr. Pershing?"

"Powell, please see a bedchamber prepared for Mr. Fletcher here. And inform Mrs. Brubbins that we will be one more for dinner."

"He'll be staying the . . . night, then, sir?"

"Somewhat longer than that." He gestured James toward the door. "Powell here will see that you have whatever you need. Dinner is served at seven."

That had all fallen into place nicely—for James Fletcher. But if putting him up for a few weeks was the price to keep the children about, then they had no choice but to pay it. At the same time, a few inquiries sent to London about Mr. Fletcher wouldn't hurt, either.

This was damned odd. And suspicious. Admittedly he didn't want Fletcher here complicating things, but at the same time the children hadn't wanted to return to London. They'd never mentioned an older brother, or even the hint of one. And they'd insisted that he and Emmeline find a family for them. They'd signed that agreement knowing they had a brother about. Whatever the devil was afoot, he meant to follow the agreement. Even if it meant continuing to look for a new family for the children, while their actual family and their pretend family resided under the same roof.

CHAPTER TWELVE

George waited until the footmen finished bringing what looked like all of Mr. P's spare coats and shirts and trousers into the bedchamber down the hall. Whatever James had said, the Pershings hadn't booted him out on his arse. In fact, they were giving him clothes.

That surprised him. The Pershings were . . . nice, but they weren't half-wits. James didn't look anything like a gentleman, and he didn't talk at all like Mr. Pershing. Yet there he was, still inside Winnover Hall, and they'd given him a room, too.

"What do you think he wants?" Rosie whispered, looking around the corner beneath his arm.

"He said he's here to collect us. He is eighteen now, I think, so I suppose he could be."

"Maybe he was scared to ask Sister Mary Stephen," she reasoned. "I'm scared of her."

"Maybe," George echoed. "You stay in here and finish dressing. I'll go talk to him."

"I'll do it, but you still shouldn't have agreed to baths for me. I didn't make you do embroidery."

"You smell like lemons. It's nice."

Lifting her chin, she turned in a circle. "I do smell lovely. I don't think I caught the ague, either. At least the water was warm. It's never warm at the stone jug. Sometimes I can't even see the bottom of the bathtub, either. But this water was clean."

"I'll be back in a minute. Get Sally or Hannah if you need help buttoning your dress."

"I know that."

Pulling in a breath, George walked up the hallway. The Pershings were probably mad that no one had mentioned James before, but he and Rosie never knew when he might appear, or if he would at all. They always made their own plans.

The bedchamber door was shut, so he knocked. A second later it cracked open. "Come in, Georgie," James said, smiling, and went over to flop down on the bed. "Don't you look pretty? I hardly recognized you."

"You, either," Georgie returned, shutting the door but staying by it. "Where'd you nick the beaver hat?"

"On the mail stage. Some chaw bacon falls asleep, it's his own fault if he loses things." He narrowed his eyes, putting both hands behind his head. "You didn't tell me you and Rosie were leaving London."

"The Pershings took us home the same morning they saw us. And we didn't know where you were, anyway."

"Why didn't you tell 'em you have an older brother to watch over you already?"

"Why would I say anything? You ran when the beaks nabbed us. I turned around, and you wasn't there. We ain't seen you in six months."

His brother grinned. "No beaks or Bow Street Runners are gonna catch me again, Georgie. You know what I told you. You have to look after your own skin, or someone else'll take it off you and sell it."

"The nuns said they were going to have us transported, James. I had to give my word not to run again.

We thought you was gone for good." He'd hoped so, too. When James was their leader, things didn't go so well.

"You managed to get out of there anyway, I see. So, who are these stiff-rumped slags? The Pershings. Tell me about 'em."

George sent a glance over his shoulder, even though the door was still shut. This was all supposed to be a secret. No gossip. Mrs. P especially made sure they knew that. "Not much to tell. It's like Rosie said; they're just borrowing us for a few weeks, to get in good with Mrs. P's grandfather."

"And who's her grandfather? Pershing gave me some bottle-headed story about a loon of an old man who dotes on babies."

James would find out. And George would rather he didn't make Rose tell it. She got confused between pretend and real sometimes, and that might make James mad.

"Her grandfather's the Duke of Welshire. The Pershings were supposed to have children, and they couldn't, so they lied about it to keep their property. Now they have to go visit, so Rose and me are pretending to be theirs."

James sat up. "Well, well. A duke. And you all set to be a duke's great-grandbabies." He smacked his hands together. "And now me here to see to it that you're treated right. I wager you've already pocketed some bits and bobs. Oh, Georgie, this is our lucky day. Finally."

"How did you even know we were gone from St. Stephen's?"

"I crossed paths with that pretty sister. The new one."

"Sister Mary Christopher?"

"Yeah. That one. I asked if she could save my soul and then, me being a good brother, I inquired about you. She said you'd gone off with some rich swells, and when I asked her nice she told me who they were and where they lived."

"You asked her nice?"

"I didn't hurt her or nothing. Just got a little cozy with her." He chuckled again. "You should've seen her shaking, like a wet dog, she was."

George didn't like that. Sister Mary Christopher wasn't very nice, but that was no reason to scare her. If he said that, though, James would hit him. "The Pershings made an agreement with us," he said instead. "And Rosie and me both signed it. We get good food, fencing lessons for Rose, and reading and writing for me, and they get to teach us good manners and dancing and such. We have to follow the agreement, or they send us back to St. Stephen's. So you can't just steal things here. You have to be careful."

James cocked his head, his gaze at his brother, assessing. "If I didn't know better, I'd almost think you don't want me around, Georgie. This is our chance; this is how we get enough blunt to stay together. I'm a man grown now, so we can be a family. A real family. Not one made up just to fool an old man."

There wouldn't be any talking James out of it, George knew. Not yet, anyway. Maybe when he'd been there a few days and saw that the Pershings were keeping their word, when he'd had a few nights of not going to bed hungry, he would realize they were better off just staying for the seven weeks left, nicking a few baubles here and there, and then leaving. Maybe together, maybe going their separate ways.

George wasn't sure how this would go. But he did know he wasn't going to give James all the things they'd already nicked. Not unless his brother could prove that he meant them to be a family and wouldn't just disappear again if things got sticky. "Where did you go after the beaks nabbed us?" he asked.

"Never you mind about that. That's our old life." James spread his arms. "This is our new one. You go do your dancing now. I'm going to take a tour of the house."

Sighing, George put a hand on the door handle. "Just remember, if you get caught pocketing things, you'll ruin it for me and Rosie, too."

James took two long steps forward and cuffed George on the back of the head. "I told you, I ain't getting caught again." Abruptly he smiled, tousling George's hair before George could duck away from him. "If we do this right, we'll have a nice little cottage with a garden, a puppy for Rosie, and no worries ever again. Just hand me whatever you nick and I'll sell it off, and just like that we'll all be plump in the pocket."

Rose was waiting just inside her door when he returned to her bedchamber. "What did he say?"

"We're to slip him the things we nick so we can be a family."

"He's not a very good family. He threw a sack of rats on you."

"I remember." George shuddered. "But he says he'll sell the things we find, which is easier than me trying to do it. When we have enough blunt, we'll buy a cottage and get you a puppy."

"A puppy?" Rose hugged herself. "Oh, I want a puppy."

"He knows that. That's why he said it. Don't be a baby, Rose. We have to be careful about this. About him. If any of us gets caught taking things that ain't ours, they can send for the constabulary. James'll go to prison, and we'll go back to the stone jug—or once the Pershings are finished lying to the duke, they'll send us to a pig farm so they won't break the agreement."

"They wouldn't do that to us."

"You don't know that. Nothing here is ours, except what we take." He hated talking to her like that, but if James did do something bad, they would have to leave whether the agreement was finished or not. She needed to be ready.

Mr. P stood up when they walked into the breakfast room, but Mrs. P wasn't there. "Have you spoken to your brother?" he asked, patting George on the shoulder.

"Yes. I'm sorry we didn't tell you. He left before, and we didn't know if he would come back."

"I understand, I think. This is complicated, but if you don't mind, Emmeline and I would like to keep looking for a proper family for you. It will give you a second choice, at the least."

George nodded. It was actually a third choice, since he and Rosie had already decided to make a run for it after the duke's party, but he couldn't tell Mr. P that. "It's in the agreement. We should hold to that."

"Just don't send us to a pig farm when you're done with us," Rosie piped up, selecting her breakfast and sitting at the mister's elbow. "You can't wear nice dresses at a pig farm."

"Who said you're going to a pig farm?"

"George," she answered.

Mr. P's gaze turned to him. George pretended not to notice as he went down the length of the side table. If Rose couldn't be quiet, he was glad she was talking about a pig farm instead of what James wanted them to do.

"Regardless of your brother's plans, you're not going to a pig farm, George," Mr. Pershing said. "You specifically requested that we find somewhere acceptable to you. I'm not a duke, but I do have *some* connections."

George turned around. "You can't use your connections

without people gossiping, and then everyone would find out that you have pretend children and the duke would take your house."

"I'm not going to argue with you, but I would be willing to wager you a shilling, say, that Emmeline and I can do better than a pig farm."

Mr. Pershing still smiled, but George knew he'd insulted their pretend father. Mr. P had insulted him, too, though. He'd been told enough lies in his life to know the difference between what somebody wanted to happen and what would actually happen. James being there was proof of that. "I don't wager against grown-ups," he said. "They never pay up when they lose."

"Why are we wagering?" Mrs. Pershing asked. When she walked into a room she almost seemed to float. She smiled, putting a hand on George's shoulder. "Are you happy your brother's here?"

"I suppose," he grumbled. It made everything four times as complicated, and it was already almost too much for him to keep track of.

"We're wagering over the family you'll find for George and me," Rosie answered. "We want you to keep looking, just in case James isn't really going to get me a puppy like he promised."

"They anticipate a pig farm," Mr. Pershing added.

"Oh, heavens no. I'll be speaking with Father John as soon as I can arrange it, to see if he knows of any good families who might be interested in adding two wonderful children to their household."

"A duke's family would be good," Rose commented around a mouthful of toast and marmalade. "Because then I could still be a duchess."

That didn't seem at all right, but neither of the Pershings corrected her. Either she had the right of it, then, or they'd figured it wouldn't do any good to tell her the truth. George was glad of that; Rose liked dressing in pretty clothes, and if she wanted to pretend to be a lady, then she should be able to do it. James might talk about pretty things and puppies, but talking about it didn't make it happen.

Mr. P cleared his throat. "Anyway, I believe you have embroidery this morning, Rose, and I thought George and I might go fishing."

"Fishing would be good," George answered. And it would keep him out of the house and away from whatever James was doing.

Rosie stood up, slamming her hands against the tabletop. "Wait just a minute. Girls can't go fishing? I want to fish!"

"We'll have more opportunities for fishing," their pretend papa said. "This is actually going to be a lesson in how to act like a gentleman, with some fishing thrown in so it's less dull."

Slowly she sat down again. "I suppose that's better. But when is dancing? I'd like to learn the waltz."

"Dancing will begin tomorrow," the missus said. "And I'm afraid we'll be starting with the country dance and the quadrille, since those are the dances you'll likely be doing if my grandfather hires musicians for his birthday soiree." She smiled. "We'll make time for a few waltz lessons, though."

"So, James has promised to get Rose a puppy," Emmie said, as Will chose a pair of fishing poles.

"He's trying to make amends, I imagine, since George said they didn't expect to see him again."

"Even so. What if he decides he's seen enough, and he bundles them off to God knows where?"

Will handed the poles to Edward. "I'm not certain he actually has a right to take them. I'll send a few letters to solicitor friends, asking their opinions. Discreetly, of course."

If Will was one thing, it was discreet. "Good. Until you hear from them, I intend to proceed as if nothing has changed except for the addition of one extremely inconvenient house guest."

"I'd like to say it would be good for them all to be a family together, but I'm not so certain. And I hope my . . . distaste for their brother isn't simply because we need George and Rose here. But yes, we need to continue seeking a family for them, until they tell us otherwise." Hefting a bucket, Will took back the poles and headed for the kitchen door. "And now I'm off to talk about fish and gentlemanly behavior."

Yes, that was good, proceeding as if nothing had altered. It hadn't yet, more or less. But promising a puppy to Rose—that was just underhanded. Emmie found Rose and Hannah in the morning room, and she leaned in. "Rose, I think you should begin with embroidering a rose. Hannah, will you help her choose thread colors? I'll be back in just a moment."

"Of course, ma'am."

Emmie hurried outside and around the side of the house to the stable. A puppy. That was unfair. "Billet?" she called as she stepped inside the large building.

"Mrs. Pershing." The head groom popped up from beside Willow in the mare's stall.

"Billet, we are in need of two ponies," she said, putting on her most confident smile. "Calm, suitable for George and Rose, and good-tempered. And we'll need them today."

"Today?" The groom squinted one blue eye. "That's . . .

Hmm. I've a prospect or two, I suppose. The beasties won't come cheap if you want them now and already trained for children, though. The Hendersens've been looking to sell off their ponies and purchase some full-sized animals for their young ones."

"Now is what matters. They've never ridden before, and I don't want them terrified." Or dreaming about a cottage full of puppies and eager to leave Winnover the moment their brother snapped his fingers. "If you purchase the animals from anyone we know, please make it clear the horses are for my visiting niece and nephew."

With a nod he glanced past her toward the house. "Niece and nephew. As you say, ma'am."

Yes, every additional lie made everything more complicated. But the children needed to be explained in a way that would not cause any gossip back in London. She'd managed it on paper for seven years, but actual children made the task trickier. And with the addition of James, it became nearly impossible. But these were the youngsters they'd chosen. And aside from keeping Winnover and Will's employment intact, if ever any children deserved a chance at a better life, it was Rose and George Fletcher.

Of course, now that she was about to add riding lessons into the mix, they had another problem. If she knew anything, it was that Rose wouldn't be satisfied without a riding habit to wear. And with less than a day to procure one, desperate measures were called for.

As soon as they finished the first, disastrous embroidery lesson, she sent Rose off to the pond to find Will and George, while she and Hannah climbed the narrow stairs up to the attic to find her old clothes. "Look for a blue trunk," she said, shifting a dreadful painting of roses and oranges to one side. Her grandmother's handiwork, most likely—Grandmother Agnes, the late Duchess of

Welshire, had always fancied herself an artist, and everyone in the family had at least one of her pieces hidden somewhere in their attic. There had been an equally gaudy pair of silver candlesticks up there, as well, holding up the painting, but perhaps Powell had decided even the hidden-away valuables needed to be polished.

"This one, Mrs. Pershing?" Hannah pulled off another sheet.

"Yes, that's it. I think these things will be too large for Rose, but we'll see what we come up with."

The twenty-year-old clothes looked both familiar and from someone else's life. When they dug out a dark blue skirt, Emmie ran her fingers along the heavy material. "This is it. The jacket should be there, as well. I'm afraid it won't be very fashionable, even given your magical skills with needle and thread."

Hannah tilted her head, assessing the garment. "I believe I can make it serviceable," she said. "I should have it for the little one in the morning."

"Excellent. I can't wait to see her in her own riding habit." And there was no point in presenting a bribe halfway.

"I'm happy to help." Hannah gathered the habit into her arms while Emmie closed the trunk again. "In fact, I've been thinking. Children—your children—would have a nanny at their age, would they not?"

Why had that not occurred to her? Probably for the same reason she'd never expected Rose to want to learn fencing; she had no experience with youngsters beyond her own childhood, and in her journals she excelled at looking after the youngsters all on her own. Adding another servant would just needlessly complicate matters. "I suppose they would," she said. "But given that everyone who meets them at Welshire Park will simply assume they do have a nanny, I don't think we need to provide one. And with a signed agreement, and now with their brother here, I don't think we have to worry about them fleeing."

"Of course, Mrs. Pershing. I just thought I'd mention it." Standing, Hannah shifted toward the attic door.

That had sounded . . . uncomfortable. Emmie looked at her longtime maid's back. *Oh.* Her well-trained, well-disciplined staff continued to surprise and please her. She needed to begin paying closer attention. "Hannah, you do far too much for me, already. I'm not about to either ask you to take on the children as well, or accept your offer to do so. Even you must have to sleep sooner or later."

That earned her a smile. "You are a very kind, and very generous, woman, Mrs. Pershing. I will say, if you ever have other duties while the children are taking their riding lessons, I'd be happy to help keep an eye on them."

Ah. "Outside, you mean? By the stable? Where . . . Billet will be?"

This time Hannah blushed. "Yes, Tom does work at the stable, but that has nothing to do with my offer."

Tom. That was Billet's first name. "Very well. I shall keep your offer in mind, Hannah. And thank you."

CHAPTER THIRTEEN

"Ponies!"

Will handed his correspondence regarding James Fletcher to Powell, then had to dodge as both children flew down the stairs to the foyer and vanished down the hallway with laughs and squeals echoing behind them. Riding lessons weren't part of the agreement, and he frowned as he followed in their wake. Perhaps a group of gypsies or a traveling carnival was passing down the road—though with Rose's wariness about being kidnapped by gypsies, he doubted the girl would dare approach them.

Emmeline was already in the kitchen, and she whipped around as he stepped into the room. "Ponies?"

"Oh. I meant to tell you."

He could make a guess at the reason for their presence, but livestock was generally part of *his* duties. "Do ponies trump puppies, then?"

"You said we should allow them to make the most of this experience," Emmeline said, hugging her scheduling book to her chest. "George is afraid of horses, and Rose is tiny. Ponies made sense."

"I don't disagree," he said. "Should I ask how much they cost?"

"No, you should not."

"Ah. Very well, then." With all of their possessions contained in two sacks with room to spare, the children needed, well, everything, including some things he and Emmeline couldn't provide. Some of the things they *could* provide, however, would be more useful than others. "We can't send ponies back to the orphanage with them, you know."

"We're not sending them back," she pointed out. "The ponies or the children. We'll find somewhere better, or their brother will . . . become their guardian, I suppose."

"Riding lessons, then. Just for a bit of fun." Will grinned at her. "Brilliant, once again," he muttered, and kissed her on the cheek. "I'd wager we won't hear any more about a puppy after this."

She didn't flinch this time. Instead, Emmeline grinned back at him. "I have no idea what you're talking about. Oh, by the way, Hannah and I found an old riding habit of mine in the attic, and Hannah is modifying it for Rose as a surprise. Her riding lessons won't be able to begin until tomorrow, though, or it won't be finished."

"I know you never thought riding worth the time it would take away from the other lessons, but James and theoretical small dogs aside, Rose will be beside herself with excitement. This is something she will never forget. And yes, riding lessons will therefore begin in the morning."

He wondered what would happen if James mentioned getting a kitten for Rose. No doubt he would awaken to see giraffes in the yard. And yes, James remained a problem, but at the moment he was one they could more or less ignore, a wiseacre who thought he could gain a few free meals and a comfortable room before no doubt asking for a large sum to support his lofty dreams—and his brother and sister, of course. When that happened, he and Emmeline would have a decision to make, and he hoped he had some answers from ~~London before~~ that time came.

George muttered something Emmie couldn't make out. "Try sounding out the word," she said. "You know the sound a 'p' generally makes, and an 'n.' When it's at the end of a word a 'y' almost always sounds like 'ee.'"

"And the 'o'?"

"Without any other vowels beside it, it only makes two different sounds."

"Give it up, Georgie," James commented from his spot lounging on the sofa. "All your whining is hurting my head." He reached over and took another half dozen biscuits from the plate on the table.

"I ain't whining," George said, his jaw clenched. "This is hard. I'd wager you couldn't do it."

His brother swung his feet to the floor and sat up straight. "Do you want to wager whether Mrs. P there gives a damn if you learn your letters or not? Go learn to shovel shite in the stable. That'll serve you better."

Emmie bit the inside of her cheek. It would be better not to say anything. James Fletcher claimed he had the right to leave with the children whenever he chose, and at this moment she and Will couldn't dispute that. She leaned closer to the eight-year-old. "Sound out what you know, and see if you can figure out the rest."

Taking a breath, George tried. "P-n-ee. Oh. It's 'pony,' ain't it?"

"Well done!" She kissed his cheek.

George grinned. "Pony."

"Sterling, Georgie," his brother piped up again. "I was wrong. Now the missus can trot you out in front of her old granddad and you can read a word you'll never use again in your life." He chuckled. "You should teach him useful words, at least. 'Orphanage' and 'constable' and the like."

"Stop it, James. At least I'm trying to learn something."

"Yes, perhaps you'd care to come over here and read something for us, Mr. Fletcher," Emmie put in.

Narrowed eyes pinned her. "I'm only saying you're wasting your time. George'll be a bricklayer or a rag-and-bone man or a whale tonguer like our pa. Nothing you teach him will change that."

Trying to keep her jaw from clenching, Emmie smiled at him. "I prefer to think that for every word he learns, a new door is opened to his future." She shrugged. "And who knows? Perhaps one day George might agree to teach you how to read and write. Even if it wouldn't aid the work you do."

George snorted. James, though, rolled to his feet and strode up to her, moving faster than she expected. For a heartbeat she thought he meant to strike her. Powell must have thought so as well, because abruptly the butler was between the two of them, a teapot in his hand.

"More tea, Mrs. Pershing?" he asked.

James turned on his heel and left the room. "You should be careful," George whispered. "James gets mad sometimes."

All the more reason to keep the brother as far away from the children as they could manage. She sent up yet another prayer that one of Will's contacts in London would know of some obscure law that would keep James Fletcher from . . . inheriting his siblings. Unless she was being selfish because they were presently under her care—and it remained vital that they stay for the next few weeks.

Perhaps this was all a punishment, more complications piled on top of complications she'd caused in the first place. "I will be cautious," she said, since George had bothered to warn her. "Thank you for telling me." She sent Powell a smile, holding up her teacup. "And thank you, Powell. Your timing, as always, was impeccable."

The butler inclined his head. "My pleasure, ma'am."

Will waited on the landing while Emmeline and Hannah went to awaken Rose with her new riding habit. The happy shouts coming from the girl's bedchamber made him smile. It was easy to forget that Rose was part of a team of pickpockets and thieves, though her task seemed mostly to be distracting onlookers. She was very good at that, and for the moment, he chose not to consider what another few years of lawbreaking would make her. They were going to change that future, he and Emmeline.

"Did they dress us the same on purpose?" George asked, stepping out of his own room.

It was rather unsettling; both of them in dark coats, buckskin trousers, and black beaver hats. "I don't think so," he said, reaching out to tap the brim of the boy's hat with one finger. "Hats are for out-of-doors," he said, indicating the one he held in his hand.

"Don't know why," the boy said, pulling his off his head. "These ones don't keep off the rain."

"Yes, they are rather useless. But they're also fashionable."

"Do we have to wait here?" George asked, leaning over the banister to peer down into the foyer. "If Rosie has a new dress, she'll be looking at herself in the mirror all morning."

With a grin Will shook his head. "We could go take

a look at the ponies. As the oldest, you should have first choice."

"I ain't afraid of horses. That's just Rosie blabbing things. You do have to watch 'em; some of 'em ain't very friendly when you walk by too close."

He could imagine, especially if said pedestrians were of the small variety *and* attempting not to be seen. "I can show you the best way to pass by a horse, if you want."

The boy nodded. "I would like that. I won't always have an apple in my hand, after all. Do you know anything about making dogs not chase you?"

"I believe it's a similar technique."

"Good. I don't like dogs much."

Will wondered if Emmeline knew that. He doubted it, because if she had, the children wouldn't have ended up with the ponies, and this entire riding adventure would never have happened. This time was meant for teaching the Fletcher children how to be young aristocrats, not how to flee dogs or dodge through carriage traffic in London—which they would no longer have to do when they found their new home, anyway.

That, though, was what George and Rose—and more than likely James—knew. That was all they knew, and he couldn't fault the lad for looking for ways to make that life easier for them to navigate. Nor would he prevent them from doing so. As far as he was concerned, the best he could hope for was that by the end of this experiment, the children would no longer feel like they had to fight for every inch of space they occupied.

"You look well put together, Master George," Billet said, straightening from his lean against the outside wall of the stable. "Had to give my coat a bath. It smelled a bit . . . horsey, it did."

George grinned. "That's because you live with horses."

"No doubt. Ready for a ride, are you?"

"I'm just looking right now," George countered. "I'll decide on the rest later."

"Ah. Very good, young sir." Clearing his throat, the groom turned his attention back to Will. "Shall I bring the steeds out for your review?"

"If you would."

Billet disappeared inside the stable. A moment later, the big doors swung open and the head groom reappeared, a pony on either side of him. "I haven't saddled 'em yet, as I don't know which is for the sprite, and which is for the scamp. Both are trained for either saddle."

They were a fine pair of ponies, half the size of their adult-carrying counterparts, with fine, full manes and tails. The taller one was a pretty gray with a black mane, and the stockier one a bay with three white hooves and a white splotch on its forehead. "Do they have names?" Will asked, when George didn't show any inclination to give the animals a closer look.

"The bay is General, and the gray is Apple. Both geldings, from the Hendersen stable."

That information sent an alarm bell ringing in Will's head. "The Hendersens? What did you say to them about our needing ponies?"

"The missus said I should tell them that you have some of her cousin's young ones here on a visit before you all go up to Cumberland, so that's what I let out to 'em. They were happy to be rid of Apple, as their daughter wants a full-size mare, and I take it the boy doesn't ride much."

"So we're your niece and nephew *and* your son and daughter?" George asked, narrowing his eyes as he gazed at the two ponies. "How many things do we have to remember?"

"For our neighbors here, you're our niece and nephew," Will said, aware of Billet's interested expression. The groom had already lied for them at least once; having him know more of the story would likely be more helpful than harmful. "Clearly Emmeline and I don't have children. Our neighbors know that, so we need to change the story where they're concerned." He took a breath. "After we do all this to save our ownership of Winnover Hall, the last thing we want is for our Gloucestershire neighbors to chat with our Mayfair neighbors about how one day last autumn the Pershings suddenly had offspring." And then have the Mayfair neighbors profess that the Pershings of course had children, which would greatly astonish the Gloucestershire neighbors. What a mess it would be.

"If we'd known all that, I could've gotten more beef stew out of the agreement," George observed, folding his arms over his chest. "I gave the missus baths for numbers; what'll you give me for us being a niece and nephew?"

Clever fellow. "We gave your brother a room and meals. Does that suffice?"

He could almost see the wheels turning in the eight-year-old's head. His young life had been mostly transactional, stealing and selling and trading for basic necessities and safety. "I suppose. And I reckon James could use a bath, too."

Well. A point in favor of the Pershings, then. Another point. "Which pony do you want to ride?" Will asked, nodding.

So they would be niece and nephew in exchange for a small kindness, and that felt like progress. Will smiled as George took a half step forward for a closer look at the animals. Any show of trust—he'd take it, and smile to boot. As Emmeline had noted, even with James Fletcher's arrival, everything seemed well in hand. Even possibly successful.

Rose took a deep breath. "Is there anything better than a queen?" she asked, turning this way and that to see herself in the dressing mirror. "Because that is what I am."

Maybe she could be a queen general, because the brass buttons that ran down the front of the blue riding habit looked very military-like. Oh, she was splendid. Marvelously splendid.

"Hmm," her pretend mama said. "An empress, perhaps?"

"What is an empress?"

"The ruler of an empire. Approximately the same as a queen, I suppose, though it does sound very impressive."

"Yes, it does," Rose agreed, twirling in the mirror again. "An empress. Empress Rose."

"Your Majesty." The maid, Hannah, smiled, because Rose could see her reflection in the big dressing mirror, too.

Hannah was a maid, and so she could never be an empress, or a queen. Of course, Rose couldn't be one either, not really, unless she married a king or a . . . "What's a man empress called? An empressor?"

Hannah snorted, then pretended to cough.

"An emperor," her fake mama answered.

"Like Bonaparte. Oh. Now I don't think I want to be an empress. I'll be a queen general." She stepped closer to Mrs. Pershing. "I know it's only pretend," she whispered, "but I like it."

It wouldn't do any good if the missus thought she was a baby. Imagining herself to be a queen general was fun, though, because usually when she pretended it was to be lost or to be looking for something she'd lost. Her favorite thing to pretend to lose was a puppy or a kitten.

Hurrying down the stairs as fast as she could while still holding on to the railing like a lady, Rose nearly ran into James coming out of the morning room. "I'm going to go riding," she announced.

"So I see," her brother said, glancing past her to where Mrs. P would be standing. "On new ponies, yet. When you come back, we'll discuss getting you a puppy when we have our own home. You'll need to think of a name."

"Of course." A maybe puppy was good, but a real pony was better. She waited while Powell opened the door for her. Tomorrow she might leave and come in a lot of times just so Powell would open the door for her each time. That could be fun.

"Look at me!" she ordered her brother when George and her fake papa came into view. "I'm splendid!"

"You look very fetching," Mr. Pershing said, giving an elaborate bow with swirling fingers.

She liked her fake papa; he'd taught her some fencing, and didn't mind when she called it swording—after all, it was about swords, and not about fences. "Thank you. Which pony is mine?"

"I think General is the best fit for you," Mr. P, as George referred to him, said, pointing at the smaller, brown horse.

"'General'? That's not a name for a lady's horse." She made a face. "What's the big one called?"

"Apple," Georgie told her. "But I'm bigger, so I should ride the bigger horse."

"But Apple is a perfect name for my horse. She's lovely, too."

"They're both boys, miss," Billet the very tricky groom said.

Bending down, Rose looked beneath the horse's bellies to confirm that. This wasn't at all right; ladies rode gentle mares with long manes. Mrs. P's horse, Willow, was a mare. "Ladies shouldn't ride boy horses."

"It's perfectly acceptable, my dear," her fake mama said, and then leaned down to whisper in Rose's ear. "I think the darker one is more spirited, and your brother may be worried about having to ride him."

Her breath smelled like tea and tickled Rose's ear, but she made a good point. Georgie didn't like horses much, and she probably should ride the more spirited one. It was hard, sometimes, always having to be brave. She sighed. "I'll ride General. But I'm going to call him Jenny, for short."

"A very good compromise," Hannah said. But when she talked, she wasn't looking at General Jenny. She was looking at Billet, and her eyes blinked a lot.

"I'll fetch the saddles, then," the groom said, and went back into the stable.

"Have Willow saddled as well, please," Mrs. Pershing called after him. "We might as well make an outing of it."

"You're going riding?" her fake papa asked, turning to look at his wife. He should have known that, because the missus was wearing a purple riding habit almost as grand as Rose's, but men didn't always notice things. Mr. P smiled at Mrs. P, but then he smiled at her more than she smiled at him. Or rather, she did smile, but not when he was looking. If it was a game they were playing, Rose wished she could figure out the rules.

"I thought I might as well," her fake mama returned, her cheeks turning a little pink. "If we can combine a few lessons on manners and vocabulary with the riding, all the better."

Well, Rose didn't want any other lessons while she was learning to ride. She opened her mouth to say so, but Georgie pinched her arm. "Ouch," she squeaked.

"Hush. Let 'em do their lessons," he whispered. "We'll get a good look around the property, so next time we'll know the best way to head out and catch the mail coach. Or we can take the horses and ride away."

"But we signed our names that we ain't running again," she whispered back. "And James is saving the money from our findings to get us a cottage."

"You think any grown-ups keep their word? Even James?"

"I don't think James is going to get me a puppy, even though he said he would."

"Exactly. So pay attention to where we ride and where the roads go, and to where there might be an inn or a mail coach stop. Rivers and streams are good, too, if we can find a boat."

She nodded, because she always paid attention to where they were. Just like she knew without even turning around that the Pershings were behind them talking to each other, and Hannah was over watching Billet saddle the horses with one of the other grooms.

"Billet doesn't trust us, you know," she said. "He nicked us and saw what we was up to."

"I know. We'll have to be careful around him. He figured out that I put his coat in horse shite, too."

"Hannah likes him," Rose stated. "I'd wager he'd like her, if he knew she was batting her eyes at him." She blinked fast, imitating the maid. "If he's looking at her, he won't be looking at us."

George grinned, lowering his head to hide it. "That's good, Rosie. After riding, make sure you be friends with her."

"That's easy. We are friends. She braided my hair and made my dress fit me." Hannah would be good to know, whether she could keep Billet distracted or not.

"George? Rose?" Mr. Pershing motioned them over. "The horses are saddled. Let's begin, shall we?"

CHAPTER FOURTEEN

It was times like this, when the house was quiet and the servants had just begun stirring to ready breakfast, that the audacity of what they were attempting, she and Will, hit Emmie the hardest. In the first place she could hardly believe that her own mother and father had accepted that they had a pair of grandchildren without ever setting eyes on them, especially after her mother's own physician had declared her infertile. Was it because they *wanted* to believe? Because they didn't want Winnover going to Cousin Penelope either?

Yes, she wrote about Malcolm and Flora all the time. Last night for the first time, she'd told the truth about them—or very nearly so. She'd written that little Flora had insisted on learning the waltz, and so they would attempt a few lessons and see if they could coax Malcolm into being his sister's partner for the dance.

She'd also stated that the children's health had been improving of late, and that they were very excited at the idea of seeing everyone at her grandfather's party. And then she'd put the letter in a drawer, because the idea of sending it to her parents' home in Bath terrified her. Once she did that, there would be no turning back.

A knock at her door startled her. "Come in," she called, twisting around in her chair.

Will stepped into her bedchamber and shut the door. "Good morning."

They would be dancing today, and he'd dressed appropriately in a dark gray coat, blue waistcoat, and cream-colored breeches with shoes. His entire figure looked very fine. Very fine, indeed. She just resisted the urge to check her own appearance in the full-length dressing mirror. Vanity wouldn't change anything, though; her hair would remain loose around her shoulders, and her dressing gown wouldn't miraculously change into the simple blue and yellow gown she'd chosen for delivering country dance lessons. "Good morning."

"I didn't wake you, did I?"

As she was sitting at her desk writing out correspondence and practice words for George, he had to know the answer already. Was he being polite? Or was he nervous? A trill ran down her spine. Will Pershing had become so competent and composed that an oddly placed query became more noticeable than it would have been in someone less . . . him. "No, you didn't," she said aloud. "I've been working on George's lessons."

He moved closer to look at what she'd been writing, bending over her shoulder. "Is he at full words already? That's impressive."

His breath warmed her cheek, and goose bumps rose on her arms. "We're going to attempt a few of them; I don't want to frustrate him, but I think he knows more than he realizes."

"He's a bright lad. I only wish he wasn't using his wiles to look for a way to escape."

"And I wish his brother wouldn't belittle him for attempting to better himself."

"Just be careful about insulting him. We don't want him taking away the children out of spite."

"I know. He was very annoying, though. I spoke without thinking."

"Oh, I approve, you sharp-tongued woman. But we can't forget why they're here." He sank one haunch onto the corner of her desk. "We have just over a month, Emmeline. Can we do this?"

"I was going to ask you the same question." Sighing, she pulled her unsent letter from her drawer and handed it to him. "I write to my mother every month. Do I send this one? Or should I begin plotting a story about the lot of us feeling ill so we can avoid going at all?"

Unfolding the letter, he read through it. When a smile touched his mouth, she knew he'd come across the bit about Rose—Flora—and dancing. "Is this letter similar to the others you've sent?" he asked, looking up.

She scowled. Letter-writing was as much a skill as dancing or organizing a dinner. "Why?"

"It's just very . . . vivid." He smiled. "You're writing from experience. Not just your imagination. And while I've read the descriptions in your journals, this feels more real."

"I . . . Thank you. If you're asking what I think you are, no, I don't believe my parents will suspect anything."

Will handed the letter back, but kept hold of her hand. "You are a marvel. I say you send it. We need to have the children make an appearance, and it may as well be now."

"I agree. It's just . . ." Why was it that when he touched her now, she couldn't think straight? This wasn't about them. It was about the children, and her grandfather's party, and Winnover. "I don't know how to quell Rose's insistence that she's a queen or a duchess. It may amuse you, but as our daughter she *could* conceivably wed a duke, which makes her silliness sound like we're relentless social climbers."

"She's five. Doesn't every girl wish to be a queen or a duchess? She also wants to be a pirate, which seems horribly dangerous, but you haven't objected to that."

"Because that could never happen." *Men.* "Don't let her twist you around her finger, Will. She needs to learn to behave appropriately."

His thumb brushed along her forefinger. "Says the woman who purchased a pair of ponies on a whim."

"It wasn't a whim. It was a strategy."

"You're worried she'll embarrass you," he countered. "*I* doubt anyone will remember anything but her charm and good humor. There are other things for us to fret over."

"Well, I didn't get James a pony. And thus far he's been harmless, if . . . how shall I put it? Insincere?"

"Oily," Will added, nodding. "He thinks he's outwitted us about something. And he may have. Unless we can convince him to sign an agreement, our future is presently in his hands. It's too late for us to start over with different children. And I wouldn't want to even if we could."

She wished James were their only difficulty. "Which brings us back to Rose. Your solution to her lack of discipline is to let her do whatever she wants, while you stand back and laugh. That's no way to raise children." Freeing her fingers, she returned the letter to its drawer. "If you'll excuse me, I need to dress."

Her husband stood. "Certainly. You might consider that constant criticism is no way to raise children, either." He paused halfway to the door. "I only came in to query whether you wanted Rose about while you give George an art lesson this afternoon, or if you'd prefer that I take

her for fencing. Unless that's not useful to you, of course."
With that he slipped out of her bedchamber again.

Emmie eyed the vase by the window. No, ladies didn't throw things. Ladies *were* responsible for their children's manners, and any fault in them would belong to her. So while Will could think Rose's spinning and dreams of elevated status endearing, she couldn't afford to do so.

Riding horses was stupid. George hiked up his nightshirt to look at his arse in the reflection of his dressing mirror. It looked the same as always, but his thighs felt bruised and stiff all the way up his back. "Damn," he muttered, after checking to be sure his door was closed. Cursing was against the agreement, and he wasn't going to be the one to break it.

If he didn't dress soon, Edward the footman would knock on the door and ask if he needed assistance—as if he hadn't been dressing himself for as long as he could remember. True, his old clothes hadn't included a cravat or a coat, but he could tie a knot, even in a fancy neckcloth.

After he finished dressing, he walked over to listen at Rose's door. She was singing, probably playing at being a queen general again. It was silly, but her imaginings didn't hurt anything. He liked seeing her happy, but at the same time he wished she would understand that this was just a few weeks. A holiday. That after the duke's birthday party, the two of them would be right back on their own again. Or they'd go with James, who so far seemed to be keeping his word. Nobody saw him around the house much, but last night he'd shown George ten quid he'd gotten for selling some of the Pershings' little baubles.

Ten quid was a lot of money. George went to his blanket box and opened it. Beneath the sack, under a spare blanket he'd allowed to remain, a folded handkerchief hid. When he retrieved it, opening it on the floor beside him, he carefully counted the assortment of coins he'd been able to gather. He might still need to learn his multiplications, or whatever it was Mrs. P called them, but he could count money. Seven pounds and eight pence. Rosie must have added some, too.

That was more money than he'd ever had at one time before. Rich folk were careless with their coins, leaving them under cushions, in pockets, and sitting on furniture. Not even counting the money James had gotten them, that much blunt could get them as far as York, but he wasn't sure he wanted them living where it got so cold in the winter. London had been cold enough, and they might not always be lucky enough to find an open church cellar.

He pocketed the money, liking the solid feel of the coins bumping against his thigh. James would want to go back to London because he knew it, knew who would buy a lady's parasol or a man's pocket watch. But he'd said they would be rich, so maybe they could all stop dipping into people's pockets.

South might be good, especially if it was just him and Rose. They could find some village big enough that any grown-ups seeing them could logically think they belonged to someone else. If a place was too small, everybody knew everybody, and he and Rosie would be noticed straightaway. That would never do.

Since the fart-catcher still hadn't arrived to make sure he was awake, George went over to look out one of his pair of windows. A week or two ago, he would have spent his morning slipping into the orphanage kitchen after an extra potato or cup of milk or anything he could get his hands on for Rosie, plus a little something for the long-haul boys so they would leave the two of them alone.

The idea that he'd never see those boys again, never become one of them, made him want to lift up on his toes, lighter. But if he'd learned anything it was that while the people around him might change, there was always a bully and a tongue-wagger and a thief, and all the other things that made his life harder. The only difference here was that he hadn't yet decided who was playing all those parts.

At first he'd figured Mr. P for the bully, but Mrs. P was turning out to be more bossy—not in a mean way, though. As long as he didn't push things too far with Mr. P, the swell just smiled and said something smart and let him do as he pleased. That could be handy, but he'd have to be careful about it. Of course James was always a bully, so George didn't even count him.

A whistle from outside caught his attention, and he blinked. Down below Billet walked Willow about the drive. The groom pointed to his eye and then jabbed a finger in George's direction. George gave the groom a two-fingered salute, which only got him a grin and a laugh in return. Yes, Billet was definitely the tongue-wagger, or at least the dogcatcher, and he knew more about skirting around the edge of the law than anybody else at Winnover Hall. The groom could watch him, but George would be watching him right back.

Rose had said that Hannah the maid liked the groom. That could be a useful tidbit of information, especially if they decided to take the horses wherever it was they were going. With whomever they were going.

But it might not be just him and Rosie. George pocketed the nice inkwell he'd found in a back room, and a tea saucer the footmen had been slow to fetch. It wasn't much, but it hadn't been noticed, and that was what mattered.

Walking over to James's room, he knocked and opened the door. His brother sat by the window, a nice tea set on the table beside him. "What've you got for me?" he asked around a too-big bite of ham.

"We have a breakfast room," George said. "The rest of us eat in there."

"*You* eat with the swells. *I* recognize an opportunity when it jumps out at me." James dumped out the sugar and put the bowl in his pocket. A spoon and the emptied cream pot followed it.

"They'll know you took those. Put them back, James."

His brother winked at him, then with his knee dumped the whole table over. It crashed to the floor, water and tea and sugar and broken pots and cups and saucers going everywhere. "They won't know anything," he said, winking. Leaning sideways, he yanked on the bell pull.

A few seconds later Edward knocked at the door and came in. "Oh my."

"So sorry, Edward," James said expansively, finishing his ham. "I tripped."

"No worries, Mr. Fletcher." Squatting down, Edward cleaned up the mess, putting all the broken pieces onto the tray. "I'll be back in a moment with cloths and a broom," he said, and left the room again.

"You see? You just have to look at things the right way."

"That was mean."

"It's what they pay the man to do, Georgie. I'm helping to keep him employed. Now. Hand over what you've got." Standing, he walked closer and leaned down. "And don't forget why we're here."

"I'm here to learn and to help the Pershings," George

stated, lifting his chin. "You're just taking things and breaking things."

"You're taking things too, whelp. Don't forget that. We got ourselves to look after. Nobody else will do it."

George handed him the inkwell and the saucer. "That's all I could get yesterday."

"I can hear your pockets jingling." Shoving George against the bedpost, James dug into his pocket and pulled out the money.

Damn it all. "That was just some coins we found lying around. I forgot I put 'em in my pocket."

With another hard push, James released him. "Don't you hold out on me again, Georgie."

George wanted to remind him that the money belonged to all of them, that it was for a cottage and a life as a family, but he thought maybe James had forgotten about that. On the chance that he wouldn't remember it again, he and Rosie needed to nick a few more things and keep them for themselves.

Once she'd dressed, Emmie went downstairs to the breakfast room. She set George's practice pages aside and selected a light breakfast of toast, egg, and tea. Will's place at the head of the table had been cleared and the newspaper was missing, so presumably he'd already eaten and made himself scarce.

Emmie paused, slice of toast halfway to her mouth. Before this latest calamity, this had been how the majority of their breakfasts had proceeded—him, eating and leaving the table before she arrived, and the remainder of the day spent separately. The fact that that . . . avoidance now seemed like a slight was something of a revelation.

"Did Mr. Pershing say where he was headed this morning?" she asked into the air.

"Into Birdlip, I believe, ma'am," Powell answered. "He said he had something to see to, but that he wouldn't be long."

He'd best not miss the dancing, or Rose would never forgive him. Later, she meant to attempt to give George an overview of drawing. He would never be an expert, and it was frivolous by Will's standards, yet there she was, permitting fun. Ha.

"Very good," she said, even though it wasn't. "Have you had time to shift the furniture in the east room?"

"Donald and Edward are seeing to it now." The butler cleared his throat. "Some of the staff have requested to watch the dancing lessons, if their duties permit. If that is acceptable to you, ma'am."

Yesterday's riding lessons had also been well attended. Emmie didn't know what the fascination was, but she couldn't deny that these were unusual happenings for Winnover Hall—where most activities proceeded like clockwork. "I have no objection," she stated, "as long as the staff is aware that they may be called upon to help keep time. Dancing without music can be difficult, especially for beginners."

"I'll see to it that they are aware. Thank you, Mrs. Pershing."

"No thanks are necessary. I appreciate all that you and the rest of the staff have done to welcome the children. I know quite well what a surprise it was to all of you."

"They're lively, for certain," the butler commented, drawing himself up straighter.

She chuckled. "That they are."

"In fact, ma'am, if I may, the sil—"

"When do we dance?" Rose asked, swirling into the room.

She'd donned the dressiest of her gowns, a deep pink confection with a purple sash and a light network of pearl beads on the bodice. The gown had been intended for the evening of her grandfather's birthday, when everyone would be expected to dress for a formal dinner after a day of presents and celebration. Seeing Rose in it now made Emmie cringe, not because she didn't look darling, but because the odds of the five-year-old spilling orange juice or marmalade all over it were very high indeed.

"Rose, perhaps you should wear a simpler gown for practicing," she said, trying not to flinch as the little girl pirouetted past the teapot on her way to the sideboard.

"That's what Sally said, but I thought it was important that I learn in my dancing gown."

George appeared in the doorway, his own attire much more subdued and appropriate for a day in the country. "She won't listen," he offered, joining his sister. "Rosie likes to look grand."

"Well, don't we all?" Emmie shut her eyes for a moment. "Rose, why don't you tell Powell what you would like for breakfast, and he'll bring it to you at the table?"

"Is that because I'm so grand?"

"Definitely."

"Very well, then." Rose listed off her preferred breakfast items before she swirled over to sit beside Emmie. "Are you dressed for waltzing?" she asked.

"I'm dressed for teaching you how to dance."

The little girl studied Emmie's attire for a moment, from the proper bun at the top of her head to her blue and yellow muslin gown with its matching blue pelisse to her blue walking shoes. "It's very pretty, but if you want to turn Papa's head, you should have more beads and sparkles." She gestured at her own front.

"I'm married to Will; I don't need to turn his head." That would mean she wanted something romantic from him. From a handsome, dashing man she evidently knew little about, and had no idea how to approach without looking like a fool. She'd certainly had an increasing number of knotty, naughty thoughts about him over the past few days, but thoughts didn't upend anything. And they still had a task to accomplish. All that aside from the fact that she was annoyed with him for saying she was too unbending. Too concerned with her reputation. As if everything they had didn't rely on their reputations. And her hard work.

"Well, I'll try not to outshine you, but I can't make any promises."

Emmie took a breath. "Thank you, my dear." She twisted to view the butler. "What did you want to tell me, Powell?"

He cleared his throat. "It was nothing, ma'am. I'll see to it."

"Nothing" didn't seem like something he would have brought to her attention in the first place, but before she could question him further, Rose declared that she should be drinking American coffee because it was all the rage, and George dared her to try some. All Emmie needed was for that to devolve into a spitting contest or something, so she informed them that coffee wasn't allowed at Winnover Hall—which wasn't true, but she almost never drank it, and Will drank it not much more frequently than she did. A small sacrifice to prevent a ruined ball gown.

As they finished breakfast and Will still hadn't returned from Birdlip, she stifled a sigh. Yes, they were accustomed to nearly separate lives, but he knew they needed to do this together, even if he seemed determined to spoil the Fletcher youngsters and indulge their every whim.

She needed him for the dancing lessons. Not even the most competent of dance masters could teach both the leading and the following steps at the same time, and definitely not while keeping the attention of a reluctant eight-year-old boy and a young girl who already thought herself skilled in the most complicated of steps.

"I can't wait any longer," Rose stated, rising from the table. "I have dance lessons, etiquette lessons, fencing lessons, and some fishing to do today."

Emmie set her napkin aside. "Yes. We may as well begin. Powell, I'm afraid I may have to ask you to step in as a dance partner."

The butler blanched. "Dancing, Mrs. Pershing? Me?"

"We'll manage," she said, reflecting that the previous her would never have asked a butler to step beyond his duties. "Come along, dears. We're off to the east room."

"Wait," Rose said, balking in the doorway. "I'm to dance in the ballroom."

Reminding herself that Will's absence was Will's fault, and that he'd probably decided he couldn't go this long without trying to shoot a pheasant or something, Emmie put on a smile. "The east room *is* the ballroom. Or half of it, rather. When we host a grand party, the wall between it and the west room opens. I don't think we need the entire span of the ballroom today, though."

"Very well," the girl said with obvious reluctance, "but I don't wish to feel stifled."

"I think you'll be pleased, Rose." Emmie offered her hand to hurry them along. "Let's take a look, shall we?"

Rose gripped her fingers. "I'll look. But I'm not convinced yet."

"I'm not convinced at all," George grumbled, falling into step behind them. "Dancing is stupid. Grown men prancing about like . . . like goats. Goats being chased by bees."

"Don't listen to him, Mama. He's just worried he'll fall on his ar—"

"Rosie!" her brother interrupted.

"His bottom, I meant to say."

"A very permissible substitution," Emmie approved. "That part of the anatomy may also be referred to as a 'sit-upon.'"

"Oh, my arse is going to be that from now on," Rose said gleefully. "My sit-upon."

"My sit-upon is going to sit upon a chair." George gave a half skip.

Goodness. That was very nearly frolicking. Emmie laughed. "Well said, George. But you are going to have to learn to dance. I would hate for us to be at the party and have someone call for a dance—and you have to stand there while all the other children take to the floor."

"I wouldn't hate that," he countered. "But I signed my name to the agreement, and I keep my word."

Once again Emmie sent up a silent thanks that Will had thought of an agreement. For that, at least, she remained grateful. Then she pushed open the double doors marking the beginning of the east room—and decided she might have been a bit harsh in her mental criticism of her husband.

A trio of musicians sat in one corner, Will standing before them and speaking in a low voice. All the windows were open, and light flooded into the large room. The servants had moved the tables and chairs to the extremities of the room, and they'd rolled up the long, narrow Persian carpet and stood it upright in one corner.

Her husband turned to look at her, and then sketched a slight bow. "I thought this might serve us better than clapping the time."

"Oh, much better," Rose said, before Emmie could answer. The girl pranced up to the musicians. "Hello. I'm Rose."

"I'm Jerry," the man with the violin responded, until the other two shushed him. "I didn't want to be rude," he whispered.

Will cleared his throat. "I've explained that we've been tasked with teaching our niece and nephew to dance," he said in a voice that would carry to all the staff still filing into the room, "and these gentlemen kindly agreed to delay their journey to Gloucester by a day in order to play for us."

"Oh! I'm so happy I'm going to faint!" Rose exclaimed, and gracefully collapsed to the floor.

"Aunt Emmie wishes you would mind your dress," Emmie said, keeping a smile on her face.

Rose sat up. "That's not a real smile," she declared, pushing to her feet again.

"No, I don't suppose it was," Emmie admitted. "But then I'd hate for your gown to be ruined before you get to show it off to everyone."

While Rose busied herself with making certain all of her shiny beads remained in place, the orchestral trio tuned their instruments and George walked over to watch. Emmie hoped he wouldn't decide he needed to learn the violin in addition to reading and drawing.

"Did I overstep again, hiring musicians?" Will murmured from directly beside her.

"You happened to stumble upon them at the inn, waiting for the northbound coach, did you?" she countered.

"Perhaps I happened to have advance notice that

Lord Sheffield is holding a party tomorrow evening in Gloucester," he said, "and that the musicians were to arrive today."

"Another of your connections, then?"

"Yes."

"It's brilliant," she said.

"Thank you." Will hesitated. "And I apologize for earlier. Neither of us had any preparation for this situation. You've been superb from the beginning—from before the beginning—and I remain in awe of your talents."

"That would have been a much more pleasant conversation," she whispered.

"Yes, well, we insulted each other. You required an apology. I did not."

With that he turned away and motioned to the musicians. The violinist tapped his foot three times, and a lively country dance filled the grand room. George took a step backward, as if the noise surprised him, while Rose leaped into the air and began twirling. Emmie kept her gaze on her husband.

She'd implied that he was frivolous where the children's wishes were concerned, but that was certainly true. Fencing for Rose? Encouraging painting for George? If the decision had been hers alone, she could have found more practical entertainments for them. Something amusing, but useful. How to play hide-and-seek without fleeing into the woods, or playing a game of cricket without using the bat to bash other children. Pitching pennies and not stealing everyone's winnings. That sort of thing.

Pointing out the truth of something wasn't an insult. What he'd said to her, though—at its base, that she was a cold fish who only cared that the Fletcher children showed well at Welshire Park—of course that required an apology. The very idea that she only cared about the results and not the youngsters made her angry.

She wasn't a cold fish. She *did* care if the little ones were happy and well looked after and had better prospects in the future than they'd begun with. For heaven's sake, she'd arranged for Father John to come visiting this afternoon so she could speak to him about that very thing.

Rose grabbed her hand. "I need to know the steps," she squealed, "or I'm going to burst into flames!"

Shaking herself, Emmie nodded. "Of course. That's why we're here. To keep you from catching fire."

"Indeed," Will echoed, taking Emmie's other hand. "I suggest you and George partner, and do your best to imitate what Aunt Emmeline and I are doing. Then we can work with each of you on the steps and timing."

Shaking his head, George backed toward the door. "I ain't dancing in front of everybody."

There were more than a dozen servants clustered in one corner of the room, and as she looked James Fletcher sauntered into the room as well, so Emmie could see why he might be embarrassed. "Oh, everyone is dancing," she announced, and gestured at the group. "Pair up."

"This is unexpected," Will murmured, lifting her hand and shifting to face her.

"I am not a cold fish," she stated under her breath.

A frown creased his forehead. "I never said you were a co—"

"That's what you meant. That I have no heart, and I'm using the children to further my own agenda."

"I didn't mean to intimate that you are uncaring, for God's sake. I only wish you would . . . relax a bit. Enjoy the madness. You used to laugh, you know. If we—you and I—don't make some changes, in a few short weeks we will find ourselves precisely where we were before all this began. And I prefer *this* spot."

Before she could decipher that, he bowed, she curtsied, and with a series of hops and skips and steps they made their way along the floor. Behind them in a ragged, loud, chortling double line, the children and five pairs of servants followed. Emmie risked a glance over her shoulder, then clenched her jaw to keep from laughing. Powell, red-faced and chest puffed out, pranced hand in hand with Hannah, while Rose threatened to yank George off his feet with her exaggerated leaps into the air. Edward had paired with Sally, and at the rear Mrs. Brubbins the cook trotted with Donald looking very thin and breakable beside her.

The only one not dancing was James. It didn't seem like jealousy, but whatever the reason for his folded arms and the sneer on his face, she wished he would take himself elsewhere before George saw him and decided he shouldn't be dancing, after all.

As she looked back at her own partner, Will met her gaze, his eyes twinkling. Then they parted, and he traveled down to the left of the pairs behind them while she went to the right, and they met up at the rear to begin all over again.

After the party at Welshire, after they'd delivered the children to a good family, Will didn't want their lives to return to their previous calm, intricate, separate dance. And she'd been considering that very same thing.

She and Will had grown up friends. Then he'd started acting . . . differently, looking at her all the time. That was when he'd stopped jesting about proposing to her. Had there still been something between them that she'd avoided examining too closely? Or had Will been the safest, easiest choice? She'd known what he wanted in life, and she knew she could help him achieve it. A good trade, it had been.

That had been what she told herself. Just as when he'd stopped visiting her bedchamber, she'd told herself it had been a mutual decision. But over the past few days, he'd made it rather clear that separation wasn't what he'd wanted. And now she had to consider that perhaps she didn't want that any longer, either.

George pulled the silverware from his pockets and dumped it into the sack James held. Beside him, Rose freed a small glass bird from her reticule. "You can't put this in with the silverware, James," she said, holding it out to their older brother. "It'll break. And it's very pretty."

"I don't want glass birds. Bring me necklaces and ear-bobs." James dropped the bird to the floor and kicked it beneath the bed. "Jewels. The missus must have pearls and diamonds. I'd look, but that devil of a butler's taken to following me like a lost lamb everywhere."

"They'll notice if we take pearls," George protested. A pair of cuff links could take near a week, between Mr. P and Powell and Davis watching him.

"It won't matter," James countered, "because once we have the rich things, we leave. I was thinking Yorkshire. That's a fair distance from here, and from any messiness we left behind in London."

"I already thought about Yorkshire, when it was just me and Rosie, because you ran off." George lifted his chin, fairly sure James wouldn't hit him; it would leave a mark, and none of them wanted to have to explain that to the Pershings. "It'll be too cold for Rosie in the winter."

James reached out his fist, his thin lips flat and almost invisible. At the last second, he opened his fingers and flicked George's cravat. "You think you're clever, George, but I'm the one who didn't get nicked by the Bow Street Runners, and I'm the one who came all this way to find you and Rosie. We go where I say, because I'm the head of this family." Shifting his attention, he pinched Rose's cheek. Hard. "Jewels, Rosie. Silver and gold and jewels. Blunt, if you can get your hands on it. Understand?"

Rose rubbed her cheek, her gaze on where her stolen bird had gone. "You kicked my bird." Gathering her skirts, she crouched down and crawled beneath the bed. "I chose it because it's pretty. You shouldn't have kicked it. What if it broke?"

"Rosie, I don't care wh—"

"Here it is." She emerged, straightening to brush off the small figurine. "Oh, good. It's in one piece."

George reached over and plucked a bit of string from her hair. "We need to get back. We have lessons. You keep the bird, Rose." They could add it to her chest, along with the other things they hadn't yet given over to James.

"Things we can sell, whelp. I'm getting tired of everyone watching me and talking behind my back, and that topsail Mrs. P insulting me with a smile. And you damned well don't need to learn to dance or draw or whatever other sodding nonsense they've got you doing. We'll have everything we want without you knowing how to sketch a bowl of fruit."

"I'm learning to read, too," George stated. "And that's not nonsense, whatever you say."

James grabbed him by the shoulder. "It *is* nonsense, Georgie. You're already what you're going to be, and you're damned lucky you have me to teach you what you need to know. Otherwise, you'd still be sleeping in church cellars and begging for scraps. Now go do what I said, or I'll thrash you."

George wanted to yell that one day he would be big enough to thrash James right back, that he'd already made a plan and James was stomping all over it. Instead, he took Rosie's hand and led her back to the drawing room.

James's idea of family was them doing what James said. Right now George didn't see a way out of that, even if he preferred listening to what Mr. P had to say about honor and manners and being respectable. The Pershings would only be in their lives for a few weeks, and after that, even if he and Rose ran, James might find them again.

And yes, drawing lessons were silly. But they were also fun. And he wasn't ready yet to see them go, especially since he'd mentioned that James was going to get them a tutor when they had their own cottage, and Mrs. Pershing had decided that teaching him to paint would be a good idea, after all.

CHAPTER FIFTEEN

Bartholomew Powell looked up from the day's discarded London newspaper as Donald entered the kitchen. "Did you confirm the count?" he asked the tall, skinny footman.

The servant nodded. "I did. Thirty-one forks, forty-four knives, and twenty-eight spoons." Standing stiff, his pale complexion gaining a touch of gray, Donald cleared his throat. "I asked about, discreetly, as you suggested," he went on in a lower voice, his glance taking in the generously proportioned Mrs. Brubbins and the waif-like scullery maid, Molly. "None of the staff here would steal from the Pershings. You recall when Edward's aunt got sickly, and Mrs. Pershing paid his mum's coach fare so she could visit her sister?"

"Yes, I recall," the butler said, sighing. He knew quite well that none of the staff had absconded with any of the Pershings' silverware; it had merely been his duty to exhaust any other possibilities. And now with Donald verifying his numbers, he'd done so. "Thank you."

"But we must tell them," Donald went on. "If we don't, all of us will look doubly suspicious when they find out how much of the silver is missing."

"I am very aware of the consequences." For the devil's

sake, he'd served as the head of staff at Winnover Hall for twenty-six years now. No one here knew the Pershings—and Emmeline Pershing, in particular—better than he did. "Please accompany Molly to Birdlip for the kitchen supplies. And be certain to tell Mr. Umber at the butcher's shop that Mrs. Brubbins wasn't jesting when she requested two flank quarters."

Donald bobbed his head. "Of course. Let's be off then, Molly. I've some polishing to see to later."

"And an extra bag of sugar, Molly," the cook said, looking up from the dough she was kneading. "Those little ones are mad for biscuits."

The little ones—and more than likely their older brother—were also mad for silverware, but Powell kept that opinion to himself. He'd been attempting for several days now to find a way to tell Mrs. Pershing without sounding accusatory or snobbish, or whatever it would be called when a long-established employee complained about a pair of orphans to the couple who'd taken them in.

As Donald had noted, though, the Pershings had to be told. He would not be seen as in league with the little miscreants. Nor did he wish to be trapped into opposing them, either. He knew why they were in residence, and he meant to do everything possible to see that this venture of his employers' succeeded. Blaming it all on Mr. James Fletcher would be easier, but Mr. Pershing had been very firm in saying the young man would be staying.

Winnover Hall and Emmeline Pershing felt inseparable. Aside from that, he'd met Mrs. Penelope Chase back when she'd been Miss Penelope Ramsey and had come to stay for the summer with the Hervey family. The girl had been a horror, and he didn't imagine her temperament would have improved as an adult. There was a reason for tales of servants spitting in their master's tea, and if he ended up in her employ, he would be sorely tempted himself.

With that in mind he finished issuing the morning's instructions to the rest of the staff, and then headed into the main part of the house. The Pershings and the children were out riding, and he didn't expect them to return until luncheon. Even that layabout James Fletcher had taken a walk into Birdlip. Powell topped the stairs, and made his way down the hallway where the family's bedchambers lay. Looking up and down the corridor, he stopped outside the younger boy's closed door.

The butler squared his shoulders and pushed down on the door handle. The door didn't creak, because he saw to it that all the hinges in the manor were kept oiled. Stepping inside, he shut the door behind him. Donald and Edward had been sharing duties with the boy, tidying his room and aiding him in dressing, but the two footmen were both bound by Mrs. Pershing's word to the children—that no one would touch their trunks.

He was also forbidden to invade the children's privacy. If he couldn't determine what was afoot, however, he couldn't proceed. This all did make him feel like a bit of a scalawag, but under the circumstances he would prefer that the children think *him* the villain rather than the Pershings.

Unable to help a glance over his shoulder, Powell knelt in front of the boy's chest, clicked the latch open, and lifted the lid.

Unsurprisingly, a blanket filled the space. Being careful not to alter the folds, he set it aside. And then he sat back on his heels. "Angels protect us," he muttered.

The cloth sack lay tucked in one corner, bulkier than it had been when the pair had arrived at Winnover Hall.

Around that, were . . . things. One of Mr. Pershing's cuff links. A teacup of fine china in Mrs. Pershing's favorite pattern. Two sets of silverware. A duck carved in mahogany that belonged in the study. A large piece of amber that he believed belonged at Pershing House in London.

The list went on and on. Coins. Paper money. Buttons. Half a loaf of bread. Scissors. A chaos of pilfered . . . things. As Powell looked through them, though, they did begin to make a degree of sense. All of them, minus the food items, were worth money, from a penny or two up to perhaps a pound. Small things that could be hidden away in a pocket and, once removed from the house, traded or sold without any one item being so valuable it might arouse suspicions about its origins.

"Clever little bastard," he breathed, replacing the blanket before he shut and relatched the box.

The girl's trunk would be much the same, and he decided not to risk digging through it. Climbing to his feet, the butler walked back to the boy's door and cracked it open to peer up and down the hallway. The corridor remained empty, so he slipped out and shut the door behind him again. Quickly and efficiently done.

He'd managed a trio of steps before the James fellow stepped out of the upstairs sitting room. "Powell."

He nodded back. "Fletcher."

"That's Mr. Fletcher to you," the lad said, stopping.

Powell clenched his jaw. "Mr. Fletcher."

With a grin the fellow headed back to his bedchamber. "Pantler," he muttered as he shut the door.

Damned insolent churl. That had been a near thing; no doubt *Mr.* Fletcher had his own box of pilfered treasures. Now he needed to figure out how to tell the Pershings that a good number of valuables were missing and in the hands of the orphans and their damned brother. Or he could simply flee the premises and take himself off to Bedlam. All things considered, that might be the more palatable choice.

Oh, his life had been so much simpler and more serene before the Fletcher children had arrived. At the same time . . . Well, it hadn't been unpleasant when young Rose had brought him a yellow daisy yesterday and put it through his buttonhole. Of course, she'd probably turned around and stolen his shoes while he thanked her for the flower, but one did have to admire the brazenness of the youngsters. And Mrs. Pershing had been . . . softer around the staff, which he generally didn't approve of, but her mood had been lighter, as well.

At least this thievery would only be a problem for the next few weeks. If Master George and Miss Rose had been permanent additions to the household, finding a solution to their sticky fingers would have been a much more pressing problem. His flight to Bedlam would have to wait; he had a bit of creative problem-solving to do.

"Why do I need to learn about dirt?" George asked, folding his arms over his chest.

Will squatted beside him, scooping up a handful of dirt and pebbles and holding it in his open palm. "Firstly, farmable dirt is called 'soil.' A farmer knows all about dirt, and his favorite is a good, damp soil. Soil with earthworms is perfection, both for farming and for fishing."

"You're a loony, ain't you?"

Chuckling, Will dropped the earth and straightened again. "Possibly, but not where dirt is concerned. I want you to have an idea of what's important about Winnover Hall. You don't need to be an expert, but other landowners know when one of their own is full of shite just by some of the words he uses."

The boy narrowed his eyes. "You said shite."

"There are no ladies present. *That* was the rule, if you'll recall."

Will watched as George processed that, his face mirroring his thoughts in a way that was somewhat reassuring—the lad hadn't become a master of prevarication yet, anyway. If he'd remained at the orphanage, or if he and Rose ended up at another one, it would only be a matter of time. The boy was far more concerned with caring for his sister and keeping the two of them fed than he was with any pesky laws that got between him and his needs.

After he lost his boyish round cheeks and bright eyes, no one would be calling him clever or inventive. They would simply call him a criminal, and he would end up in one of three places—prison, Australia, or the gallows. Could a few reading lessons alter that?

"Are we going to stand here and look at dirt—soil—now?" George asked. "Because I'd rather go fishing, if it's all the same to you."

God's sake, maybe Emmeline had a point, after all. Learning anything that could give the children a better future far outweighed "fun," especially when fishing and fencing did nothing to keep them out of trouble. Even his commentary on soil versus dirt was more useful than the silly things he preferred to do with them, especially since he would much rather the boy become a farmer than a highwayman.

"Are you having an apoplexy? Mr. P?" The boy muttered what sounded like a curse under his breath. "Papa?"

Will shook himself. "No. Not an apoplexy. A thought.

If you had any life you wanted, George, where would you be in ten years, say? What would you be doing?"

The boy frowned, kicking a rock as they headed off toward the pond again. "What do you care, as long as Rose and me are off your hands?"

"I'm interested. What's your dream for yourself?"

George blew out his breath. "She said you'd do this."

"Who said I'd do what?"

"Mrs. P. Whatever we're supposed to call her. She said you're good at getting people to like you, but charm don't work for everything. So, I reckon that now you're worried you've been too nice and Rosie and me won't be ready for that party. Are you going to be mean now?"

Out of the mouths of babes. "I have no reason to be mean," he said, his jaw clenched. Damn Emmeline. She'd stated her opinion of his "frivolous" ideas, and he'd told her his reasoning. To pass her thoughts on to the children was highly inappropriate. And not at all helpful.

"Good. Because I like fishing."

"So do I," Will said absently. First Emmeline accused him of having no sense of humor, and now she thought him too frivolous. It would be helpful if she made up her damned mind about his faults.

She was the one with no sense of humor, anyway. If it had been up to her, George would be in starched neckcloths and Rose in a ball gown at all times, standing at attention and bowing and curtsying on command, with no concessions to their wants and needs at all.

After they'd married, and after months of nocturnal . . . conjoining while she showed no sign of ease in his presence, he'd wondered if she didn't want to have a child with him. If that was somehow the reason she'd never become pregnant. Of course, he'd been a fumbling idiot, as much a virgin as she'd been, but her ongoing reaction to intimacy with him had made it clear that this marriage was a business and social partnership—and nothing more. He'd jumped into marriage with his heart, and she'd stepped into it armed with a social calendar.

Eight years together hadn't changed that. And now even this very uncharacteristic insanity had done nothing to alter their supremely frustrating status quo.

"Hey, I found earthworms in your damp soil," George called from close by the pond. "It *is* perfect."

Yes, at least the dirt knew what it was doing.

Rose tried to pretend that embroidery was like fencing only with a very small rapier, but it didn't work. She still hated it. If the needle *had* been a rapier, the handkerchief she was trying to stitch a rose into would have been very, very dead by now.

"Be patient, Rose," Mrs. P said from beside her on the sofa. "Big stitches can be a delightful effect, but smaller stitches show more artistry."

"I'd rather have sword artistry," Rose commented, beginning to wish her name had been a simpler kind of flower.

"Yes, but this will be more useful."

It wouldn't be, because Georgie had said once the duke's party was over, they would be leaving, and James said it wouldn't even be that long. She didn't want to go with James, but at least out in the world they could do what they wanted, and people would give her coins when she danced. That was her favorite—that, and going into the sweet shop afterward.

At least the dancing lessons she was getting here would earn her more coins, because she was becoming very good at country dances and quadrilles and maybe even waltzes, though they'd barely touched on that one. The only problem with all those dances, though, was that she needed a partner. James was too tall, and too old, and he liked to be behind the crowds, picking their pockets, anyway. And the way George frowned when the Pershings made him practice, no one would throw money at him. Vegetables, maybe.

"What are you grinning about?" the missus asked, a pretty smile touching her face.

Rose couldn't tell her, because then there would be another lesson about how the Pershings were going to find them a good family and she wouldn't be dancing in front of people for coins any longer. "This afternoon is more dancing lessons," she said aloud. "I like those almost as much as fencing."

"I'm glad you do. You're very good at them, too."

"Thank you, Mama."

Her fake mama blushed a little bit, like she always did when Rose called her that. It was funny how much the Pershings liked being called Mama and Papa, even though everyone knew it wasn't true. If they liked children so much, they should have had some of their own. That was none of her business, though, and she liked all the things she'd been collecting, even if James said they were stupid. *She* thought they were pretty, and so she would keep them for herself, or let Georgie sell them. He liked her baubles.

Powell knocked at the open morning room door and then walked inside the room. "Ma'am, Father John has arrived."

The missus set aside her embroidery and stood. "Splendid. I'll speak with him in the library. Rose, perhaps you'd best not tell James about the pastor."

"I won't. No pig farms, though."

"I shall keep that in mind. In the meantime, keep practicing. Remember, it doesn't have to be perfect. You just have to try your best."

"Yes, Mama."

Powell sent her a look that made her feel like he'd seen her put the pretty blue and white porcelain thimble in her pocket, but he hadn't even been in the room when she'd done that. Rose smiled at him, and with a humph he left again, but didn't close the door.

Well, she was glad he'd left the door open, because Georgie had told her to try to listen to what the missus told the pastor, and she especially wanted to know if Father John did say anything about them going to a pig farm. If he did, then they would definitely have to leave with James, even if he had almost broken her bird.

Putting her embroidery on the sofa beside her, Rose stood up and tiptoed to the doorway. Edward hurried by with a tray, so Mrs. P and the pastor were going to have tea. Briefly she wondered if that meant Mrs. Brubbins had made lemon biscuits, but finding out would have to wait even if the cook had baked dozens of them.

Slipping directly behind the footman, she trotted up the hallway, her skirts in her hands so they wouldn't swish. He knocked on the library door, and then when Mrs. P answered he pushed it open and went inside. The library had a million excellent hiding places, and once the footman started serving the tea she crawled through the doorway and around the corner behind the bookshelf that smelled like old potatoes.

Shifting the heavy book at the bottom up to the next shelf, she squirmed onto the empty lowest shelf, folding her legs up beneath her stomach and resting her head on her folded arms. Anyone looking at her would probably think she looked like a big, very pretty bunny.

"I apologize for not accepting your invitation sooner," the pastor said. "Between Mrs. Packem's rheumatism and her sick cat, Whiskers, and Ben Holder's broken leg and trying to organize his neighbors for harvest, it's been a busy fortnight."

"I had no idea Ben Holder broke his leg," Mrs. Pershing replied. "We would happily lend him a team and a wagon."

"If you don't mind, I shall inform him of that. I know he's a bit . . . cantankerous, but I remain hopeful that the charity of his fellow parishioners will open his eyes and soften his heart."

They muttered agreement to each other. After that at least one of the grown-ups ate a biscuit, and Rose was sure she could smell lemon. Blast it all, Mrs. Brubbins *had* made lemon biscuits, and with her stuck on a bookshelf, someone else—probably frowny Powell—would eat them all.

"Now, Mrs. Pershing, your note mentioned needing my resources for a task. I must tell you, after eight years of marriage, the Church is very unlikely to grant an annulment, even with no proof of matrimonial . . . relations."

"What?" The missus sounded shocked, whatever an annulment was.

"I . . . I beg your pardon," the priest stammered. "I thought . . . Well, with the phrasing of your request, I assumed—"

"I assure you, Father, I am not pursuing an annulment. And neither is Mr. Pershing."

"Oh, splendid. You and Mr. Pershing are a much-admired example of matrimonial harmony in the community, I must say."

"Thank you. We strive to be so. Which makes me ask

the question: Why would your first thought after seeing my note be that I wished for an annulment?"

The priest cleared his throat. "Just a silly stray thought, Mrs. Pershing, I assure you. I mean, I *have* seen a number of annulments requested, and in most instances, there has been a failure to produce offspring."

"Yes, well, there are also marriages of great renown without children. I don't know if ours is one of them, but we are quite happy. And that isn't at all why I requested your assistance."

"Please, then." A slurping sound of drinking tea made Rose wrinkle her nose. Slurping wasn't at all proper, she knew now. "I'm all ears."

Now Rose wanted to imagine a man in black pastor's attire but with giant elephant ears. She put a hand over her mouth to cover her giggle. She couldn't laugh now. Georgie said this was important.

"I must have your discretion, Father John. Everything rests on that. Do I have your word?"

"I couldn't very well remain in my position if I were a gossip, Mrs. Pershing. Of course you have my word."

"Very well." Mrs. P took a loud breath. "Will and I have recently taken two young people into our home. Children."

"My heavens, Mrs. Pershing," the pastor exclaimed, sounding like he had another biscuit in his mouth. "That is very charitable of you. I had heard that your niece and nephew are visiting; did something happen to one of your relations? It's not everyone who will step forward to assume such a grave responsibility after a tragedy. Oh, I shouldn't have said 'grave.'"

"It's not—"

"My condolences, of course. Lady Graham's cousin

recently passed away. They say he drowned, but there is some speculation that he was . . . overly inebriated when he fell into the Thames. Thankfully, he was without issue, and Lady Graham graciously arranged for his funeral. It was quite a lovely ceremony, and very moving, if I say so myself, and of course with no mention of his drinking. How may I assist you, though?"

For a minute nobody said anything. They were probably eating the rest of Mrs. Brubbins's biscuits. "Yes," the missus finally said, drawing out the word. "Well, now this is doubly difficult. You were correct earlier, or at least partially so. Will and I have found our . . . interests diverging somewhat, and I wanted to ask if you had any advice. It's nothing serious, but I don't wish it to become so."

That didn't make any sense at all. While Father John and his elephant ears started talking about praying and Mrs. P doing her wifely duty, which she probably already did because the house was very clean and the food was the best Rose had ever tasted, she tried to figure it out. Mrs. Pershing had said she meant to ask Father John about any good homes that might want two children. It had been part of the agreement that nobody was going back to an orphanage. But Mrs. P hadn't asked about that at all. She hadn't even mentioned the word "orphan," and that was her and Georgie.

Maybe George would have a better answer, but to Rose it looked like the Pershings had been lying when they'd said they would find a place for them. And if they were lying, then all of this was just about Winnover Hall. Nobody cared about her and George, or their agreement, or if they ended up at a pig farm or an orphanage. Stupid Pershings. She'd been liking it in Gloucestershire. James had the right of it, after all, and she didn't like that, either. For one time, *she* wanted to be right.

"Thank you, Father John," Mrs. Pershing said after a long time. "You've been very helpful. And as you already mentioned it, having my niece and nephew here has made me wonder: What do you recommend for children who *don't* have a relation willing to take them in?"

Wait. This sounded better. Rose shifted a little, turning her head to where she could just see the grown-ups' feet. Father John's were far apart, and Mrs. P's were close together, a little on her tippy-toes.

"Well, the Church has a plethora of orphanages," the pastor replied. "Two in Gloucester alone. St. Michael's has a splendid reputation, or so I've heard. Are we speaking of children with no means? Because that does make a difference, of course."

"They're hypothetical children, but say they did have an inheritance, or a recurring allowance. Surely there would be somewhere more pleasant for a lively youngster or two."

"Boarding schools are quite popular, in those instances. There are several for girls in London, and at least one nearby, in Pitchcombe."

"Is it the practice to separate siblings, then? That seems rather harsh."

"Unless they can be placed with a family, that's generally what happens."

"How do children come to be placed with a family to whom they have no relationship?"

"Well, there are always farmers looking for another hand or two, or millers, or the occasional shopkeeper. If the youngsters have an income or an inheritance, that makes them a bit more palatable. Folk dislike taking on an additional worry, however Godly charity may be."

"So the children are generally put to work?"

"Everyone must earn their keep. If the children are

very wealthy, the Crown would appoint them a guardian, I suppose. Your own niece and nephew aside, children are quite a burden, or so I'm told."

"Mm-hmm. What about paying a family to take them in and raise them? Has that ever been done?"

"I . . . Not that I know of, but I don't see why that wouldn't suffice, though in a purely hypothetical scenario one would have to find a suitable family rather than one simply after additional funds. If whoever it was paying the youngsters' way didn't wish to take them in, that is— which would seem to be the more likely scenario." He cleared his throat. "Is that what's afoot here, Mrs. Pershing? Are you looking for someone else to take over the care of your nephew and niece?"

"What? No! My cousin and her husband are alive and well, I assure you. Having them here, though, seeing how . . . innocent and vulnerable they are, it made me wonder, is all."

"Understandable. With some effort and God's blessing, there is still time for you and Mr. Pershing to be, well, blessed with your own."

"Indeed. And now, I happen to know that Mary Hendersen has been after a cutting of my orange roses. She won't ask me directly, of course, but if I give you a cutting, would you take it to her?"

"I'd be delighted. I've been meaning to call on the Hendersens, anyway, and this will give me the perfect excuse."

"Follow me, then, and we'll get the cuttings and a bouquet of fresh autumn roses to go with them."

The feet shifted, and then walked out of view. When it got quiet, Rose rolled out of the bookshelf, stood up, and dusted off her dress. Mrs. P had asked for some advice, but she hadn't asked about her and Georgie specifically.

And where all the money to pay a family was supposed to come from, Rose had no idea—James had taken all their blunt, nearly fifteen quid now, plus most of the things they could trade for some rhino.

Maybe George could make some sense out of it, because she had no idea what was going on. But she did want to run up to the music room so she could look down into the garden and see how big Father John's ears were.

CHAPTER SIXTEEN

George frowned. "I don't care about his ears, Rosie."

"But they were huge!" She fanned her hands out on either side of her head. "I don't think he can wear a hat."

"Mrs. P didn't ask him to find us a home, though. That's the important part. Are you sure?"

"Yes."

He squinted his eyes, wondering if he was about to discover what a megrim was. "Tell me what she said. Exactly."

"Fine. She asked where poor children without parents would go, and where rich children would go, and whether people could pay a family to take in children. But she never said our names, and she never said the word 'orphan,' and she never asked Father John for his help—except for her and Mr. P, because she said something about marital relations and he told her to pray."

This would have been easier if he'd been there when Father John had come calling. "Did she ask about orphanages?"

"I told you. She asked where children with no one to take them in would go, and he said orphanages. That's when she asked about children with money." His sister shifted from one foot to the other. "Wait. Do you think that means the Pershings want to pay someone to take us?"

"It could be." And that could be trouble, both because people who earned money by keeping children didn't sound at all good, and because if James could find a way to get money for them, he would take it.

"What do we do, then? Because I think I'm worth a great deal of money, and they might not be able to give anyone that much."

George rubbed one eye. "We're not waiting for that, re-member? And it doesn't matter, except to see if they're keeping their word." And from what he could decipher, they seemed to be doing that, and if they were, they still didn't know they were being robbed. He could convince James to let them stay a little longer. The more time he had to learn reading, the better.

"I still don't understand," Rose said, flapping her hands against her skirt. "They gave money to the stone jug to take us, and now they're giving more money to get rid of us. I don't think they know what they're doing."

"It won't be up to them, so don't worry about it. But be careful; Mr. P asked me what I wanted to do when I was bigger, but I didn't want to give them any hints where we might be going."

"I wish we could stay here. I don't know why they don't want us."

With a sigh, ignoring the sudden pinch in his chest, George sat on one of the chairs in his bedchamber. "Be-cause everybody here knows they don't have children, and everybody in London thinks they do. They only want to be able to keep living here. They don't want us."

Rose flopped into the chair opposite him. "But I like it here. Everyone's nice and wants to be friends, and they call me Miss Rose." She sighed. "We've been good, and

I've only taken a few bigger things because James is making us. Don't they like us?"

Sometimes it seemed like they did, but that didn't matter. And it didn't matter that he liked going fishing with Mr. P, who didn't ever try to cuff his ears or shove him. Just because someone asked every morning if he'd slept well and what he wanted to eat, and just because Mrs. P said nice things and kissed his forehead or his cheek when he learned to read a new word, didn't mean anything. Even if once in a while, he wanted it to. Even if sometimes it made him want to curl up his fist and punch James right in the face.

"I don't know, Rosie. But family are the only ones we can rely on. You know that."

"Yes, I know. Not even our whole family. Just you and me." Lowering her shoulders, she sank back in the too-large chair. "Sometimes I wish we didn't know so much. Then we wouldn't have to worry all the time."

"Don't wish for things that can't happen."

Somebody knocked at his door. "George? It's time for our reading lesson," Mrs. P said in her silky voice. "And do you know where Rose is? Will is out in the garden for her fencing lesson."

Rose pushed to her feet. "Today is wooden swords!" She jumped up, pulled open the door, and galloped out of sight.

The missus leaned in. "Ready, George?"

"I suppose," he said with another sigh, standing.

"Is something wrong?" Mrs. P asked, gliding into the room. "I hope Will didn't keep you out in the sun too long." Before he could protest, she'd put her hand on his forehead, then on both of his cheeks. "You don't feel warm." Bending down, she took a close look at his face.

"And you don't look flushed, or sunburned." She touched the tip of his nose. "Does that hurt?"

"I ain't sunburned," he said, backing out of her reach. "We sat in the shade to fish." He didn't need some woman fawning over him like he was a baby; he couldn't even remember the last time anybody had asked him if something hurt.

Slowly she straightened again. "Is something else troubling you, then? You've said you enjoy the reading and writing lessons. Is there something else you'd rather be doing?"

"No. I just wish I was learning it faster." He was learning it all as fast as he could because James was going to get them caught, but the more he discovered about reading and writing, the more he realized that a few weeks wouldn't be enough time for him to master anything. Maybe he could nick a few of the books they'd been using so he could keep practicing after they escaped and James made them go to York or back to London. He'd have to hide them from his brother, but he could manage that.

"George," Mrs. P said, gesturing him toward the doorway and falling in beside him, "you are giving yourself an advantage that many your age could never hope to equal. And we still have time for a great many more lessons." She walked with him down the stairs, which didn't seem quite as far apart as they had been a week ago. Was he getting taller? "In fact," she went on, "I would like to give you the books we've been using. The end of this holiday doesn't have to equal the end of your learning."

George stopped on the landing and looked at her. "You're giving them to me? Why?" No one gave him things. The only reason the Pershings had been giving him meals and lessons was so they could keep their house. To give him the books after they were back from the party—that didn't make any sense.

"Because you like them, and because I can," she replied, her smile lighting her eyes.

It only lasted a few seconds, but George caught himself smiling back at her, and not because she expected him to, but because what she'd said felt . . . nice. Warm. Shaking himself, he whipped back around and trotted down to the foyer and up the hallway to the library.

He understood Rose liking it here, because Rose was barely more than a baby, and she adored anything that was frilly or shiny. If someone was nice to her, she considered them a friend. She was too young to know it wasn't that simple, that nice nearly always expected something in return. Even this time, he would have been willing to wager that Mrs. P was giving him books because she didn't want to feel bad when she sent them off to live on a pig farm. It did make him feel bad that he'd nicked a pearl necklace from her bedchamber and handed it over to James this morning, though.

Taking his seat at the worktable, he pulled one of the books over and opened it. "Rosie said Father John called on you yesterday," he commented as the missus sat beside him. "Did you ask him to find us a family?"

"Not specifically," she returned, which was more honest than he expected. "I did ask him about various strategies we might use to find you a home."

"But you didn't tell him to find us one? I thought that was why you wanted to talk to him."

She grimaced. "Father John is a very nice man, but I don't always agree with some of his . . . opinions about things. And he's also something of a gossip."

That explained it. If Father John went about telling everyone that the Pershings had taken in two children and now wanted to be rid of them, not only would it make them look very bad, but it would give away their game and lose them Winnover Hall. It always came down to the blasted house.

And now he was mad because he was mad. He wasn't surprised, after all, that the house came first, but that didn't explain why it made him want to punch his fist into the table. What had he expected—that she would have been thinking about him and Rose first, about what might be best for them?

"Oh," he said aloud, because at least she'd told him the truth. "What did you decide to do, then?"

"I don't know yet. I'll need to discuss it with Will, and with you and Rose." She sighed as she leaned over to flip the book to the page they'd been reading. "What sort of family would you wish to live with, George? If you had your choice? Would they have other children? Would they live in a city, or a village, or out in the country?"

For the devil's sake, she was just like her husband, asking him about what he *wanted,* when real life had nothing to do with that and would only make what they actually ended up with seem even worse than it would have.

Well, he knew how to put a stop to that. It had worked with the nuns, and it had worked with Mr. P. The mister had hardly asked a question for the rest of fishing, and just kept muttering to himself. "I know it doesn't matter to you," he said. "Mr. P told us you just want everything to go back the way it was before, that we're just a disruption you can't wait to be finished with."

The missus opened her mouth, then snapped it closed again. "Don't forget," she said, much too brightly, "you need to practice calling him Papa." She took a breath, then another one. "And you are not a disruption, George. I've become quite fond of you and Rose. I want what's best for your future." Pushing to her feet, Mrs. Pershing hurried over to the nearest window and put both hands on the sill.

Damnation. Now he felt bad again. He didn't care about the nuns, and Mr. Pershing had acted angry, but he didn't like it if he'd made Mrs. P cry. She'd been good to them, whatever her reasons for bringing them there. The ice cream had been her idea, and it had been so good that he dreamed about it sometimes—and that was much better than dreaming about rats crawling all over him.

The trouble was, as often as Rosie talked about living here forever and how perfect it would be, there were times, especially in the last day or two, that he could imagine it, too. And that didn't help anybody—him and his sister least of all.

Scowling, George tipped back his chair. Reaching behind him, he nicked a small purple and yellow blue john stone bowl from the shelf and shoved it into his pocket. It didn't quite fit, so he shifted it to the inside coat pocket over his chest. That didn't completely hide it, either, so he had to slouch forward to make the other side of his coat poof out in the same way.

By itself the bowl would be worth almost a quid. Put with the other things he and Rose had managed to acquire even before James had started making them nick more expensive baubles, they could afford lodging and food for a year or more. When it ran out he would be almost ten, and could find better-paying work toting boxes or delivering packages or letters for rich people. Maybe James would even decide that being paid for work was better—and safer—than stealing.

"Why don't you read that first line to me, George?" Mrs. P said, not moving from her spot by the window.

"Remember, if you don't know a word, sound out the letters."

He'd barely made it through "the cat liked cream" when she turned around and sat beside him again. That was good, because he wanted to keep learning to read and write, but she looked like she might have been crying. How she managed to hide it so well, he had no idea. When Rosie cried, her face turned red and blotchy, and her nose ran.

"I want you to know, I have never called you a disruption, or thought of you as one," she said abruptly. "I did say that our lives have been turned upside down, but that might have been a good thing."

George shrugged. "I don't mind. It ain't—isn't—the first time someone's called us disruptive. We disrupt things a lot, I reckon."

Mrs. Pershing turned in her seat to face him. "I like you, George. You and Rose. Very much. I hope you understand why you can't stay here. And it's not because of anything you've done. Or anything Mr. Pershing and I might or might not want, or even because your brother wants you."

"You told us already. Some people think you have children and other people know you don't, and if we stay, everyone will know you lied and you'll lose your house."

"Yes. Exactly. The only good thing about my lie is that because of it we met you two. And I can never thank you enough for helping us save Winnover Hall."

This conversation needed to change, because it was making him feel mushy inside, and he didn't like that sensation. He liked being hard inside, except where Rosie was concerned, because he had to be ready for anything around James. Soft meant he was thinking too much about other people, and that was the opposite of being ready for trouble.

"If you want to thank us, send us off with some blunt in our pockets."

"We intend to do that. In fact, we would like to open bank accounts for each of you." Her cheeks turned pink. "I should probably wait for Will to be here before I explain the rest, but we won't abandon you, George. And again, I do not think you're a disruption. I don't know why Will would say that."

Well, Mr. P hadn't said that, actually. George had told the story, though, and now he needed to keep it aloft or he and Rosie would have to run with James before they were ready to go. Lying to adults and getting caught at it was the worst. Especially now that he knew the Pershings meant to give him and Rose some money—unless that was a lie, just like the ones he'd been telling. Even if it wasn't a lie, James would make sure the money went to *him*. *Ugh*. Now George was almost certain he was getting a megrim.

"Keep reading, George. You're doing amazingly well."

"Thank you, Mrs. P—Mama."

She sighed. "You really should practice calling me that, my dear. Pretend you're studying lines for a play, if it helps. You don't have to mean it."

"That won't make you feel bad?"

"It isn't about me. At the moment, every time you say it, you scrunch up your nose, like the words tastes bad."

"It ain't bad," he countered. "It's just odd. I had a mama, and then I didn't think I'd ever use that word again." Stifling his own sigh, he bent over the book again.

Lips touched his temple. "I'm not trying to replace her," Mrs. P said quietly.

Sharp, deep pain bit at him, harder than he'd felt in

three years. Since she couldn't see his face, he scrunched his eyes closed tight. He was *not* going to cry. He'd stopped doing that a long time ago. All of this was too damned soft, with her being nice, and the stupid kissing on his head. Next, she'd want to hug him. "Just help me read, please," he said aloud, even though what he really wanted to do was run outside and keep running until he couldn't even breathe.

For a few seconds she just sat beside him. "Of course, George. Let's get back to work."

Ah, splendid. Another dance lesson without musicians. That was the way Emmie had thought they would be practicing from the beginning, but since Will had surprised them with music on their first day of practice, every lesson after that seemed too quiet—and too awkward.

She couldn't blame the silence on the lack of music this time, however. For three days she and Will had barely spoken. In the beginning, she'd figured that her methods had been effective, and that he'd realized he was being given the cold shoulder. First implying that she was a cold fish, and now telling the children that she considered them a disruption and couldn't wait to be rid of them—it was the first time she'd known him to be cruel.

A day or so later, though, she'd caught him glaring at her, then swiftly looking away when she met his gaze. And then instead of joining her and the Fletcher children and James in the drawing room after dinner, he'd claimed to have correspondence to see to. His having evening correspondence had been extremely common until a few weeks ago, but she knew for a fact that he'd informed the trade minister's office that he would be on leave for two months.

They seemed to be ignoring each other, then, which made the whole thing silly. Why, though, was *he* slighting *her*? Had he begun it when he'd noticed her slighting him? For heaven's sake, this was difficult enough without him saying disparaging things about her, and however absurd it was, she wasn't going to apologize—she'd done nothing wrong. Well, nothing recently. And she'd already apologized for the lie that had begun this mess.

"If you keep your head down when you curtsy," Will was saying, one hand gripping Rose's as she folded herself nearly in half, "you may find that you end up on the floor on your face."

"But if I keep my head up, I can't see if my feet are in the right place," the girl complained.

"That's the part you'll have to memorize. Where your feet go."

"This is impossible. I already have to memorize where my feet go in four different dances. They don't remember where to be when I curtsy."

Shaking herself, Emmie stepped forward. "Let me show you," she said, lifting her skirts almost to her knees. Yes, it was highly improper to do so, but Will's advice wasn't helping anything. "Stand beside me."

With a heavy sigh Rose did so. "The nuns say only hoydens lift their skirts," she observed, hiking her pink muslin up to her own knees.

"I'm not a hoyden. Are you?"

"I don't think so."

"Then the nuns are wrong." Perhaps that was a bit of an oversimplification, but Will was glaring again and it annoyed her. "Now. Turn your toes out like a duck, like this." She demonstrated.

Rose mimicked her, giggling.

"Now bend both knees, but keep your weight on your

right foot and shift your left one forward. Arms out like you want to be soaring in the air, and head up with a smile." She dipped a deep curtsy as she spoke, then straightened again. "In short, you're a duck preparing to fly."

"Oh, I like that." Dipping down, Rose flapped her arms and stretched out her neck.

"Remember, you're only testing the air to see if you want to fly. You aren't trying to become airborne."

"Don't flap so much," her brother advised.

"I wish I was a boy," Rose panted, trying again. "Bowing is easier."

"If I'd known ladies were lifting their skirts, I would have come in for more dance lessons," James said, stepping into the room.

Before Emmie could straighten, Will moved between them. "I'll thank you to keep your opinion to yourself in my home," he stated, his voice flat.

She couldn't see his face, but James could, and a moment later with a mock bow, the young man left the room again. It meant something, that they could not even be speaking and Will would still defend her honor without a second thought. *Goodness.*

"Mrs. Pershing," Hannah said, entering the room from another door, a wooden box in her hands. "It was in the attic. I took the liberty of winding it."

"Thank you, Hannah." The music box had been a Christmas gift a year or so ago, and while it wasn't the most attractive thing, with giant flowers carved on the lid and sides, it did play a waltz, something only the very newest of the mechanisms did. "George, shall we attempt a waltz?"

The boy backed away, his hands going behind his back. "Not me."

"I'll waltz with you," Rose stated.

"The two partners have different steps, my dear. Each of you should have an experienced partner."

"I ain't doing it until I see it." George plunked himself into a chair. "I heard a man can get a woman pregnant dancing the waltz with her."

"Ah. No," Will finally contributed. "Not unless you're doing it very, very badly."

Emmie shot him a look, rather grateful that James wasn't there to say something worse. "That isn't amusing. No, George, a waltz, well or poorly done, will not cause a woman to be with child."

"Oh, my apologies," Will snapped back. "I forgot; there's no time for fun or amusement in this household. Back to work, then. Dance, children. Dance."

"But I want someone to show me, too," Rose said, her face scrunching into a scowl. "I want a baby, but I'm still too little."

The pregnancy-through-waltzing story must have come from Deirdre at the orphanage—the girl seemed to have a theory about nearly everything. Before she could consider a better response to it, Will walked up to Hannah and flipped open the music box. As the tinny sound of a German waltz tinkled into the room, he strode up to Emmie, took her hand, and half pulled her into his arms.

"Rose, watch Emmeline's feet," he instructed. "George, watch mine. The steps repeat, so once you learn the first six, you've learned the entire dance."

As he spoke, he demonstrated, leaving Emmie no choice but to join him or be spun to the floor. Previously he would never have dragged her into anything without first asking her permission, or without them already having coordinated an entire evening to decide with whom they would be dancing each dance. Given his lowered opinion of her, he evidently no longer felt it necessary to bother with coordinating. Or asking permission.

"You're supposed to be encouraging them to participate," he muttered, his mouth close by her ear. "Or is dancing too frivolous now?"

"What?" she whispered back, hiding a scowl behind a much-practiced smile. "I suggested the dancing lessons, if you'll recall."

"Ah. Dancing is acceptable, then."

Whatever this was, she didn't like it. She was the one who'd been insulted, even if he'd done it behind her back. Meeting his glare straight on, Emmie kept the smile on her face. "In the future," she whispered, "it would be helpful to the cause if you didn't inform the children that I see them as a disruption and can't wait to be rid of them. I never in my entire life thought of you as cruel, Will Pershing. Even if you meant to hurt me, there was no reason to do that to the little ones."

"'Cruel'?" he repeated. "No, you made it quite clear that you think of me as a charming, whimsical fool. Which is odd, since you previously didn't think I owned an ounce of whimsy. And don't you dare lecture me about carrying tales to the children. I know full well you gave them your opinion of me."

Emmie blinked. "What the devil are you talking about? I told you to your face that I envy you your charm and ease with the children, and I have never said a cross word about you in front of them, no matter the provocation."

As they argued they twirled about the room, faster and faster, the pace of the music box left far behind. Peripherally she noted that Hannah had set the mahogany box in a chair, and that she and the children had joined hands and fled the room.

"Is envy why you—What do you mean, you've never

said anything cross about me in front of the children?" Will demanded. "George told me precisely what you said. Do not lie t—"

"I am not lying. And George told me what you said that I said, which I didn't say, so pray climb down from your pedestal and—" She stopped midsentence. This disagreement had one thing in common: *George Fletcher.*

At the same moment, Will stopped their dizzying dance around the room, though he kept his grip on her waist and one hand. "George," he said out loud, making the name a curse.

"Why would he do that?" she panted. The boy had pitted them against each other, and given that he didn't seem a mean-spirited soul, either she'd misjudged him or he'd had a reason of some sort.

"I have no idea," Will replied. "He seems to be enjoying his time here. I even caught him laughing when he hooked a five-pound trout yesterday. This feels like sabotage. Deliberate sabotage."

"I still don't understand the purpose of it. We haven't violated the terms of the agreement, we're in the process of finding him and Rose a permanent home if they choose not to go with James, and I informed him that we would be willing to contribute a sum to see the two of them well settled."

"It seems very specific," he commented, his tone more thoughtful. "He meant to have us arguing, or not speaking to each other. What does that gain him?"

She considered his question. "When he told me what you'd said—allegedly—I was asking him what sort of household he imagined himself in, what sort of family he wanted."

Will's eyes narrowed a fraction. "I believe our conversation was along similar lines when he informed me of your disparaging remarks. Why wouldn't he want us asking those questions, though?"

She considered that for a moment, and only one answer came to mind. "He has other plans," she suggested. "Or one of the Fletchers does."

"I'd guess the young ones still mean to make a run for it, as soon as we return from Welshire Park, would be my guess. With or without their brother. Damnation."

"We can't blame this on James, either. He's someone they're accustomed to not being able to trust. It's us. We brought them here because of a lie, Will," she said. "They have little reason to trust adults as it is. We may well be their worst nightmare—offering food and comfort, with the assurance that we will turn them out when we don't need them any longer."

"That's a horrible thought." Will looked down at her, then turned them back into the dance, this time moving in time with the music-box tune. "I've missed waltzing with you," he said softly.

"You have? We agreed to only share one dance at each soiree."

"Yes. The last dance. Which generally isn't a waltz."

She glanced up at him, then leveled her gaze at his cravat. "Dancing with our guests and friends is important."

"I don't disagree. But I always have looked most forward to that last dance. Especially when it's a waltz."

For a moment they glided about the room, silent but for the tinny waltz. As the music began to slow, her heart did the opposite. Will took a breath and removed his hand from her waist. Shifting his grip on her fingers, he led her over to the couch by the wall.

"I find myself rather relieved, despite George's prevarications," he said, sitting and drawing her down beside him. "We aren't at odds after all, it seems. We've been friends forever, and I always thought we had a good . . . partnership, and lately I've thought that we . . ." He stroked a thumb along the back of her hand. "I've enjoyed spending more time in your company, Emmeline."

Oh. Of course they were friends, but now he was regarding her very intently. A damned handsome man, he was. She'd tried telling herself they were practically brother and sister, growing up in each other's pockets, but that had never been it. He'd been a boy, and she'd wanted a house. She had the house, but he wasn't a boy any longer.

The shiver that ran down her spine now, though, was nerves, but not . . . nervousness. A heightened awareness. For goodness' sake, he was distracting, in a way she couldn't before recall. She did know all about his charm, though, because she'd helped him refine it. "You thought me a cold fish, Will."

"I never called you that, for God's sake," he countered, his fingers warm around hers. They hadn't held hands for this long in ages. Ever, really. "I have long admired your precision. Your logical bent, the way you see a challenge and unfailingly find a way to both succeed and exceed all expectations."

"That's nice of you to say. Thank you. And I have long admired, and envied, I suppose, your ability to win over an entire room with a well-placed smile or a single word or two."

"But you do have your doubts that my charming ways will suffice where the Fletcher children are concerned."

"I did not say that to George," she stated. "Though if we're being honest, I may have mentioned to Hannah that on occasion I have found your charm . . . aggravating, as it leaves me to wield the metaphorical hammer."

She thought that statement would more than likely end

the conversation, but Will only turned his gaze toward the windows on the opposite side of the room. "I have maintained that it's more important to make certain the children enjoy their time here than that they learn some of the minutiae we've put before them. I was wrong. But I think we need to alter our approach, regardless."

"I agree. We need to be united, Will, or those two will take over Winnover Hall and have *us* running for the hills."

He looked at her again, the serious lines around his eyes easing. "Agreed. They're children, but they're also wily. We need to be wilier. And united." With that, he leaned closer and kissed her, very gently touching his mouth to hers. "To our new partnership."

Now the flutter down her spine felt more like excitement, though she should have been far too long-ago-married to feel such a thing. Before she could think herself out of being impulsive, Emmie tipped up her head and kissed him back. "To success."

CHAPTER SEVENTEEN

"And who is this?" Emmeline asked, bending down to tuck a yellow strand of the little girl's hair behind one ear.

"That'd be Margaret," Mrs. Pennywhistle said with a confused-looking smile. "My youngest. You know Robby, my middle boy. He's the one delivers you the mail."

"Oh yes, Robby! He's a fine young man."

"A bit of a scamp, if you ask me, but I'd be proud to see him postmaster one day," his mother responded.

Will, standing to one side of the women, took in Mrs. Pennywhistle again. She was a tall woman without curves, and while she didn't have the look of utter exhaustion about her that Jenny Dawkins with her fourteen children did, neither did she seem even remotely ready to take on the Fletcher children—even if she'd wanted that task.

"Emmeline," he said quietly, as the women continued chatting. "No."

With a slight nod she bade the Pennywhistle females good day, and returned to wrap one hand around his forearm. "We're running out of families," she said, giving a smile and wave to Peter Grumby, Birdlip's stablemaster.

"We'd probably have better luck in Gloucester."

"But Gloucester is miles away." She sighed as they continued down the cobblestoned street in the direction of the church. "Yes, I know, distance from Winnover isn't the point. It's about finding a suitable family for George and Rose."

"And budding felons though they are, it wouldn't please me never to be able to see them again, either. Logically, the more complicated having the children about becomes, the more eager I should be to see them gone, but it seems to be just the opposite." Every mishap only reminded him how very clever they were, how enterprising and imaginative, and how much he wanted them to have a life where they could simply be children.

"I know what you mean, Will," she murmured. "But what choice do we have?"

"None. And luckily Gloucester isn't that far; it's better than London or York or Cornwall."

"Those are our only alternatives? A town or a city—there are too many places they could hide in either, and too much trouble for them to get into, don't you think? A village or a farm seems a much wiser choice. And there are a plethora of both in just the surrounding five miles."

"None of them may be the best place for the children, though. We can't settle simply because it means we can stop by for tea on a whim." Even if that idea was damned tempting.

"But we need to be thorough, because somewhere close by we might find the perfect place." Her gaze lifted, her fingers jumping. "Dash it all, it's Mary Hendersen's barouche. And she's with that horrible Prudence."

Will chuckled. "Prudence wasn't so much horrible as she was perfect and mild," he returned, but guided

Emmeline toward the jeweler's shop. "Back here," he said, nudging her into the narrow alley and following.

"I should apologize to her, I know," Emmeline whispered, peering around his shoulder back toward the street. "But then she'll suggest tea and cricket with our niece and nephew, and Rose and George are simply not ready for polite company. I will not have my ship sunk by Mary Hendersen."

The barouche rolled past them up the street. "Wait here a moment, just to be certain they aren't doubling back to purchase earbobs," he murmured, leaning down to smell Emmeline's hair as she pressed against him. Lavender. God, she was arousing.

Thank God they'd figured out what George was up to with his slanderous comments, even if he hadn't quite satisfied himself with the purpose for it. He had twenty-eight days to figure it out, after which time they would be at the Duke of Welshire's estate, head home, and then send the children off to . . . wherever he and Emmeline could find a place for them.

After that, he would have to spend at least a week in London catching himself up on any new business in the trade ministry. Emmeline would busy herself with planning one of their dinners for the local gentry and her correspondence with the spouses of whomever he needed to rally to whichever cause was next assigned him.

Separate lives again, coordinated and peaceable and efficient—and damned unsatisfying. It seemed the height of selfishness to complain about perfection, but there it was. He wanted . . . more. From her, from himself, for their lives.

"I think they've gone on," she said, looking up at him from the circle of his arms.

Now he wanted to kiss her again. Evidently it had taken eight years for him to figure it out, but he was still in love with his wife. "More than likely," he agreed, unmoving.

"What?" she asked, grinning.

"Just gazing at my wife," he said, and took a reluctant step backward. He'd been on this road before, after all, and then she'd informed him that there was no reason for them to share a bed any longer. Preparing the children to meet the Duke of Welshire wasn't the only thing it took both of them to manage. And he refused to be in love alone.

"Who should we try next?" Emmeline asked.

"This would be easier if you'd included Father John. He knows far more about the local families than we do."

"I just . . . He *might* keep our confidences, but this is too important for 'might.' And he was very quick to mention orphanages and money after he told me all about the unfortunate demise of one of Lady Graham's relations. I didn't feel comfortable confiding in him, Will. Nor do I trust that his idea of a good family for the little ones would equal our—"

"Then I shall trust your judgment. We need to find someone we *can* trust, though, because we are . . ." Abruptly he realized he was speaking to the air, because Emmeline had stopped several feet behind him. He turned around. "What is it?"

Her gaze remained on the front window of the jeweler's. "I—It can't be."

Frowning, he rejoined her. As usual, Mr. Rippen the jeweler had several items on display in the window. Today, a pretty glass diamond brooch, pearl earbobs with a matching pearl necklace, a jadestone bracelet, and an onyx cravat pin enticed shoppers to come inside and see more treasures. "Do you fancy something? Because I find myself very much in the mood to purchase you whatever you—"

"I misplaced my pearl earbobs, and then my matching necklace went missing day before yesterday," she murmured. "You know, the one with the gold roses forming the hasp?"

Nothing specific came to mind, but he could clearly see the gold rose hasp on the necklace in the window. "Are you absolutely certain?" he muttered back.

"I always knew which way to put it on, because the left hasp has a bent petal. I knew the children were making off with items, but this is not a carved bird or a silver fork."

"I'm at least as concerned over how they managed to sneak into Birdlip without us knowing," Will stated. "And how they convinced Mr. Rippen that the pearls belonged to them."

"If it was them." Rolling her shoulders, she pulled open the jeweler's door and walked inside.

Will followed her, already seeking the proper phrase to discourage George and Rose's thievery without breaking their spirits. Did that make him a fool? A gullible idiot? Even deeper down he wondered if that made him a father, but that was a question that would never find itself in the light of day. It had more than likely been James— and if it had, that could be the moment they'd been waiting for.

"Mr. Rippen," Emmeline was saying, her most appealing smile on full display. "Good morning."

"Mrs. Pershing," the diminutive jeweler exclaimed, rising from his work stool at the back of the shop. "An unexpected delight! How may I serve you? And you, Mr. Pershing. Yes, of course. Both of you, in my shop!"

"May I ask where you acquired the pearls in your window?" Emmeline asked, gesturing with one hand.

"They're exquisite, aren't they?" The shopkeeper sprang past them to lift the necklace and earbobs from their velvet display. "It was just the luckiest thing, really. A lad came in and said he'd found them in a clutter of luggage that had fallen into a stream. Very muddy, they were, but I could see the quality."

"Before you bring them any closer," Will said, "may I ask if the left-hand hasp has a bent petal?"

Mr. Rippen flipped them over in his hand, his expression shifting from elated to horrified in one swift second. "I . . . Oh dear. Oh my goodness. I would never—these are—"

Emmeline put a hand on his arm before he could leap through a window. "I do not doubt you for one moment, Mr. Rippen," she said warmly. "I wonder if you could answer us three questions, though."

His Adam's apple bobbing, the jeweler nodded. "Of course. Anything you require of me, I will do my utmost. I—"

"What was the age of the young man who brought you the pearls?"

"I . . . I'd say he was somewhere between seventeen and twenty, Mrs. Pershing. A stranger to me, long-haired and wearing fine clothes, very apologetic about bringing in found items and saying it was the luckiest he'd been in a year."

That described several young men around Birdlip, but Mr. Rippen attended church with them and their families every Sunday. A stranger, though, narrowed things considerably. Will imagined he should be furious, but it wasn't anger drilling through him. It was relief. "Dark hair? A thin mouth and a beaked nose?"

The jeweler nodded.

"Did he give you a name?" Emmeline asked, always after absolute proof and the last detail.

"No, he did not. He did say how pleasant it was to find an honest businessman about, and that given his luck hereabouts, he might begin digging beneath bridges in the area and bring any findings to me."

"Lastly, how much did you pay for the pearls?"

His fair skin turned even pinker. "I'm ashamed to even say, but with no provenance I offered the lad ten pounds for the three items. He accepted without bargaining."

Wordlessly Will reached into his pocket for a tenpound note and handed it to the jeweler. "If you should see this young man again, please purchase what he offers you. We will reimburse you."

Now Mr. Rippen looked like he meant to begin weeping. "I was the fool, Mr. Pershing. Please take them back, and I could never ask you to reimb—"

"Simon," Will broke in. "We've all been fooled on occasion. I do not expect you to pay for someone else's dishonesty."

The jeweler's fingers curled around the money, and he brought it up to press against his chest. "I've always said the Pershings are the very best of landlords, and you've proven me right yet again. I shall certainly send word immediately if I set eyes on him, and I apologize for my lapse of judgment. It will not happen again. I swear it."

Emmeline slid her hand around Will's arm again as they walked back into the street. "I think we can agree that that was not a description of George," she said, keeping her voice low, "or of Rose standing on George's shoulders and pretending to be a gentleman."

That image made him snort. "No. I believe we need to have a conversation with James Fletcher."

"And the pearls aren't the only things missing." With a grimace, Emmeline kept hold of his arm as they strolled down the lane. "Do you think the children are involved?"

"I'd say so. This is what they know. He's the one who should have seen this eight weeks for the opportunity it is, rather than risking George and Rose's freedom and their future along with his own."

"I wish they'd told us about him," Emmeline went on.

"They've lived on the streets of London for most of their lives. Even if it wasn't a question of loyalty, I don't doubt there are several unspoken rules about carrying tales."

"I should have realized everything was going too smoothly. Reading, writing, dance, a bit of petty larceny, and now this." She made a face. "I suppose our family-seeking is finished for the day."

At least they'd known something about the pilfering going on behind their backs, though the pearls meant the thefts had escalated far beyond the porcelain-cup level. He and Emmeline had to be the children's best opportunity in ages, if ever, and they were still so accustomed to being self-sufficient that they were unable to stop hoarding goods. And evidently handing them over to James to sell.

"I've been thinking," he said aloud, "about why George created chaos rather than answer our questions about what his ideal future would be. Perhaps it wasn't nefarious. I wonder if imagining a good thing is, for him, a road to disappointment."

She moved in closer against his side. "That makes sense. I wish he'd simply said that instead of trying to begin a war between the two of us, though."

"What would you tell me if I asked you the same question, Emmeline? Where would you put yourself, if you could be anywhere?"

Emmeline paused. For just a moment she shut her eyes, and he wondered what she might be imagining—and whether it included him. Then she opened them again and glanced away, wiping a hand across her cheek. "I think George had the right of it," she murmured, and continued on.

Hmm. Considering that he'd already spent some time imagining the future, and that it included Emmeline as well as George and Rose, he knew what she meant. At the same time, he wanted to know what her perfect world looked like, and if it was at all similar to his.

Bartholomew Powell seated himself at the head of the long kitchen table, and the rest of Winnover Hall's staff, less the three stable boys and Hannah, took their seats on the long benches set at either side. "My friends," he said, as the platter of thin-sliced meats went around the luncheon table, "I'm afraid the time has come to discuss a serious matter."

"Is something amiss, Powell?" Mrs. Brubbins asked. "You have been looking rather pale over the past few days."

"You're ill, Powell?" Sally put her hands to her mouth, her eyes flooding with tears.

"No, I'm not ill. Wipe your tears, Sally, for heaven's sake. While I'm touched by your concern, this isn't about me." The butler took a breath. "I think it's time we have a discreet, honest discussion about the children."

"Is that why you waited until Hannah wasn't about?" Billet commented around a well-buttered slice of bread. "Because you reckon she'd champion the little ones?"

"I didn't know Hannah wouldn't be present until she headed upstairs ten minutes ago," Powell returned, though her absence had somewhat influenced his timing. Hannah might well feel obligated to discuss their private conversation with Mrs. Pershing, and he preferred that not happen.

"What about the children, then?" Mrs. Brubbins asked. "I've never seen anyone enjoy lemon biscuits as much as little Rose does."

"Yes, yes, they like biscuits," Powell said, pushing against his impatience. There were moments when he found the little ones amusing and charming himself, but that didn't erase the rest of the nonsense that surrounded them. "First, discretion. None of this must get back to the Pershings."

"I am not a gossip, Powell," Mrs. Brubbins declared. "None of us are, or the Pershings wouldn't have us here."

Murmured agreements followed that, and he nodded. "Even so." Measuring what he wanted to say, he met the gaze of each member of the staff, daring them to interrupt again. "Have any of you, especially Sally and Lizzy, noticed anything missing from the house? Baubles from shelves, things like that?"

Lizzy and Sally exchanged a glance. "There've been a few things," Sally said slowly. "But the missus is forever shifting decorations, depending on who's visiting the house. You know that."

Davis cleared his throat. "Cuff links," the valet said. "Two pair. I thought I'd left one behind at Pershing House, but now another pair's gone missing. And a hat, the blue beaver. And a shoe. And as of this morning, a scrimshaw box that was dear to Mr. Pershing."

"Why would the children take one shoe?" Mrs. Brubbins demanded.

Kate Brubbins had a very soft heart, and Powell wasn't surprised to hear her defending the youngsters, but facts were facts. "Facts are facts," he said aloud, liking the logic of that thought. "We may not know the reason for something, but we do know something has happened."

"But you don't know for certain who did it," Edward pointed out unhelpfully. "Their brother is here, the ne'er-do-well."

This was the tricky part; he *knew* George, at least, had taken items from the house and put them in his trunk. He'd seen them. But as they'd all been forbidden to look in the damned things, he couldn't admit that he'd done so. He also suspected the older Fletcher, but he couldn't prove anything. "We've all been employed here for years," the butler said aloud. "Edward, you're the last one to be hired, and it's been over four years for you. Nothing—nothing—has ever gone missing before, with the exception of that hand mirror we all know Lady Graham's mother slipped into her reticule."

"Daft old lady," Edward muttered.

"Yes. But if none of us removed an item from its place, and it is no longer there, we have a very limited number of suspects. Three, actually."

"You'd best be certain before you go accusing them," Billet added, still being obvious and unhelpful. "I don't know about the older one, but the Pershings need those babes for the next few weeks."

"I'm aware, Billet. I'm also aware that in six or seven

weeks the Pershings may want all of their pieces of silverware for some occasion or other, and when we can't produce them, *I* will be the one on whose shoulders the blame will fall."

"You're missing silverware," the groom pursued. "What else have *you* noticed, then?"

"Several things. Mainly baubles, as I said, but lately a few items that are rather valuable. If anyone else had noticed additional things gone missing, tell me."

One by one, with clear reluctance, the Winnover Hall staff began to raise their hands. Sally noted that an ebony-wood bird and a pair of candlesticks had gone missing. Donald thought he had mislaid a silver salver. Lizzy thought perhaps a blue john bowl in the library had been moved into the master's private quarters, though she couldn't guess why. Edward couldn't find part of a tea set. "I thought perhaps one of the children broke the cup and didn't want to admit to it," the footman said. "That's to say, I don't know for certain it's been taken. Yesterday I couldn't locate the pot either, though. That doesn't count the set that Fletcher sent to the floor and shattered."

Powell sat and listened. Most of the things he knew about, but not all of them. This was utterly dismaying and unacceptable. "Well. That's that, then."

"That's what, Powell?" Billet asked. "If you accuse the children, it'll be you versus them for the next four weeks. If you tell the Pershings, you'll have them both fretting, and you'll *still* set the young ones against you."

"Yes, yes. You're grand at pointing out difficulties, Billet," Powell finally snapped. "I would much prefer if you had a solution."

"Take the things back," the groom said, finishing off his tea and standing.

"We are forbidden to open the children's chests, so how, pray tell, do you suggest we recover the items?"

"What you and the little ones have, I believe, is a mutual reason to keep things quiet. You can't tell anyone you've gone into their things or you'd have to admit to breaking your word to the Pershings. The children can't complain if you break into their treasure chests because then they'd have to admit that they stole things from the house. It would seem to be a similar situation with Fletcher. Seems fairly straightforward to me. Now, unless you've another problem for me to solve, I have some horses to exercise."

Powell watched the groom go out the kitchen door. By God, it *was* that damned straightforward. He wouldn't be carrying tales about the children, and they wouldn't be able to do anything about the return of their purloined items to their rightful places in the house.

"I believe we have a plan, then," he said, sitting back in his chair to sip his tea.

"But what about the chests?" Sally asked faintly, a frown drawing her generous brows together.

"The children aren't supposed to be robbing the house. We will know what's happened, and they will know. The Pershings will not. This is an extreme action, I know. But our reputations are at stake, as well."

"As you say, then," Mrs. Brubbins muttered. "I don't like it, but it does seem the path that ruffles the fewest feathers."

"Yes, it does." He wished he'd been the one to think of it, but even with his annoying habit of being clever, Billet had done well this time. "And with the children headed out for a riding lesson this afternoon, we will have our opportunity to act. I will empty the chests of any stolen items myself, and will hand them off to whichever member of the staff sees to that area of the household. We must move quickly and precisely. Are we all in agreement?"

The unanimous, if unenthusiastic, ayes were reassuring—it truly would take all of them to see this done successfully and without the Pershings hearing a whisper of any of it. Lord knew the master and mistress of the house already had enough on their plate without him adding to it. His job had always been precisely the opposite of making more trouble, anyway. This was simply a more literal interpretation than usual.

"Did you see me?" Rose asked, flopping down on her very soft bed. "I was trotting!"

"You weren't trotting," Georgie argued, slipping a white beeswax candlestick out of his trousers. "General Jenny was trotting."

"We were trotting together. You should get the other one out of your trousers before it melts."

"I know that. Open your chest; mine's nearly full. We need to give over yesterday's haul to James."

Her trunk was nearly full, too, but she'd found a nice, dark corner of their shared dressing room to use for additional things. "Do you think they'll have riding at the duke's party? I would show very well, I think. And I have a lovely riding habit."

"I don't think so. There's too many people coming." With some frowning and wiggling, he freed the other candlestick. "These are real beeswax, you know. We could get a penny for them. Each, maybe. I think I'll keep hold of these. James won't want 'em, because they ain't worth enough."

"I've been keeping the birds I find. He only throws

them away, anyway." Groaning at the memory, Rose sat up and slid off her bed to unlatch her trunk and lift the lid. "Why would Mama and Papa go to all the trouble of teaching us to ride if we won't even be using it? You have to make more sense, Georgie."

"Don't call them that," he snapped, his voice hard.

"I'm just practicing. You should practice, too."

He walked over to her trunk. "Rose, where did you put your things? You can't hide them all in the hatboxes in the dressing room. These chests are our only safe place. And we need to be able to get the things to James without having to rummage through the house again."

"I only put the lace and handkerchiefs and that white box in the dressing room," she said, and looked down.

Her chest was empty. Not quite empty, because her old clothes from the orphanage were in there, and a few buttons, and the leaf she'd found that was her very favorite color of orange. But all of the findings—as she liked to call them—she'd acquired and kept for herself since leaving St. Stephen's were missing.

"Georgie," she whispered, "I've been snabbled."

"Damnation," he muttered, leaving the candles in the almost empty box and charging into his own bedchamber. A second later he cursed some more. "So have I," he called. "Snabbled rotten. They left the damned coins James didn't take, but everything else is gone."

Oh, this was bad. Very bad. Georgie always said the only thing they could count on was what they had in their own two hands. Now their hands were empty. Gasping, she ran into the dressing room and pulled out the third hatbox from the top. *Oh, thank goodness.* "Georgie, my lace and buttons and the box are still here. That's something, isn't it?"

"I don't care about your stupid buttons, Rosie."

"That's mean," she retorted, stomping into his bed-chamber. "You're as mean as James."

"Don't you see?" he countered, his face very pale. "The Pershings know we stole from them."

"Maybe it was James."

He thought about that for a second. "No, the chests are the best hiding place in the house. He knows that. And he couldn't carry everything at once to go sell it. It had to be the Pershings."

"We only took what we needed."

"That doesn't matter. We stole from rich folk. And they're feeding us and clothing us. We'll be stuffed in a coach going back to the stone jug by nightfall, and with nothing we can sell to run again. I'll wager they'll take the blunt they left behind right in front of us, just to try to make us cry."

She stared at him for a minute, a hundred ugly things going through her head like nightmares in the daytime. "We shouldn't have taken anything." A tear ran down her face, and she didn't care.

"We had to, or we'd just have been stuck again. And James made us take the other things. I'd wager that's when the Pershings noticed. Stupid James."

"I'd rather live on a pig farm than at the stone jug."

Even worse than that, the look on her brother's face told her that the daydreams she'd been having, the ones where Mr. and Mrs. P changed their minds and decided to be their real mama and papa, would never, ever happen. More tears began plopping on her pretty riding habit. Would it still be hers? Or would they have to give back their clothes, too?

"Don't cry, Rose," George said, and walked over to put

his arms around her shoulders. "I'll figure things out. You know I always do."

"But what if James makes us go with him today? We don't even have any biscuits to take with us."

A knock sounded at her door. Oh no, it was time to stuff them in a coach already. And she hadn't even had a chance to say goodbye to General Jenny, who really was a very nice pony, and she would miss her terribly.

"Rose?"

It was Mrs. P's voice. Rose gasped. "I'm not ready to leave yet, Georgie," she whispered.

"Rose?" The door opened. "Oh, there you . . . What in the world is the matter, my dear?" Her fake mama glided into George's room, then hurried forward and sank to her knees in front of Rose. "Please, tell me. Has someone frightened you? Been mean to you?"

So many things were wrong, and James had been very mean. "I—"

"She bit her tongue," Georgie said, before she could ask if she could keep her dresses. He hugged Rose very hard, then let her go. "She doesn't like it when she cries."

Well, that wasn't really true, because she was very good at crying when they were pretending things so people would give them money. But George knew that, which meant he was up to something. Which meant . . . what? She looked up at him, and he frowned at her from behind Mrs. P's back, angling his chin toward their fake mama.

"Yeth, I bit my tongue," she said. "It hurths."

"Well. Let's get you out of your riding habit and we'll go downstairs for some lemonade. That'll help, I imagine." Standing, she offered her hand.

Rose took it. "Yeth, I think tho. Thank you, Mama."

Something had happened. Mrs. P wasn't mad at them. She didn't seem any different at all, really. So, if the Pershings didn't know about the findings she and Georgie had taken, who had snabbled them?

CHAPTER EIGHTEEN

Mrs. P hadn't acted like she knew they'd been stealing things.

That meant two things, as far as George was concerned: first, they might not be sent away on the first coach headed to London after all; and second, that someone else had gotten into his and Rose's chests after the Pershings had given their word that that wouldn't happen.

For a second he wondered if it might have been James, impatient for his next haul of baubles. But he'd been correct when he'd said their chests were a better hiding place than any James had in the house. Plus, James knew their things were in there, and if he'd wanted something to sell he would have just come in and taken it. He wouldn't have taken everything.

Who, then? Donald and Edward both talked to him and especially Rosie like they were babies, but they seemed to like working at Winnover Hall. Breaking promises didn't seem like a good idea for a fart-catcher who liked catching farts.

If someone from outside had broken in, then he and Rosie wouldn't be the only ones to be snabbled. He'd listen for that, to see if anything else was missing, even if he didn't think a real housebreaker would have left behind near five quid in coins. That made him frown as they went downstairs for lemonade.

But if whoever had taken their things didn't say anything to the Pershings, it also meant that Rosie and he had a chance to gather more supplies before the time did come for them to make a run for it. They just had to be smarter and more careful about protecting their finds. And explain to James why nothing would be going in his pockets today.

As he sat down, he caught sight of the black wood bird on a table in the corner. He knew Rose had nabbed it, because he'd seen it in her trunk the day before. And yet there it was. George turned his head. The fancy book with the colored drawings inside was back on its shelf, too, and just a few hours ago it had been wrapped in cloth inside his trunk waiting to go to James. *What the devil?*

Powell knocked at the door and walked in, Donald behind him carrying a tray with glasses and a pitcher of lemonade. While the footman poured and handed out the drinks, the butler looked at George. George looked back at him.

"Is there anything else I can get you?" Powell asked, turning from George to look at the table in the corner, the mantel, and then the bookcase with the painted book before he looked back at George again. Then he lifted one tufty eyebrow and turned away.

The butler had done it. Powell, the stuffy, patchy-pated, stiff-spined pantler, had snuck into his and Rosie's bedchambers, opened their trunks when the Pershings had told everyone not to do that, and snabbled all of the goods they hadn't already given to James. And he hadn't even kept them or sold them. He'd just put them all back.

Even with James's share handed over, he and his sister had managed to sneak a lot of things into their trunks.

Because whether they were family or not, he recalled quite clearly when James had vanished without a thought for them the second the Bow Street Runner had appeared that day. He'd never trusted his brother's word, even before the rats.

George took a slow breath, letting the realization that they weren't about to be booted out of Winnover Hall fill him up. It felt like a warm breeze. They didn't have to leave. Not yet, and not until they had time to finish their lessons and meet the duke. Unless James got mad and dragged them off, that was.

Powell had put them back to five quid, plus the things Rose had hidden in that hatbox. Their trunks weren't safe any longer. He wouldn't put it past Powell to search their entire bedchambers—the entire house, even—if something went missing again. And he and Rose needed to snabble more things. Or the same things again.

Therefore, they needed a better place to hide them, and James should probably find another one himself. Luckily, George had been figuring out his way around adults for his entire life. He glanced over at Mrs. P and Rose, currently chatting about lemonade and why sour things made their mouths pucker up. He was glad Rose had some time to be a little girl and not worry about anything but how fast she could spin without falling over.

Maybe it was good James had come. It reminded him that this place, being able to sleep soundly and eat as much as he wanted, was only temporary. At the end, either he and Rose would leave on their own, or James would make them go with him. The worst choice would be to go to some family who didn't want them anyway. There was no fourth choice, and whatever he might think about on occasion, there would never be a fourth choice.

* * *

"Ah, James. There you are."

Will strolled into the billiards room as the oldest Fletcher scattered balls all across the table. "I had a shot lined up," the lad grumbled. "You startled me."

"My apologies, then. I only wanted to mention that we've evidently had neighbor children or squirrels in the house; some of Emmeline's jewelry has gone missing. If you've come up missing anything yourself, let me know. Hopefully it won't occur again, but I will keep an eye out."

James leaned on the cue stick, smugness radiating from every inch of him. "I'll be sure to tell you if I see any squirrels wearing gemstones, or young lads in pearls."

Mentioning pearls wasn't a confession, but gaining one hadn't been Will's intention. Not today. Young Mr. Fletcher had been made aware that the Pershings knew things had been taken. If he had any sense, he would stop stealing—or stop encouraging it. He might even realize he could be considered a suspect. At best, this little chat would frighten him away, and he would vanish into the night without his siblings.

As he left the room, Will rolled his shoulders. The moment he heard back from his friends in London, the moment he could be certain that James Fletcher had no right to make off with George and Rose, he would remove the proverbial gloves holding him back from direct accusations and a visit to the constabulary. That was, of course, if the news was what he hoped for. If James could indeed claim his siblings, that would mean an entirely different set of problems—both for him and Emmeline, and for George and Rose. The idea of having to watch them slip back into a life of poverty and crime with nothing he could do to prevent it, with no opportunity to find something better for them . . . "No," he muttered, heading for the stairs to see if the day's mail had yet been delivered. "No."

Hannah Redcliffe let out a sigh, then set aside young Rose's bonnet. With the ribbon reattached, it looked fresh and pink and good as new, as long as the girl didn't return to running through the garden and towing the hat behind her like a kite.

"You've had a sight more work to do, these last days," Mrs. Brubbins observed, giving the bonnet an approving nod as she made her way from the larder to the cutting board, an armful of carrots held against her bosom.

"I suppose I have, but I'm enjoying it," Hannah said, moving on to sew a loose hem in one of the girl's pink gowns. "I'm frightfully busy when we're in London, but the year slows down so much when we're at Winnover. The children have . . . livened thing up, haven't they?"

The cook chuckled. "I'd agree with that. They're still eating like no one's ever fed them before, poor things. I've had to send Molly down to the village again today for an extra five pounds of sugar just for all the sweets I'm baking."

"I've been enjoying those treats of yours far too much myself," Hannah said, grinning. "I may have to let out my own dresses if this continues much longer."

Mrs. Brubbins's smile faded. "Less than four weeks till they ride off to Cumberland, isn't it? A shame, really. Even with all the tomfoolery, there's been so much smiling and laughter here, it'll seem quiet as a mausoleum after they're gone."

The small clock in the hallway chimed ten times, and

Hannah set her sewing back in her basket. "Yes, it will, but we haven't arrived to that point yet. And I've been invited by the little ones to go apple picking."

"Bring me a dozen, will you? I'll bake up a pie or two for tonight."

Nodding, Hannah left the kitchen and trotted up the short hallway, through the door, and into the main part of the house. Hannah liked Mrs. Brubbins, just as she liked Powell and Davis and Edward and Donald and Sally and Lizzy and Tom Billet and the other staff here and at Pershing House in London.

The Pershings expected a well-run, efficient, and effective household, and the servants had long ago learned that performing as a unit made things go much more smoothly. They relied on each other, everyone did their duty and carried their weight, and as a result, the Pershing household was universally praised and admired. She couldn't count the number of barely disguised invitations she'd received to serve in other London households. She'd never even been tempted.

"There you are, Hannah," Rose said, and immediately handed over an enormous basket nearly half the girl's size. "Powell said we could use whichever baskets we wanted, but I've never picked apples, so I think we should be ready for anything," she went on by way of explanation.

"That's very sensible," Hannah returned. "I have a request from Mrs. Brubbins for a dozen apples. Is it to be just the three of us?"

George, another giant basket draped over one of his skinny elbows, nodded. "The Pershings are going to Birdlip again. I don't know why, because they didn't tell us."

"Ah." They hadn't told her, either. She wished they had;

the shawl Mrs. Pershing had with her this morning was probably too heavy for a walk in the sun.

"Let's go. I heard that worms get in apples in the morning, and I don't want any worms in mine." Rose wrinkled her nose.

"If you do find any worms, let me know," George put in. "It'll save me from having to dig 'em up and learn more things about soil from Mr. P."

"If you're going to be living in the country, it's important to learn about soil." Hannah smiled. "Though, honestly, I don't know much about it myself."

Powell pulled open the front door, practically waving them outside. "Have fun, sir, miss, Hannah," he said, and closed them out of the house.

"I don't think Powell likes us," Rose observed, skipping down the drive.

"I think he has a broomstick stuck up his arse," George contributed.

"He likes order," Hannah offered. "This has been an unusual autumn for him."

"Because of us. I know." The girl veered around the side of the house toward the stable.

"Miss Rose, the orchard is on the other side of the house, past the pond," Hannah pointed out.

"Oh yes. But I need to know how many apples Billet needs for the horses."

At the mention of the groom's name, and before she'd realized what she was doing, Hannah put her hand up to check her hair. Immediately she lowered it again. Since she didn't have hooves and her hair didn't look like a mane, Tom Billet wouldn't even look in her direction. She knew that for a fact, because she'd been looking in his for the past three years. *Stupid, thickheaded man.*

"Billet!" It took two tries for Rose to get herself and

her giant basket through the stable door, but she finally made it inside, Hannah and George close behind her. "Billet, how many apples do you need for the horses? We're going to pick some."

The head groom emerged from the tack room. Cleaning his hands with a rag, he took in the three of them standing there with their absurdly giant baskets. "The horses are mighty fond of apples," he noted, a smile just pulling at the corners of his mouth. "I'd say thirty, if you can manage that many."

"Oh, we can manage that many." Rose dropped her basket, putting the handle over her shoulder when she picked it up again. "Do you think thirty apples weigh a lot?"

Billet tossed his rag into a bucket. "What say I join you? I reckon I can tote a basket or two, and that'll leave your hands free for picking."

"That would be good," George said.

Well. New surprises every day. George had made no secret of his antagonism toward the groom since the day Billet had found them in mid-escape in Birdlip. Her suspicions aroused, Hannah glanced at the groom, to find him looking at her, one eyebrow raised. She had no idea what to say, because the first thing that came to mind was to thank Rose for deciding the horses should have apples.

"No arguments, then?" Billet asked, finally turning his gaze back to the boy.

"No," George answered. "Rose found enormous baskets, and I don't want to have to carry hers and mine and Hannah's back from the orchard."

"Well, it looks like you have a use for me, then." Chuckling, Billet picked up a horse blanket, then ushered them out of the stable.

With Rose leading the way, they traipsed through the

garden and around the right side of the pond. The grove consisted of fifty or so apple trees, with the fruit available to anyone from the estate, neighboring farms, or the village to come and take as they chose. That still left a great many apples for pies, horse snacks, and treats for the local deer and other wildlife in the area.

"Look at them all! Georgie, have you ever seen so many apples?"

"No, I ain't."

"Don't pick up the ones from the ground unless they're for the horses," Hannah advised, as Rose began piling apples into her basket. "Those will be the ones most likely to have worms."

"Ew!" Immediately the little girl tipped out her basket again. "But I can't reach the ones still on the trees. Are there ladders? I'm good at climbing."

"Not necessary," Billet said, and spread the blanket beneath one of the trees. "That's where this comes in." Picking up a broken branch, he trimmed off a couple of twigs with a boot knife, then poked it up into the tree. Shoving it against a laden branch, he used it to shake a score of apples off the tree and onto the blanket.

"Oh, that's brilliant!" Rose exclaimed, scampering to retrieve the new-fallen apples. "I want to try that next!"

"I'll do it," George countered. "I'm stronger."

While the children argued over "the shaking stick," as they named it, and went about dragging the blanket from tree to tree and knocking down apples, Billet strolled over to stand beside Hannah where she'd taken a seat on a stump. "Well done," she said, smiling at him.

He inclined his head. "I'm an apple thief from way back. Besides, we don't want them climbing the trees and ruining their fancy clothes. That would mean more mending for you to do, aye?"

"Yes, it would. I don't mind, though. I'm glad they're able to have adventures. My childhood wasn't terribly exciting, but I had both my parents and the occasional picnic, and once we even went to see the Royal Menagerie. Those lions were massive; they still give me the shivers."

Squatting down on the ground beside where she sat, Tom Billet plucked a stem of grass from the ground and stuck one end between his teeth. He wore a brown and gray vest, the sleeves of his plain white shirt rolled up to his elbows and revealing sinewy forearms that looked much more attractive than arms should. "You're from Town, then?" he asked. "London?"

"Yes. Born and bred. You?"

"Hereabouts. My parents have a farm about halfway between Birdlip and Great Witcombe."

"You said something about having a great many brothers and sisters." He hadn't said it to her, actually, but it had only taken a little bit of coaxing to get Mrs. Pershing to relay the details of her conversation with the groom.

"Ten of us, there are. And not enough work to keep us all at home," he conceded, nodding. "What of you? Brothers or sisters?"

"Two younger sisters. Meg married a pastor and they moved to Chelmsford two years ago. I see her at Christmastime. Jane still lives with Mama and Papa."

His paying attention to her made her feel twittery and fluttery, and she took a slow breath to remind herself not to giggle or otherwise sound insipid. Her . . . infatuation, she supposed it was, didn't make sense, anyway. He worked in the stable, even if he was the head groom, while she had a privileged place in the great house. His large hands were calloused, his eyes had fine lines in the corners from squinting in the sun, and he smelled of hay and horses.

But they were just chatting, for heaven's sake, while the children picked apples. There was no harm in chatting, certainly. "Are any of your siblings married?"

"Five of them are. The youngest four aren't yet grown, but my mama's a fine hand at seeing us married off. She'll say, 'It's time,' and three weeks later whoever she's pointed at will find themselves standing in front of the pastor." He grinned. "I think she might be a witch."

Chuckling, Hannah looked at him all over again. He'd been employed at Winnover for five years now, and had improved upon what had already been a well-run stable. A capable man, as well as a handsome and well-built one. "Did she never point at you, then?"

His cheeks reddened a little, and he ducked his head. "Oh, she pointed at me."

"You must tell me. What happened?"

Blue eyes met hers. "I'll have to let you know."

Goodness. Had that been a flirtation? Had he just flirted with her? Heat flooded her face, and she made a show of standing and picking an apple to give herself a moment to think. A groom. If he hadn't been as handsome as Apollo and clever to boot, she wouldn't have been having any kind of conversation with herself about him, but he was, and so she was.

Hannah cleared her throat as she sat again. "Is this where you want to stay?" she asked.

"Here at Winnover, you mean? I like it here, and the Pershings are kind and generous—and they have high expectations. It makes me hold my head a little higher, knowing they're pleased with the work I do."

"I know what you mean." And yes, even though some of the work she did was exacting and tiring, it was also appreciated, and she was well compensated for it. In addition, there was the satisfaction in giving a sound "no, thank you" to the Society ladies who had tried to lure her away from Mrs. Pershing and into their employ. "I feel very lucky, sometimes."

"Aye. Lucky." Now he smiled at her, and she wanted to just look at his mouth and imagine how his lips would feel on hers. The idea that this wasn't a daydream, that he was actually squatting on the ground beside her, talking to her and looking at her with those . . . eyes, was both glorious and terrifying. What might happen next? What did she want to happen next? What . . .

Hannah shook herself out of her hazy thoughts. Around them birds sang in the trees, insects buzzed lazily, a few frogs croaked from the edge of the pond, and in the distance, she could hear cows mooing. Quiet, idyllic, and pastoral. *Quiet.* She shot to her feet. "Where are the children?"

Tom Billet straightened beside her. "Little damblers," he muttered. "You look by the pond. I'll check in the direction of the road."

"Do you think they've run again? Oh no. I'll be sacked!"

"They haven't run," he countered. "They went somewhere."

"How do you—"

"Whatever they've got in their heads, I'd wager a month's pay they wouldn't do anything that would get them sent back to the orphanage. That doesn't mean they aren't up to something, though."

"But what would they be up to in the apple orchard?" Gathering her skirts in her hands, she hurried toward the pond. "Miss Rose! Master George!"

"Something they don't want us to know about," he said as he veered off to the left. "They're close by; I'd wager on it."

While she didn't know what a dambler was, she imagined it had something to do with being rascals or rogues,
which the Fletcher children were. They were also darlings,
and while she couldn't quite reconcile the two sides of them
yet, she was certain that she didn't want anything bad to
happen to them. At this moment she was also annoyed
that they'd either arranged for her and Tom to distract
each other while they scampered off, or their departure
had managed to interrupt the most interesting conversation she'd ever had. Little damblers, indeed.

Rose peeked around the edge of the fallen tree. "They're
still making moon eyes at each other," she said, sitting
back to blink her lashes.

"Good. Let me know when they notice we're gone."
Keeping his voice at a whisper, George continued digging
beneath the log. It was a little too close to the house and
the stable to make a perfect stash hole, but it was out of
Powell's territory. James had his own hiding place, about
which he hadn't enlightened them. So this was only fair
play. They needed a place to put things, and the orchard
provided its own excuse for frequent visits.

When he decided he'd made the hole deep enough, he
pulled a sackcloth out from under his shirt and lined
the bottom of the hole with it. "Give me your things," he
whispered.

His sister sat sideways, lifting her skirt to dig into the
top of her stockings. The buttons, beads, and green ribbon she handed over weren't precisely valuables, but they
meant something to her. Carefully he set them on the
cloth. "Is that all you brought?"

"Just a minute." Twisting, she pulled a pair of silver

spoons and a fork from the hem of her dress. A carved bird followed those, though he had no idea where she'd hidden that. "That's all I could fit. Are you sure James won't be mad?"

"He doesn't want birds, anyway. And if he gets nicked or runs, we need to have our own treasures. Are they still talking?"

As she checked on Hannah and Billet, George pulled the blue john stone bowl from his pocket and set it into the hole. Powell could look for it all he wanted, but the butler would never find it this time. His other pocket held more silverware and some coins, along with the yellow rock with the mosquito inside it that he'd found at Pershing House and rediscovered in the Winnover library. It wasn't a lot, but they'd only one day to nick things for a brother who wanted gems and silver and was going to be mad already because they'd been avoiding him since yesterday afternoon, and furious after they told him they'd been robbed of their stolen goods. All that with a household staff that knew they'd all been outsmarted once. Grown-ups hated being tricked, especially twice.

"They're standing up," Rose hissed in her version of a whisper. "And they didn't even kiss!"

"Hush, Rosie. Help me cover this up."

He folded the cloth over their treasures, then piled dirt on it. Rose added some fallen leaves and twigs, until he was fairly certain no one would walk by and notice anything unusual. Then he took his sister's hand and, keeping low, hurried toward the road that led to the village.

"Remember, you saw a bunny and chased it, and I chased you," he informed her.

"That's silly of me, but very well."

They entered a small glade, and he let her hand go.

"This is a good spot. You think the rabbit went in there," he said, pointing at a thicket, "and you're not listening to me telling you that we need to go back to the apples."

"I'm very wicked," she observed, but obligingly went down onto her hands and knees to peer into the thicket.

"Come along, Rosie," he said in his normal voice, trying to sound a little annoyed. "We need to get back. We promised apples to Mrs. Brubbins and Billet."

"I'm not listening to you," Rose returned. "I'm finding a rabbit."

"You're going to get your dress dirty."

At that she stood up, looking down to brush at the green gown where dirt showed across her knees. "Dash it, Georgie! I don't want to ruin my dress."

Brush rustled behind them. "Then you shouldn't go crawling after rabbits," he improvised. "You're going to get us in trouble."

"There you are," Billet said, stepping around an oak tree and into the glade. "What are you doing down here?"

"I saw a bunny," Rosie said, still brushing at her gown. "I tried not to get my dress dirty."

The groom folded his arms over his chest. "A bunny," he repeated skeptically.

"Yes. We don't have bunnies in London. Just squirrels. And they bite."

Oh, that was a nice touch. Rosie tended to see things the way she wanted them to be, but she could spin a good tale when they needed one. "Did you think we ran again?" he asked, folding his own arms just like Billet.

The groom narrowed his eyes. "No. Not with less than four weeks until you meet the duke." He looked from George to Rose. "Did you stash something hereabouts?"

There were times George almost liked going up against the groom, because Billet knew things. At other times, though, he reckoned the groom knew too many things. "Did we?" he returned, narrowing his own eyes.

Billet sighed. "None of my affair. If you or anyone else nicks something from the stable, though, I'm going to fill your shoes with horse shite."

"You said shite," Rose observed. "In the presence of a lady."

His jaw twitched. "My apologies, Miss Rose. If you nick something from my stable, I'll fill your shoes with manure. Do you believe me?"

For a moment George weighed what he'd been learning about servants against what he'd observed of the head groom. Finally, he nodded. "We won't nick anything from the stable." He'd have to inform James, but there wasn't much there he wanted, anyway, except maybe for the ponies. If they did nick Apple and General Jenny, though, his and Rose's shoes would be on their feet while they rode for Gloucester. George sighed inwardly. Or York, blast it all.

"Good," the groom said. "Now, let's get you back. You scared Miss Hannah."

"I like Hannah," Rose declared, allowing herself to be nudged back toward the apple grove. "She helps me choose pretty thread colors, and she doesn't try to make us learn things."

"I thought you liked learning things," Billet countered, falling in behind them.

"I do, but only some things. Dancing is good, even though we still haven't done enough waltzing, and I like fencing. Embroidery is horrible. And so is sewing."

"I believe Hannah is a fine seamstress. You might ask her to give you a few pointers."

"Oh, I have."

They passed by the fallen tree, which George made a

point not to look at. It was just a tree, and there were a lot of trees. Behind him, though, Billet's footsteps slowed a little. "Can a falling apple kill someone?" George asked quickly.

The footsteps resumed. "I suppose, if it cracked some-one right on the skull. An apple falling on him is how Sir Isaac Newton discovered gravity, though, and it didn't kill him, so who knows?"

"What's gravity?" Rose asked.

"It's the thing that makes apples fall when you let them go. Without gravity, I reckon we'd all be floating about in the sky."

"Like birds? I don't want gravity, then."

"I don't think you have a choice, Miss Rose."

"Well, that's stupid."

"Oh, thank goodness!" Hannah came running toward them, a frown on her face. "Where in the world did you go? I thought you might have fallen in the pond, or some-thing."

"Why does everyone think we've fallen in the pond?" Rose asked, a scowl bringing her eyebrows together.

"Rose saw a bunny," her brother explained.

"A bunny." Hannah took a breath. "Well, there are a great many bunnies here on the property. Perhaps we can go look for some another day. Today we promised apples to people, and we need to give Mrs. Brubbins enough time to bake her pies. And remember, no worms."

"No worms," Rose echoed.

George sent another glance at Billet, but the groom was busy looking at the lady's maid, and didn't seem to care if they *had* stashed something from the house. And Han-nah was too distracted by the head groom to be suspicious of anything. That mutual distraction had been what he'd hoped for when he'd told Rose to pick baskets that were too big for them to carry, but grown-ups didn't always co-operate.

Now they just needed to arrange a few more trips out to the orchard, and they would have enough here to support them in case James ran off with their valuables—if they ever got them back. He wished James *would* run off, because the Pershings were . . . nice, and he didn't like taking their precious things. The two of them only needed small things, because with some blunt it wouldn't matter who the Pershings might find to be their new parents, or how many times Powell—or James—raided their treasure chests.

Whoever their fake parents found, they wouldn't be better than what he and Rosie had found here. And if it couldn't be here—which it couldn't, of course—then someone needed to look after Rose's best interests. Just giving people money to be their parents wouldn't work; he'd seen the nuns take the money donated to them and use it to buy chairs and beds and plump chickens that the children never got to see, much less use or eat.

And it was James's fault they'd ended up at the stone jug the last time, anyway. If James had stayed and distracted the beaks, he and Rosie might have gotten away. No, he had no intention of trusting anyone but himself where his and his sister's future was concerned. Nothing good had yet happened from trusting anyone. Even if sometimes he thought about it.

None of that mattered, though, because eventually the Pershings *would* realize that some of their very valuable things were missing. They would make a stink about it, and Powell would say he'd known all along, and had been doing his best to put things back where they belonged.

That would be the excuse they needed to break the agreement and send Rose and him back to St. Stephen's the minute the duke's party was over. At least this way he knew it was coming, and he'd prepared both for that, and for James dragging them away. The only question right now was who was going to lie first—or at least which of them would be caught at it first.

CHAPTER NINETEEN

Looking up from his desk as Emmeline walked into his office, Will sent her a grim smile. "You'll be relieved to know that my pistol hasn't yet gone missing, but the pocket watch Liverpool gifted me is gone. That was engraved, damn it all."

"I have no gold jewelry left. They even pilfered that giant red campion brooch from my aunt Hetty, and I had that ugly thing stashed in the back corner of my unmentionables drawer."

Will opened a drawer and pulled out a letter. "It's not all bad news. I just got word back from London. James Fletcher spent some time at Newgate Prison, and was released to become an informant on his fellow thieves. Evidently he hasn't been seen since."

"Thank God." Emmie grimaced. "That doesn't sound very charitable of me, does it?"

"I nearly began dancing."

"That's truly it then, isn't it?" She sank into the chair opposite his desk with an ease he hadn't seen in her for years. Was she becoming more comfortable with him? With the idea that they weren't merely partners, but a married couple? He hoped so, because he'd had to get out of bed twice last evening to splash his front with cold water. And that had been just from thinking about her. "If he ran, then no doubt the magistrate would be happy to see him again. And they'd never trust him to raise young children."

"I would think not." He sighed. "There is still, however, the chance that if we approach this the wrong way, he might take George and Rose and flee with them, anyway—whether he has a legal right to do so or not."

"I agree. As much as I'd like to be present when you boot him out of the house, it'll be safer for the children if Hannah and I—and Edward and Donald—go close ourselves in the conservatory after dinner, at which time you . . . go boot him."

Will nodded. She'd chosen the largest room in the house with locks on the doors, of course. Practical, smart, and quick-witted, she was. "I would say we should inform the children first, but since we've already decided not to report him to the law, which is likely what would worry them, I propose that we see to his exit and then let them know."

She sighed. "I wish we could prepare them. He is their only family. They may not react well to his departure."

"I'll risk it. His absence will be the best thing he could do for them." He pocketed the letter on the chance that the one Fletcher who could read a bit might find it before they were ready. "If necessary, I suppose we could resort to bribery again."

"Ah. Puppies?"

Will snorted. "Hopefully it won't come to that."

"Yes." Humor touched her face. "A few weeks ago, I would have been horrified at the idea of a houseguest robbing us. Now we have three of them doing it, and my first thought is how to protect two of them."

"You, my dear, are not alone in that."

"I'm pleased to hear it."

"What do you mean, 'snabbled'?" James glanced past George toward the far side of the drawing room, where Powell was replacing the old flower bouquets with new ones. "You got outsmarted by *him*?"

"He's tougher than he looks," George grumbled, not looking at all happy.

"Or you're not as clever as you thought," James retorted. "What's he doing in here, anyway?"

Rose looked. "Powell is the butler. He makes certain everything is where it should be. Even us," she said. "And some of our findings."

"Maybe it's time for Powell to fall down the stairs, then," James muttered.

"Don't say that." George frowned at their brother. "He's stuffy and a bother, but he could've told the Pershings, and he didn't."

"Not yet he hasn't, but we can't be certain he won't. Pershing's already sniffing at me, damn it all. This is on you two." James said some more curse words, the kind she and George weren't allowed to say in the house. Rose almost told him that, but telling James what not to do had never been a good idea.

"We'll just snabble them back," George whispered.

"You'll have to. We've got eight quid between us, and that's not enough to rent a room for more than six months."

Rose cocked her head. "George said you had twenty-five quid the other day."

"Shut it, Rosie. I nearly had us fifty quid until that

damned coachman drove in and took all my luck with him."

She'd heard about people taking his luck before, mostly after she'd spent a good day dancing while James and George dipped into pockets. James would go out to buy them a real supper, and then come back hours later with bread—or nothing at all—and say someone had stolen his luck. "You went and played gambling," she said.

He curled up his fist, looked over at Powell again, and opened his fingers. "You two are finding me stupid little things. I have to do something to turn our money into more money."

"I already got you pearl earbobs like you said," she protested. "And now all of our own things are gone. We have less than you."

James leaned forward, turning his face to look at George. "*Your* things? *My* things. I'm the leader here. And if you've been keeping baubles back, I'm going to thrash you, Georgie. Do you hear me?"

George looked straight back at him. "I hear you."

"Good. I want at least five quid worth of things by tomorrow. Or maybe I'll just decide it's time for us all to leave and we can go back to London. It's not like the Pershings could stop me. You two belong to me. The sooner you understand that, the better."

"If we go back to London and we get nabbed again, they'll transport us," George said, his expression grim. "Back there's St. Stephen's. And Newgate. You don't want to go back to Newgate, James."

James stood up. "Let's go for a walk, shall we?" he said with his big smile.

Rose didn't really want to go for a walk, because her legs were already tired from apple picking, but if

James was going to yell, he should do it outside where he wouldn't break the agreement with his slanging and cursing. She followed him toward the door.

"Where are you off to, Master George, Miss Rose?" Powell asked, turning to face them.

"Just going to get some biscuits," James said. Then he reached sideways and with his hand brushed two vases with flowers in them off the side table. "Mind your own business, pantler," he said, grinning as water and roses and glass went all over the floor.

"You shouldn't have done that," Rose said, frowning. "Powell just finished those."

"And now he ain't snooping after us, is he? I almost had a painting from the attic this morning, until he came waddling up to look for some damned thing or other."

With Powell gone they had to open the front door themselves, and then they circled around toward the garden. Rose hoped they weren't going to one of the follies, because she'd already gotten lost in there once.

"Where are we going?" George asked.

James grabbed George by the arm and tucked him up under his shoulder. "To the garden, Georgie. Where nobody'll be listening to us. Because we have a problem here, and we need to figure out a solution before it's too late."

That made sense, at least, and James didn't look as mad as he did before. "We should pick some more flowers for Powell," Rose said, pirouetting into the lead.

"Why don't we start with you asking me that question again, Georgie?" James said, walking faster and passing Rose up again. George had to keep up, because James still had one arm around his neck and shoulder.

"Which question?" George asked, pushing against James's ribs. "Let go, James."

"The one about whether I wanted to go back to New-gate or not."

"I didn't mean anything by it. You said before that you weren't ever going back there. If we're not in London, it would be easier to not be nabbed and sent there, don't you think?"

"What I think, Georgie, is that you should keep your damned mouth shut. You aren't nearly as clever as you think you are, whelp. And—"

"Children?" Hannah came up from behind them. She looked out of breath, like she'd been hurrying to catch up. "Oh, good. You're late for your embroidery lessons, Miss Rose, and Master George, Mr. Pershing has found his atlas for your geography lesson."

James stopped and let the maid catch up to them. "What is it, Hannah?" he murmured. "You think I'll hurt the boy? My own brother?" He shifted his grip, grabbing George by the wrist, and half dragged him up to Hannah. "Or are the little ones an excuse for you to chat with me? I've had my eye on you, you know."

Hannah stepped back a little. "I'm . . . I'm just here to collect the children, Mr. Fletcher."

"I don't think the Pershings sent you at all." James moved up closer again. "I think you came out here all on your own, just to see me."

"She said we have lessons," George muttered, trying to pull his hand away.

They didn't have embroidery or geography lessons right now, because today was manners, but Rose didn't say that. This was not good. She and George had made James mad. And now he was mad at Hannah, too, just for trying to help them. "Stop it, James," she said, "or I'll scream."

"If you scream, I'll throw you in a rosebush," he retorted.

Those thorns would hurt. She closed her mouth, trying to think where everyone was. The Pershings were probably in the breakfast room getting ready for good and bad manners practice. She couldn't see the gardeners. Billet and the grooms were the closest, then. "No, you won't," she shouted, and ran.

James Fletcher grabbed for his sister, and with a quick breath Hannah shoved him in the shoulder. He stumbled, and the little girl vanished behind the corner folly. When he straightened again, he grabbed for her, too, but Hannah ducked away from him.

"Let George go now, please," she said, wishing she could keep her voice steadier. If she hadn't glimpsed them out the library window and been suspicious . . . Oh, this could still be very bad.

"Don't worry, Hannah. I'll let him go. We're just having a chat. Aren't we, George?"

"Let me go, James. Then we can talk." The boy tried to yank his arm free again, and skidded onto one knee.

James bent, grabbed on to George's leg, and hefted him into the air. Taking a dozen strides forward, he heaved George forward—and threw him into the pond. "What did you want to talk about, Georgie?" he called. "I can't quite make it out!"

Hannah screamed as the boy went under. Flailing, he grabbed on to a handful of reeds, but they came loose in his hand and he submerged again. "George!"

"I can't sw—" He went under again.

James stood there, laughing, as his brother splashed and sputtered. She wanted to kick him, punch him, but she didn't want to end up in the water herself. Instead, she ran for the dock and the punting pole lying across the small boat.

A hand grabbed her shoulder. "He won't learn his lesson if you get him out too soon."

"Let me go!"

"Not so fast, sweet Hann—"

Billet leaped over the hedgerow and plowed into James, knocking him flat on his face. "Hands off, you bastard," the groom growled, rolling to his feet.

"The pond!" Hannah yelled, pointing. "George!"

Leaving James where he'd fallen, Tom Billet sprinted to the edge of the water, throwing off his coat as he went. He didn't dive, but waded in, reaching out toward the boy. "Calm now, scamp," he said. "Johnny, keep Mr. Fletcher there on the ground."

The two stable boys had arrived just behind Tom, she realized. Johnny, a pitchfork in his hands, stood over James and aimed the tines at the young man's chest. "Stay right there, you."

Finally, up past his shoulders, Billet caught hold of George. Drawing him close, he backed up, keeping the boy high and tight against his chest. "I've got you, George. Slow breaths, lad."

Abruptly Mr. Pershing was there, as well, wading in after them without hesitation, despite his fine boots. Powell and Mrs. Pershing were right behind him, and most of the rest of the staff after them. "Where's Rose?" Mrs. Pershing demanded, her voice tight.

"Roger's with her at the stable, ma'am," Johnny said. "Billet told them to hold for a whistle before they came over here."

Tom managed to turn around, facing the shore, and he handed the boy off to Mr. Pershing before he stumbled out of the reeds. For God's sake. Hannah had known he had a good head on his shoulders, and a better education than a groom might strictly require, but what he'd just done was much more than those parts. When he straightened up again, his thin shirt wet and clinging to his wellmuscled chest, her heart started pounding all over again.

"I'll get Rose," Hannah volunteered with a squeak.

Mr. Pershing gave her a nod, and then Mrs. and Mr. Pershing and most of the household staff hurried back into the house, George still in Mr. Pershing's arms. Billet, shaking water out of his hair, walked straight up to her. "Did he hurt you, Hannah?"

She shook her head. Her tongue seemed to have swollen up so she couldn't get a coherent word out.

"I saw you trying for the pole. That was quick thinking."

"You were quick thinking," she managed.

His mouth curved. "I'll go with you to fetch Rose," he offered. "She'll be scared about her brother."

"What about Fletcher here?" Johnny asked.

"Oh, I reckon Mr. Pershing will want a word with him. Keep him there."

Will sat George in a chair at the kitchen table. The boy had already coughed up a good portion of the pond, but he seemed to be breathing well now. "Does your chest hurt?" he asked, squatting in front of him.

"No." George coughed again. "I saw a fish when I was under water."

"That's very observant of you. Can you tell me what happened?"

The boy's eyes narrowed a little. "Ask James. I don't remember," he said.

"Mm-hmm. Mrs. Brubbins, perhaps some cake might be called for."

George straightened up, coughing again. "I think cake would help, yes. Definitely. Where's Rosie?"

"I'm here," his sister said, hurrying into the kitchen with Hannah and Billet.

Will straightened and Emmeline took his place, holding the boy's hand and kissing his temple. "What the devil happened?" he asked the maid, keeping his voice pitched low.

"I'm not certain," Hannah said, answering him. "I was in the library fetching books, and I saw the three of them out in the garden. James had his arm around George's head. It . . . bothered me, so I went out after them." Tears filled her eyes. "I hope I didn't make it worse, but Rose ran, and I hit James, and then he picked George up and just . . . just threw him as far as he could into the pond."

"The sprite came running up, bellowing that James was killing George in the garden," Billet took up. "We ran that way, and I saw Fletcher shoving Hannah while she tried to grab the punter's pole. I knocked him down and went in to get George. That's all I know, sir. Except Johnny's still got Fletcher out in the garden, at the end of a pitchfork."

"That's a good place for him." Will looked over his shoulder. "I'll be back in a moment, Emmeline," he said, and walked back outside.

"Get this ass off me," James ordered, shoving at the pitchfork.

Will took the pitchfork. "Thank you, Johnny. I've got him now." He waited until both stable boys were out of sight. "You may sit up now."

With a groan James sat up and brushed at his coat. "You lot interrupted a family argument," he said. "I'd like an apology. And that Billet needs to be sacked."

"I can't decide if you actually wanted George to drown, or if you're just an idiot." Will gripped the pitchfork hard, but kept it pointed toward the ground.

"It's none of your affair, Pershing. I told you, I'm their family. No damage done."

"No thanks to you."

The young man rubbed his jaw, which had a red mark on it, hopefully from Billet's fist. That man was getting a bonus. "I lost my temper. You know how they are, minds all full of clouds and butterflies. What do you expect?"

Will smiled. "I'm glad you asked. I expect you to collect your things and vacate the premises."

The young man didn't even blink. "I thought I was your guest. And I'm judging your ability to look after my brother and sister."

"The next time you steal jewelry, don't sell it back in the same village where the owners reside, James."

"What?" James put a hand to his chest. "Those were your things? I found them in the stream. How was I to know where they come from?"

Resisting the urge to throttle the young man, Will took a breath. "I'm not going to debate you. Get your things and leave. Now. Before I change my mind."

"Or what, you'll send for the local constabulary?" James shook his head. "Why don't you tell me how that would go. Like I said, it was a family disagreement."

"What if I mention that you were a guest of Newgate, released under certain circumstances you haven't lived up to?"

That hit the mark. He'd always enjoyed the part of the negotiation where he set an opponent back on his heels. At this moment, though, he was too angry to feel anything but a grim satisfaction that this man would be going away. Without his siblings.

"You wise old bird," James said after a moment. "You think you stumbled onto something, didn't you?"

"Not so much stumbled as asked."

"Well, I asked some questions, too. You and Mrs. P pretending you have children to answer her old granddad's dying wish or whatever nonsense that was? Ha. Georgie told me what's what. Firstly, that poor old Granddad is the Duke of Welshire; secondly, it wasn't a wish that you had young ones—it was a contract. And you broke it. You're trying to lie to a duke about his having grandchildren so you can keep hold of this estate. Wouldn't it be a shame if the truth of all this got out and you got the boot from the missus's granddad, then? Especially if I was to add that you stole two babies from the orphanage for your little game."

Damn it all. He didn't blame George; the children had been rightly wary of their brother. He only wished he'd realized sooner that it had been fear of James and not suspicion over his and Emmeline's motives. In his defense, the idea that a man would hurt children, especially his own siblings, seemed the sort of thing that could happen only in Shakespeare.

"That's right, Mr. P. Maybe I'm a wanted man, but that's just Bow Street, all the way in London. And it's been three years. I doubt they'd make the effort to drag me in even if I was in Charing Cross, much less all the way in Gloucestershire. The cove who made me the bargain got himself transported to Australia, anyway." He chuckled. "You can ask about that, too. I ain't lying."

There were moments in a negotiation that Will didn't like; the ones where the man across the desk turned the table on *him*. He didn't think, though, that even counting seasoned statesmen, he'd ever been handed his hat so deftly. "I see," he said, keeping his voice flat. "What do you want for all this mess you've made, then?"

"Oh, I reckon I'll stay on at Winnover, for now. If you want me quiet, it'll cost you . . . twenty quid. A day. For as long as the little ones are here. And you'll keep quiet if you happen to notice things going missing. I'll go with you to—what was it? Welshire Park. And then I'll leave you George and Rose. I don't want the little fleas. You do whatever you want with them. Send 'em back to St. Stephen's." He stood, brushing dirt and grass off his coat sleeves. "That's what I want, if you want me quiet."

"I have to admit, that's a brave thing to say to a man with a pitchfork." Will took a step forward, noting that James retreated the same distance. Not as collected as he pretended to be, then. "You've managed a standoff," he said aloud. "Not to brag, but I regularly dine with the prime minister. I suggest you take a few minutes to consider which of us would pay the higher price if all of this were to unravel."

"I d—"

"I'll let you know what I've decided to do with you," Will cut in deliberately. "In the meantime, yes, remain close by. If you lay a finger on either George or Rose again, however, I guarantee that you will disappear, and no one will ever find you. Is that clear? Those are my terms, James."

Obviously the boy didn't know how to take that. A frown pulled his brows together before he straightened, lowering his hands. "I'm getting what I want. I have no reason to damage the little darlings and queer your— our—trip to Cumberland."

"Then we have an agreement." With that Will turned his back and headed into the house.

"Rose, please try another tune on the pianoforte, will you?" Emmeline asked, wincing at the cacophony.

"I'm learning it," the little girl insisted.

"Which song is it? I don't quite recognize it."

"I made it up."

Over at the easel by the window, George snorted. "It sounds like a bird dying."

"Your painting looks like a dead bird," his sister retorted.

A short time ago this conversation, this attempt to tutor the children in two very different mediums at once, would have had Emmie pulling out her hair. Now, though, she only hid a smile and walked over to show Rose a more harmonic set of notes. Evidently a slice of cake had revived George except for some sniffing, and he'd felt well enough to paint. The resilience of children continued to amaze her.

The music room door opened. She turned, expecting to see Will give her a solemn nod, informing her that James Fletcher had been sent on his way. Yes, she would have preferred to consult with the children first, but she understood Will's reasoning. From what Hannah had said, James might have thrown both children into the pond if the maid hadn't interfered.

Will's expression, though, looked icy enough to freeze flame. Silently he closed the door behind him. "George, Rose, I asked your brother to leave Winnover. He—"

"Good," George interrupted. "I'm glad to see the hind end of that white-livered sneaksby." Already a little pale, his face went gray. "I slanged, but it's not my fault."

"You may slang today," Will said, before Emmie could reassure the boy herself.

"He's a rat," Rose stated. "And that's not slang. He got mad at George once and threw a sack of live rats on him while he was sleeping."

"That's despicable!" And it explained so much.

"I wish you'd told us about him from the beginning." Will still looked grim. Too grim to be withholding good news.

"We didn't trust you, and he said we had to keep quiet so we could be a family. Then he gambled and lost all the blunt we'd been saving to get a cottage and a puppy." Rose sniffed. "I'm glad he's gone, too."

Abruptly Will grabbed Emmie's hand. "You two, stay in here for a moment," he ordered, and headed for the door.

"What is going on?" Emmie demanded, once he'd pulled her half the length of the hallway. "Clearly it's nothing good."

Will kept a hard grip on her hand. "I informed James that if he didn't leave we would send for the constabulary, at which time he said he would remain here, in the house, and that we're to pay him twenty quid a day—I presume for his continued silence—and we're to allow our valuables to be pilfered as he sees fit. If we don't do that, or if we attempt to have him arrested, he will inform the constabulary, and all and sundry, that we've been lying to Welshire about having children. And that we kidnapped them from St. Stephen's."

Emmie stared at him. "I think I may faint," she announced.

"Please don't. If you do, I will run screaming through the fields until someone bundles me up and takes me to Bedlam."

The vision that conjured, and how out-of-character it would be for him, actually bolstered her a little. "With neither of us here, the children will sell Winnover to the Hendersens and use the proceeds to become pirates."

Will chuckled. "The fact remains, we are in trouble, Emmie. We can't force James to leave now without jeopardizing Winnover. Or the children, as I happen to think that a man who throws a boy into a pond—knowing he can't swim—just because he lost his temper, shouldn't be trusted with the care of either of them." He made a disgusted sound. "At least he doesn't want them going with him after he's taken everything we own. He said they can go back to St. Stephen's for all he cares."

"Just when I'd begun to think we had this figured out," she muttered, leaning back against the wall. "Even if we *could* have him arrested, the children would never trust us again. He is their family, however horrible he is to them."

"George and Rose are quite a bit smarter than he gives them credit for. They were happy enough at the idea of him being gone."

"'Gone' is not the same as being imprisoned. Or hanged. You can't think they would side with us," Emmie countered, wishing that were so. She tugged her hand free of his. "What a mess I've made of your life. I'm so sorry, Will."

Will placed his palms flat on the wall on either side of her shoulders. "Our getting married was not a mess, Em. You may have surprised me, but I have yet to do anything against my will. And you surprised me again with the information that we have two children, but I'm still here. And I intend to remain."

Oh. "Will," she murmured, holding his gaze. "Thank you for saying that."

He leaned down, catching her mouth with his. Heat twined down her spine. If she hadn't taken advantage of him, used him, then the fact that he'd agreed to marry her, and the fact that he'd agreed to this mad scheme in which they were presently embroiled, meant something important.

Sliding her arms around his shoulders, she kissed him back. Will Pershing was not that same twenty-year-old boy whose will she could bend with a smile. Goodness. That realization was . . . arousing.

It was also distracting. Their houseguest who insisted on remaining their houseguest was robbing them, and meant to continue to do so. "Will," she murmured. "We can't allow that boy to chisel away at Winnover and then yank it out from under us out of spite."

"Then what are you going to do about him?" George asked from a few feet away.

Emmie ducked under Will's arm. It wasn't wrong to be caught in her own husband's embrace. It was just . . . unexpected. "For the moment I think we have to do as he asks. You may not think well of us at times, but we do wish to avoid hurting you and Rose."

George folded his arms, half defiant and half little boy. "What did he ask, then? That you treat us good?"

"He asked that we give him twenty pounds a day," Will took up, "that we allow him to remain in the house, and that we give him free rein to take whatever he wishes from here."

"Are we still going to the duke's party?"

"He wants to go with us." Will clenched his jaw. "His Grace has a great many valuable things in his home."

Rose walked up behind her brother. "Why didn't he go away?"

"If we send for the law, he means to tell everyone how

we've broken the duke's agreement. I'm sorry, Rose. We could have him arrested, but that wouldn't help any of us. And it would lose us Winnover."

"He shouldn't get to win," George declared. "I heard what you said, that he don't want us with him when he's finished here. He lied. Again. About everything. He turns everything bad. Even our mama said so."

"He is your family," Emmie said, then wondered if she shouldn't have kept her mouth shut. The bully had nearly drowned George.

"He seemed fairly certain Bow Street doesn't care that he's still a fugitive," Will said. "But if we *could* see him arrested, that's . . . It's serious. He might never go free again."

"That's a lie about Bow Street," George cut in. "He's terrified of 'em. And Newgate. He got nicked once, when one of his friends turned conk for the beaks. They put him in a court, and a pettifogger agreed to get him out—but only if James would turn conk himself. He said no, and they put him in the real stone jug with a view of the drop until he changed his mind. As soon as they let him out, he ran for it. We didn't see him for a year, until he got word that the limb of the law got himself arrested and transported for running his own ring of fingersmiths. In fact, I reckon that's what he's trying to do to us now, make us his kiddies, who have to do what he says."

That . . . was a great deal to decipher. Emmie glanced at Will. "Did you catch that?"

"I think so. It meshes with what Bernard wrote me about. Bow Street arrested James when one of their informers pointed him out, and they sat him down with a solicitor who agreed to get him out from under his charges if he would also become an informant. When he refused, they imprisoned him in Newgate with a view of the gallows until he changed his mind, and when they released him to inform on his fellows he fled, only returning to London when he learned that the solicitor was found guilty of running his own thievery ring and sent to Australia. Is that correct, George?"

"That's what I said. You said I could slang today."

"So I did."

"Don't forget the part where I said he's trying to do to us what the . . . solicitor did to him."

"Oh, we won't forget that," Emmie said, trying to keep her jaw from clenching. Thank goodness she and Will had been honest with the little ones from the beginning. Thank goodness they'd arranged for an exchange of beneficiary services, and doubly thank goodness for that agreement.

"I don't want him to hang, though," Rose said, putting her hands around her neck. "I just want him to go away."

Clearing his throat, Will abruptly turned down the hallway. "Perhaps we should slip in a dance lesson."

"Beg pardon?" Evidently Emmie had just lost the plot again.

"I could dance," Rosie agreed, and turned to follow him.

They made their way to the east ballroom, and Will walked over to wind the music box before he opened it. "We don't want anyone to realize we're plotting," he said as the waltz tinkled into the air, "and this should keep anyone from overhearing."

He held his hand out to Emmie, lifting an eyebrow at George until the boy took his sister's hand. Once the siblings had begun rocketing about the room, he put a hand on Emmeline's hip and swung her into the dance.

"If we see him arrested, he *will* hang," she whispered. "And aside from that, he's already threatened to wag his tongue about our plans to anyone who'll listen."

"The trick would seem to be to get him to run, and to not make it profitable for him to return or to gossip." Will bent his head close to hers.

His nearness aroused her. Just his presence had been enough to distract her lately, but it was more than that. He was her dear friend Will Pershing again, but he was also a man grown, an honorable, witty, scheming, and supremely desirable man. She'd wasted eight years figuring that out.

She swallowed, trying to turn her thoughts back to the very serious problem at their feet. "All we need is a corrupt solicitor whose services we can purchase to frighten the devil out of him, and a handful of determined but inept Runners to catch him and then lose track of him."

His steps faltered before he caught up to the rhythm again. "By God, Emmie, have I mentioned lately that you are a brilliant, beautiful woman?" he murmured, and kissed her on the cheek. "Give me two days, and I think I may be able to keep Winnover for you."

CHAPTER TWENTY

Will closed his pocket watch and put it away. Half three, which would put the children a good way through their music lesson. After that it would be reading for George and should have been fencing for Rose—an appointment he'd informed her that he would be missing.

The little girl had been very understanding, considering that he'd promised to make up the lesson first thing in the morning, before they went riding. It helped that he'd implied this was in regard to James, but he wasn't going to say anything more until he had actual results.

The idea of leaving any of them in the house with James still there made his blood boil, but he couldn't be in two places at once. Asking Billet and Roger the coachman inside would hopefully discourage Fletcher from doing anything more than snatching some jewelry, but Winnover could not be maintained as an armed camp. Hence his destination now.

Kneeing Topper, he sent the bay gelding down the left-hand fork in the road and over a small stone bridge. The village of Brockworth was perhaps twice the size of Birdlip, right in the pretty center of the Cotswolds, and he had two reasons for being there. Emmeline knew about one of them, and he felt damned guilty over not telling her the other.

Having the children at Winnover, having this scheme together, had changed more than their daily routines. Previously their lives had barely intersected. Now they chatted, looked, and touched more frequently every day than they'd likely done over the past five years together. Hell, he'd knocked on Emmeline's bedchamber door last night for a good-night kiss, and for God's sake, he'd felt it. She wanted him. *Him.* A lack of patience had hurt them before, though, and this time he meant to do it right. This time, the next step had to be hers. And he hoped to the devil she would take it.

Crossing through the center of Brockworth, he turned up a side street and stopped in front of a small building that housed a tobacco shop on one end and a solicitor's office on the other. For a moment he almost sent Topper on his way again, back through the village and back to Birdlip.

Instead, he blew out his breath and swung to the ground, looping the reins around the cast-iron hitching post and walking up to the solicitor's door. It had a little bell set at the top, which rang tinnily as he pushed the door open and stepped inside.

"I'll be with you in a moment," a male voice called from one of the two back rooms separate from the small desk and chairs in the narrow front of the office. "Mrs. Garvey?"

"No," Will said, noting the faint smell of tobacco that evidently crossed the barrier between the two shops.

A chair scratched against the floor, and a stocky man appeared in the doorway of the right-hand office. "Pershing? Will Pershing?"

"Hello, Michael," Will said, stepping forward to take the solicitor's outstretched hand.

"By God, Will Pershing." Michael Fenmore shook hands for a moment longer than called for by custom, before he gestured at one of the two chairs in the foyer. "Sit, sit. What brings you to Brockworth?"

"How are you and Caroline?" Will responded. "It's been what, two years since we last spoke?"

"Three, I think. We're fine. Little Patrick is five now. You and Emmeline?"

"We're well, thank you," he said, trying to shake off his impatience with the idle chatter. Small talk was his forte, for God's sake. A little bit of nonsense about the weather or the Derby to create a solid foundation for a more serious discussion. This time, though, nerves jangled along his arms and up his spine, and he had a ridiculous desire to flee the premises. "I should ask you and Caroline to join us in London more often. It's been too long since Oxford, and you were a good friend."

"Likewise. But not all of us crave rubbing elbows with the rich and influential." Michael gave a short grin. "My last efforts were for water rights for a local farmer, and he paid me in pigs."

"Hmm. Good pigs, I hope."

"They were delicious. So, what does bring you to Brockworth? If you're here to invite me to go hunting with you, I accept."

"We'll have to do that. But no, that's not why I'm here." Will sent up a quick prayer, though he wasn't entirely certain what it was he was praying for. And that was the difficulty in this, damn it all. "Two things bring me here, actually. You may not like either of them."

"Well, this is more interesting than petitioning the

court to limit the number of cats Mrs. Vendle is allowed to keep on her premises."

"Oh, it's definitely interesting." Will took one of the seats. "I suppose I should begin with the longer tale. I . . . Emmeline and I have a quandary, and I thought you and Caroline might be the ones who could solve it for us."

"The two of us?" Michael frowned. "I'm listening."

"Yes. We . . . came into the possession of two children, and for a variety of reasons, we cannot keep them. You and Caroline are good people, and I thought you might consider taking them in."

Michael stared at him. "Say that again?"

"There are two young orphans living with us at Winnover Hall. George is eight, and Rose is just five. They are, quite frankly, mischievous and clever and wonderful, and badly in need of someone who can love them forever."

"Aside from the question of how you came to have them, why is it you can't keep them?"

Thus far only he and Emmeline and the servants—and the three Fletchers, of course—knew the truth of that, and he was loath to include anyone else. On the other hand, the lies were beginning to pile up, and causing nothing but more tangles and troubles. He took a breath. "I'm telling you this in confidence, Michael. No one other than Caroline can know."

The solicitor held out his hand. "Give me a shilling."

"What?"

"Or a quid, or a penny. Whatever's in your pocket. Then you will be my client, and what you tell me is privileged."

Most of his spare change had been going into the children's trunks, but he found a shilling in one pocket. He handed it over, and Michael pocketed it. Symbolic or not, it left him feeling a bit steadier, though not because of the exchange of money. Without knowing any but the broadest of facts, Michael had agreed to keep this secret, and he'd done so in a way that was not only personally binding, but legally so. "Thank you."

"You're my friend. And my client. Now. What's afoot?"

Will told him. The agreement he and Emmeline had signed, their inability to produce children, Emmeline's lies to both their families and the journals she kept about their faux children, her grandfather's invitation, and the trip to London and St. Stephen's. And the promise they'd made to find George and Rose a good home afterward.

"That's . . . not at all what I expected to hear," Michael said into the silence when Will had finished. "If I didn't know you any better, I'd say you'd gone queer in the attic."

"Perhaps I have. The fact remains, though, that we—I—promised the children a good home, and that I thought of you and Caroline." The more he considered it, the better they seemed. The only reason they hadn't been among his first choices was that he'd been hoping to find the youngsters a home that was less than a long hour away from Winnover Hall.

"Will, I get paid in pigs. I can't afford two additional children, even if Caroline was amenable."

"You could for an additional thousand pounds a year, I'd wager."

The solicitor blinked. "That's extremely generous."

"It goes along with the provision that Emmeline and I could continue to visit them on occasion." The idea of never seeing the children again made his throat tighten and his chest hurt, like someone had reached a hand in and was trying to rip out his heart.

"God, Will, find a way to keep them."

"We've tried. We've spent nights awake trying to

figure something out. Keeping them there as our niece and nephew and not bringing them into London with us for the Season nearly won, but if either of our families who think them our children came calling and decided to take the little ones into Birdlip . . . We'd be done for. It's easier to hide faux children than real ones."

For a long moment Michael looked at him. "Let me speak with Caroline. God knows what she'll say, but I'll do my damndest to convince her."

He'd done it, then. It should have been a relief, he supposed, but he didn't feel relieved. "Thank you," he said anyway.

"She could still say no," Michael pointed out. "I'll send word. How long do I have?"

"Eleven days. I'll need an answer by then."

"You'll have it."

This was a good thing, Will reminded himself. This was the way it had to be, and he'd found good, kind people for the Fletcher children. But these good people needed to know the rest, especially with the favor he meant to ask of Michael. "There is one other reason we can't keep them, however."

"Would this be your second reason for calling?"

"Yes. Before I tell you, though, I feel as if I should give you more than a shilling. It's . . . a bit mad."

"Well, now you must tell me."

"As I said, George and Rose are orphans. They do, however, have an older brother. He appeared at Winnover shortly after we brought them home, saying he was of age now and wanted to claim them. Out of the goodness of his heart he would allow our little ruse to continue, though, for what I assumed would be a monetary compensation later. However, he's been stealing from us, directing the children to steal valuables from us, and he's been selling the items in Birdlip and the surrounding area."

Michael made a sound in his chest. "Ah," he said aloud. "I'm afraid I can't take them in, then. Not with Patrick in the house. It's a bit reckless, don't you think?"

"No, no, no. You misunderstand. We mean to be rid of James Fletcher, and the children intend to help us."

Standing so quickly his chair went over backward, Michael scrambled away. "I cannot hear this! For God's sake, Will, you're talking about murder!"

"What? No, I'm not. Sit down, Michael, and listen. Closely. Then tell me your opinion."

Half an hour later he had something of an agreement and a renewed measure of hope—not just for the children, but for him and Emmeline. Of course it could all just as easily end in disaster, but he'd paid his shilling and tomorrow the newest play would begin.

Returning to Topper, Will headed back toward Winnover Hall. He'd conducted another successful negotiation, or at least the bones of one. This negotiation, though, was personal, and whichever way it went he could still find ruination.

Even if they succeeded tomorrow, they had eighteen days until the duke's party began, and perhaps five after that to return to Winnover, get the children packed, and take them to their new home. He meant to make the most of those days. Once he figured out a way to tell Emmeline that he'd done what she hadn't been able to bring herself to do, that was.

Even in a month of daily surprises, this morning had a good chance of winning the trophy. Emmie looked about

the private room at the Blue Rose Inn. Winnover staff, se-
lect friends, one stranger, and all of them together the
last hope of wrenching George, Rose, and Winnover Hall
out of James Fletcher's greedy, dangerous fingers.

"Mr. Pershing, are you certain this is absolutely necessary? Mrs. Pershing?" Farmer Harry Dawkins tugged
at the crimson waistcoat hugging his frame. The fit wasn't
horrible, but with the way he kept pulling at the clothes
he might well rip them off before they could be of any
use.

Emmie smiled at him. "I'm afraid it is necessary,
Mr. Dawkins. And Will and I can't thank you enough for
agreeing to help us. We could not do this without you."

"You've servants aplenty at Winnover. Couldn't one of
them do this? I mean, it's red."

"It is, indeed," she agreed, handing him another item
borrowed from Will's wardrobe, this one a dark blue greatcoat. "Red and blue, the colors of the Bow Street Horse Patrol. It's the closest we could come to an official uniform.
And James Fletcher is acquainted with every member of
our staff. It's why we're here at the inn to begin with."

"I understand that. It's just . . . I'm not much for pan-
tomimes and such. I don't want to ruin it for you."

Will walked up and clapped him on the shoulder. "We
wouldn't have asked if we didn't think you could help.
Mr. Allen there will take the lead. All you need to do is
support him, just as if you were truly law officers."

Emmie followed the farmer's glance over to Mr. Francis Allen, solicitor, seated at the long inn table with his
law partner, Michael Fenmore. "Both Mr. Allen and his
partner are legal scholars, Mr. Dawkins," she decided.
"You're doing nothing wrong, and you are helping free
two innocent children from the clutches of a thief and lawbreaker."

The farmer straightened. "I'll do everything I can. It's easy to imagine my little ones being caught up in something before Jenny and I could stop them."

Hannah jumped up from her seat in the corner, another red waistcoat over her arm. "All finished. I hope it will suffice; I haven't much experience with gentlemen's garments."

Mr. Allen took it from her, the solicitor nodding his thanks as he pulled it over his plain white shirt. "It fits well, Miss Hannah," he said. "My thanks." He sent a glance at his partner. "If someone yesterday had told me I'd be playing a Bow Street Runner today, I'd have laughed at them."

Hopefully Allen wasn't having second thoughts, too. If they lost both officers, they would have to ask the innkeeper, and Arnold Highwater would not fit in either waistcoat. "We are extremely grateful, Mr. Allen," she said aloud.

"Don't you worry, Mrs. Pershing," the stout solicitor said with a brief smile. "I excel at pantomime and charades. And I'm always ready to champion a good cause."

"Now, Harry," Mr. Pershing said, handing the farmer the pair of irons they'd borrowed from the local constable—a favor that had cost them one of Mrs. Brubbins's pies—and giving the key to Mr. Allen, "are you certain you haven't seen James Fletcher about the village, or wandering through your fields?"

"I'm certain of it, Mr. Pershing. You described him, and I've never seen anyone like that. I'd know if there was a stranger roaming my wheat. We've more than enough pairs of eyes for that."

Will smiled. "Then we've gone over your roles; Harry, you are Mr. Dawkins, and Mr. Allen is . . . Mr. Allen. Bow Street Horse Patrol."

"Does it matter that we've no horses?" Mr. Dawkins asked, fitting a black beaver hat on his head. The top hat was too fine for a Bow Street officer, but the only wardrobe they'd had to borrow from for the farmer had been Will's.

"Fletcher will assume you've left them out of sight somewhere. Just be confident and stern, and do as we rehearsed."

As Mr. Allen straightened his coat, Rose pocketed the cuff links Will had given her and wandered over to Michael Fenmore. The solicitor had barely said a word since his arrival this morning, instead sitting at the table to fill out some official-looking papers.

"I'm Rose," she said.

"Hello, Rose," the barrel-chested man answered with a warm smile. "I'm Michael Fenmore, today playing the role of Michael Shavely."

"Oh. Are you Peter Shavely's brother? Because James hates Peter Shavely. Shavely nabbed him and threw him in the big stone jug."

"He's pretending to be Shavely's cousin," Emmie said, taking the girl's hand and leading her back to her brother. "We didn't want to confuse you, because all you need to know is that when Mr. Dawkins and Mr. Allen and Will appear, you run to Billet."

"I can run very fast."

Will pulled out his pocket watch for at least the tenth time since they'd gathered in the inn's one private room, the only outward sign of his nerves. "If everyone is comfortable with their roles, we should begin," he said, clicking the watch closed again.

"Yes, let's get this over with," Emmie said, suppressing a shudder. All of the pieces needed to fall into place, or they would be well and truly sunk. "George, you and

Rose and Hannah and I will take the carriage back to the house. At my signal Powell will tell James that you want to meet him at the stable, where you will give him your prizes."

The boy, his expression more serious than Emmie was accustomed to seeing, nodded. He'd seen some horrible things in his life, but George remained a young boy with a poor upbringing and not enough age or wisdom to decide on the course of his own life. The fact that he'd chosen to help them spoke volumes.

"We'll do it," George said, taking his sister's hand and heading for the door, "but be careful. James really don't want to go back to the stone jug. The big one."

"We'll come up the hill behind the stable," Will took up. "If he happens to see us, he'll assume that's where our Runners left their horses. Give us ten minutes after you return to Winnover, Emmeline, then send out the children."

Emmie nodded. After the near tragedy at the pond, she had no doubt that James Fletcher could be dangerous. She only hoped that in attempting to dispose of him as the children wished, rather than through the actual magistrate, they weren't going to get anyone—particularly Will or the children—hurt. "It's just another tale," she said, sending him a smile. "We excel at those."

As the women and children left, Will took a breath. If he'd had more time he might have brought in another friend or two from Oxford, but each additional day Fletcher remained at Winnover meant a greater threat to the futures of two small children and the estate that had become the focus of Emmeline's entire life. It had to be Harry Dawkins, or one of the other farmers who by chance had never run across Fletcher in Birdlip or the surrounding countryside.

Harry, though, continued to look petrified, and that wouldn't serve, either. Before Will could conjure more words of support, Francis Allen walked over to the farmer. "You'll be fine," he said in a low voice. "I'll take the lead, and you follow."

Dawkins nodded, his Adam's apple bobbing as he swallowed. "I'll do my best. Didn't expect Winnover's future to rest in my hands, though."

God's sake. This *was* the future of Winnover Hall. Trying to slow his breathing and the abrupt pounding of his heart, Will led the way out the side door of the inn. "We'll see you in half an hour, Michael."

"I'll be there."

They arrived below the stable in twelve minutes. With a last nod Harry Dawkins slipped inside the building's back door, while he and Francis circled around to come from the direction of the house. Michael would make his appearance later, after they had Fletcher corralled.

Up ahead he caught sight of the children with their brother outside the main door of the stable. Abruptly James grabbed George by the collar and shook him. "You think you're better than me now? Because you can spell 'pony'? Because you think there's a difference between stealing shite and stealing valuables? There's no difference, Georgie." Straightening his arm, he shoved George into the dirt. "The Pershings don't give a damn about either of you. As soon as this is over and I have what I want, you two go back to St. Stephen's."

"Stop it!" Rosie shouted, squatting down beside George.

That was more than enough of that. Will broke into

a trot, Francis Allen beside him. "What's all this, then?" the solicitor bellowed.

"Bugger me," James rasped as he jerked upright, his ruddy face going gray. Fumbling to dump the jewelry into his pockets, he moved backward toward the open doorway.

"Going somewhere?"

The young man whipped around as Dawkins appeared in the doorway. Swearing, James whirled back around and grabbed for Rose's skirts as she and George fled to Billet, who bustled them around the rear of the stable and back toward the house.

Half hoping Fletcher would make a fight of it, Will stepped forward to trip the lad as Mr. Allen shoved him to the ground. Before he could twist upright again, Dawkins pounced on him like a wildcat. The solicitor took a kick to the knee before the farmer could drag the wrist shackles out of his pocket, but neither of them hesitated. "Bind him up, Mr. Dawkins," Francis grunted, grabbing for an arm.

With surprising dexterity Harry Dawkins fastened the cuffs around James Fletcher's wrists. They should have got them behind his back, but Fletcher was caught, and that was what they needed. Mr. Dawkins jerked Fletcher upright, while Mr. Allen made a show of pocketing the key to the irons. "Be still!" Francis ordered.

"I only took what the brats gave me!" Fletcher yelled, sitting upright.

The solicitor hesitated. They were supposed to mention bad happenings in London, but apparently Francis had lost the thread. Will stepped forward, trying to figure out how to get them back on the path without giving away the game.

"Do you think we'd ride a day out of London for some jewelry?" Harry Dawkins demanded, yanking the boy to his feet before Will could say anything. "We've been following you for some time, James Fletcher. It was just luck a messenger came in to Bow Street yesterday and told us where you've been hiding yourself."

Thank God for the farmer. "Thank you for arriving so promptly, gentlemen," Will added.

"You tell them to let me go," James yelled at him, "or I start wagging my tongue!"

Will stopped in front of him. He'd been looking forward to this bit. "Young man," he said, "I have long supported London's efforts at policing and justice. You may say whatever you wish, but I do feel it my duty to warn you that anything you say may be used by these gentlemen as evidence of your ongoing criminal activity. And from what I've learned, you've done a great deal well before now. You're not as forgotten as you'd hoped."

"He kidnapped my brother and sister." James tried to wriggle away from them, but the solicitor clamped a hand on his shoulder.

Of course, this would be the pleading bit, but they all knew enough of the story that none of them had any sympathy for the boy. "Shut it, you."

"The Pershings have been lying to the Duke of Welshire about having children, so they took Rose and George from the orphanage. Paid for the use of 'em, too."

"They paid for the children?" Harry—Mr. Dawkins—asked.

"Yes. Paid for 'em."

"That doesn't sound like kidnapping then, does it, Mr. Allen?"

Mr. Allen shook his head. "It does not, Mr. Dawkins."

"It was! And they lied! They had to have children to keep the house, and they didn't!"

"The affairs of the gentry aren't my concern," Francis said, clearly remembering his dialogue. "*You* are, James Fletcher. You were released from prison in order to fulfill an agreement. You didn't do that. In fact, you went right back to thievery. A man doesn't cross the magistrate and escape justice."

"Fletcher? I ain't Fletcher. I'm Reed. James Reed. Ask any of these coves."

Dawkins snorted. "Mm-hmm. Come along, then. You'll stay in the stable until he gets here."

"Who? Who, for God's sake?"

Francis smiled grimly. *A nice touch.* "You'll find out soon enough."

He and the farmer dragged Fletcher into the stable and sat him on a stool. "I have information!" the boy wailed as Will and Harry Dawkins left the building.

The farmer paused. "Good. We'll see if it can save your hide."

It hadn't been anything they'd rehearsed, but damn if it didn't feel good to hear the farmer say it. Will clapped Mr. Dawkins on the back as they headed to the house. "Perhaps you have a bit of actor's blood in you, after all."

"Ha. After this, I'm never doing a pantomime again."

CHAPTER
TWENTY-ONE

Will paced. It could be a delicate balance, the difference between giving a man enough time to panic and enough time to seize on another strategy. "It's been an hour," he said, turning from the window. "I don't think we should wait any longer."

"Mr. Pershing," Harry Dawkins said, the borrowed beaver hat in one hand as he tugged again at his red waistcoat, "this has been a day I won't forget. I am worried for Mr. Allen, though, alone with that fellow."

"I suppose it's my turn, then." Michael Fenmore, seated at the small table in the morning room, closed his leather satchel and buckled it. "I still don't know how you talked me into this, Will," he said, "or how *I* talked Francis into it, but let's get it over with."

Nodding, Will gestured at the farmer. "Harry? Mr. Dawkins, will you lead the way?"

"Certainly, Mr. Pershing. I'll never have it said that Harry Dawkins didn't do his part for Winnover Hall."

It had been a stroke of luck that he'd had a red waistcoat and an older blue greatcoat, that Michael owned a similar coat, and that there'd been enough of that old red curtain in the attic that Hannah could sew a second waistcoat for Francis. The entire staff had jumped in to support his plan, in fact, without a complaint among them. Mrs. Brubbins, with a nephew at Bow Street, had been especially helpful. All this from a respected, respectable staff of servants he'd thought dutiful, obedient, and unobtrusive. It seemed everyone had a surprise for him these days.

They headed for the kitchen and the servants' entrance. A few weeks ago he would have thought this a mad idea, and he still did. But neither had they been able to summon a better plan. And after seeing James going after George and Rose even after he'd been warned, Will couldn't wait to see the back end of young Mr. Fletcher.

As they entered the kitchen, Emmeline and the children were seated at the table together with Hannah and Billet, while Mrs. Brubbins set biscuits onto a platter and Powell lurked. His wife, the one who could balance a social calendar in one hand while organizing a soiree honoring the prime minister in the other, had been just as deft at putting together this play. Her imagination had become as mesmerizing as the rest of her.

Will shook himself. There would be time for ogling later. "Are you two well?" he asked, looking at George. "You played your parts magnificently."

"We are magnificent," Rose agreed, daintily taking two biscuits from the platter. "Especially me."

"No regrets?"

"Nothing's happened yet." George took a quartet of biscuits for himself, but then both little ones had had a trying morning. "Just don't turn your back on him, Mr. P . . . Papa."

"I shan't. Stay here until I return."

"What if this plan of yours goes awry, Will?" Michael whispered as they left the house and walked to the stable. "You've never been one to wager on luck."

"I am today."

"Oh. Splendid."

How odd that he, the one who'd helped create faux children, was the only one playing himself in this theater. Yes, he was accustomed to assuming a role of sorts during his negotiations, but this wasn't about a canal or a bridge. This was about Winnover, and even more it was about Emmeline and those two children. Another few years under James's leadership, and they all would see the inside of Newgate prison. Or worse. That couldn't be allowed to happen, any more than he would let bad luck or circumstance see Emmie removed from her beloved home.

He walked into the stable. "Thank you again for getting here so quickly, Mr. . . . . I'm sorry, what was your name again?" he asked over his shoulder.

"Shavely," Michael Fenmore said. "Michael Shavely."

The boy, seated on a stool in the corner, made a sound very like a whimper. Will, though, had no sympathy for him. They were giving him better than he deserved, and James could thank George and Rose for that. "Yes. Shavely," he said. "I apologize; it's been an eventful handful of days."

"No doubt." Michael motioned at Francis, who obligingly pulled up another stool. "So. You're James Fletcher," the solicitor said, sitting in front of the young man and making a show of opening his satchel. "Before your name crossed my desk yesterday, I thought you would be one of those people whom one knows all about but never sets eyes on. I'm glad I was wrong on that count."

"I'm James Reed," James said, his face a pasty gray. "I don't know who this Fletcher is. And I don't know you."

"Of course you don't know me," Michael Fenmore went on. "I'm Peter Shavely's cousin. He's the one you're acquainted with. In fact, your disappearance after you agreed to inform for him is the reason the magistrate's court began looking into his . . . activities."

"I didn't—"

"Hush now." Michael glanced up at the boy, almost as if James was an afterthought. "As it happens, Peter will be returning to England in six months. You are definitely a loose bit of netting he—we—would like to see tidied up. So to speak."

"I have information," James rasped, sweat dripping from his longish, unkempt hair. "I know the Pershings violated the conditions of their agreement with the Duke of Welshire, and I can tell you how."

Michael lifted an eyebrow, glancing at Will. "Do you, now?"

The boy leaned forward. "I do. I'll tell you everything I know if you take these shackles off me."

Deliberately the solicitor patted his plump breast pocket. "Well, it so happens that Mr. Pershing and I have spoken. At length. And you know, gossiping about your betters, especially when they have no interest in being gossiped about, is a very good way for a foolish young man to end up at Bethlem Hospital, say."

James jerked upright. "Bedlam? You'd send me to Bedlam?"

"That's up to you, I suppose. If you continue wagging your tongue like a madman, then I imagine you could well end up at Bethlem or one of its sister institutions."

Will watched as James absorbed that bit of information. Stopping him from gossiping had been the main goal here, but it was just as vital that James Fletcher go away.

"If you don't want me to talk, then I won't talk. I swear it. Just let me go."

"You're being foolish again." Michael stood. "Mr. Pershing, I wonder if you would favor me with a cup of tea before we travel back to London."

"It would be my pleasure, Mr. Shavely," Will answered.

"Good, good." Michael smiled. "Mr. Dawkins, please ride down to Birdlip and query if the constable has a patrol wagon we might borrow. And perhaps one of his watchmen, so that we may return it once we've delivered this fellow to Newgate."

The farmer saluted, which wasn't entirely correct, but he did it with such enthusiasm that it seemed natural. "At once, Mr. Shavely."

That would leave Francis Allen alone again with James. If the solicitor did as they'd discussed he should be fine, but there was always the chance that something would go wrong. *Faith,* Will repeated to himself. Or luck. It had been with them thus far today.

As the farmer exited, Will gestured at Michael. "This way then, Mr. Shavely. And perhaps we might discuss future endeavors from which we might mutually benefit."

"Delighted to, Mr. Pershing."

James Fletcher watched them leave. He was damned, all over again. Worse than before. Now he could admit that he'd overreached, thinking he could match up against a rich cove who knew the prime minister and could pay magistrates and solicitors to do whatever he wished— even if that meant locking someone up in Bedlam with the loonies.

Damnation. He wasn't dim enough to think George might slip into the stable and save him, either. Not after he'd pitched him into the pond, even though that had just been to teach him a lesson. Rose might help him if he promised her a kitten or some such, but he couldn't count on it. Useless little whiners, they were. No, he had only himself, and himself had already proven to be a disappointment.

Staying at Winnover Hall, eating beef and pork and pheasant, he should have let it be. George was right. He should have been patient and then at the end asked for a hundred pounds to help him look after the young ones. After that, he could have left them anywhere—back in London, or York, or wherever he was when he decided he couldn't stand their questions or Rose's fancies any longer.

The stout beak, Mr. Allen, remained in the stable, so he couldn't just up and run. Especially with the irons around his wrists. He hated those things. "Don't you want to get some tea?" he asked.

Snorting, Allen leaned back against the far wall. "You're going to get me a fat bonus from Richard Birnie himself. You're not very popular at Bow Street." Mr. Allen took a look around them. "I will make myself comfortable, though. Tea with Shavely could take some time."

Dragging the second stool closer to the wall, Allen sat down, tipping it back on two of its three legs. If James had been a bit taller, he might have been able to kick the stool out from under him, smash the buzzard in the face, and make off with the key to the irons. Even his size was against him today, though. *Jesus.*

Angling his beaver hat forward over his eyes, Allen folded his arms over his chest. *Damn it all.* It was so close to being a simple thing, getting away from Bow Street and the magistrate. Surreptitiously James tried to pull his hands free, but the irons were too snug. He'd grown some since the last time he'd worn the bloody things.

Something slammed into the back wall of the stable, so hard that hay drifted down from the loft. The beak leaped to his feet, nearly falling over after all. "You stay here," he ordered James, and sprinted outside as the sound repeated. As he left, he kicked something into the near corner. Something that sounded metal.

Hardly daring to breathe, one eye on the doorway, James knelt down and felt about the dark corner. *The key.* The beak had dropped the damned key. Snatching it up, he twisted his left wrist until he could just reach the clasp. One second later, and he was free.

Setting the irons down, James crouched, stuck his head out the door, then ran for the woods as soon as he saw it was clear. He stayed hunched over, waiting to hear a pistol fire, waiting to hear a whistle or someone shouting, and to feel a hot lead ball burrowing into his back. But no alarm sounded, no one shot at him, and he kept running.

He couldn't go to York now, because he'd mentioned it to the brats. Manchester would do him, or Sheffield, though somewhere like Newcastle would give him access to a port and the sea, and everywhere beyond.

Yes, Newcastle would do. And George and Rose could go ride their ponies until the Pershings sent them back to the orphanage, for all he cared. He was free now, and he meant to stay that way.

Billet slipped back into the kitchen. "He's gone, Mr. Pershing," the groom reported. "Headed north at a dead run. I doubt he'll stop until he reaches Scotland."

George took a breath, then went back to devouring biscuits. The grown-ups seemed to think he and Rosie would feel better if they had all the sweets they wanted, and he wasn't about to argue with that. If he was supposed to feel bad about helping Mr. P and his friends scare James, though, he didn't. Mostly he felt relieved. It was just him and Rosie again, like it was supposed to be. Easier, and no one else making them do things that put them at risk.

And best of all, James could take the blame for everything with him. For the jewels already gone, for the birds Rosie kept finding, and all the utensils and coins and vases and candlesticks. "Did you get the necklace and cuff links back from him?" he asked around a bite.

The farmer's face flushed, and he dug into the pocket of the borrowed blue greatcoat that was too loose across his shoulders. "I beg your pardon, Mr. and Mrs. Pershing. Here they are."

Mrs. P took them from the farmer, smiled, and put a hand on his shoulder. "Thank you, Mr. Dawkins, and please don't distress yourself. I would happily have parted with all of these things in exchange for having him gone. We owe you a great deal." Her smile went away then, and she turned and looked at George and Rose again. "Though I'm sorry we couldn't have managed things a different way."

"If he'd been honest about his reasons for coming, we might have been able to help him find honest work," Mr. P put in, taking his wife's hand. He touched her a lot more now than he did when they'd first met the Pershings in London. She seemed to like it.

George shook his head. "He didn't want to find work. He always just wanted what he could take from other people, and he never watched Rosie as close as he should have. Maybe I'll miss him, but I don't want to see him again. We just want to do our part of the agreement so you can find us a good family."

They all smiled and nodded, because that was what

they wanted to hear. So he and his sister would keep learn-ing their lessons and hiding their baubles, and then when they'd visited the duke and saved Winnover for the Per-shings, they could go where *he* wanted to go, and Rosie would be safe, and he wouldn't have to be a long-haul boy or a pig farmer, or a despicable, blasted fellow who didn't even care about his own family.

CHAPTER
TWENTY-TWO

Emmeline cast a glance about the drawing room. Even with a good portion of her jewelry returned, something was still amiss. The room was beginning to look bare, with only the clock and a single candlestick on the mantel, and nothing left on the bookshelf nearest the door but a trio of books on birdwatching. Originally, they'd been complemented by an ebony carving of a raven, but that bit of decoration had gone the way of a great many portable objects in the house.

She had no idea how the children had managed to hide everything. It certainly wouldn't all fit in both of their blanket chests together, and she doubted James Fletcher could have hauled about that quantity of items without being noticed.

And even more puzzling, none of the staff had said a word about the missing items. Not the maids, nor the footmen, and not Powell—who'd vigorously supported the removal of sticky-fingered James from the household. It could be possible he believed all the thefts had been James's work, but the disappearances had begun well before his arrival.

Just as strange was the way some things vanished

and then reappeared a day or two later. Regardless, the plan she and Will had conjured to ignore the thefts in the hope that in the wake of their brother's departure the children would stop stealing hadn't been at all successful.

Will strolled into the drawing room. He'd dressed for the evening, as she had, and his dark green and gray waistcoat brought out the green in his eyes to a rather startling degree. "Good evening," she said, standing to offer him a curtsy.

He bowed. "Good evening, Emmeline. You look lovely. I would say that purple is definitely your color."

She did like the way the purple and black formal gown glimmered around her, tight beneath her breasts with beading throughout the bodice and flowing out in a full skirt. That was why she'd chosen it for this evening and for the day of her grandfather's party. "Thank you. Any sign of the children?"

"Not yet. I imagine it'll be a while; I did hear Rose complaining that she needed more ribbons in her hair as I passed by her doorway."

"I suppose it's better to discover now how many ribbons she'll require rather than wait until after we've traveled to Welshire Park." That was the main reason for the formal dinner this evening; the children needed the practice of an entire meal. This was a rehearsal, and hopefully it would go well. Time was the one thing that kept marching forward regardless of their progress and the other brambles that kept landing in their path.

He motioned for her to take her seat again, and sat down beside her. "We leave in a week, and everything's been remarkably calm. I'm beginning to believe we may pull this off."

"I hope so," she said. "They've been working so hard.

And they helped with James; I think they do want a better life."

"As do I," he agreed, nodding. "But they aren't the only ones who've worked to bring all this to fruition. You continue to astound, Emmeline."

Her cheeks warmed. "As do you," she returned, "though I have to say that Rose's fencing skills strike me as haphazard, at best."

Will chuckled. "She's as likely to wound an ally as an enemy. But she'll do it very enthusiastically." He took her hand, twining his fingers with hers. In response, a quiet thrum began humming through her, warm and deep. Once he'd been a playmate, a sharer of adventures, and then someone she thought she could use, as long as she helped him achieve what he wanted. And it had taken eight years for her to begin to realize that they'd both changed, both grown, and that she very much liked the man he'd become.

"I wrote out a paragraph this morning, using words I've been working on with George, and he read it perfectly," she said. "And he's learning to sound out the words he doesn't know. I don't envy the next adult who attempts to censure him or Rose in writing."

"That does lead me to another topic," he said slowly, pausing as thunder rumbled through the house. "You know we've run out of local residents to query about taking in the children."

That wasn't a question, but she knew what the question was. "I just don't—I meant to make another attempt to ask for Father John's help, but—I still don't have much confidence in his criteria for finding a family for the children." She sighed. "But not only have we run out of neighbors, we've run out of time. I'll send him a note in the morning."

"Emmeline, y—"

"We promised to find them parents," she interrupted. "It's in the agreement. I just . . . I haven't gotten to that particular task yet."

How could she explain it to him? She, who'd had every intention of shedding the orphans once they'd played their part, couldn't make herself take that last step. Once she did, she would have to put a date to the end of this experiment. This different sort of life she enjoyed more than she'd thought possible. A life much more interesting than the one she'd conjured in her journals.

"In fact, I've been thinking," she went on. "We don't have to be back in London until February. That would give us much more time to find the perfect place for them. I doubt St. Stephen's would object. We haven't intended to return them there since nearly the beginning, anyway."

"I want to agree with you," he said after a moment. "But if we have them here through Christmas, I don't know that my heart could withstand seeing them go." Will took a breath. "Not a very manly thing to say, I suppose, but because I want them to stay, the sooner they go, the better."

Emmeline wished she didn't know exactly what he meant. "I've become very fond of them," she whispered. Any louder, and she would begin weeping.

She couldn't even say how or when it had happened. On the day they'd visited St. Stephen's she'd seen George and Rose as a godsend—poor little darlings whom she and Will could spoil and return to London with a bucketful of fond memories. Five weeks later they'd become clever little scamps who stole everything not nailed down, presumably to fund their inevitable flight from the house. And at the same time, they'd turned on their own brother when he'd threatened to take even the nailed-down things. One day that might make sense, but today she was simply . . . grateful.

They were smart and devious and far wiser than she'd been at their age. They considered themselves to be self-sufficient and independent, and she had no idea whether to fear more for them or for England if they returned to their previous lives of petty thievery and hiding in church cellars.

That was the rub, though. She had hopes for them. She wanted good things to happen for them. She wanted them to have parents who loved them and cared for them and who could ensure that they had safe, happy, and comfortable lives. And with every ounce of her being she refused to think the next sentence, the one that would pull everything together, because that could never happen. It couldn't. Even if her mother had been wrong in saying she wasn't meant to be a parent, Emmie had created still more circumstances to make it impossible.

When she'd begun her lies, she'd made a mistake; she'd created children on paper and in London, but hadn't carried it into her life in Gloucestershire. All she would have had to do was purchase some children's clothing in Birdlip, add a pony or two to the stable, mention from time to time during one of her Winnover Hall dinners that the children had wanted to attend, but she'd promised them a trip to the fair instead. That was all it would have taken.

She knew several couples socially, knew for a fact they had children, but had never met the youngsters. There was no reason at all that she couldn't have created her children in precisely the same way, and then George and Rose might have stayed.

"I found a family for them," Will said into the silence, and she whipped her head up to stare at him, every thought in her head crashing together.

"What?" she gasped, barely remembering to keep her voice down.

"I have possibly found one," he amended. "Michael and Caroline Fenmore. I didn't go see him just to gain his aid with James."

"But he's in Brockworth. That's an hour away."

"Yes, it is. But the Fenmores are a good match. Their son, Patrick, is five now. Brockworth is a small enough village that the children couldn't disappear into it. The family isn't wealthy—some of Michael's clients pay him in pigs—but I told him we would be willing to support the expense of adding two children to their household with an annual stipend of a thousand pounds."

"You didn't ask me." With all the noise in her head, that statement was the loudest. "You just went and gave them away."

"Emmeline, I didn't give them away." He scowled, his grip on her hand tightening as if he worried she would flee. "You know that. Michael and Caroline are good people. They don't live far away. They don't. We've considered every single adult in the area, and none of them satisfied either of us. Who else would we ask?"

"I don't know." A tear ran down her face. "You mean they're leaving?"

He swore under his breath. "Michael was to speak with Caroline and send me word within the next few days. He's met them now, so he has an idea of what they'd be in for."

It might not have happened yet, but it would. The children had a family. Two adults who would love them and not send them away because of a stupid lie begun years earlier. Will should have told her what he meant to do before he'd done it, but she would have come to the same conclusion. Michael had helped them when he had no incentive to do so but friendship. Even if they didn't travel in the same social circle, she knew the Fenmores, and she knew Michael and Caroline *were* good, kind people.

"A penny for your thoughts," Will murmured.

"You don't want to know them," she returned. "They're full of regrets and poor decisions made far too long ago for anything to be done about them now."

"I hope marrying me wasn't one of those poor decisions."

Emmie shifted to look him in the face. "I chose you because you could help me, and I could help you. I trusted you, and logically you made the most sense."

"Th—"

"Over the eight years we've been married," she continued over his interruption, "I . . . fulfilled my part of the bargain. Over the past few weeks, however, I've realized that I had a partnership, and not a marriage. I—you're honorable, and witty, and warm, and . . . I just didn't see it." In fact, as she put it all into words, it seemed that after eight years she'd fallen in love with her husband.

"And I wanted a marriage, but settled for a partnership."

"I know. I'm sorry it's taken me so long." She swallowed. "Not too long, I hope."

"No, not too long," he murmured. "When our lives are back in order, though, how do we keep this?" With his free hand he gestured between the two of them.

What did she say to that? Could they maintain this easy intimacy when they no longer had a mutual challenge in front of them? "I don't—"

"Do the cows have a place to go when it rains?" Rose asked, prancing into the drawing room. She'd worn her best pink gown again, despite Emmie's reservations about whether it would still be wearable by the time they actually needed it. There must have been at least a dozen pink ribbons wound through her hair.

"The cattle don't mind the rain," Will said, letting go of Emmie's hand and standing to bow.

Rose sank into a decent curtsy. "If I were a cow, I would be mad at the horses, because they get to be in the stable."

The things this child thought of. "We'll pay an extravagant amount of attention to the cows tomorrow, then," Emmie suggested. "Perhaps an extra bale of hay? We can tell them it came from the horses."

Pursing her lips in consideration, the little girl nodded. "That might do."

George walked into the room behind his sister. Like her, he had worn his best things, a deep gray coat, a pale green waistcoat with a simply tied cravat, and brown trousers. Though they weren't related, he looked very much like a miniature version of Will. If everything went as well as she hoped, no one would ever realize that George and Rose Fletcher weren't Malcolm and Flora Pershing.

Good heavens, they might actually manage to fool everyone and keep Winnover Hall out of Penelope's hands. After that . . . Well, she just wouldn't think about it. Not yet. Caroline Fenmore hadn't agreed, after all, and for all they knew she might never do so.

Emmie stood, curtsying. "Good evening, Malcolm," she said with a smile. "And also to you, Flora."

"Thank you, Mama," Rose said, curtsying again. "I am Flora Pershing. And this is my brother, Malcolm Pershing." She giggled. "I like that Flora means flower, and my name is Rose, which is also a flower."

"Tonight, your name is Flora," George pointed out. "You can't say things like that, or you'll get us stagged." He winced. "You'll get us discovered, I mean."

"I wouldn't say that in front of people," his sister retorted. "I know I'm supposed to be Flora." She wrinkled her nose. "But what do we call the duke? Grandpa Duke? Grandpa Malcolm?"

"You will call him Your Grace," Emmie supplied. "If he wishes to be addressed in a more familiar manner, he will tell you so."

Powell pulled open the far door. "Dinner is served," he announced, ringing the small gong in his hand, and stood aside.

Rose clapped, but subsided when Will lifted an eyebrow at her. Her eccentricities could be a problem, but Emmie imagined that most five-year-olds were a bit silly. Stepping forward, Emmie took Will's arm. With a sigh, George stuck out his forearm and Rose grabbed on to him.

"You're escorting me," she whispered.

"Yes, I know," he said.

"Because I'm a lady."

"Rose—I mean Flora—hush."

"He said the wrong name!" Rose crowed.

"You're not supposed to try to make me make a mistake. If we do, then the agreement's off."

That wasn't strictly true, because she and Will were not going to send the children back to St. Stephen's, regardless. "All we ask is that you do your utmost."

"We have to fool the evil king," Rose said with an excited grin, "or he'll send a witch's curse at us."

Very well, then. "Yes, do try to keep us from being turned into toads, children."

They giggled as they took their seats, Will holding her chair for her, and George doing the same for Rose. When all four of them were seated, Emmie took a look at the table. It had been set for a formal dinner—a pair of polished silver candlesticks as the third in the trio couldn't be located, plates and utensils placed so precisely that Powell and the footmen used rulers when setting them out, sprays of flowers, crystal glasses for wine or lemonade, and seven courses for the dinner.

She'd chosen mutton stuffed with oysters for the main course; it was old-fashioned, but so was her grandfather. Yorkshire black pudding, flavored with lemon thyme, was a favorite of the duke's, so she'd requested that, as well. All but a few of the other courses were stuffy and not her particular favorites, but she wanted George and Rose to experience what they would be facing in Cumberland. Spiced damson cheese, scones with oats and beans, and all the other silly things adults liked to pretend made them feel sophisticated.

One by one the footmen presented the courses, while she and Will demonstrated how to eat them properly. Rose refused to taste the oysters, which led to another discussion about how to move them aside without drawing attention. There were so many things she'd learned as a child, Emmie was realizing, that she'd simply absorbed by watching her parents and their friends. Things that these children had never had the opportunity to observe, and so needed to be taught. Not just about food, but utensils, dress, manners, speech, the world in general—it was, she supposed, like learning a foreign language in a foreign country.

"They look like slugs," Rose whispered, jabbing her fork at one of the oysters gathered at the side of her plate.

"There's no need to give your opinion of something you dislike," Emmie said. "By setting it aside, you've made that known."

"Do I say anything about food I do like? Or does everyone know that I liked it because I ate it?"

Will grinned behind his glass of wine. "A word or two of appreciation is always welcome. The hostess went to a great deal of trouble to choose the meal and the setting, and it makes her happy to know that you like what she's done. Or in His Grace's case, *he* chose everything for his party."

"Sister Mary Claude always said if we left something on our plates, we were insulting God. But sometimes there was weevils. She didn't like hearing about that."

"Flora," George said, elongating his sister's faux name, "we aren't supposed to talk about the orphanage when we're at Welshire Park. Remember?"

"I remember. But we aren't there."

"We're pretending we are."

She blew a raspberry. "How many more courses are there? If I eat much more, I might burst my seams."

"Ah." Emmie dabbed at her mouth with her napkin, and set the blue cloth back on her lap. "Generally, for a large dinner, the hostess—or host—will inform the guests of the courses ahead of time, or will have a menu printed. The trick is to look at the menu, and decide which courses to merely sample, and which to enjoy."

"So I could have just a bite of the mutton and oysters and eat all the scones?"

"Something like that. When a footman brings the platter to you, you may ask him to be sparing, or to be generous."

Rose said the words to herself. "This is very complicated. I did use the correct fork, though."

With a grin, Emmie nodded. "Yes, you did. Well done."

"Maybe we should tell everyone that Flora can't talk," George suggested, only a swiftly hidden grin giving away the fact that he was jesting. "She could make hand gestures, and I could translate for her."

"Here's a hand gesture," Rose said, and gave her brother a two-fingered salute.

"Rose!" Emmie chastised.

"Ha! That was a trick. You called me the wrong name, too," the little girl quipped.

Will snorted, covering the sound with a cough. "Let's concentrate on helping each other rather than tricking each other, shall we?" he commented, sending Emmie a sideways glance, his green eyes dancing.

"Yes, Papa," Rose agreed.

"What about desserts?" George asked. "Can we ask for extra?"

"That's considered rude," Emmie decided, though she could sympathize. "I will say that the duke is quite fond of cake, so I imagine there will be more than one, and that they will all be enormous."

"I hope they're enormous. I could eat one all by myself." Rose poked at the oysters on her plate again as if she expected them to slither away on their own. "I would make an agreement to behave just so I could have cake."

"So would I," George seconded. "If you'd put Mrs. Brubbins's strawberry cake in the agreement, you might've gotten manners and dancing and no cursing just for that."

"Well," Will said, "I am going to begin my next negotiation over trade rights with an offer of cake, then."

The children laughed. All in all, they were doing splendidly. If they could avoid calling each other by the wrong name and referring to the orphanage or the agreement, they all might actually succeed. It was odd, because originally Emmie had thought fooling her grandfather and her family would be a simple matter. After two days with the Fletcher children she'd nearly lost hope, and now it all seemed possible again.

CHAPTER
TWENTY-THREE

Hannah Redcliffe tied off the last stitch in the hem of Rose's yellow gown and bundled it over her arm. Generally, she assumed that one let out the seams of a young girl's dresses as she grew, but with Rose her hems seemed to be coming out every other day.

Leaving the kitchen and her basket of work behind, she headed upstairs to return the dress to the youngster's wardrobe. Rose's door was closed, and she pushed down on the latch and nudged it open. The room looked as it always did, except for one vital difference—Powell, up to his elbows in the girl's blanket chest. "Powell!"

Yelping, the butler shot to his feet and whipped around to face her, one hand over his chest. The other held a trio of spoons. "Good heavens, Hannah, you frightened the wits out of me."

"What are you doing? The Pershings gave their word that no one would look through the children's things." Earning their trust had been difficult enough. If they even had a suspicion that someone was digging through their belongings, there was no telling what might happen.

"I'm not touching the children's things," he stated, cradling the spoons against his chest. "I'm recovering items belonging to the household."

"Th—"

"Haven't you noticed?" he pressed. "Candlesticks going missing? Silverware gone from the table at the end of dinner? Earbobs and necklaces and cuff links gone from Mr. and Mrs. Pershing's rooms?"

"I . . . Well, I noticed the jewelry, but nothing since the other Fletcher boy left. And while I've mislaid buttons and such on occasion, I've always found them again."

He shook his head. "You didn't mislay them, Hannah. They were taken, and I returned them to their rightful place."

"But they're just children." Even as she spoke, though, she had to acknowledge that Powell's statement did explain a few things that she'd found rather odd. She'd thought her mind had gone soft here and there, when something went missing from where she *knew* she'd put it.

"They are miniature varlets. It's taken all of my wits to keep the Pershings from discovering the thefts and tossing the little rogues out on their ears just as they did the brother. Even now there are items I *know* they've absconded with that I still can't locate. We've been searching every dark corner and deep drawer in the house for days. On occasion we root out something, but we haven't discovered their main hoard."

"'We'?" she repeated.

"The rest of the staff and myself. We thought you might feel obligated to inform the Pershings, so we've attempted to keep you out of it. You and Billet, who seems to find these miscreants amusing."

So Tom Billet didn't know, either. She liked that. She liked that Powell's actions had, in a way, turned her and the groom into partners—even if it was partners in ignorance. "But if you had told the Pershings, you might have been rid of George and Rose by now."

"Yes, well, they're needed at the moment."

Hannah looked at the stern-faced butler. "You like them," she stated, grinning.

"Nonsense," he mumbled. "I enjoy outsmarting them."

"Perhaps so, but if you truly thought them varlets, you would have told our employers they were being robbed by three Fletchers instead of one. But you've been keeping it all a secret."

Powell narrowed his eyes. "I don't know what you're talking about." Turning again, he shut the lid of the chest and then reversed course for the door. "Now if you'll excuse me, I need to see these cleaned and polished in time for dinner."

Still gripping the utensils, he strode out of the room. Well. While she'd had a suspicion that the children might have been secreting away a few choice items, clearly she'd underestimated the scope of the thefts. Hannah returned the dress to the wardrobe and closed the heavy mahogany doors.

During her time employed by Mrs. Pershing, she'd seen the butlers at both houses work miracles, organizing the staff and resources for flawless grand dinners, balls, and charity fetes. Now, however, one of the houses had fallen into complete disarray because of two children under the age of nine.

Chuckling, she left the room and trotted downstairs, through the kitchen, and out to the stable. "Tom?"

"He's out behind the stable, Hannah," one of the stable boys informed her as he pitched hay down from the loft.

"Thank you, Johnny." Passing through the door at the

far end of the long building, she found Billet walking Topper, the groom's attention on the gelding's feet. She watched for a moment, a bit mesmerized as the man moved around the horse, every step graceful and sure and calm.

"Hannah," he said, straightening.

Topper snorted, jumping at the sudden movement.

"Damn." Billet caught the bay's bridle with one hand, patting him on the neck with the other. "Easy, lad. It's just a pretty girl."

Her cheeks warmed. "Is Topper well?"

"Aye. I trimmed his hooves this morning and just wanted to see if it's enough, or if I need to send for a farrier."

"Oh."

"What brings you down here?"

Oh yes, that. She'd nearly forgotten. "I just happened upon Powell, digging through Rose's blanket chest. Evidently the little ones have been stealing since before their brother's arrival, and the staff have been attempting to recover the items and return them to their rightful places. It seems to be a bit of a war, and I think the children may be winning."

The groom snorted. "I knew Powell planned to go hunting for missing bits and bobs. No one's come out here to look, though, so evidently I'm in on the dodge, or I'm sympathetic to the snabblers." He grinned. "Or as I might say to a proper young lady, the rest of the house either thinks I'm in on the thefts, or thinks I'm not of a mind to stop them."

"Are you? The second one, that is."

Shrugging, he led Topper over to a fence where a blanket and saddle waited. "I think I understand why the little ones are taking things. If I had nothing and knew I was to be cast out of such an opulent palace, I might be nicking everything in sight myself."

Hannah frowned. "They aren't being cast out. The Pershings are finding a nice home for them."

"I don't know that the scamp and the sprite believe that." The groom saddled the horse as he spoke. "How often do you reckon anything nice has happened to them? I know their own brother told them he'd find them all a proper place to live, too."

"They don't think it'll last, you mean."

"Exactly. They're accustomed to looking after themselves."

"Poor darlings."

Billet swung up into the saddle. "So, when I tell you that they've been spending a fair amount of time in the orchard behind the old fallen tree, I'm thinking you might choose not to pass that bit of information on to Powell."

He did know where they'd been stashing their treasures, clever man. She wondered if Billet was always so aware of everything going on about the property. He certainly paid more attention than she'd realized. "As I wasn't included in the original plan," she said, "I'm inclined to keep any information to myself."

He grinned, the sight making her feel a bit lightheaded. "Good lass." Tom reached down an arm. "Come for a quick ride with me."

"A ride? I—I have duties in the house. I cannot be galloping about the—"

"The family's at luncheon," he broke in over her rambling. "We'll be but ten minutes. Twenty at most. No galloping." He kept his hand outstretched.

She should be thinking of her reputation, of what the

rest of the staff would think to see her riding off with Billet, but instead she took his hand, stepped into the stirrup as he indicated, and flew into the air to land across his thighs. *Good heavens.* Reflexively she put an arm around his shoulders.

"I've got you," he said, smiling at her.

"Where are we going?"

"Just down the hill a bit. I want to show you something."

Before she could ask for more information, he'd tapped his heels against the bay's ribs, and they set off at an easy canter. It was the first time she'd ever ridden a horse, though this was actually more like just sitting on one. Tom was definitely the one doing the riding.

They descended the hill on the road to Birdlip, crossing the small stream on the stone bridge that she always thought of as marking the difference between Winnover Hall and the rest of the world. The Pershings owned the land here, as well, and all the way past Birdlip, but this was where their tenants lived, and it wasn't the Pershing gardeners or staff who cared for it.

Tom pulled up the horse as they reached a small cottage at the edge of the village. It was a pretty thing, with a white fence half obscured by climbing roses, and baskets of flowers hung between the pair of windows overlooking the road. She looked up at the groom to find him gazing at the cottage, as well.

"Why are we stopping here?"

"What do you think of it?" He gestured toward the building.

"It's lovely. Why . . . are we here?"

"I bought it yesterday," he stated, as calmly as if he'd just said "horses eat hay."

She twisted to look him in the eye. "You bought it? Why? You sleep in the stable, do you not?"

The groom nodded. "I told you that my mother pointed her finger at me."

Did that mean he'd met someone? A rock dropped into the pit of her stomach. Ah, so they were friends, and he wanted to show her where he and his wife would be living. And she was supposed to smile and be happy for him, blast it all. "Yes," she said, realizing she needed to say something.

He narrowed his blue eyes a little. "Yes," he repeated. "I reckon it's time for me to get married. A man can't keep his bride in the stable with the lads."

Hannah dug her nails into her palm, concentrating on the sharp pain to keep herself from weeping there in his stupid, manly arms. "That makes sense," she offered, wishing her voice didn't sound quite so mousy and miserable.

"Will you share it with me, then?"

"I'm sure she'll adore it." As she finished speaking, his words sank past her ears and into her mind. "The—we—me?"

"That's right, Hannah. I'm asking you to marry me. Will you?"

Noise, confusion, and a stealthy, growing excitement all swirled about inside her. Certainly they'd always been friendly, but she'd mostly embarrassed herself by hanging about him whenever she could and laughing too loudly when he told a joke during meals in the kitchen. "We haven't even kissed."

Cupping her cheek with his free hand, he tilted his head and touched his mouth to hers. Warmth spread through her, all the way out to her fingers and toes. Wrapping both arms around his neck, she kissed him back again and hoped she wasn't being horribly awkward about it.

After a long set of moments, he lifted his head a little. "Now we've kissed," he said, his voice a bit rough. "I'd like to do that again. Say you'll marry me."

"Oh, goodness," she breathed. "Yes, I'll marry you, Tom."

His grin made her insides heat. "Excellent. Do you want to go look inside?"

When she nodded, he swung down from Topper, then reached up and lifted her down beside him. *Goodness, indeed.* He took her hand as they walked up the short pathway to the blue front door. Her own house, her own husband, only a wedding between her and them.

She froze. *A wedding.* "Tom, we can't say anything until after the Duke of Welshire's party. The Pershings have enough to worry over, and so do the children. They certainly don't need another distraction."

"We're not a distraction from my point of view, Hannah," he returned, "but I take your meaning. We'll tell them after—as long as you come out to the stable for a kiss now and then."

Hannah took a deep breath. Dreams did come true sometimes, it seemed. "Agreed."

"I don't see how dinner last night could have gone any better," Emmie said. "One or two slips, but they recognized them immediately. I slipped once myself."

"They are accomplished prevaricators," Will commented, shuffling through the day's correspondence across from her. "Which reminds me, we should make a point of informing them that nothing at Welshire's estate is to come back here in anyone's pockets."

"Perhaps we could say something, but it would mean letting them know that we know what they've been up to all along. I worry that might be a blow to their confidence at this point, and we're so close to success."

Will laughed. "Did I just hear you say that you don't want to let them know that we're aware of their thievery because that might hurt their feelings?"

"Oh, I don't know." She flipped her hand at him. "Nothing here makes sense any longer. Including me."

"I think it makes perfect sense," he said mildly. "But then I married a woman three days after she proposed to me." He shook his head, a swift grin touching his face. "And is it odd that I find their thievery endearing?"

"If it is odd, then I'm odd, as well."

As he glanced down, the amused expression on his face froze. That made alarm run up her own spine. Will lifted a letter and unfolded it. "Damn," he muttered. "Powell!"

"What is it?" Emmie asked, holding her breath.

"A note from Michael Fenmore."

As Emmie's worry slid into a deep, pinched pain, the butler skidded into the small dining room. "Yes, sir?"

"When did this arrive?" Will held up the letter.

"It came this morning, Mr. Pershing. I wouldn't put it past that little scamp who brings the mail to have forgotten to bring it with him yesterday, though; he came quite early, and seemed in an extreme hurry for some of Mrs. Brubbins's honey-and-oat biscuits."

Will nodded. "Very well, then. We'll be having visitors this afternoon. Please inform the staff. I don't know if they'll be staying for dinner or not."

"Very good, sir." With a nod of his own and a twitch of one cheek, Powell left the room again.

"Today? But . . . we haven't said anything to the children. Can't we send the Fenmores away until after we return from the party?" Emmie felt out of breath, as if her chest was shrinking.

"No, we can't. Caroline wishes to meet the children before they decide. They'll be here any m—"

"Coach on the drive," Edward called out from the foyer.

"—minute," Will finished. "This has to happen, Emmeline. You know that."

Yes, she knew it, because she was the one who'd invented the circumstances in the first place. "We could keep them as our niece and nephew," she whispered. "Staying with us for a time. Eventually it would be permanent, and no one would be the wiser. In London they could be our son and daughter, miraculously recovered from their illnesses."

"Aside from the fact that we would be stripping them of their names and asking them to lie to every acquaintance they ever meet, one of them—or one of us—would make a mistake, and everything would unravel like a worn sock." He took a breath. "Don't make me into the villain, Emmeline. Please."

She put her hands over her face. "I know, I know. I just . . ."

A moment later warm hands came down on her shoulders, and a kiss brushed her hair. "I've become extremely fond of the little pilferers myself."

It wasn't just the children. Everything had become better since they'd arrived. It was all different now, and she liked it that way. She loved it that way. For God's sake, she'd left her bedchamber door open for the past two nights, hoping Will would call, wanting his strong, warm body in her bed.

Powell stepped into the room. "Sir, ma'am, Mr. and Mrs. Fenmore and their child are in the morning room. Shall I offer tea and lemonade?"

"Yes. And biscuits, please. Are the children still at the stable?"

"I believe so. It's been far too quiet for them to have returned to the house."

"Send Donald out after them, will you?" Will returned to his seat. "Have them meet us in here. And have them brought in through the kitchen."

Will was being logical and organized, of course, two things at which he excelled. And he was correct; if the children stayed on with them, they would be forever lying about who they were, what their names were, where they came from—everything. The quiet calm she'd so missed when the little Fletchers had first arrived now seemed foreign and faraway, and she much preferred the barely controlled chaos of the household now. It just wasn't meant to be, though. Lady Anne, Mother, had been correct. It had never been meant to be.

"Dry your eyes, Emmeline," Will murmured. "You'll frighten them. And no, you're not the only one hoping that something goes amiss and the Fenmores decide against taking them."

That short statement reassured her. He was doing as they'd both agreed, but he didn't like it, either. She lifted her napkin and wiped her cheeks, set it back on her lap, and put a smile on her face just as the children trotted into the room.

"I'm teaching General Jenny to curtsy," Rose announced. "It looks like a bow, though."

"Billet said a coach came up the drive," George said. "Who are we supposed to be this time?"

That was the rub. The children might not mind the lies and subterfuge now, but eventually they would. And by then it would be far too late to straighten out the stories.

What if they fell in love? Married? Which name would they use? Who would they be?

"Today you are George and Rose Fletcher," Will answered when Emmie didn't. "You remember Michael Fenmore? You'll be meeting him and his wife, Caroline, and their son, Patrick. I didn't tell you, but Michael is a friend of mine from school, and he knows all about you."

George glanced from Emmie to Will. "These are the ones you chose for us?"

"If you like them, yes."

The eight-year-old narrowed his eyes. "Did he know that when he came here before to scare James?"

"Yes. He's a good man, George."

"We'll see."

"How old is their son?" Rose chimed in.

"He's five years old. Your age, Rose."

"You're certain I'm Rose? I've been practicing Flora all morning."

With a hard breath, the smile still pasted on her face, Emmie stood up and walked over to take Rose's hand. "Yes. You are Rose, my dear. A fair flower and a queen general."

"That's me, for certain." Rose scowled. "I'll go meet them, but I still like it better here."

"And we love having you here," Emmie murmured, not trusting her voice enough to speak any louder. "Let's go, shall we?"

Will had done his part, and she would do hers, but no, she didn't like it. At all.

CHAPTER
TWENTY-FOUR

George had almost managed to put this bit out of his mind, the part where he and Rose would have to meet whomever the Pershings had chosen to be their new parents.

All of his free time had been taken up with keeping count of how many treasures they'd nicked, and how long the blunt from selling the baubles off would see them fed and clothed, even though he still hadn't even decided for certain where they should go—because he actually didn't want to go anywhere. But what he wanted didn't matter; this was about what *had* to happen.

With the servants all interfering it had gotten even more complicated, because he and his sister had to take the things they needed, plus some things they didn't so that the staff would have things to find and put back where they belonged.

In a way it had become a game, and as he followed Rose and the Pershings into the morning room, he realized that pretending this was a contest between him and Powell had been a mistake. It could only be a game when the winner didn't matter. But everything kept moving forward, and now there was a family for them to meet.

Staying here at Winnover Hall wouldn't last. No miracle had happened.

"George, Rose, you know Mr. Fenmore. This is Mrs. Fenmore and young Patrick. Caroline, I am pleased to introduce George and Rose Fletcher to you."

With that statement Mr. P stepped out of the way, and George looked at the Fenmores. The man, Michael, had been polite before, but now George knew why he'd looked at him and Rosie so much. He was broad and soft-looking, not all hard edges like Mr. P. But he looked nervous today. The lady had blond hair in a high bun, with little curls in front of either ear. From the way she looked at him and then Rose, she wasn't convinced that her family needed two more children in it. Well, neither was he.

"I'm Rose," Rose said, making a curtsy. "I'm five years old." She walked up to the skinny little boy with yellow hair standing beside his mother. "Are you five years old, too?"

"Yes," Patrick answered. "Five and a half."

"I'm still the youngest, then. That's good. But I'm not a baby."

George watched her with these new people. Rosie made everyone like her, and he wished he knew how she did it. He never knew what to say, because he didn't trust anyone not to try to use it against him later.

But then Rose had him to protect her, and he didn't have anyone. Not even when he'd been littler and pretended James cared about them. For a while he'd managed to forget that good nights of sleeping and a full stomach and the knowledge that nothing bad was about to happen wouldn't last forever. Here, though, was the proof that no one would look after him and his sister as well as he did, because the Pershings were giving them away.

"Hello, George," the stout man said, holding out his hand. "You know why we're here today, yes?"

"Yes." George shook his hand, even though he wanted to leave the room, collect his clothes, and head out to the orchard for their treasures. "Hello again."

"I've told Caroline that you're an impressive young man. And although previously I was pretending to be a solicitor, I actually am one. I help people with rules and laws."

A solicitor was almost as bad as a Bow Street Runner. "You help people take blunt from other people, you mean," he stated.

"I actually specialize in land purchases and water rights, with some inheritances thrown in for flavor. I like to think of myself as a navigator on a ship. The captain is my client, and I help him avoid the rocks and whirlpools."

"Our papa was on a ship. He's in Davy Jones' locker now." Rose sent her brother a glance, clearly proud that she hadn't said "locket" this time.

"I'm sorry to hear that, dear," Mrs. Fenmore said, finally stirring. "Were you very young when it happened?"

"I was a baby. I don't even remember him. George does, a little, but I think sometimes he pretends to remember when he really doesn't."

Well, he wouldn't have to pretend if she didn't keep asking for stories about their father and pirates and whales and Frenchmen. This was stupid, and he didn't like it. He didn't like that she was just saying things like she didn't care who they lived with, because he *did* care. And if it couldn't be the way he wanted, then they would live on their own.

"George, Rose, why don't you show Patrick your ponies?" Mrs. P suggested.

"Oh yes," Rose gushed, grabbing Patrick's hand. "Mine is a boy and he's named General, but I call him General Jenny because a lady should ride a lady horse."

George didn't want to go, because he knew what would be happening in the morning room while they were somewhere else. Mr. P would say what fine children they were, and Mrs. P would say they were high-spirited but sweet darlings. None of it would be his decision, but they would all expect him to go along with it because he was only eight years old.

"You're a damned pettifogger, is what you are!" he burst out, jabbing a finger at Michael Fenmore. "Rubbing elbows with bugaboes and Philistines! And you don't want us at all, Mrs. Princum Prancum." Clenching his fists, he whipped around and bolted out the door.

He was halfway up the stairs when a hard hand closed on his shoulder and pulled him to an abrupt stop. "George," Mr. P said in a low voice. "We have an agreement about slang."

George twisted to look up at the tall man. "I just insulted your friend, and you're mad about slang?" he asked, frowning.

"Michael is a solicitor; do you think he's never been insulted before? And if I'm not mistaken, you actually called Caroline a well-dressed woman, isn't it?"

"A snooty one," George corrected.

"Ah. I'm more concerned that you're trying to break the agreement only a few days before the duke's party. I've brought you some prospective parents, which is my part of the agreement. An agreement you signed, if you'll recall."

"I don't care." George shrugged out of Mr. P's grip, but he didn't try to run again. He wasn't sure where he wanted to go. "I don't want them."

"You don't even know them yet."

"I don't want to know them." Squeezing his hands into fists, he tried to find the words to explain why he was so mad. He knew what he wanted to say, but he couldn't say those words, either. "Just cross out that part of the agreement. We'll go to the party, and then just leave us alone."

"You know I can't do that. We want you two to be safe and happy and . . . and loved, George."

"Then why can't we stay here?"

As soon as he yelled the words he turned around and rushed up the rest of the stairs. He didn't want to see Mr. P's face if he looked disgusted or annoyed or any of the other expressions that meant the Pershings didn't want them, had never wanted them, and would be happy to see the last of them.

This time Mr. P didn't chase him, so he ran into his bedchamber and closed the door, then crawled under the bed. Little spaces, dark spaces, were safer when you didn't know where to go. Hopefully he'd made the Fenmores mad enough that they would leave and not come back, so the Pershings would have to start looking for a family to adopt them all over again.

Will sat on the stairs as George fled. Damn. *Damn, damn, damn.* The boy wanted to stay. George wanted him—*him*—and Emmeline to be his parents. The thing he'd been avoiding in his mind for weeks, the thing he and Emmeline never discussed, had now been spoken, and by an eight-year-old boy.

Warm wet plopped onto the back of his hand. For God's sake, now he was weeping. He wiped at his cheek, taking a deep breath and reminding himself that he'd brokered agreements to open trade routes, thereby ending wars, and that the dilemma here was a small, insignificant one compared to that. Except that it wasn't.

Pushing to his feet, he returned to the foyer, took another breath, and opened the morning room door. Rose and Patrick were gone, presumably to see the ponies. "I didn't expect that. My apologies, Michael, Caroline. I'm certain he didn't mean any of it, if that makes a difference."

Fenmore shrugged. "I've been called worse. That doesn't trouble me as much as the reason for it; the boy clearly doesn't want to go with us."

"He's comfortable here. That doesn't mean this is the best place for him. Emmeline and I have tried to figure something out, believe me." He sat beside his wife, and she wrapped her hand around his arm. "They're here because of lies, and those lies would remain with them if they stayed."

Caroline sat forward a little. "They aren't dangerous, are they? Michael said they grew up on the streets of London."

"No, they're not dangerous," Emmeline answered. "They are very independent, however. With an exaggerated belief that they will do well if left to their own devices." She sighed. "It will take them time to learn to trust you."

"I have no worries about the little girl; she's darling. But the boy . . ."

"They go together," Will said, sounding sharper than he meant to.

"Will," Emmeline murmured.

"You mentioned a thousand pounds a year to help us see to them. How long do you mean for that to continue?

That is to say, until they come of independent age? Or until they marry? I just want everything to be decided before we make our decision." Caroline sat back again.

Money. It always came down to that. Still, Will could see why she'd brought it up. Children were expensive, and the Fenmores were being asked to take on two more than they'd planned for. "We'll set up a fund. The money will go to you, five hundred for each child, until they turn eighteen. At that time the money will go directly to them, for . . ." He glanced at Emmeline, who nodded, leaning her head against his shoulder. "For the remainder of their lives."

"That's very generous, Will, for two children you've known for but a month."

"They're enabling us to keep our home. I—we—could do no less."

Could they do more, though? That was the question that would keep him awake nights for the rest of his life. And it wasn't as if the children were only gifting them with Winnover Hall; they'd also given him a wife who'd once again become the smiling, witty woman who'd tangled his heart practically from the moment he'd met her. He'd attempted to will himself out of love with her when she clearly didn't love him back, but even so, he'd always admired her. Now, though, he couldn't imagine being without her. *Love.* The children had brought it with them, somehow, and now they were sending them away.

The Fenmores put their heads together to confer, and Will faced Emmeline. "George asked why they couldn't stay here," he whispered. "I didn't have a damned answer for him."

"They'll understand when they're older," she returned

in the same low tone, her voice catching. "They would come to resent all the lies, and us. You know that, just as I do."

He nodded. "I do know. And I still don't like it."

"Neither do I, Will. But I don't have a better solution."

"Neither do I," he repeated. "Though I wish to hell I did."

"We'll take them," Michael said into the quiet. "Hopefully they will eventually come to trust us as much as they do the two of you." He stood, drawing Caroline up after him. "I don't think we should stay, though; I doubt today will convince anyone of anything. What say you accompany them to Brockworth after you return from Cumberland? We don't have the room to put both you and the children up, but there are some fine inns in the village."

Will stood up and offered his hand. "Yes. And thank you. Thank you, Michael. Caroline. You have no idea how much easier this sets my mind, to know they'll be well cared for."

The solicitor tilted his head. "I have an idea. I am a parent, too, you know."

I am a parent, too, you know.

For better than a week those words had been echoing in Emmie's mind.

They'd dug into her when she'd gone upstairs to find George after the Fenmores had left. She'd discovered the boy beneath his bed, Rose under there with him. The little girl had an arm over her brother's back, and she'd brought a pair of pillows into the makeshift cave with her, one for each of them.

Four days ago, when they'd packed for the trip to Cumberland and George had asked if their things would still be at Winnover Hall when they returned, she'd nearly broken down into tears. The children were giving them Winnover Hall, and in doing so, were ensuring their own exile from it. That was how it felt, anyway.

If this was parenthood, she'd never realized how very much it hurt. And yet she'd felt all the other emotions, too, when one of the little ones smiled at her or hugged her or asked her to read them a story or demanded an explanation for lightning. She adored it, she would miss it more than she could ever express, and she didn't regret a moment of it.

There was even more to it than that. The warm arm currently draped across her shoulder, long fingers twined with hers—that was not . . . new, but at the same time, it was. The way she felt having Will there in the bed with her, sleeping beside her, that was new. The fondness and humor in his eyes when she looked up at him, that was new, as well. It had taken her eight years to figure out, but evidently procreation wasn't just about making children, and a friend could also be a very passionate—and very patient—lover. And without that burden . . . well, *good heavens.*

"Good morning," he murmured, followed by a kiss to the nape of her neck.

"Good morning," she said, shifting onto her back so she could see him.

"How are you?"

How was she? Relaxed, a bit aroused, comfortable—all things she hadn't been in his presence for eight years, until the past few weeks. And especially the past few nights. "Feeling a bit naughty."

"I—" He narrowed his eyes. "Which kind of knotty?"

Chuckling, she reached out and ran one finger down his well-muscled chest. "This kind."

"Ahh." Will closed in for a long, slow, heart-pounding kiss. "Another reason I'm glad we've taken an additional day for travel," he murmured, shifting his attention to her throat.

She sighed. If only they could turn the coaches around and head back to Winnover. Today . . . Today they would secure Winnover Hall. There was no sense in thinking otherwise. "I'm worried about this afternoon."

"Yesterday would have been more difficult, with a hundred people arriving and settling into rooms, and a large formal dinner. We've avoided that by being late."

"Which will raise questions, because we're never late to anything."

"Yes, but this time we have sickly children with us. They'll garner some attention when we first arrive because they've been much mentioned but never seen until now, but with the party already begun, hopefully any greetings will be brief. We've made it as easy on George and Rose—Malcolm and Flora—as we can."

"Yes." She put a palm against his cheek, rough with its morning stubble of beard. "Regardless of what happens, though, I . . . I don't want things to go back the way they were, Will."

"I don't want that, either." His fingers, still twined with hers, tightened. "I like being in love with my wife."

She lifted up and kissed him. Love was . . . extraordinary. And unpredictable. The peskiest thing about it was that once it awakened, there was no telling who it would surround and encompass and make vital. And it had seized on two precocious little children with the same fierceness that it had this connection between her and Will.

The door to the inn's adjoining room rattled. "Are you awake?" Rose's muffled voice sounded through the keyhole. "We want to go have breakfast."

"Go ahead," Emmie answered. "We'll be down shortly."

She'd brought Hannah along, because she wasn't about to do her own hair with a hundred relatives there to pass judgment on it, and she slipped on her dressing robe to go fetch the maid and have Davis, Will's valet, come see to him.

"I keep reminding myself it wouldn't be fair to the children to keep them," Will said, as he pulled on his black, formal trousers.

"Yes," she agreed, not certain why he wanted to revisit this same argument again. "Too many lies have been told. That's on me, I know, but they would be the ones to suffer for it if they stayed."

"It's not on you," he stated, straightening. "You kept us in our home. But I keep trying to find a path where we can untangle everything and have them stay. I want them to stay."

"I want them to stay, too, Will. But we can't even ask them if that's what they wish, because they simply don't understand the consequences. Or the responsibility of pretending to be other people for their entire lives."

"I detest problems without solutions; I don't believe in them," he countered, scowling.

Emmie looked at him for a long moment. Of course he expected to find a solution, because that was what he did. "If you think of one, please tell me. I promise I will be amenable."

"Likewise, my dear."

When she headed downstairs, Rose in her festive pink

dress was explaining to the innkeeper that she liked visiting different inns every day, because she could ask for trifle after dinner every night and it wasn't too much burden on any one cook—which it evidently was for Mrs. Brubbins.

"All of Mrs. Brubbins's desserts are delightful," Emmie said, sitting beside Rose and opposite Will and George. "Making the same one every night would be tiresome, don't you think?"

"Yes, but eating them isn't at all tiresome."

With a chuckle the innkeeper gave the little girl a bow. "I shall tell my wife that you adored her trifle. You'll have her smiling for days, young miss."

After he left the table, Rose leaned over Emmie's shoulder. "I didn't want to tell him," she whispered, "that Mrs. Brubbins's trifle is better than his wife's. He doesn't need to know that."

"Very wise of you," Emmie whispered back, and kissed the girl's cheek.

Rose giggled. "I am *so* wise."

That was the way to do this. The way she and Will had been proceeding—giving the children the best experiences they could manage, giving them time to have fun, to laugh, to be children. The worrying and crying—well, that was for her to do. Not George and Rose.

"Are you two ready?" Will asked. "The easiest approach would probably be not to speak unless you're spoken to. You can always pretend to be shy."

"Well, we've been sickly," Rose stated. "Should we cough every now and then? I could faint. I'm a good fainter." She put the back of her hand to her forehead and sank down on the bench.

"The idea is to be unnoticed," her brother said. "Don't say much, and don't be remembered."

"But have fun," Will put in. "Remember? Cakes and pies and God knows what else."

"How many days do we stay after the party?" George picked at his eggs. "Doing all the pretending today will be easy. It's always easier to lie when everyone's paying attention to something else, like dancing or a party. After that, though, I'm worried Rose might forget that she's supposed to be Flora."

"I wrote my grandfather that we would only be able to stay for three nights because of Will's—your papa's—work, and we're already a day late."

"Because the coach threw a wheel," Rose recited. "I wasn't scared, though."

That had been the simplest story, and Roger their driver had agreed to tell it as well, if asked. The Winnover staff making the impossible possible for them once again. "You were very brave, Flora."

"Thank you, Mama," the girl quipped. "By the way, you look lovely. I think I might like a lavender gown, too, one day. A very fancy one, with beads like yours."

Out of the corner of her eye Emmie saw George open his mouth then shut it again. That was George, looking out for his sister even if it meant declining to remind her that the daughter of a solicitor likely wouldn't have many occasions to wear a fancy lavender gown. Of course he might well intend to go live under a church again, which would also preclude fancy attire. She and Will were going to have to post guards when they returned.

"You would look lovely in lavender," Emmie said, smiling. "But my goodness, you are spectacular in pink."

"Yes, I am. George—I mean, Malcolm—looks handsome, too. Davis tied his cravat for him."

"Davis helped me tie my cravat as well," Will said, tugging a little at the simple ruffles.

"I tried it first, but I made a knot," Emmie confessed, chuckling.

Will buttered his toast. "Nearly strangled me, she did."

Even George grinned at that. *Good.* "Please have fun today, dears. You've worked very hard, and I know you'll do your best. That's all we ask of you."

George took a bite of egg. "I'm not supposed to tell," he said, "but I heard Billet talking before we left. He asked Hannah to marry him. He bought a cottage at the near end of Birdlip for the two of them."

Emmie blinked. *Her* Hannah? The woman had never said a word about it. Of course, everyone knew that she'd been making moon eyes at Tom Billet for better than three years, but this . . . "Are you certain?"

The boy nodded. "I know things."

Grasping her hands together, Rose squealed. "A wedding? Can I be the flower girl?"

Before anyone could point out that the Fletchers wouldn't be at Winnover by the time a wedding took place, Emmie grinned at her. "I think we should wait until Hannah tells us her news, and then we could suggest it. If perhaps she should need a flower girl, you would make yourself available. Something like that."

"But—"

"Because, as you know, Brockworth is only an hour away," Emmie pushed over George's objection. "So, wherever you are, you would be available."

"Does that mean we would still get to see you?"

Emmie pressed her palm against her heart so it wouldn't break and fall out of her chest. "I insist upon it, Rose."

"Flora," Rose whispered. "We're still practicing."

"Yes. Right you are, Flora. Now, you and Malcolm finish up your breakfast. We're only an hour away from Welshire Park, and the birthday celebration will have begun in earnest."

CHAPTER
TWENTY-FIVE

Hopefully they had reviewed everything the children would encounter. Emmie's parents, Sir Fitzwilliam and Lady Anne Hervey, were to be addressed as Grandmama and Grandpapa, and the little ones would have no reason to recognize anyone at all. They had gone over the names and relationships in general, so once they met Frederick Chase they would know he was Cousin Penelope's oldest, and when they were introduced to ten-year-old Roderick, Lord Ramsey, they would know to bow, as he was third in line to inherit the dukedom.

But they were little, and couldn't be expected to remember everything. As long as they kept to their manners and their names and didn't mention the orphanage or larceny, everything should go swimmingly. Emmie crossed her fingers. It *would* go swimmingly.

After breakfast they took the first coach and headed down the lane, leaving Hannah and Davis and the majority of their luggage to follow. "Flora and I couldn't help noticing," George said as he turned away from the window and sank back on the plush leather seat, "that you've been sharing a bedchamber at the inns where we've been staying, Mama and Papa."

Emmie's face warmed. "Malcolm and Flora are far too young to be paying attention to such things."

"And I saw you kiss this morning," Rose pointed out, making smacking sounds with her lips. "I think it's romantic."

"As do I," Will noted from his seat opposite Emmie.

"Mm-hmm. So, tell me, Flora, who is Lucy Chase to you?"

Rose squeezed her eyes closed. "She is our second cousin, and she's six years old," she said, opening them again. "She has curly blond hair."

"Very good. Malcolm, tell me about Roderick Ramsey."

"He's Lord Ramsey," George said, sitting straighter. "He's ten, and his father is Lord Talmot, the Duke of Welshire's oldest grandson. Talmot's father is Lord Heyton, the Duke of Welshire's oldest son."

"Good. And what rank is Lord Ramsey?"

"He's a viscount. His papa is an earl, his grandpapa is a marquis, and his great-grandpapa is the Duke of Welshire."

"Excellent. If you don't know who someone is, just ask. With so many relations there, I'm not certain even I would know them all. Oh, and Malcolm, don't forget—you are seven years old."

George made a face. "I'm much older than that. Seven is little."

"Yes, but eight would mean that Emmeline and I had a child out of wedlock," Will quipped.

"Deirdre was had out of wedlock," Rose supplied.

"And who is Deirdre, pray tell?" Emmie asked, lifting an eyebrow.

"Oh. Deirdre is a friend of ours from back at Winnover Hall." Rose leaned forward. "Is that right?"

"Yes. But please try not to mention anyone from the stone jug. It will complicate things greatly."

George laughed. "You said a slang."

Emmie put on an innocent look. "Did I?"

They settled into a reasonably peaceful rest of their drive, though the children sitting on the edge of their seats was a good indicator that they remained nervous. She was nervous, as well; she would be piling more lies onto the ones she'd been telling everyone up to and including her own parents for the past seven years.

But the three days at Welshire Park would be easy compared to the one after they returned to Winnover and she'd have to help Rose and George pack for the last time before they all drove to Brockworth and she and Will returned alone. Emmie took a breath. That was for later. Thinking about it now wouldn't help anything, her nerves least of all.

"Mr. Pershing, we're in view," Roger called from the driver's seat above them.

Immediately the children clambered onto the seats to look out the windows. "Good glory, it's spanking huge!" George declared. "It makes Winnover look like a doll-house."

A very lovely and warm and comfortable dollhouse, but yes, Emmie could see the comparison. Her grandfather's land accounted for over half the shire, after all. It was only fitting that his house should match the grandeur of his properties.

"There are people *everywhere*," Rose said, holding on to her pink bonnet with one hand as she leaned out the window. "Are we related to all of them?"

"Most of them, yes. Are you ready? Because I think you're going to do smashingly."

"I'm ready," Rose said. "And we can have all the cake and sweets we want?"

"Just don't cast up your accounts on anyone's finery if you eat too much, Flora," George added.

"I won't. I'm not a baby, Malcolm."

As the coach stopped and a pair of red-and-yellow-liveried footmen pulled open the door, Emmie exchanged a glance with Will. This was it. The next few hours would decide their fates, and they'd wagered it all on two orphans who'd spent the last weeks robbing them blind.

"His Grace is in the garden," one of the footmen said. "You're the last to arrive."

"We'll go say hello, then, shall we?" She walked through the foyer with the children, waving to a cousin sitting in the morning room with three other people she vaguely recognized. While she had been her parents' only child, her mother had six brothers and sisters, and some of them had had at least that many offspring themselves. They had rightly been referred to as "Welshire's Horde" in the past.

The main hallway went on for ages, and while she tried to ignore the family portraits that lined every bit of wall not covered by a window, the children were clearly fascinated. "That one looks like you," Rose noted, pointing at a painting of a pretty girl in pearls.

"That's my mother," she whispered, offering her hands to the youngsters. "Lady Anne. Don't get distracted now. You'll need all your wits about you."

"I have all my wits," the little girl returned.

In the garden the staff had set up several large canopies, with drinks and delicacies offered beneath them, and scatterings of chairs all about the large grounds. As she'd expected, they—or the children, rather—received more than a few curious looks as they headed for the largest of the canopies and the cluster of people beneath it.

Will took Rose's free hand, smiling over the girl's head at Emmie. "I wouldn't wager against us," he murmured. "We are splendid."

"Oh yes, we are," Rose agreed.

"There you are," a gravelly voice came from the shaded depths beneath the canopy. "I'd begun to wonder if you meant to ignore my birthday entirely."

With a deep breath, Emmie released the children and walked forward as the crowd parted. The shifting skirts and breeches revealed an iron-straight man with iron-colored hair sitting on what might as well have been an iron throne rather than a plush red-velvet chair. "Your Grace," she said, curtsying before she bent down to kiss one gaunt cheek. "Grandfather."

He glanced up at her, then beyond her again. "Emmeline. William. And these are my great-grandchildren, are they? They don't look sickly."

"They're much recovered this year, I'm relieved to say," she responded. "Malcolm, Flora, come meet your great-grandfather."

Will had to nudge them from behind. First Rose and then George stepped forward like they were walking on broken glass. "I'm Malcolm," George said, and bowed deeply at the waist.

"I'm Flora Pershing," Rose put in, curtsying so deeply she nearly sat on the ground. "Hello, Your Grace."

"We know who you are, don't we?" the duke said to the growing crowd at large. "Been waiting for you since yesterday."

"Our coach broke a wheel," Will said. "We sent a note."

"Yes, yes. All full of politeness, everyone is. Go on, then. Mingle with the other vultures. We're serving luncheon inside. It's too bloody hot to do it out here."

A moment later Emmie's mother and father approached. "Well, hello, Malcolm and Flora," Lady Anne said, tapping Rose on one cheek with a forefinger. "You are darlings, aren't you?" She kissed Emmie on her cheek. "I'd begun to think they were lepers," she whispered. "They look perfectly normal, though."

The things that came to Emmie's mind in reply to her mother's comment would have been judged much more harshly than slang. "Flora, Malcolm, these are my parents. Your grandmama and grandpapa."

"Sir Fitzwilliam and Lady Anne," Rose muttered, and flung her arms around her faux grandmother's waist. "It's very nice to meet you, Grandmama."

"Oh! It's very nice to meet you, Flora. And you as well, Malcolm." She reached over to pat George's cheek.

As Lady Anne straightened again, Will shook Sir Fitzwilliam's hand. "I see His Grace is as warm as ever," he muttered.

"Some things never change. Malcolm Ramsey, chief among them." Emmie's father patted his pretend grandchildren on the head, like they were dogs. "I'm glad you finally decided to allow these young ones into the daylight, William. A man wants to see his line continue, even if it's under another family's name."

Will shrugged. "I blame the physicians, telling us to keep them away from everyone. Thankfully, they've improved this autumn."

"Is Penelope here?" Emmie asked, even though she already knew the answer to that. Cousin Penelope would never miss a chance to ingratiate herself with their grandfather.

"Yes. They arrived a day early, I believe, she and Howard and the three little ones. The children are playing down by the pond, if yours would like to join them."

"Do you wish to join them?" Emmie asked.

"Yes, please," Rose answered, and George nodded.

"Very well. Nothing too strenuous," she instructed, since they had been invalids for most of their pretend lives, after all. "And we'll see you inside for luncheon."

Holding hands, the Fletcher children trotted off toward the Welshire Park pond, and Emmie sent up a quick prayer that at the end of the next three days she and Will would still be calling Winnover Hall home.

Two hours later, Penelope Chase took the seat to Emmie's right, roughly in the middle of the absurdly long dining table. "I was wondering if you would make an appearance at all," her cousin said without preamble.

"Hello, Pen. It's good to see you, as well. And thank you for your concern, but we're fine. Luckily the coach was on level ground when the wheel came off."

The blond-haired woman leaned backward to peer around Emmie's shoulder. "William. You've finally deigned to acknowledge your children. I was beginning to think you'd made them up."

Emmie forced a laugh. "We can't all have children as healthy and round as yours. Speaking of which, where are the little ones?"

Her cousin gestured toward the east wing of the house. "You know how Grandfather is, with his 'Children are best neither seen nor heard once they've been added to the family.' He set up a separate table for them in the small ballroom."

Oh dear. She'd wanted a few moments to ask Rose and George how they'd fared, if they needed any more information, and if they were enjoying themselves. They'd considered Winnover to be opulent, so Welshire Park must have been like a maharajah's grand palace to their eyes.

"I spoke with my Frederick," Pen went on, naming her oldest. "I told him specifically to make Malcolm and Flora feel welcome, since they've never met any of their own relations before."

"That's very kind of you." As she recalled, Frederick was a spoiled little twit a few months younger than George, but that only meant that George and Rose would have no difficulty outsmarting him.

"Are you ever going to confess that you played me for a fool, Emmie? Or at least admit that the entire time you were congratulating me for winning Winnover Hall you and Will had a plan to wed first?"

Emmie smiled. "When I spoke to you, I had no idea I would be marrying Will." On her other side, his fingers brushed her elbow. "I am, however, very happy to have done so. And not just for the sake of Winnover."

Her cousin's eyes narrowed. "Keep your nasty little secrets to yourself, then, you and your perfect life. I don't care."

At the moment her life didn't feel so very perfect, but they seemed to be close to keeping their secrets, which would have to be enough.

Down at the far end of the table, so distant he might have been in another shire, the Duke of Welshire stood. Picking up a glass and a knife, he rapped one against the other, even though the room fell silent the moment he rose.

"Thank you all for coming to my birthday party," he said. "Most of you know what I think of you, but it does my soul good to see so many who carry the Ramsey bloodline gathered about me. Watered down as it's become, it's still my legacy. And some of you are even respectable. So, happy birthday to me." He lifted his glass.

Everyone stood, echoing the birthday wishes but not the insults, and drank. They all sat again, and as the servants brought around the first course, Emmie heard a sound in the distance. A distinct, high-pitched shriek that sounded like a very angry, and very familiar, young man. *Oh no.* She pushed to her feet. "Excuse me."

She hadn't been to Welshire Park in years, and it took her a moment to find the small ballroom. As she searched, the sound of glass breaking led her past two more doorways and down a short hall, and then she stepped into . . . hell.

"Say that again, you ass!" George demanded.

Ten-year-old Lord Ramsey pushed the boy in the shoulder. "I said, you don't belong here. The servants eat in the kitchen, and you're not even fit to be there."

"In the stable, maybe!" Frederick Chase chimed in—and abruptly took an egg to the forehead.

More raw egg hit Emmie in the shoulder, the sound an odd combination of crack and squelch. Wet dripped down her cleavage and her lavender bodice, down to the ribbon at her waist, a sickly yellowish green further marred by flecks of eggshell.

"Malcolm!" she said in her sternest voice.

"I came for the cake!" George shouted, his face beet red and his fists clenched. He climbed onto the table. "Stupid Frederick Shits-in-His-Pants Chase says there's no cake, and I ain't being polite while these wormy-tongued gundiguts call me names!"

"You know you didn't come for the cake," Emmie said, keeping her voice low and calm.

"That's what you think!" With that George pulled another egg from the bucket he'd commandeered.

"Don't do it," she warned him, shifting a little to put more distance between her and the already splattered quartet of shrieking children nearest to her.

Whoever had decided an entire separate room should be set aside for the youngsters to have luncheon was clearly an idiot. At the same time, she had to admit that no one could possibly have anticipated her children. The cook certainly hadn't, or she wouldn't have left a bucket of fresh eggs anywhere the resourceful eight-year-old could find them.

He threw the egg. This time Emmeline saw it coming and ducked. Directly behind her, the thud and crack was answered by a low grunt. She risked a glance over her shoulder, to see her husband framed in the doorway, frozen as his previously white cravat dripped with yellow yolk and light brown eggshell.

Will took a breath, eyes narrowed as he assessed the chaos of the room. "This is going well, I see," he commented, motioning her to circle left as he veered around another patch of food-smeared youngsters to the right.

"We nearly made it through luncheon," she returned, smiling grimly.

"I'm rather proud of us, my dear." He slipped behind a pillar and ducked out of sight.

"Come down from that table, young man!" she ordered, trying to keep George's attention on herself until Will could work his way around behind the food-strewn battlefield. "We use our words in this family. Not our fists. And certainly not eggs." A handful of spring peas rained down around her, at least one of them bouncing down the neckline of her gown and squishing coldly into her bosom. "Or vegetables!" They hadn't even served peas; heaven knew how they'd ended up in his pockets.

"There *is* cake, Georgie!" another familiar voice announced from somewhere behind the table where a dozen more children cowered behind chairs and pillars and their parents, as the grown-ups began arriving from the dining room. "I found it in the kitchen hallway!" A plate teetered up over the edge of the table, atop it a misshapen white lump of what had most assuredly and very recently been a finely decorated cake. Rose's white-icing-and-pink-ribbon-streaked brown hair and oval face popped up behind the rounded blob. "It was too big, so I brung you the top part of it."

"It doesn't matter now, Rosie," George responded, bending down to take her hand and pull her up onto the table beside him. "We don't want it. Stupid, noddy Roderick Lord-Pig-Face Ramsey said we was gutter rats not fit to eat their fine food, and he said you had fleas in your hair."

"I don't have fleas!" Rose yelled, dipping down for a handful of cake and flinging it at the cowering Roderick, Viscount Ramsey, where it added to the dripping egg already covering the young viscount's front. "It was a beetle, and you put it there, you pig-widgeon!"

The flung frosting added a festive patina to Emmeline's gown as well, but most of it went to her left, across the front of her second—or was it third?—cousin's torso. "This isn't helping your cause, dears," she said, keeping her voice level.

"We don't have a cause. We did what you asked, and look! Stupid and fancy and snobbish is all they care about, and that ain't us. I reckon you should send us back to the orphanage!"

Rose bent down and picked up a table knife, pointing it at Roderick. "En garde, you niffynaffy scrub!"

At that moment Will launched himself forward out of the destruction, grabbing a child beneath each arm.

Emmie swept in from the front, shoving the bucket of eggs well out of reach. "Take one," Will grunted, lifting Rose in her direction.

Emmeline wrapped both arms around the squirming, yelling five-year-old, bending her head to reach Rose's ear. "This is my fault," she whispered. "Just take a deep breath. We'll take care of everything."

As she turned around, though, she froze. The huddled relatives young and old, children dripping with egg and cake and God knew what else, parents all frowning and yelling at the food and abuse being hurled at their offspring, grew quiet. A heartbeat later, she saw the reason for the sudden silence.

The Duke of Welshire himself stood in the doorway. "What the devil is going on here?" he asked, his low voice tight and clenched.

Taking a deep breath, Emmie hefted the sobbing Rose to her other shoulder. As she did so, a silver fork fell from the hem of the girl's pink gown and clattered onto the floor. "Yes. I believe I owe you an explanation, Grandfather."

CHAPTER
TWENTY-SIX

"*I* was the one who ruined it," George muttered, pulling against Will's grip on his arm. "Rose said she liked when Mrs. P—and not Mama—read to her at bedtime, and I tried to distract everyone by saying I could pitch pennies and would take anyone on, and then everything . . ." He put his hands out and wiggled his fingers as if dirt was trickling through them. "It just fell apart."

"Who started calling whom names?" Will asked in a low voice, keeping pace behind Emmeline and Rose, who in turn followed the Duke of Welshire into the depths of his rambling house. "The truth, because I heard you using some rather colorful descriptions."

"They figured out we didn't belong to you, and they started calling us gypsies, and then said the gypsies had sold us to you, and then Rose said we were orphans. That damned Lord Ramsey put a beetle in her hair and started yelling that she had lice, and then Frederick Chase said we belonged in a stable. I had to hit him with an egg to shut him up."

"Can't say I blame you, lad."

"But I ruined it."

It *was* ruined, undoubtedly, unless Emmeline meant to spin another of her masterful stories about how vivid her children's imaginations were, and that they always took turns making up stories to pass the time while they were in their sickbeds. *Hmm.* That might actually work.

Catching Emmeline's shoulder, he whispered the basic outline to her. "Welshire's more likely to believe you than the pompous little brats teasing our children, anyway," he finished.

She nodded. "It could work," she whispered back. "Well done."

As they reached the duke's large study, he bent down toward George. "It's not ruined yet. Stay quiet and listen."

The boy nodded, wiping tears from his face.

The duke took a seat behind his massive mahogany desk. Steepling his fingers against the well-polished surface, he nodded. "Sit down."

With Rose on her lap and whimpering, Emmeline sat in one of the chairs facing the desk. Will gave the second chair to George, and he stood beside his wife, one hand on her shoulder.

"You made a mess of things, young man," Welshire stated, glaring at George. "More importantly, you made a wreck of my house. Explain yourself."

"I—"

"Malcolm and Flora have spent most of their lives with only each other for company," Emmeline interrupted before George could confess anything. "And for much of that time, they've been quite ill. We make up tales, tell stories, things to keep their imaginations engaged and quell their boredom. Evidently Flora told one of our stories to the other children, and it got her teased. Malcolm stepped in to defend her when they began calling her a liar."

"And a baby," Rose added.

The duke pinned each of them with a hard look, no

doubt meant to induce them to confess any falsehoods. Well, he'd chosen the wrong family to intimidate. Not one of them so much as blinked.

"Humph," His Grace grunted. "A reminder, then: This party is about me. My legacy. I will not have it disrupted again. And especially not by your family, Emmeline, when I gave you such a generous gift, and you produced such sickly offspring. Any of your cousins would gladly take it from you if they could."

"I am aware, Your Grace. Thank you."

"Yes. Go now. And apologize to your betters, boy, for throwing food at them. Ramsey's a damned viscount." He snorted. "*Your* father works for the government."

Emmeline stood and gestured at George to follow her. Not quite certain he'd heard what he thought he'd heard, Will followed them out to the hallway.

"And shut the door. I need a moment of quiet away from the vultures."

Will pulled the door closed, then took Rose from Emmeline's arms. "Well."

"Well," she echoed. "Evidently, we've done it."

"But all the other children were calling us orphans and poor and stupid," George muttered, his fists clenching again. "They know everything."

"Knowing and being believed are two very different things," Will said. "I suggest we change out of these egg-soaked clothes, take a walk to give everyone time to calm down, and then retreat to our rooms until dinner."

"I ain't apologizing."

"No, you aren't. We're going to ignore it."

"So, we won?" Rose asked, putting her hand on Will's chin and turning his head toward her.

"I think we did." There was still a chance they would be challenged, especially if Penelope Chase's son told *her* about the conversation, but Emmeline had set the story perfectly, with a firm base and light details. "Emmeline has a way with words."

Rose sighed. "Well, that's good. I was worried you wouldn't get to keep Winnover Hall, and we wouldn't have done the agreement like we promised."

Emmeline stopped midstep. For a moment he wasn't even certain she was breathing. "Emmeline?"

With a blink she returned to life again, whipping around to face him. "I think I have a solution," she whispered, and put her hands on his cheeks, cupping his face much as Rose had done. "Are you with me?"

"Always," he murmured, his heart pounding.

She gave him a swift kiss before she released him again. "Come with me." Gathering up her skirt, she not so much walked as marched back to the door of the duke's study.

Rose pushed away from his chest, so he set her down, and she stomped after Emmeline, a lady in miniature. George went next, and he brought up the rear. Without even pausing to knock, Emmeline shoved open the door and walked back into the duke's study.

"What the devil are you doing?" His Grace demanded, setting aside a half-empty glass of what smelled like whiskey.

"I lied to you, Grandfather," Emmeline said, not stopping until she had put her hands flat on the surface of the desk. "Will and I tried to have children for months and months after our wedding. We were unsuccessful. But I knew a child was an integral part of our agreement to reside at Winnover Hall, so I invented one. I invented two of them, actually."

The duke blinked, then turned to Will. "Your wife is touched in the head. Please remove her."

Will, though, looked at Emmeline. She *had* found a solution, by God. "I only work for the government," he took up. "But she is telling the truth. Now, that is. Earlier, she was lying. We all were. When we received your invitation and knew we needed to bring our offspring along, we visited St. Stephen's orphanage in London and borrowed these two children. Tell His Grace your names, children. Your real names."

George puffed out his chest. "I'm George Fletcher, Your Grace. And I'm not seven. I'm eight years old."

"I'm Rose Fletcher," Rose said, and curtsied again. "I'm five years old, like I said, so I didn't lie about that."

"Orphans." The Duke of Welshire looked as if he'd just stepped in horse shite with bare feet. "You *borrowed* orphans. From St. Stephen's Home for Unfortunate Children. Where they specialize in the children of dead sailors and dockworkers and other unfortunates from along the Thames."

Huh. He hadn't known that. "Yes," Will said anyway.

"So, you are childless."

Emmeline lifted her chin. "No, Your Grace, we are not. Will and I intend to keep these two, if they'll have us."

Beside him, George gasped. Rose squealed and threw her arms around Emmeline from behind. Reaching over, Will took George's left hand in his. The boy was shaking. Emmeline, while she gripped his other hand hard, was not shaking. And neither was he.

"That was not the agreement you signed," the duke stated. "These aren't my blood. They aren't part of my legacy."

"No, they aren't, Your Grace. If you'll do us the favor of thirty days, we will remove ourselves from Winnover Hall. I know Cousin Penelope has been itching to get her hands on it for years. I imagine she'll be delighted."

Malcolm Ramsey scowled. "You're trying to sway me to allow you to remain. It won't work."

"I'm not trying to do any such thing. Will and I have been searching for a month to find a way to keep these two without turning the entire rest of their lives into one large and innumerable small lies. I was quite stunned when I realized a moment ago that the best way to accomplish that was simply to tell you the truth."

"You grew up at Winnover. You've told me countless times how much you adore it. What's your game, Emmeline?"

She shook her head. "There is no game. I love these little ones more than I love a heap of wood and stone, no matter how beautiful it is. We did not fulfill our part of your agreement. It goes to Penelope Chase." She took a breath. "And since we need to vacate it, we will be leaving Welshire at once to begin packing. Thank you for your hospitality, Your Grace. Happy birthday to you. And best wishes for your legacy." She turned around.

"Just a damned minute, Emmeline."

"No. I believe I've spoken my piece. Did I miss anything, Will?"

"Not a thing comes to mind, my dear. Happy birthday, Your Grace."

"Happy birthday, Grace. I'm sorry you're not my grandfather anymore, but I'm glad we won't get turned into toads." With a curtsy, Rose headed for the door.

"I'm not sorry," George said, taking his sister's hand. "You're a Captain Huff, trying to bullock all of us."

Will opened the door, ushering his brood—*his family*—back into the hallway. "Well said, George."

"Out!" the duke bellowed, and George closed the door on the old man.

That was it, then. Will tugged Emmeline against his side. "You did find a solution."

"I hate losing Winnover," she murmured, as the excited children bounced around them, "especially to Penelope, but look at them. They can be ours."

"It'll take some maneuvering," he said, "especially if Hannah and Billet have just purchased a home in Birdlip. And you know Penelope won't keep the staff on."

She nodded. "I know. We will lose a great many friends over this, as well. I've been lying to most of them for seven years. And you will lose your position."

Will shrugged. A few months ago, that would have flattened him. "I won't have time for it. I'll be occupied with being a father."

Rose spun around, grabbing Emmeline around the waist again and looking up at her. "Am I Rose Pershing now? Or Flora?"

"You are Rose Pershing, my sweet. Or you will be, once we sign a few papers."

"That's very good. I like being Rose. I didn't want to say anything, but Flora is a silly name."

Emmeline's mouth twitched. "Well, Flora was pretend. You are real."

"I wish we didn't have to stop living at Winnover Hall. It's lovely there."

For a long moment Emmie considered what Rose had said. Winnover *was* lovely, and stately, and warm, and familiar. She would miss the green hills and yellow stone and the way the sun sparkled on the pond in the mornings. "I will miss it," she said, fixing a strand of hair at the girl's temple. "But missing you would be much harder."

"Oh, I know," Rose agreed. "George and I know some good places in London, if we need somewhere to sleep."

"We still have Pershing House, silly thing," Emmie answered, "and a very small cottage in York called Arriss House. No need to sleep in any church cellars."

"Thank goodness for that. I don't want to ruin any of my dresses." The girl straightened, looking down at her egg-and-cake-streaked pink gown. "Any more of them. I *am* worried that we're ending up in York, though."

"James won't be there, will he, do you think?" George asked.

"If he is, he has good reason to stay well away from us," Will said, ruffling the boy's hair. "And with the truth out, nothing about which to threaten us."

As they climbed the stairs to the rooms they'd been given, George stopped on the landing. "There's something you should know. Even before James, *and* after he left, Rosie and me've been taking things from Winnover Hall we thought we could sell. Because after we finished here, we were going to make a run for it, maybe to live in Gloucester."

Will nodded. "I did notice a few things going missing. Thank you for telling us."

"But Powell found us out, and he's been taking things back. But we knew that, so we found a better hiding place, but we didn't want to hurt Powell's feelings, so we kept putting a few things where he could find them."

"You took extra things so Powell could find and return them?" Will's jaw twitched, his eyes merry.

"Yes. He didn't snitch on us when he could have, so we helped him back some."

"And Hannah kept fixing my hems, even when the silverware was too heavy and pulled them out," Rose announced. "They can stay with us, can't they?"

That explained the hems. Clever darling. "We'll figure something out, my dears," she said, because some response seemed to be needed. What that thing would be, she had no idea. More than a dozen staff called Winnover home, and several of them had families in the area. Penelope wouldn't keep most of them on, but for goodness' sake, they'd all become like family. Good God, they *were* a family now. All of them, together.

"If we sell Arriss," Will said, on the tail end of that thought, "we might be able to purchase something close by Winnover. It would make your cousin our neighbor, and it would be . . . a great deal less than what you're accustomed to, but it wouldn't upend the household."

Emmie grabbed his face and kissed him, right on the stairs. "I love you, William Pershing," she declared.

"I have waited a very long time for you to say that, Emmeline Pershing," he said vehemently, and kissed her back. "I love you."

This would be their lives, then. Upended, pecked at by lost friendships and uncertain alliances, responsible for a possibly reformed pair of thieves and helping them grow into kind, responsible adults, and keeping their partnership tangled, together, and loving. Messy and daft. And perfect.

EPILOGUE

"No, Hannah, leave that," Emmie said, looking up from setting a pair of candlesticks in a wooden box and covering them with straw before adding another pair. "I think it came from Uncle Harry."

The lady's maid put the yellow vase back down on the table. "It is rather hideous, if I may say so."

"You may." Emmie chuckled. "At least I have the satisfaction of leaving all the things I never wanted behind here. Let Penelope figure out what to do with them."

William appeared in the morning room doorway. Hands on either side of the doorframe, he leaned into the room. "Em. Come look at this."

Leaving the candlesticks behind, she followed him to the library windows that overlooked the garden, part of the pond, and the apple orchard beyond. A large, dirty sackcloth stretched out between them, Rose and George were leaving the orchard. Whatever was in the sackcloth looked to be extremely heavy, and the middle of it bumped along the ground.

"Their ill-gotten goods, I reckon," Will observed.

"Good heavens. It's a wonder we have any furniture left in the house."

He put his arm around her shoulders. "Our darling little miscreants."

Snorting, she slid her arm around his waist. "Have you heard back from Michael Fenmore?"

"Yes, just this morning. Evidently, he wasn't terribly surprised that we decided to keep the children. He's offered to write up the paperwork for the adoption."

"That's very kind of him. We should have them over to our new home once we find one."

"We'll find one. Our finances will be pinched, though, without the income we've been getting here, even after we sell Arriss House. The new house will be smaller. Much smaller." He leaned closer. "With less need for servants," he whispered.

"They all come with us," she murmured back. "We'll save money by hosting fewer soirees."

"Because we'll have fewer friends."

She nodded. "I wrote my parents and told them everything. I don't expect to hear back from them for some time." Her mother would be full of "I knew it" and her previous "some women aren't meant to be mothers," but Lady Anne could put a cork in it, the gunpowder cat. *Ha*. She'd learned some new things herself.

"Likewise. I have no idea how my mother and father will react."

Looking up at him, she sighed. "I hope you at least put the blame on me. There's no reason your parents should be angry with you."

"We are partners," he stated, as if that explained everything. In a way, though, it did.

As they watched, Powell appeared in the garden. The children set down their bundle, and after a moment of speaking, George held out his hand to the butler. To her surprise, Powell shook it. To her even greater astonishment, the butler took Rose's side of the sackcloth and helped George carry it toward the house.

"It's good to see the entire family getting along," Will said dryly, making her laugh.

"You weren't playing on my sympathies, then," a gravelly voice came from the doorway.

Gasping, Emmie let Will go and spun around. "Your Grace?"

The Duke of Welshire walked into the library as if he owned it, which technically he did. For once, her first thought on seeing him wasn't to recollect which lie she'd last told so she could keep her stories straight, but rather, how disappointed Powell would be to have missed admitting the duke to the house.

He glared at her as he crossed the room, ivory-tipped cane in one hand. "I reckoned you'd be sitting here, nothing packed, figuring I'd send word that you'd softened my heart and I'd decided to let you keep Winnover," the duke said, joining them at the window. "Nonsense that that would be." He looked out at the garden. "What's that?"

"George and Rose are returning all the items they stole from the house," she said.

"They stole from you."

"Well, yes. We told the children we were borrowing them for eight weeks, and that we would find a good home for them after we returned from your party. I imagine they were making plans on the chance they didn't like the home we selected. There was some worry over a pig farm, as I recall."

Her grandfather looked at her. "You've changed, Emmeline. I don't like it."

"Yes, but I like me much better now, so I'm not apologizing."

He glanced toward the window and back again. "That little brute called me a Captain Huff."

"It means 'bully,'" Will supplied.

"I know what it means." The duke harumphed again. "The minute you left, Penelope came and found me, yelling about orphans and cheats. Your cousin demanded I give her Winnover Hall." He scowled. "That's what you all want me for, isn't it? The things I can give you."

"That's why most of us come and see you when you ask, yes." There didn't seem to be a point in lying now, Emmie decided. She'd had her fill of it. "You can be unpleasant."

"I'm old. It's expected."

Had that been humor? If so, she didn't quite know what to make of it—or him. "But not necessary," she said after a moment.

"Ha. Shows what you know. I'm having Christmas at Welshire this year, for the entire brood, hens, vultures, and the other carrion eaters. You'll come."

It wasn't precisely an invitation, but it was unexpected, nonetheless. "We've ruined your legacy and embarrassed you in front of the *ton,* have we not?"

"Yes, you have. *You,* at least, are still family, though, Emmeline."

"We'll consider it. If we do join you, we're bringing the children. And there will be rules about the behavior of your legacy toward them."

"Oh, so now that you don't need me, *you* make the rules, do you?"

"Where my children are concerned?" Emmie countered. "Yes, I do. We do."

"That was implied, I think," Will contributed with a grin.

She faced him. "Oh, good, because I didn't want you to think—"

"I didn't."

"For God's sake," the duke burst out. "Keep it."

"What?" Emmie looked at her grandfather again. Her first thought was to wonder what it was she should keep. When she realized what he must have been referring to, her heart skipped a beat. "If you're toying with us, or getting some sort of revenge on us for our lies, I am going to go find some eggs and throw them at you."

"Ha." He stood there solemn-faced, eyes narrowed but . . . amused? No. It couldn't be that. "Penelope's a sycophant. Makes me feel as if I need a bath after a conversation with her. Never trusted a word she said, because none of it's genuine. You were the same, or so I thought. Inventing children, for God's sake. I've never heard the like."

"So you're—"

"Heh. As I said, I'm old. And I'm unpleasant. I can change my mind when I like. Keep Winnover Hall. I'd like to see if Penelope has the spunk to argue with me. I'd wager she doesn't." Turning around, he walked to the door.

"You just arrived," Emmie said, walking after him and still feeling bewildered. "You're welcome to stay."

"I'm headed for London to see to some business, alter some paperwork, and then back to Welshire again. Aside from that, I don't want to stay. Too much noise, and you'll be unpacking."

"Thank you, Grandfather."

Welshire faced her again. "You be honest with me, Emmeline. From now on. No lying." His shoulders lowered a touch. "What you did took courage. Spleen. Not the lies. The truth took courage. Didn't think you had it in you."

"I . . . Thank you. Again."

"I haven't decided about Christmas. I wanted to know what you'd say. You agreed to come, even without Winnover Hall. That's spleen. Still not certain I like it."

With that he left the library. Emmie turned around again to find Will looking at her, both eyebrows lifted. "God's sake," he muttered.

"I don't even know what to say." Emmie kept her gaze on the doorway, waiting for her grandfather to reappear and state that he'd been jesting all along, and they needed to get out of the house by sunset.

"He came all the way from Cumberland to get the last word," Will mused.

The children rushed into the room, most of the servants behind them. "I saw the duke," George said, scowling. "What did he take away from us now? Do I need to go mill him?"

"That means murder," Rose supplied helpfully.

"No. You don't need to mill him." Emmie knelt down, opening her arms. When the children ran forward into her embrace, she started laughing in pure, giddy delight. "He said we should stay here," she managed when she could take a breath.

"What?" they demanded in unison.

"His Grace said we could keep Winnover Hall. We don't have to leave!"

The squealing and screeching from both children and servants nearly deafened her, but she didn't care. This was the feeling, the one she'd craved without knowing what it was. Joy.

Read on for an excerpt from

Every Duke Has His Day—

coming soon in trade paperback from
Suzanne Enoch and St. Martin's Griffin!

"Do I conduct electricity?"

"The human body does conduct electricity, though not well. If you're asking about you, specifically, I would say that's a matter of opinion."

She faced him, leaning back against his worktable. "And what is your opinion?"

Michael knew what he wanted to say. He wanted to tell her that he practically saw sparks when he looked at her, and that in her company over the past few days he felt positively enough charged that the hairs on his arms lifted.

Instead of answering, he took a half step forward, leaned down, and kissed her on the mouth. Her lips molded against his, and while he'd expected another of those pleasant, enticing shivers, the heat spearing down his spine took him by surprise.

Elizabeth slid one arm around his neck, the other hand splayed against his chest. He noted it distinctly, because everywhere she touched him felt like fire. Slipping his arms around her waist, he tugged her closer. The days he'd spent in her company—if they'd been an experiment, he was now reaping the very successful results. And she kissed him back.

He blinked as down the hallway Huston said something to one of the other servants, his voice echoing. Whether or not he thought himself a suitor, or suitable, he was certainly capable of ruining Elizabeth's reputation. And she was nine years his junior, and popular, and she enjoyed dancing and being around people—things that made him cringe. The social niceties at which he failed. Miserably.

Releasing her took all his willpower. Lifting his head, he stepped back again. "Science doesn't have opinions," he commented, turning to pull the wires out of the water and disassemble the pile to render it inert. "Luncheon?"

She straightened, lifting her gaze from his mouth to his eyes and her expression slamming shut to that mask of politeness he frequently saw on those occasions he mingled with his peers. "What was that, one of your experiments?" she demanded.

Yes. And there had definitely been combustion. "Curiosity," he said aloud. He had no business interfering with her life. None. And they both knew it. "Luncheon?" he repeated.

"I . . . suppose I knew from the beginning that you have no manners," she stated, an edge to her voice.

Michael inclined his head, trying to keep his gaze off her sweet, soft mouth. "I did warn you. Are you going to stomp off, then?"

Elizabeth cleared her throat. "If flight is what you expect, then of course I will stay for luncheon," she said, moving to put the worktable between the two of them. "I'm famished, and not a coward."

"Good," he said, though he almost wished for a few minutes to gather the shambles of his thoughts back together, himself. "We need to refine our search area for Galahad and Lancelot. The sooner we find them, the better."

No, she wasn't a coward. He felt like one, though. Rather than offering his arm, Michael led the way back into the hallway. Huston glared at him, clearly disapproving of his manners. The servants could say he was being obtuse again, his mind on nothing that didn't have tubes and wires attached to it. More often than not, their assessment was correct. Today, though, the kiss had been the accident. What followed had been on purpose.

Circumstance had literally thrown them together, and she required his assistance. Her beginning to feel some . . . affection for him made sense from her point of view.

As for him, well, she wasn't a vial or a voltaic battery. She was unique. And unique had always interested him. That didn't make them compatible. It didn't even make them friends, though at the moment he was loath to let go of that title—because they still had two dogs to find, of course. It had nothing to do with the arousal he felt from being in her presence, much less kissing her. That was just emotion, and emotion was unreliable.

While all he'd told Huston was to set luncheon in the garden, the servants had outdone themselves. A proper table, tablecloth, candelabra—supremely useless given the light breeze—a vase of garden roses, the best silverware and china, and a footman standing behind either of the two chairs. "Good God," he muttered.

"This is lovely," Elizabeth noted, gliding to a seat before he could even think of holding a chair for her.

"I suggested sandwiches. The rest is none of my doing." Michael sat opposite her.

She kept her gaze on her plate. "No, we don't want anyone thinking you like me."

"*You* shouldn't like *me*," he stated, then cleared his throat. *Civility.* He could be civil for a few bloody minutes, even if he did want to peel off all her clothes and claim her for himself. "I believe it's more about my servants wishing to remind me that I have good silverware and should entertain more often." It was actually far more likely that his staff wanted him to make a good impression on a female in whose company he'd been seen, but he'd ruined that by losing what little self-control he possessed.

"You know, if you don't want me here, I can go," she said, lifting her napkin and then setting it down again. "I feel like I've been foolish, and you've just handily pointed that fact out to me. I *should* go. This is a mistake."

"It's not—" Michael swallowed the awkward lump of what he'd been about to say, and attempted to weigh the fact that she was quite right against the fact that he didn't want her going anywhere. And the fact that he was not going to apologize for kissing her. Ever. "Perhaps view it as me making a point of my own impropriety. Not yours. Aside from everything else, we're partners until the poodles are found, Elizabeth, and we both did quite a bit of work this morning. Eat a damned sandwich."

She narrowed one eye, gazing at his face intently, then nodded, settling the napkin across her lap. "Very well. You are provably objectionable."

Well, that hurt, but it had been his misstep. Not hers. "Thank you."

"Thank *you* for continuing to state that the dogs will be found. I've thought of the other alternative, endlessly, but I don't want to hear it said by anyone else—by you, specifically—until every other possible path has been explored."

A roundabout way of saying she believed in his abilities, even if she wanted to slap him. "Agreed," he said. "They are alive and well until we have proof otherwise.

And as of this moment, given that we've offered a great deal of money and no one's seen or found anything in the Thames or some alleyway somewhere, I do believe both dogs are still alive."

"I hope so. Very, very much."

Tim and Bradley served more of the ridiculously tiny sandwiches, fresh-sliced peaches, and champagne. "I hope there are more of these," he muttered, sending Huston a glare as he lifted a delicate cucumber sandwich between his thumb and forefinger and then popped it into his mouth. It could barely be considered a mouthful.

"What do you mean to do with the information you gathered today?"

All business now, she was. Well, that was his fault, so he'd have to live with it. "I'll look into the half dozen sightings that seemed credible, and then I intend to go for a walk in the area your performing poodle was spied. You're welcome to join me, of course."

"I'll have to consult my calendar. Lord Peter Cordray evidently means to propose to me again, this time with my father's blessing, so I'll have to give him the opportunity to do so."

A bit of bread went down his windpipe. Coughing, Michael grabbed for his glass of champagne and tried to wash it down. She said it very matter-of-factly, which should have had his approval, but he didn't like the damned content. At all.

"Do you want me to pound you on the back?" she asked, sipping at her own champagne.

"No, thank you." He coughed again. "Do you mean to accept Cordray's suit, then?"

"I haven't decided. We do enjoy many of the same things, and though Galahad detested him, well, logically I cannot have my life dictated by a dog's whims. But ignoring Galahad's very strong opinion doesn't sit well with me, either. And now neither of them can attempt to make amends."

"So your main objection is due to your affection for Galahad?"

She blinked long lashes at him. "Of course."

Even a failed experiment contributed an opportunity to gain knowledge, and Elizabeth was presently handing him a very sharp lesson over what he thought had been a rather spectacular—if poorly timed—kiss. "Hopefully we'll find Galahad quickly, and you *will* be able to take his wishes into account."

"Does science believe in hope?" she asked.

Well, that struck its mark. "Elizabeth, I . . ." He stopped, not certain what he could say to take his insult back without making it clear how much he liked her. *Him. The curmudgeon.* "Science doesn't care what anyone believes. It simply is," he finally said. "Not always sufficient, that, but it's the main rule."

"Science can't explain everything."

"It can."

"Then explain this." She stuck her tongue out at him, and went back to eating her tiny sandwiches.

Michael snorted. "I stand corrected. Science cannot explain you." Or his damned attraction to her.

"Good."